For Julia

AN

Englishwoman's
Guide

TO THE

COWBOY

best wishes!

June.

(I've heard so much
about you — you sound
wonderful!!)

JUNE KEARNS

Chapter 1

'When a woman seeks to journey independent and unprotected, it must be borne in mind that she puts herself at risk, both physically and morally.'
  Margaret Mary Whittier,
  'The Gentlewoman's Guide to Good Travel'

There was a moment, somewhere between Arizona and Texas, when the bile rose in Annie's throat and she thought, this is awful. Close to hellish, in fact.

She should have known, of course. I mean, when did things ever work out the way cheap novels led you to expect? Then again, what woman in her right mind would travel from one side of America to another wearing whalebone. Laced tight. Over layers of petticoats. And gloves! Buttoned up.

An Englishwoman, that's what. This one, anyway - Annie Haddon, here present - in the company of an aunt and cousin whose authority on matters of dress was absolute.

Not that there'd been any discussion on the matter of corsets. One glance at her aunt's own ramrod stiffness had been enough. Laced tight as a sausage.

And if Aunt Bea said, 'Button gloves' – you buttoned them.

Even if you were hot and cross and couldn't for the life of you see what the fuss was about.

It wasn't just the heat in the stagecoach, though that was bad enough. Nor the shaking and swaying, the smell of cigars or the chewing tobacco. It was everything. The dust. In their eyes, their ears, their hair, and anywhere else you could think of.

'Salts! For pity's sake, someone! Find my salts.'

Snatching up the tiny bottle, Annie waved it under her aunt's nose. 'Deep breaths, aunt. That's right.'

Aunt Bea was not wearing well, but Lord knows that was hardly surprising. Her face was now the colour of claret, her nose covered with a cambric square, as she tried in vain to shut out the worst whiffs of fellow un-bathed traveller.

A man with an enormous stomach leaned against Annie's knees. A weary-eyed widow with a baby behind. Nine inside and two on top and one in the driver's box. And the men all given to hawking and spitting, as they passed bottles of ranch whisky round.

Only one man wore city clothes, and he had shifty eyes and smoked a filthy pipe of black plug tobacco, and didn't look open to any discussion about it.

Oh, to remove an item of clothing. Annie fingered her collar restlessly. Just one, only one, that would do it. Oh joy. To unhook, unbutton, or even loosen something a little. Before this heat sucked the very breath out of you.

A slight shake of her head dislodged her small beribboned bonnet.

'Hat miss, hat!' Her aunt's hiss took less than a minute. 'It can't be more than an hour, two at most, since we left the last way-station, and I distinctly said - did I not say to you - that a lady never travels hatless. Under any circumstances.'

'We left at dawn, Aunt.' Annie pointed out. 'Five hours ago at the very least. It's now past midday.'

'What! Is that insolence?'

No, arithmetic.

'Don't be pert. Hat and gloves. It is the wearing of those accoutrements - must I remind my own ward - that separates us from the lower orders.'

Lucky lower orders, then. And what of everyone else? Were they to melt into puddles and ooze clean away? Mustn't take off your hat. Mustn't take off your gloves. Mustn't get flushed or perspire. Mustn't, mustn't.

Cousin Charlotte, of course, still looked porcelain pale and pretty. How had she managed that? How could she stay neat and composed in this furnace?

'Water! A little water!'

Examining gloved fingertips, Charlotte ignored her mother. It was left to Annie to peel herself wetly from the burning seat. 'Here, aunt.' She tipped the flask to her aunt's lips. 'A little more?'

Settling back, she stared blankly outside. One thing, anyway. She had no quarrel with the landscape, none at all. Wide and wild, it matched her very highest expectations. Red rocks rearing into brilliant blue sky, lonely way-stations and piles of bleached bones marking their route.

But where exactly *was* it? The wild, wild West. That was what she wanted to know. Where was the excitement, where the freedom? She'd seen herself hitching up skirts, flinging off hat and riding over purple plains with people she barely knew.

Aunt Bea, of course, had other ideas and saw impropriety everywhere.

'Never,' she'd warned, spotting Annie in conversation with the stagecoach driver, 'never *ever* speak to men here who have not been properly introduced. You do not know where it might lead!'

Annie had blinked at their driver. He'd lost his hair, one arm and an eye in the Indian wars and creaked when he walked.

'I was just being civil,' she said now, to her cousin. 'He was telling me about the war.'

'What! Which war?'

'You know. Southerners and Northerners and how one sees the other as being far too overbearing. They resent being bossed around, that's all.'

'Who does? What are you talking about now?'

'Southerners. Apparently, Robert E. Lee still adorns many a parlour wall round here. They hate the abolitionists. No-one wants to free their slaves, either.'

'How unbelievably dull, how... *dreary*.' Charlotte yawned.

'Not that it was just about that, about slavery. The driver says –'

'Oh, the driver, the driver! Why do you encourage these awful people?'

'No, it was interesting, Charlotte. Do you know what he said?'

'I don't care what he said. What could be interesting about someone who spends his days staring at a horse's fundament?'

'Language, Charlotte! I heard that!'

'Of course you did Mama, you haven't been out of earshot for five days.'

'What? Speak up.'

'I *said* this must be near the spot where that stage was attacked by five braves.'

A pitiful cry floated up from her mother.

'And don't think being nice to everyone sets you above the rest of us,' Charlotte muttered, through her teeth. 'Because it doesn't, you hear? It certainly doesn't.'

Mustn't smile at strangers. Mustn't speak unless spoken to. Mustn't mix with the lower orders. Mustn't, mustn't.

Why in the world then, had Aunt Bea insisted on this detour? What had been in her mind? The long sea voyage from England and around the Horn had been bad enough.

They'd recovered though, in San Francisco, enjoying the

bustle of that brash, get-rich-quick Spanish town. There had been a buzz in the streets, an air of fashionable lives, fast money. Charlotte had been in her element.

Then, Aunt Bea had made her announcement. 'We are leaving,' she'd said. 'Going on.'

On?

'To Texas.'

'But Mama,' Charlotte had wailed. 'It's so civilised here. Aren't those other territories still wild? Barely settled. There's nothing there!'

'Texas.' Aunt Bea had waved all protests aside. 'Then, to New York to meet Mr Hewell. From there, God willing, we'll return home together. To England.'

Henry Hewell? Annie had felt herself stiffen. The man half-marked as her match? Brutish, bumptious, physique of a porter barrel. Not yet, she wasn't ready. Did he have to come and spoil everything?

'Ding-dong, ding-a-dong,' Charlotte had sing-songed, slyly. 'Mama is set on wedding bells, cousin dear, whether you want it or not.'

'Oh, we barely know each other. Mr Hewell and I are not betrothed.'

'But you will be, I'll wager you will be, before we leave New York. Look, you're hardly the green side of twenty-five anymore, Miss Particular. He's got family name, hasn't he? What have you got? Don't screw your face up like that, you look like a prune.'

'I'm entitled to some say in this, surely, some choice.'

'Wouldn't count on that if I were you,' Charlotte had said, airily. 'Hoo, noo.'

That thought had lodged in Annie's mind like a splinter. It had been bad enough when he'd first been presented. A suitor! That port-swilling old fogey, blinking short-sightedly behind his eye-glasses?

Not that she was anything to write home to a fond mama

about, she knew that. Even so, she had her pride, hadn't she? Her self-respect.

Henry Chewton Hewell. Even his name sounded like something stuck between your teeth. Well, she wasn't going to think about him yet, not until she had to.

And *Texas*? Some wild blank sprawl on the map, some part of the new frontier. What possible business could they have there?

As far as Annie knew, her family had one American connection, one only. That was with her father. A father, she had neither known nor seen; a father who hadn't shown the slightest interest in her since the day she was born.

After all this time, was this trip something to do with him? Out of the question to ask, it would only set corset laces snapping again.

No mention of Annie's father was ever made in the Haddon household. *Black Sheep*. And one thing she'd learned after living so long with her relatives. The more you pestered for information, the less likely you were to learn anything.

Well, if they *had* to go on, could they consider the railroad? You know, the modern way to travel?

'Far too piecemeal!' Aunt Bea had dismissed the idea, with withering British superiority. 'Too many bits and pieces not meeting anywhere in particular. No, we will take the stagecoach. I have made my decision.'

A decision clearly regretted, from the first giddy-up.

Their route: San Francisco to St Louis, via Los Angeles, Tucson and El Paso. Three thousand miles and a four week trip. Not an ideal itinerary for an aged aunt. Or anyone else, come to that. Careering along like a chariot race on trails so rough, they fairly rattled the teeth in your head.

'*Fan!* Find my fan!'

Annie saw Charlotte look round for something to kick. 'Get Mama's fan!' She shot her cousin a poisonous stare. 'Now, for pity's sake. Are you deaf?'

Rising to the call, Annie swayed, teetered.

'Oh, watch your feet!' Charlotte was beside herself. 'If I don't die of boredom, I'll be crippled by your boots.'

'Fan, Annie - fan, fan.'

'Annie! You take up too much room!'

Fanning her own face with the flat of her hand, Annie inspected grimy gloves. She had dirty boots too, and a grubby hem, from forays at way-stations for food. Aunt Bea and Charlotte, often declining to get out, always complained bitterly about anything brought to them. 'Old beef. Tough as boots!'

Tough, yes. Beef? Most probably not. For some time, Annie had harboured grave suspicions about the origins of all this grease-sodden meat. If it moves - eat it, seemed to be the first rule of the prairie. And who could say for sure, which awful animal was being served up?

'Oh, my.' A ridge of striated rock soared up on one side of them. A vast, rippling wall of orange and ochre hues. Glittering gouged lines, sharp angles.

'Look, Charlotte!' Annie's eyes followed it up, up into painted blue sky. 'Just look at that view.'

'That's not a view, you dolt. It's another lump of rock. Nasty wild, barren place, and no sight of a proper gentleman since San Francisco.'

'What do you mean? We've met plenty of gentlemen, haven't we? All those officers at Fort Reno and ... '

'Girls! What are you talking about, what are you saying? I insist on hearing.'

'Nothing, Mama.' Charlotte's voice rose over the creaking coach and clattering wheels. 'We were speaking of the weather.'

'Do not whisper, then. It is impolite.'

'I didn't say there was a shortage of men, muttonhead.' The hiss came in Annie's ear. 'Just the right kind.'

'When I was a gel,' Aunt Bea quavered. 'I ... '

'But surely, Charlotte. Captain Calhoun for one. Remember? So charming and courteous.' Hadn't Charlotte flirted shamelessly with him behind her mother's back?

'... when I was a gel, I *never* indulged in private conversations. A mark of rudeness!'

'Courteous! He was rude to Mama, chiding her for travelling without escort.'

'You said how distinguished he looked in his uniform; you admired his horsemanship!'

'I expect I was charming. I can't help it, it just leaks out. Look, why do you insist on liking everyone? Why would you want any of these uncouth, ill-bred Western types to like you?'

Annie's eyes flicked up to meet those of the uncouth, ill-bred Westerner sitting directly opposite. He was taking a surreptitious swig from his flask at the time and winked as he caught her glance. She looked away, hurriedly.

At home men gazed at Charlotte, or gawped at Aunt Bea's finery and feathers. They rarely noticed Annie - except perhaps, to mark her limp, her slight, uneven gait. Step gimp, step sway - and a clump you could hear coming.

Was Charlotte right about the men here, then? Did they *all* look at women in that way? As if they were hungry. Forty to one, they outnumbered females in the West, apparently.

She turned her face to the window. No roads, no neat fields, no fences. No people either, not one. Just glorious, unending wilderness. Unfamiliar trails through wild, wild country.

There'd been times when she'd yearned for something like this. Something less suffocating and settled. And she couldn't help feeling that somewhere out there, was the life she had always dreamed of.

And something else. *You are here.* That calm, quiet voice, echoing and re-echoing in her head since California. Whose voice? What did it want?

'Annie! Stop fidgeting.'

'It really is magnificent country,' she murmured. 'Isn't it? So grand and beautiful. Almost mystical, you might say.'

'You might. I'd say these gloves were once the palest dove grey. Look at them now, just look. Ruined!'

'It's the feeling it gives. Of freedom, I think.'

'Are you mad!'

'Can't you sense the timelessness, Charlotte, the –'

'Oh shut up about the scenery! Shut up, or I'll be sick.'

Annie shifted her weight on the cracked leather seat. She hadn't slept well since San Francisco, hadn't changed her underwear for a week. If only she could rest.

Sore eyes drooped to the beat of hooves, the squeak and creak of the stagecoach. A huge horsefly buzzed by her ear.

And then, it began.

A scream of gunfire. Another, and one more. Pulled up sharp in the stage-coach, they sat like statues - breath held, eyes wide - swapping quick pale glances. In heavy heat, everything shimmered silently. White powder smoke drifted past the window.

Suddenly, a whoop, a yell, a volley of shots. Bullets ricocheted on rocks, horses reared. As the baby began to wail, they were off again, weaving wildly, careering out of control.

Jagged rock hit the Concorde coach headlong. Flung high into the air, it jack-knifed and twisted over in clouds of dust. Horses thrashed and whinnied shrilly. Someone screamed.

Annie knew nothing of this. Having been violently thrown against the door, consciousness had already left her.

Chapter 2

'Women of a delicate frame should be mindful, that long days of exertion in the open air can be seriously debilitating.' – p.17

Thoughts unwinding, drifting. Back to England and half-heard conversations, odd events.

Hadn't it all started in her aunt's conservatory, on the last big occasion before leaving home? Concealing silk skirts carefully, Annie had taken refuge behind a screen of potted palms.

She *had* been dancing, it was true, but knew herself to be someone men never asked for a second waltz, not with her limp. Her timing was good, but her balance was not and few were prepared to risk looking ridiculous. Not that she blamed them for that.

She'd been tired, that was all. Tired of being grateful for any attention. Brave Annie, with the plucky smile and that gammy leg. There had to be a limit to the amount of humiliation a person could be expected to stand in one evening.

Besides, there'd been a hole in the foot of her stocking and her toe had kept poking through.

Then, Aunt Bea's penetrating voice and a waft of powdery

cologne. 'Did you notice Annie? Was she still on the floor?'

'She was not.' Another aunt. Eugenie. 'Skittered off, I suppose, to skulk in some corner. You realise Beatrice, that gel has no prospects. Too much reading and not near enough time in society. Oh *sit* down Bea and move the dog, he hangs all over you. Don't give him any more chicken either, he'll be sick.'

Just imagine, Annie had thought, being introduced. *This is Annie. She reads.* Yes, a dull sort of gel. Solid and rather dreary. Like porridge.

Both aunts were formidable. To their small niece, they'd always seemed elderly and remote, like mountain ranges with ice on their upper slopes.

From the time she could first walk and talk, Annie had tried Eugenie's patience. ('That child can never stay clean and quiet for more than two minutes ... stubborn and wayward, just like her father.')

And Beatrice, exasperated by her habit of arriving late for meals with muddy petticoat, blackberry-stained face and another hole in her stockings, would sigh, 'you see what I have to put up with?'

'And her *hair*.' Eugenie's voice again. 'All puffs and rats and that nasty carroty colour.' Sniff. '*His* side of the family, of course. Gypsies! Fortune-tellers!'

'Well none of this is *my* fault, Eugenie. I've done my best to set her in society, and make sure she never mentions her affliction, or calls attention to anything ... unpleasant about herself.'

Annie's eyes had rolled. Could a lop-sided leg, like some dreadful disease, actually make a person a social outcast? Better pass the bell then, and the 'unclean' sign.

'Look there, Eugenie, just look at Charlotte. Doesn't she look *fine*. She's sure to have an offer soon.'

'The sooner,' Eugenie had said, thinly, 'the better. And what then? Shall you keep Annie as companion?'

By then, Annie's mouth had been dry, her palms wet. Not that she hadn't considered her own prospects. She had, often. Resigned to being passed over by marriage, she regularly reviewed other options. Trouble was, what were they? She was fit for nothing except being a wife. And none too well fitted to that either, if Beatrice and Eugenie were anything to go by.

Of course, she would always be grateful to her aunts. When her own mother had died giving birth to her, they'd taken her in, reared her.

But to spend the rest of her life as companion? Interminable evenings in dusty rooms, playing piquet. Was that really all there was? She'd rather pray for the grace of an early death.

Then, the announcement. 'Well, there *has* been some interest lately. From a certain quarter. Most unexpected.'

Annie had stiffened. Not that widower again, surely, with the brood of motherless children. Hadn't she turned him down flat? Wait. Could it be ... the curate? Yes! John Dickon!

'Henry Chewton Hewell.'

Who? Her mind had gone blank. That forbidding man of fiftyish, with florid complexion and carefully combed scant hair?

Then from somewhere, the sound of loud lapping. Ming, Aunt Bea's pampered Peke, supping milk from its own little silver salver. Eugenie didn't keep a lap-dog. She did all the biting herself.

'Was he not married before?'

'Years ago, yes. Pale, sickly sort of woman. Died.'

Lapping had stopped. Crackle, crack. Ming now crunching busily on something.

'What of those rumours? Scullery maid, wasn't she? Barely sixteen years old, or so I heard.'

'Gossip. It was never proven he was the father. Although I have to say, he's always been more than a little ... profligate.'

'Why on *earth* then, would he want Annie?'

'Ah ... ' Her aunt's voice had sunk to a confidential murmur and Annie had needed to strain really hard to catch it.

Unfortunately, Ming had chosen that moment to sniff behind the palms. Blinking suspiciously, he'd begun to growl.

'Shhh,' Annie had hissed, pulling a face at his strings of dribble.

'Last letter ... to make recompense ... a considerable sum from the goldfields.'

'Good boy, Ming ... shush!'

But Ming had refused to be shushed. As beady-eyed and irritable as his mistress, he'd snapped at Annie's ankles with an enthusiasm usually reserved for chopped liver. She hadn't dared kick him away. Until he'd mounted her leg and begun making passionate love to it.

'What's wrong with that dog! For goodness ... '

'Quiet Ming! I've decided to take her to America ... murmur-murmur, blah-blah ... Charlotte too, of course. Mr Hewell will accompany us as far as New York ... business prospects.'

Frantically freeing her foot, Annie only half-heard. What *was* all this about? As the dog snuffled off, another hoo-ha had started up.

'He's been sick! What did I tell you Bea, too many tit-bits! A pinch of this, a piece of that – he's ruined.'

Later, having picked the conversation clean of meaning, she'd still been confused. America? Well, her father was there somewhere, but what was that to do with anything? There'd been no communication with him, ever.

And Henry Chewton Whosit. A face scorched by whisky, a whiff of stale pomade and old pipe dottle. She'd as soon marry her uncle's lurcher.

In the weeks that had followed, he'd become a regular visitor. ('Why, it's Mr Hewell! What a pleasant surprise!') She'd dreaded his coming, hated the humiliation of being prodded out to greet him. ('For pity's sake smile, Annie! Is it too much to ask?')

After hours of toe-curling embarrassment in his company, that smile had become fixed and glassy.

Most times, he'd been as gloomy and silent as an old piece of furniture draped in a dust sheet. Splayed in a chair, eyes drooping with boredom or whisky, he'd seemed utterly fatigued by the whole business.

Annie had known just how he felt.

Then, when they'd been alone together, his behaviour had changed and become creepily familiar. The way he'd leered had made her think of Ming and want to bolt for cover. She'd started to feel nervous.

She had prayed for an angel.

Could *this*, be the response? *Oh Lord.*

Chapter Three

'I have learned that in some countries – South America, Albania and Iceland, for example – it is customary for women who have to accomplish long distances on horseback, to bestride the horse man fashion.' – p.14

Annie was travelling, travelling fast, towards a harsh bright light.

Eyes opened to glaring white sky and flickered in agony. The light burned. Something whooshed in her ears. Her head hammered … *thump, thump-thump.*

She was on her side, with the stagecoach propped by a wheel, tilting precariously overhead. Staring at the canopy of hanging nails and splintered wood, she wondered why no-one was helping her.

Was she hurt? Was she *dead!*

Through a blurry haze, she saw her own stained skirts. And someone's boots. Moving away over hard ground. Circling slowly back. Closing her eyes, she shifted, painfully.

The boots stood stock-still. Dimly, she saw long legs sink to the ground and a man's face, shadowed by the low brim of a hat, stare in at her, eyes narrowing in disbelief. One long-fingered hand held a gun.

An incredulous pause. Then, 'Who in hell are you?'

Annie struggled to speak. Who was *he*? No-one from the stagecoach, that was for sure. She didn't care for his tone, either.

Weren't Confederate soldiers still roaming round here? Their driver had said something. Roughnecks and renegades, he'd said, respecting neither life nor law. When she'd asked why they didn't go home, he'd said, 'Lady, they ain't got no homes.'

Out of the corner of one eye, she saw her aunt's abandoned umbrella. Reaching out for it, her hand touched something else – a small bundle, wrapped in cloth? soft skin? – and she quickly tucked it into her sleeve.

'Miss … ' Her voice seemed to come from a long way off. 'Annie Haddon.'

'Are you hurt?' The man was studying her intently.

'Not sure. My head hurts … and my arm. Ouch! This arm.'

'Can you move? Try your legs.'

She responded, gingerly. Everything else seemed all right.

The man nodded. He had a suggestion. He would put his back to the stagecoach and try to lift it a little. When he yelled, 'move' - she should do just that.

As his legs straightened and his feet spread, Annie's mind wandered. What had happened? Where were the others?

He took the strain and she heard him shout.

Who *was* this and what would he do to her when she left the security of the stagecoach? That stagecoach which now slowly re-occupied the six or so inches above her head.

The man sank back on his heels, hat too far down for Annie to read his expression. His mouth though, was a tight line and she dimly recognised someone hanging on to their last shreds of self-control.

'Miss … Harden?' Her name was spat out, like a half-chewed plug of tobacco. 'If you don't get out of there right now, this whole thing'll be down round your ears. Got that?'

She'd barely rolled clear of the carriage, when there was a shuddering sigh and it collapsed creaking between its shafts. Clouds of dust rose high in the air, one wheel spun wildly.

Then, silence.

Annie knelt in the dust, clutching her aunt's umbrella. Hot wind rushed her face, loosening hair, stirring clothes. Aunt Bea? She looked round, straining an ear to the silence. Charlotte. They must be here, somewhere.

Ahead, empty landscape stretched to the horizon. Behind, the heap of wrecked stage-coach. No rocks, no trees, no sheltering shade. No sign of anyone else. Just huge black birds wheeling endlessly overhead, watching, waiting.

She felt a shiver of superstition.

'Where am I?' She tried to get up, but the ground slid away.

The man held onto her. 'I'd guess a long way from home. What happened here?'

'Gunfire.' She flapped a hand at the horizon. 'Horses. Where *is* everyone?'

Her gaze swivelled, nervously. Dry empty land, in every direction. Just this towering silhouette between herself and dizzying sun. She couldn't see his eyes. 'My aunt. The driver?'

'Gone, I guess. We need to go, too. Preferably, at a gallop. You up to it?'

'I can't *leave*. They'll come back. My aunt and my cousin.'

'Miss ... lady, they've gone. So have the horses. Look at these tracks.'

'They wouldn't go! Not without me.'

'Maybe they had no choice. Look, this isn't helping anyone, is it? Fact is, I'm here and they're not. Think about it.'

Shading sore eyes, she looked him up and down. Dark clothes, tough leather, straight, unblinking stare. Perfectly still, like some animal predator. For a few slow seconds, she imagined herself the prey. *Steady.*

'But don't take too long.'

'I can't just … go off with you, can I? I don't know you.'

'Better get to know me, then. Real quick.' Taking off his hat, he slicked black hair back. 'What do you want?' Restless eyes raked the horizon. 'Formal introductions? Calling cards?'

Annie stared. 'I am English.'

'Congratulations,' came the indifferent reply. 'I'll mention that to Lone Cloud, as I go by. Comanche,' he said, to her quizzical look. 'He's with a few braves, over that rise. Been trailing me all day.'

'I didn't see any Indians.'

'No, they're not in the habit of coming up and introducing themselves. So, you coming with me or staying put? What do you want to do?'

Dizzy with heat, she swayed. One thing was beginning to dawn with a sort of awful inevitability.

'Ma'am?'

She'd been abandoned. In bandit country. 'Do I have a choice?'

'Ride with me, save your skin. Stay, lose your scalp.' He shrugged. 'Like it or not lady, I'm your huckleberry.'

Oh Lord, Annie thought. What use were *Bædeker, Bradshaw* or her *Gentlewoman's Guide To Good Travel* now? Dealing with any sort of native was always airily dismissed: *'Try offering bonbons or scraps of bright cloth.'*

'Well look, thank you for your concern, but … '

'Concern, hell! Lady, I'm scared! Listen, Miss … Whateveryourname, let's keep it real simple, shall we? Forget sweet talk and la-di-da. I'm not asking anymore, I'm telling. Get on the goddamn horse. I'm not getting staked out and skinned alive for anyone.'

She flushed. 'That's very gallant.'

'I'm gallant on Sundays. This is Thursday, as I recall.' He looked around. 'You need a hat.'

One lay amongst the baggage, strewn all over the ground, next to a cloth doll and a Bible. Small and pert in purple ruched silk, prettily finished with feathers. Charlotte's hat! Annie stared, appalled.

'I said a hat, not some fancy folderol. Here.' The man retrieved a grimy felt, large and battered, from the ground. 'Put this on before you fry. Now, let's go!'

'My clothes.' She waved at scattered bags and boxes. 'My trunk!'

'On one horse?'

'My portmanteau, then. All I have is ... '

Ignoring her, he steadied his horse and tied a blanket over the forward arch of the saddle. 'Give me your foot, Miss.'

'Haddon. Please. If I could just – '

'Your *foot*.'

Offering up a dusty black-buttoned boot, Annie tried to grab the saddle. When her injured arm took all her weight, she yelped out loud.

'May be broken,' the man said. 'When we get away from here, I'll take a proper look.'

The way he said it didn't make her feel any better.

Grabbing her waist, he lifted her high into the saddle. A moment's dizzying panic and then he was up hard behind, arms around, urging the horse off at full gallop. And nothing more said.

Slumped in the saddle behind bunched petticoats, staring at her own white knuckles, Annie swallowed hard. Since the accident that had caused her limp, she'd avoided all horses. Never before, had she ridden astride. Never in her life, had she been as close to a man, not like this.

In the lap of a stranger. Someone grimmer than a reaper with a gun on his hip.

She kept her head down against the glare as they rode headlong over hard ground, dust rising furiously all around them.

Kicking his horse even harder, the man soon swerved away from the trail, through tangled brushwood that swatted their faces, round rocks and gnarled stumps. He spurred them on, up and over sharp rises, that dipped down again, abruptly.

Sweat ran into Annie's eyes. Her head was pounding. Thrown about on the horse, she tried not to groan from the pain in her arm.

After hours of this hellishness, when her thighs were chafed and aching, he reined the horse in with a jerk and zigzagged them slowly to the crest of a hill.

'Can you see anyone?' She squinted blearily into the distance.

'No.'

'Those Indians ... perhaps they're friendly.'

'We're killing off their food, stealing their hunting grounds, robbing them blind. Would you feel friendly?'

'They wouldn't really do what you said, though, would they? You know ... take our scalps!'

He took his time answering. 'I may have exaggerated,' he said at last, his breath unnervingly warm on her neck. 'A little. It's not always like you read in dime novels.'

Sliding from the saddle to half-crouch behind some boulders, he stared out over dusty landscape beyond the ridge. Looking, listening.

Drenched with sweat, Annie sat and listened, too. The horse's ears twitched up, back. Nothing. The man didn't move.

After a while, she swung painfully down to crouch behind him.

'Did the Indians attack the stage-coach?'

'No.' He didn't look round.

'How do you know that?'

'You wouldn't want me to tell you.'

'I would!'

'Lady, it's not sport. Or some game. Bodies wouldn't have

been taken away for decent Christian burial.'

Oh! Her breathing grew ragged. 'Murderous heathen savages!'

'What's that?' He turned to stare. 'Don't be so quick to judge. They're only fighting to hold onto what's theirs. There's some savage in us all, surely.'

Ho, ho. A frontier philosopher. 'What do they want, then?'

He shrugged. 'They're all stirred up. Railroad's coming through, grabbing land, scattering the buffalo. Pushing them out.'

Annie sucked in her breath. He wasn't interested in making her feel better, was he? He wasn't a talker. Well, bad luck. She'd nowhere else to go.

In full glare of the sun, the heat was brutal. Strings of hair fell down round her face and she pushed them away with a sticky, horse-smelling hand. 'Won't it be years though, before the railroad gets going properly?'

'Lady, I couldn't rightly say.'

'I read something about it in my journal.'

Her journal! In her trunk. Along with just about everything else that she owned. Not that this man would understand how much those things meant to her. Probably couldn't even read or write. Gross ignorance, vulgar manners, both so widespread here.

He stood up, stretched and walked back to the horse, Annie stumbling behind.

'Almost everything I own,' she murmured, 'was in that trunk. The one you made me leave back there. Bound copies of Dickens, an entire set of - '

'That's OK,' he said, heaving her onto the horse and boosting himself up behind. 'Comanche love Dickens. Apaches now, they're more partial to Edgar Allan Poe.'

A flush rose on Annie's neck. Staring ahead, eyes sliding out of focus, she felt his contempt oozing into her back.

'I need to visit a railroad camp,' she said, with a rush. She didn't know why, it just popped out.

'What in the world for?' He walked the horse slowly up and over the ridge.

'I have ... good reason. I believe this one's near Sedalia.'

'Respectable women with any sense, don't visit railroad camps. No matter where they're at.'

Annie didn't tell him about the crumpled scrap of paper she'd found on her aunt's dressing-room floor. Her father's name had been on it, and an address: *Care of Missouri-Pacific Railroad, Sedalia*. She hadn't told anybody.

'Do respectable ladies here all ride astride?'

'A few have fancy female saddles, but most fork it like the rest of us. Side-saddle doesn't suit serious riding.'

'Women used to ride astride in England. I believe the wife of Richard the second introduced the side-saddle.'

Kicking the horse into a trot, back to some sort of rough dirt track, he said, 'Lady, for someone who wanted a proper introduction, you do a helluva lot of talking.'

Closing her mouth, she stared at the horse's neck.

Then, a long time later, 'Did you say you were from Texas?'

'I *didn't* say.'

She lurched against him as they flew over a wheel rut.

'Well, do you mind if I ask - ?'

'Do *you* mind if I don't answer,' he said, irritably. 'We'll move faster if you stop chattering. Unless you want to share your thoughts with the Comanche. And try to loosen up.' Against her back, he was easy and relaxed. 'Sit stiff and you'll suffer. There's more to this than sitting with your feet hanging down.'

Annie didn't care for his logic, or his manners either. His horse, though. No point asking him to leave. 'One question,' she said. 'Where are we going?'

'Red Rock. Nearest town, day and a half's ride away. Maybe the rest of your party will be there.'

She brightened immediately. 'And ... you are?'

'That's two questions,' he shot back, before drawling, 'name's McCall.'

McCall what, who McCall? Annie chose not to ask. Second name terms were entirely appropriate here. She would put up with this man until reunion with her relatives. Then goodbye McCall and oh, the relief!

The man's heels squeezed hard on the horse's flanks, driving them on through heavy dust.

The track ran out, wilderness closed in. No more words, no attempts at conversation. Just the thud of hooves on hard baked earth and the rasp of the horse's heavy breath.

She longed to ask more questions. Was this Texas? Were those Comanche still following? Was he this insufferable with everyone? That sort of thing.

Mile by weary mile though, panic subsided and she shrank back inside herself. Half-delirious and dizzy, she was drawn back against him, her head snapping up again when the horse stumbled and pain shot through her arm and head.

Every so often she pulled away, uneasily aware of unfamiliar scents. Warm male skin after hard riding, tobacco, raw leather.

'Relax,' McCall muttered once, feeling her shiver of resistance. 'I'm on your side.'

Oh, that was all right then. It bothered Annie more than she could say, to think that she'd sometimes dreamed of something like this. A mysterious stranger, a daring rescue. Being carried off on a wild-eyed horse, westward into the sunset.

Ha! Be careful what you wish for.

Chapter 4

'When embarking on long and fatiguing expeditions, ladies should endeavour to avoid those garments which constrict the vital organs, as far as modesty allows.' – p.22

'Hey! Hey, take it easy.'

A man's voice in her ear, someone's arms supporting her.

McCall. He splashed cold water in her face and Annie floundered away, staring up at blazing blue sky.

'What happened?' she croaked, tasting grit. Her throat was parched. She felt nauseous from the heat, dizzy from lack of food and drink.

'You fainted. Needed to rest, I guess, after being knocked out. Wasn't time. We had to get away from there fast.'

An apology? Good as she was likely to get, anyway.

He offered water, warning her to take small sips, then ran a careful hand over her arm. 'Out of line, is all. Reckon I can fix that.' He shrugged at her alarmed expression. 'I've done it with horses. Bones are bones, aren't they?'

Annie looked doubtfully at his horse, still sweating and shaking nearby, and felt a stab of fellow-feeling. 'Does it always work?'

'Not always, no. If it doesn't, I shoot the horse. Take off one of those petticoats, will you? I'll need something for strapping.'

She stared pointedly until he turned his back, then hitched up her skirts to wrestle with yards and yards of creamy calico.

'Best get the rest of your clothes off while you're at it.' The suggestion was thrown casually over his shoulder. 'Un-strap, unhook. Get out of those corsets. You'll feel far more comfortable.'

Turning back, he ran into Annie's outraged stare. 'Better close your mouth, ma'am, it tends to invite flies. Look, that dress isn't suitable for riding astride and it's too damn hot for all that whalebone. How many bolts of cloth are you actually wearing?'

Was he always right? What a perfectly vile habit. 'What *will* I wear, then? You wouldn't let me - '

'I've spare pants and a shirt. They'll do for now.'

Annie swallowed, with difficulty.

'Something wrong?' he said.

'I'm not very comfortable with this situation, that's all.'

'I'm not turning cartwheels myself.'

She stared at his retreating back as he loped over to a group of stunted trees and started rummaging about in yellow-dry brush. He was making it very, very hard for her to feel grateful.

'Now, don't move a muscle,' he said, coming back with a stick. 'This is likely to hurt.'

There was a sudden, hard pull on her arm and her ear-shattering shriek scattered birds from nearby trees. 'Guess it did,' he muttered, binding her arm tightly to the piece of wood. 'There. How's that feel?'

'Oh, tip-top,' she said, her voice thin as tissue-paper. 'Good as new.'

His sudden smile, revealing perfect teeth, afforded Annie

her first almost-human sensation, since sun-up.

Dazed, she looked all around. They were by a river. Wide, brown and sluggish, fringed by low trees. 'The Red,' he told her. 'May as well rest up here.'

Red River? The Pecos, Amarillo, Rio Grande.

Annie stared at open, empty land beyond the water. Names that had charmed her on maps, suddenly seemed to have lost their appeal.

Heavy afternoon heat was now slowly softening. The air was still and breathless and carried rich scents of something - sagebrush? sun-baked grass? As shadows stretched, setting sun changed the colour of distant rock. Red, umber, orange to purple, misty blue.

It was very quiet. Just the low murmur of moving water, the rustle of a breeze through ragged grass.

In welcome shade, her back to a rock, she watched McCall. As he started a fire and made a meal, she could do little else. Her eyes followed lethargically, as he set a tin pot to bubble over the fire.

Long and lean, without an ounce of spare flesh, he still managed to suggest something powerful. No sign of the bone-aching weariness she felt herself, he barely seemed to have broken sweat.

Someone in his own element, well able to look after himself.

When he offered scraps of food on a stick, she sat up stiffly. 'Thank you, I can manage.' She was more used to doling out this sort of treatment than receiving it. ('A little quince jelly, aunt? Here, try some on this spoon.')

'Oh, just rest up.' He stabbed at more meat. 'We've a way to go yet. If you start swooning every few miles ... '

'I won't!'

'Wouldn't bet on it. Sun's rough here and you English ... your blood's too thin.'

Annie chewed in resentful silence, her eyes on birds

gathering in low branches of nearby trees. They flicked down to feed, skimmed the river shallows, then spun giddily off again.

Half-blinded by the sun, she almost choked when she caught the glint of metal. McCall had taken out his gun! He was raising it high!

As the butt came down on coffee beans to crush them, birds rose in a wave of panic and she exhaled, shakily.

Settle down, she told herself. Stay calm. It will be all right.

One by one, the birds floated back. McCall passed her a tin mug of coffee and settled himself opposite.

She did her best to hold onto a pleasant expression, but it kept slipping into a rabbitty one. Other times, other places, she would have been over those hills by now, and safely back home with a book.

Because here - only a fool would deny it - was a particularly disturbing kind of male beauty. Dark and brooding. Dangerous. The sort of man that most women would forgive anything. The sort of masculine ideal that Aunt Bea despised. ('The man's either a fop or a rascal! It's how the Devil fools us.')

Well, he wasn't a fop. As for the other ... jet hair was now wet and sleek from washing and a faint stain of stubble gave him the look of someone who had been up for far, far too long.

'So, what happened back there?' he prompted, rubbing his chin. 'Can you remember?'

Annie dragged her mind back. To the gunshots, eerie silence, panic-stricken faces. It was all a blur, she told him. A series of shocks, a nightmare. She wouldn't know where to start.

'Try right back at the beginning,' he said, but when she did, he kept stopping her with sharp questions. 'How many? Two, more?'

'Not sure. I didn't see. I was looking at my aunt, you see, concerned – '

'Gunfire all around, though? Both sides?'

'Err ... '

'Voices? What about voices?'

'I believe ... it may have echoed, the gunfire echoed. What?' The intensity of his stare started to frighten her. 'I really can't. I'm sorry.'

Something did come to mind though, suddenly. Something long-forgotten. 'One thing,' she muttered, fumbling in her sleeve. 'This was under the stagecoach.'

Holding out the small skin bundle, she watched him frown down at it.

'Medicine bundle. Handed down from father to son. Reckoned to have special powers.'

'You mean magic?'

'An Indian might say so. Of course, a good-living, God-fearing Englishwoman would likely call it a heathen charm.'

Ah, yes. Aunt Bea claimed to see the works of Beelzebub everywhere in this wild country. Stay on the lighted paths! Don't stray into dark woods! 'What do *you* think?'

'Me? I've some respect for the ancient ways.'

She coughed. 'Do you not believe in a Christian God then, Mr ... '

'Couldn't we start with something easier? Look, can I have that?'

'What? Oh, yes ... here.' A small pause. 'You told me that Indians didn't attack the stagecoach.'

'They didn't. Someone wants us to think they did.'

A fitful breeze flattened the grass and stirred leaves. Shaken loose from a nearby bush, a bird clacked off in a flurry of feathers.

Annie looked round sharply. There was a sense of something here. You could almost touch it. Something melancholy, mysterious. Some other world? It made her shiver. 'What is this place? It has a very odd feeling to it.'

His head jerked up.

'A while ago ... the wind seemed to carry voices. Is there a settlement nearby?'

'No. That's prairie wind playing tricks on your ears.'

'I know what I heard,' she said, and was met with a long slow stare.

'There was a battle,' he said, at last. 'Near here. Many killed.'

'Recently?' Annie shot another sharp look round, expecting men dragging bloodied, injured stumps to hove into view at any moment. Moaning.

'I'm talking years back.'

'Between North and South?'

'Indians and whites.'

Her blood quickened. 'What are you suggesting?' Shamans? Spirits! She felt chilled.

'Not suggesting anything, I'm just telling you what happened.'

'I'm a Christian, Mr McCall. I don't hold with pagan superstition.'

'Won't feel spooked by the place then, will you? Like I said, the wind plays tricks.'

He didn't seem in the mood for further explanation or any more questions, either. Annie *had* heard something, she was sure of it. Not exactly rattling bones, but it wasn't the wind, either. The same wind which was now whispering, faintly.

Trees stood gaunt and ghostly, the spaces between them deep and mysterious. It was quiet, strangely portentous. Superstitious or not, she was more than ready to leave now. If spirits *were* here, she didn't want to see them. Or hear them, either.

Why then, this feeling? The thought came to her as clearly as if it had been spoken. She was *meant* to be here.

Chapter 5

'In many places, it is possible to travel securely at night. However, the inexperienced traveller may find herself alarmed by the isolation and unaccustomed sights and sounds.' – p.172

In the evening's heat Annie felt an icy draught, cold and distinct. Gooseflesh rose on her arms. Wasn't it time to go on? Surely it would soon be dark?

'Mr McCall? Isn't it getting dark?'

'Yip. Happens every day. Something to do with the sun and us spinning round it.'

She drew a sharp breath. Don't let him rile you. You need his help. Don't answer back.

For some time, they sat in silence. Strangers in uneasy intimacy. Dusk came thick and blue, the world closed in. Birds that had been cutting through the air disappeared. And suddenly, it was dark.

She gazed up at the black bowl of sky, at a crescent moon and thousands of stars. Dead stillness was all around them now. Only night birds broke the silence.

The low-burning fire flickered and flared and pungent smoke coiled upward. A sharp smell stung her eyes and caught the back of her throat. 'That wood.' She coughed. 'It's very strong.'

'Dung.'

'I beg your pardon?'

'Dried dung. Keeps the mosquitoes away.'

He was never going to be easy company, this man. He unsettled her, with his air of ... what? Bored insolence? Been-everywhere, done-everything? Which was he, then? Hoodlum or gentleman?

Her gaze was drawn to the zigzag scar at the corner of his mouth. Somehow she didn't think he'd got that by tripping over his own feet. Perhaps he only pretended to bite legs for a living. After all, he knew about books. Cursed a good deal, though. Airs, but few graces.

'Tell me,' she said, fidgeting. 'Did the people who stopped our stagecoach want money?'

A weary shrug. 'Who knows? The war sucked the gold out of the South. Left some pretty desperate people around.'

'But why bother with harmless travellers?' Her face was pale, drawn. 'And why leave me there? What would make them do that?'

'We'll find out soon enough, don't fuss about it now. You'll wear yourself out.'

She waited, her stomach tightening. 'Do you think they'll be all right?'

'Your relatives?' He poked the fire with his boot. 'I'd like to say everything'll be just fine.' He weighed his words, carefully. 'Fact is, since the war, life's been pretty cheap.'

Annie's eyes slid to his low-slung gun-belt, thick and wide and studded with cartridges. Light from the fire glinted off the gun's handle.

'Is that why you carry that weapon?' She tried to keep her voice natural. Not just to crush coffee beans, was it?

'A man needs to show he can defend himself. If people think he can't, he's in trouble.'

'But, you might shoot somebody!'

'That's the general idea.'

'Do you have to wear it all the time?' she said, shaken. 'Can't you leave it on your saddle?'

'Unfortunately, my horse isn't a very good shot. Look, this isn't England. The West belongs to the meat-eaters. The meek don't inherit much, west of Chicago.'

'People can't just do as they please though, surely. The law –'

'There is no law.' He returned her stare. 'Not for a hundred miles, anyway. Since the war, people make their own rules.'

Annie didn't want to get drawn into any discussion about the war. It always seemed to end up with someone hitting someone. She shifted, uneasily. 'Violence isn't the answer though, is it?'

'You don't think so?' His tone was polite, condescending.

'I saw men fighting over money in San Francisco, and a man take his fists to another at Fort Reno. Over a woman. Didn't resolve anything.' Over Charlotte, as it happened, but she didn't go into that.

'Fighting over a woman's one thing,' McCall said, drily. 'Survival or defending a matter of principle's another.'

'So for *principle*, it was all right to set brother against brother in the war?'

'Certain wrongs have to be righted, I reckon.'

'By killing? Vengeance is mine saith the Lord.'

'How about eye for eye, tooth for tooth?'

'Oh, that.' Annie said. 'That's the *Old* Testament.'

'Would you stand by while others died trying to protect you? Defending your kin and your home?'

'I couldn't kill. Not another human being.'

'What about Indians?' He watched her, closely. 'Savages. Could you kill, then? To protect yourself?'

'No. Well ... I'm not sure. I've nothing against them, of course.'

'Well, they'll be real happy to hear that.' He waved flies away irritably with his hat. 'You've got a helluva lot of opinions for a newcomer. You always so argumentative?'

Annie plucked at a square of silk skirt, pinching it between her fingers. 'I'm just trying to see both sides, that's all. It's better than the person with the biggest stick winning all the time, isn't it?'

'Oh, we'll learn the lessons, don't worry about that, we don't need help doing it.' He paused, his stare menacingly polite. 'Of course, you're English, aren't you? One thing I've learned. You don't tell the English, *they* tell you.'

Annie's tongue touched dry lips. A thought struck her, a particularly unsettling one. Why did he snarl whenever the English were mentioned? Wasn't just politics, was it? Something else was prickling. Was it the whole English race he held a grudge against, then? Or just her?

'Don't get me wrong,' he was muttering, stonily. 'I'm not exactly disagreeing with you. It was a dirty war, real dirty.'

'Were you in the war?'

'With the Rangers, Texas Rangers. Heard of them?'

'Our stagecoach driver said they're the finest mounted soldiers he's seen.' She hesitated. 'You no longer ride with them?'

'No.'

'So ... what is your business now?'

McCall raised an eyebrow. 'The mind your own sort?'

'I beg your pardon,' Annie said. 'I just – '

' – don't trust me. Well, maybe you'd better start. Listen, lady. If I'm *not* on your side, you're in pretty big trouble.' He reached for her mug. 'Can you stand more coffee?'

'Err ... no.' Awful stuff. 'Thank you.' Thick, black, foul.

'Tea drinker, huh?' He made it sound like an insult.

'Do you have any?'

'No. Look,' he said. 'It'd be OK with me not to say anything for a while. If we don't talk so much, maybe we'll communicate better.'

Annie was too tired to try and work that one out.

Peering into inky blackness, she thought about that battle. There *was* an atmosphere, here. Of secrets, bloody secrets. Danger and trespass. If Moses had suddenly appeared, waving a stick and offering to lead the way, she wouldn't have been especially surprised.

Her eyes probed the shadows. Even with the moon up, it was hard to see more than a few feet. Dark shapes and silhouettes, all perfectly still. Trees, rocks, scrub. She sensed life but could see no movement, nothing to suggest they were not entirely alone. It was eerily quiet.

'Are those Red Indians still behind us?'

He didn't answer straight away. Then, 'Yep. Right on our tails.'

'I can't see any sign of them.'

'You can't hear them either, but they're there.'

'Why don't they say what they want?'

A careless shrug. 'They'll get around to it, eventually. Right now, they've got everything their way, they're not in any hurry.'

'Can't you just ... parley with them or something? Ask them to go away?'

'You mean offer a handful of beads and greetings from the Great White Queen? England Rules,' he drawled, as colour rose in Annie's face again. 'I wouldn't count on conversation if I were you. I don't think that's what they have in mind.'

'Why don't we go on, then?' she said. 'Now that it's dark. I'm feeling much better. Couldn't we creep away while they're not looking?'

A faint snort. 'Comanche are always looking. We're not creeping anywhere, we'll hole up here.'

'Hole?' she said, warily. 'Up?'

'Make camp. Sleep, rest the horse.'

'Here?' Staring round, Annie stiffened. 'In the open?' Her

voice rose sharply. 'Together?'

'Good water, some shelter. What more do you want?'

Doors, she thought. With locks. Walls. Privacy! She was covered in confusion.

'You can rest easy.' McCall's mouth twitched. Clearly he'd managed to add mind-reading to his list of talents. 'I never move in on a woman without a clear invitation. No matter how alluring.'

Oh, ho. Annie's eyes rolled. Very funny. She didn't need mirrors to know that she looked a fright. Face scorched by wind and sun, hair a wayward red bush down her back. Probably blood-shot eyes and a coated tongue, as well.

But men like McCall had never shown the slightest interest in her before, even when she'd been well-dressed, nicely shod and prettily groomed. Why would things alter now?

He passed her a blanket, then stretched out full-length, propping his head on his saddle.

'Are you sleeping there?' She shot him a startled, side-ways look.

'Yip.' He tilted his hat over his eyes. 'This is as private as it gets. Just you, me and the lone prair-ree.'

'But ... what about those Comanche?'

'Whatever they're planning, they won't come in tonight. They rarely risk dying in the dark. Think their souls might lose their way.'

In spite of everything, Annie felt stirrings of interest. Hadn't she yearned for travel and adventure? Epic journeys to far-flung parts with an elderly female relative as chaperon? Well, here she was. Another dream shattered.

'That battle I told you about? Indians think their spirits stay in the place of their death. We're close to sacred ground here. They won't come near.' He hesitated. 'Still think you heard voices back there?'

'I heard something.' Felt something, too. Something exerting a powerful, supernatural pull. 'It wasn't spirits, though.' Or the restless dead. '*And when they say unto you, seek unto them that have spirits, should not a people seek unto their God?*' Isaiah. Chapter eight, verse nineteen.' Her lips set, primly. Even unbelievers deserved enlightenment.

'Thought you didn't reckon much to the Old Testament. My advice'd be to go easy on the '*And he said unto them, Go ye into all the world and preach the gospel to every creature*'. Mark, sixteen, verse fifteen? Piety don't go down too well round here. May get your tongue cut out.'

Fortunately, he couldn't see Annie's mouth hanging open in the dark. She did hear him mutter something under his breath though, something scathing and disagreeable.

Well, Amen to that. There endeth another of his wretched lessons.

It was some time before she could settle down. So many strange and unfamiliar sounds. The whisper of water, wind in the cottonwoods. Rustlings, night noises. Birds, and – a covert glance at McCall – beasts.

Had the man no consideration? Couldn't he climb a tree, sleep in that?

When a harsh wail echoed a way off, she sat up sharply. 'Mr McCall!'

He didn't stir.

'Was that a wolf? A coyote?'

'I sure hope so.' The drawl drifted up from beneath the brim of his hat.

And that was it? No reassurances, no sleep well? No keeping watch?

'But, what if - '

'I sleep with one eye open. Try it yourself.'

Hauling the blanket up round her ears, she lay down in semblance of sleep. Eyes though, were wide, fixed on black velvet sky and a million stars over her head.

'If you need anything,' he said, amusement clear in his voice. 'I'm only six inches away.'

Annie lay stiff as a board. The lamb stretched out next to the lion. But would the lion be licking his lips in the morning?

He'd *said* he wouldn't make a move in her direction, hadn't he? He knew his Apostles from his Isaiah, didn't he? But, was he a man of his word?

Fingering the crucifix round her neck, she sent up fervent private prayers to that effect. And as the embers of the fire died down, she slept.

Chapter 6

'When traversing rough country, I strongly advocate a good thick travelling costume. Loose skirts of heavy serge and high boots are ~~both picturesque and practical.' – p.24~~

Waking at dawn, Annie sat blinking in early eggshell light. Stiff and crumpled, bleary-eyed. Dress was rucked up, a twist of petticoats round her legs. Hastily, she covered herself up.

The horse had already been saddled and everything else packed up. McCall looked remarkably fresh, she thought, resentfully. Sluiced and shaven. How had he managed that?

'Sleep well?' he asked.

'Yes. Yes, thank you.'

'Thought so. You were snoring like a wounded buffalo. That's a dandy of a black eye, by the way. Looks like you were in a bar-room brawl. How're you feeling?'

She touched her bruised cheek, cautiously. As if marauding elephants had trampled her in the night? As if her head belonged to someone else? 'Better,' she lied, through tightening teeth. 'Much stronger, thank you.'

He challenged her with a look, but made no comment.

'Here, try some coffee. And don't spit it out this time, it'll help get you started.'

She took a swig of thick black liquid. It tasted like tar and the smell made her want to gag, but she kept swallowing, one gulp after another. One violent shudder brought it all boiling back, and she vomited a thin black stream over parched weeds.

'Was it that bad?'

'The chicken,' she croaked, her stomach churning. He held out a cloth and she wiped her chin. 'Last night. I thought it tasted odd.'

'That wasn't … never mind. You're wrecked, that's all. But we can't afford to hang round here much longer.'

'I'll be all right.' She swallowed the bad taste in her mouth. Another lie. Her stomach was boiling and she would rather stick needles in her eyes than get back on that horse.

'Right. We need to leave. Soon as you're ready.'

Struggling up, legs like jelly, she wobbled as far along the river bank as she dared, away from McCall's gimlet eye. He'd warned her to shake her boots back there. Snakes, he'd said, scorpions. Shuddering, she flicked fierce-looking flies away.

She'd never liked insects, she was sensitive to them, always had been. Other things, too. Salt water, coarse grass. She came out in blotches. Well if the Indians and the food didn't get her, the wild-life surely would.

Her toilet took ages. Wriggling out of corsets, pulling off petticoats, battalions of baby hooks and eyes. It felt like armour. Eighteen pounds of voluminous clothing, one useful hand and her stomach rolling, rolling.

Undressing within a circle of trees, she started anxiously as a dry wind stirred leaves, rustled grasses, snapped twigs. When birds called a warning, she stared sharply back over her shoulder. Eyes flew over outlines of rocks, bushes, boulders. Imagination ran wild.

Nothing moved. No-one there. Not that she could see,

anyway. She had that funny feeling again, though, a vague uneasiness. That someone was nearby. Something?

Outdoor living, she decided, made her very nervous. Wading into unexpectedly cold, copper-coloured water, her feet stirred red mud in the shallows. Or maybe – she splashed herself with ice-cold spray – maybe it was just McCall.

Her thighs were chafed and raw. Was cross-riding really so injurious to health? Her aunts thought so. But then, her aunts believed that too much thinking made a woman infertile. Better to bleed, she decided, than risk McCall's wrath.

For a while, she wrestled with the stiff canvas pants and huge creased shirt he'd insisted she wear. They smelled musty and faintly of him. But button-holes were stiff and everything hard and scratchy, and in the end she gave up.

Thinking wistfully of her trunk, squashed to its straps with silks, soft chemises and frilled lawn, she flapped back to her companion – his shirt held tight over her camisole.

'This is silly,' she said. Morning bath in a creek, male clothing? 'I'm lost in these, it's … fancy dress.'

Without a word, the shirt was pulled over her shoulders and slowly buttoned. Long fingers grazed her skin and she didn't speak, barely breathed, just fixed her eyes on a spot in the middle of his chest.

There was a pause when he'd done and she felt his eyes still on her. Her own stayed firmly downcast.

Turning trouser hems over, he cinched the waist with thick twine. 'There.' Tying a tight knot, he flicked her a disapproving look. 'Silk and hoops are fancy-dress out here. This way, you don't stand out. Now can you fix your hair up? And pull your hat down real low.'

'Why?' She was uncomfortably aware of flaming cheeks.

'So you'll look like a boy. We can't be sure what sort of company we'll be keeping. Just a precaution,' he said, seeing Annie's eyes widen. 'Anyhow, it must feel pretty good getting rid of those petticoats.'

Uneasily, she took off her hat, freeing her hair with a shake. As the damp tangle of gingery red tumbled to her shoulders, she trawled it ineffectually with her fingers. Her aunts abhorred the colour. Too brash, too vulgar. Her cousin, too. So reminiscent, Charlotte said, of bad temper and freckled skin.

For Annie, though, her hair was one frail link with close family. She'd inherited the colour from her father, apparently. And knowing that, she rejoiced in it.

She sensed McCall's stare, before she saw it. Dark eyes were reflective, making her blushingly aware that she was in danger once more, of missing impropriety by a whisker.

Loosening your hair in front of a man was practically wanton behaviour, best kept to the privacy of the boudoir. Not that she'd had much choice here. What should she have done? Stood behind a tree?

Her companion seemed oblivious to such niceties. He had something else on his mind. 'I knew someone once,' he said, thoughtfully. 'A friend with hair that colour. Unusual. Just the same.'

'Is that so?' murmured Annie. A woman. She could tell from his expression. Some head-turning, heart-stopping red-head most probably, with hair more flame than her own carrot.

She felt a small surprising stab of something. Resentment? Envy? 'An old friend?' she asked, offhandedly.

'We were pretty close.'

Ah, yes. A seductive, red-headed vision came to mind, swaying on his arm. Not that his sort of woman was of any interest to her, of course. Not in the slightest.

Bundling her hair back into her hat, not caring if it were neat or secure, she limped towards the horse - step limp, step sway - and waited to be helped onto its back.

'What's wrong with your leg?'

'Oh.' She flapped a cloud of gnats away. 'A runaway horse. Years ago. My foot caught in the stirrup and I was dragged along. It left me lop-sided.'

'You get this, the same time?' Frowning, he traced a small scar's path on her face with the tip of one finger. His hands smelled of leather; his eyes were dark and very steady.

The gnats came whining back. Annie barely noticed, just nodded, swallowing heavily, several times. No man had ever touched her like this, or noticed so much. What was it that made him so alarmingly affecting?

With Henry Hewell, she'd always felt herself shrink, like an oyster squirted with lemon. Not that he'd minded, he'd seemed to relish her response and had loomed over her, grinning like a crocodile. ('Afraid of me, Annie, hmm, hmmm? Like that, yes, like a woman who's afraid. And if a woman were to tell the truth, she likes a man who makes her feel that way.')

Then, she had experienced a sharp sense of dread. Here, the feeling was entirely different. Of course, her aunt would have thrown McCall out by now, and his hat after him.

A lecture would have followed. On Appropriate Behaviour For Young Ladies Of Refinement In The Event Of … Situations Arising.

Yes, well. Aunt Bea wasn't here, was she? Nor was anyone else, thank Heaven. No-one need be any the wiser.

'You were lucky,' he said. 'Could've been worse.'

Tired as she was of being patronised and pitied all the time, Annie found herself now, for some reason, wanting sympathy. 'I can't dance,' she said.

McCall's mouth twitched. 'That's tough,' he said, gravely. A slow smile. 'Oh, real tough.' And his head went back for a huge shout of laughter.

As the horse jerked its own head, appearing to join in, Annie felt aggrieved. Until now, this man had been as mean with smiles as with words. Now he was laughing, at her affliction. How much longer must she put up with him? 'Mr McCall.'

'Colt.'

'I beg your pardon?'

'I've seen you undressed and we've spent the night together. I think it's about time, don't you?'

'Colt?' Annie was thrown into confusion again.

'My Pa was Mike McCall,' he said, 'known as Mustang, on account of his way with horses. As a kid, I was all legs. And I'm in the horse business, too.'

She devoured this scrap of information. After a day and a night together, it was the most he had offered, one solitary clue to his character. Was he feeling more disposed then, towards conversation? 'So, those Comanche … '

'What about them?'

'Are they still with us?'

He gave her a level look, a certain tightness to his jaw. 'Try not to worry about the Comanche. They're part of life here.'

'Maybe so,' murmured Annie, 'but until now, the worst thing to chase me has been a neighbour's goat. Aren't I bound to be concerned about a band of bloodthirsty – '

'Why are all European women obsessed with the same thing?' he said, a twist to his mouth. 'Not death or disease, but this everlasting dread of captivity by male savages. They'd do things to you you'd never even dream of. There. Thrilling enough for you?'

Dismayed, she studied his face. His expression warned her off. He had a habit, she thought, of closing a conversation down when it suited him - bam, just like that - leaving a person just hanging, confused.

A rush of wind through prairie grass made her suddenly aware of other sounds.

A bird she couldn't see was calling softly to its mate, a strange persistent cry. When the answering two-note call sliced the air close by, McCall stiffened.

'What is it?'

He held up a hand. The throaty warble came again.

'Time to leave.'

Chapter 7

'To rest, and renew strength and courage in the desert, some shade must be procured against direct rays of the sun.' – p.102

Conversation ceased then. They rode again, hard and fast, and the dust cloud rose around them. Hot wind rushed by, sending hair and mane streaming.

Once more, Annie found herself awed by the landscape. She'd seen pictures in books, attended lectures with lantern slides. Nothing had prepared her for this. Vast open space, the widest vista. Fluted rock on the horizon soaring to meet limitless blue sky. Stunning silence.

Enthralled, she stared at the grandiose scene unfolding around them. The throat-catching beauty, the loneliness. So different to tidy England.

Just herself, the man and the horse, lost in vast mysterious space. Dwarfed by it. She thought, there's a spirituality in this, a closeness to God.

When McCall spoke again, his voice made her start. 'There's a water-hole ahead. We'll stop a while, give this feller a rest.'

'How much further?' Though she had every sympathy with the horse, her own driving need was to reach Red Rock. Back with her own kind, God willing.

'Couple more hours. We'll wait here 'til it cools down. Be there before dark.'

At least they'd be spared another nerve-wracking night together.

She had no desire to eat, just to drink and drink and rinse the dust from face and eyes. Her head, her whole body ached with travelling. Oh, for a bath. A bed!

'Water hole's low,' McCall warned. 'Go easy.'

With sticks and a saddle-blanket, he erected a sort of awning. Dozing in that sweltering shade, Annie drifted in and out of a fretful sleep.

All around, parched earth, as far as the eye could see. Scorched grass stretching out to a nearby bluff and boiling blue sky. No escape anywhere from the blinding sun, and heat so thick you could barely think.

'It's so *hot!*'

'You get used to it.'

She didn't want to get used to it.

'Look!' she said, struggling up to a sitting position. 'Over there! Is that a snake?'

'Sure looks like one.'

'Is it harmless?' She squinted at the motionless spiral, next to a pile of stones.

'Nothing's harmless here, unless it's dead. Go kick it, see if it rattles.' A beat, then he shook his head. 'Of course it's dead! Take it easy, for pity's sake.'

She didn't want to do that, either. Questions kept nagging.

Were Aunt Bea and Charlotte safe? If so, where were they now, and how were they managing without her? Charlotte could never cope with her mother alone. Since leaving England, Aunt Bea had demanded more or less permanent coddling.

They may have been mad with worry themselves, but she doubted it. She irritated her relatives and gave them headaches with her restlessness, her red hair, her reading. ('Bor-ing! You're bor-ing me!')

At that moment though, she would have welcomed any number of their complaints. If her relatives were to come flying out of that canyon, she would have forgiven them anything. But they wouldn't - a lump rose in her throat - so she couldn't, could she?

Overhead, the fringe of the saddle blanket waved and fluttered in the wind and she felt herself shrivelling. Wilting, withering in the brutal heat, along with everything else.

Everything, except McCall.

Because nearby, silent and preoccupied, her companion crouched, hat as ever shadowing his face. He hadn't moved a muscle in an hour - barely a twitch, a shift or a scratch. He didn't get tired, he didn't get hungry. Was he even breathing?

She studied him, warily. Was he *human?*

What was he thinking, then, this off-hand man? She had never, in her entire life, known anyone so utterly devoid of small-talk. 'Loosen your boots.' Those had been almost his only words in the last few hours. 'Or you'll get foot-rot.'

Words were of use to convey or obtain information, that was all. Anything else was a distraction. And if *you* talked too much, he'd simply lower his visor and clang - cut you off.

Although mindful of her injured arm, hadn't he unbuttoned her boots himself? And easing them off, gently rubbed her swollen feet and ankles. An action so sharply at odds with his brusque manner, that Annie's face had flamed like a beacon.

What if she'd been wearing hose, she wondered, what then? Would he have fumbled for her garters? Slid stockings down over her ankles? Would even *he* dare to act so indelicately?

She stared up at the sky. He was everything that had ever alarmed her in a man. Could she trust him, then? Had to, didn't she. There was no-one else.

'How would a person get to Missouri?' she said, suddenly.

He stared, narrow-eyed.

'Sedalia?' she tried again. 'How would you get to there from here?'

'I wouldn't, 'less I was taking a herd. Wild cowboy town. Stink of stockyard animals under a dust cloud.'

'The railroad camp, then?'

'Forget it, is my advice.'

'I don't think that I can.'

He shrugged. 'Your funeral.'

Another lull. Annie's eyes flicked to her grimy hands, then back to McCall's face.

His attention had already wandered. He was staring at the horizon, tracing a line from massive rocks in the east, to the yawning wideness of plains in the west. Watching, measuring.

His face wore that familiar closed look. *Keep Out.*

She felt a prickle of irritation. A friendly word would have cost him nothing. She wouldn't expect his life story and he hadn't shown the slightest interest in hers. There had to be something that would engage him though, surely.

'Mr McCall? What do you think of Andrew Johnson?'

He raised an eyebrow. 'Is he here?'

'No. No, I mean your president. He's in trouble, isn't he, he – '

'I know who he is. Can't say I think of him much at all.' He held out his flask. 'You ready for another drink? We'll fill up again before we go on.'

Taking a mouthful, she handed it back, wiping her mouth on her hand. 'Didn't men on the Santa Fe trail once drink the contents of a buffalo's stomach, when they had no water?' She'd get a conversation going here, if it killed her.

'Very likely.' He gave her an odd look. 'Want to try it?'

'I'd rather die!'

'If you were thirsty enough, you'd drink anything.'

'I can assure you – '

'Look,' he said. 'You don't have to keep making conversation. If you've nothing to say, save your strength. Keep your mouth shut and breathe through your nose. Or be real sorry later on.'

Annie shut her mouth. She breathed through her nose. He wasn't going to reveal anything about himself, was he? A stone would have been better company.

How did he do that though, shut everything down? Wasn't that what fish did? Well, she wasn't a fish or a fossil, not yet. Nor some hard-bitten Westerner, either.

Another Great Silence. As heavy and oppressive as the murderous heat. Time seemed to have slowed, the world was drifting in slow motion.

She rubbed her arm, convinced that it hurt more than yesterday. Was that normal? She daren't ask. McCall would expect her to behave like one of his horses - bravely mute.

Closing her eyes, she drifted back to a cool, damp English morning and her last walk with John Dickon. Narrow English lanes, knee-deep in cow-parsley, the air smelling of rain and wild garlic. And sweet, sensitive John. *They* had talked. Oh, yes.

Well, the Lord giveth, Annie thought, and the Lord taketh away. Indeed He does.

Yawning, she froze in mid-stretch as an odd sound reached her ears on heavy afternoon air. A distant rumble growing steadily to deafening roar.

As hard baked earth shuddered beneath her, tremors moved up through the ground, right into her bones. Something was coming. She sat transfixed, unable to move. Coming fast. The ground was shaking; the whole world shaking.

McCall's hand closing like a clamp round her wrist, shocked her to her senses. Hauling her up to the top of the bluff, he gave a low whistle of disbelief. 'Well, I'll be,' he said, softly. 'Will you look at that.'

Annie looked.

Here, land dropped sharply away to a flat plain of rippling

grass. At first, all she saw was a wide moving mass of dust. Then, beasts. Hundreds of them. Strong animals with glossy hides and huge shaggy heads, stampeding over the grass.

'Buffalo,' breathed McCall. 'A real big herd. That'll get the Comanche off our backs. I'd bet folding money those braves are high-tailing home to round up the rest of their men. Let's hope no-one else beats them to it.'

Annie stared at the crazily running animals, bunching and bumping, matted hair all over their eyes. Dust rose up after them, in clouds.

Covering her mouth, she coughed. 'Why? Is it sport of some kind?'

McCall's eyes were on the horizon, his mind adrift. 'Only civilised white men kill for pleasure. Indians think it's wasteful and insulting to the Great Spirit.'

'Food, then?'

'And the rest. Life and death. Trouble is, everyone's starting to know it.'

'I don't understand.'

'Hardly your concern, is it?'

Annie sighed. 'Don't patronise me, Mr McCall. I want to understand what you're saying.'

'You know anything about the Indian situation?' His blank expression matched her own.

'I know they attack defenceless white people, chop off their heads and play lacrosse with them. They impale infants on sticks sometimes, too, don't they? And grill them?'

'Whaat!' He swore under his breath. 'Where'd you hear that?'

'Books. I read a lot.'

'Yeah, well let's stick to fact not fiction, shall we?'

'Are you saying it's all untrue?'

'Not entirely. There's good and bad on both sides.'

'My book said – '

'I don't give a damn what your book said. Indians have land, that's the real rub, protected by treaty. Railroad companies and others want that land. So, they kill the buffalo, let carcasses rot and hope the tribes move off somewhere else. They stir up other trouble too, between Indians and settlers, to bring the army in. Get it?'

'I think so,' said Annie. 'If you can't catch the fish, drain the water in which they swim. Even my feeble brain can put two and two together and eventually arrive at the right answer.'

Dark eyes narrowed again. '*Have* I patronised you, Miss Haydon?'

'Haddon,' Annie said, wearily. 'It's all right, I'm used to it. Englishmen rarely think Englishwomen capable of grasping the strands of an argument. Unless it's to do with joints of mutton or rhubarb. I'd hoped it would be different here.'

'Ouch,' McCall murmured.

'You bullied me, too,' she said, 'yes, you did. When I was hurt and confused at the stagecoach Mr McCall, you –'

'Colt,' he cut in. 'And you couldn't have stayed put. Sure, you were shaken up and confused. I had to get you going.'

'You said we'd be staked out and skinned. I saw myself smeared in syrup and pegged out in the path of soldier ants!'

'It was that or a sharp slap.' He turned to watch the dark mass of buffalo roll in an unswerving line over the plain. 'Wonder what spooked 'em.'

'How can you be sure,' Annie said, 'that those Comanche have turned back?'

'I told you. Buffalo are their life-blood, their sole means of survival. Their gift from Wakan-Tanka.'

'Who?'

'The Great Spirit.'

'You mean God.'

'Do I?'

'Our Christian God, you know, the – '

'God of retribution and punishment? That Hellfire and Damnation feller? Indians believe Wakan-Tanka is in all things. The air we breathe, the wind, the water.'

'Oh. Very ... Genesis.'

'Too simple for you, is it?'

'No, no, it's interesting,' she said, quickly. 'We think of Indians as devils in war-bonnets. Dancing to tom-toms. Whooping – '

'Yeah thanks, I get the picture. It's insulting, a joke. Once there were hundreds of tribes. Now, a few are fighting to hold on to what's left. The red world's ending, a white one beginning. You won't find that in any damn book, either.'

Annie studied him, thoughtfully. The buffalo herd had gone, an eerie silence in its place. 'Have you studied history, Mr McCall?'

'No. I just live here. History is what you see, isn't it? The rest is guesswork. Better go back,' he said, 'and fill those water-bottles. I'll go further up. Try and see back along the trail.'

She did as he asked.

Then, trudging back with canvas-covered flasks, she spotted the sheaf of furled paper sticking out of his saddle-bag.

Her honest intention, she told herself later, was not to pry. God's truth, it was not. Her instinct, foolish though it may have been, was to try and organise the saddle-bags better. To take out, re-fold, tuck back.

Something though, caught her eye - a word? a name? - something, and she found herself straightening out the crumpled sheet of yellowing paper.

She read it once, then once again, her mind refusing to believe what her eyes could clearly see. A chill spread through her and her heart began to pound. Trying to make sense of it, she went over every word.

McCall's name was there and a grim likeness, in black and grimy white. He looked dark and vicious. Below the rough daguerreotype, some chilling words: '*WANTED: DEAD or ALIVE: HORSE THIEF AND MURDERER.*'

Something about a reward, something about him being

dangerous.

Hot and unsteady, a pulse beat in Annie's throat. This man, the man she had been alone with for two whole days, was a thief. Murderer!

Shifting stones warned of his approach. As he came closer, she stared with new eyes. The faint sense of security she had started to feel, had been sorely misplaced. This was a stranger. Tall, cold-eyed. Dangerous!

'Comanche have gone,' he told her. 'Someone up there's looking out for us.'

Annie swallowed, thickly. Someone up there might be looking after him. But what about her?

Chapter 8

'Ladies should always be alert to the prospect that some native peoples are dangerously unpredictable and barbarous in their habits.' – p.42

Get away! *Hurry, hurry.*

That thought filled Annie's head, blocking out all else. But how? She was trapped. Afraid of being on her own, terrified of the man at her side.

For a few seconds she wobbled between making a mad dash for freedom, and battering McCall with her aunt's umbrella - fetching out his eye with its sharp ferrule.

The chance soon passed by. His hands settled round her waist, lifting her high into the saddle. 'Better lose that parasol.'

Annie froze. 'Umbrella,' she corrected, unsteadily.

'It's a hundred and ten in the shade!'

'In England, it's … an essential fashion accessory. For men and for women.' And all she had left of her own.

'In Texas, Miss Hatton, we don't go much for accessories.' Prising it from her, he lobbed it into thick brush. 'Useless baggage.'

Which, her - or the umbrella? Annie's heart thumped. Wasn't it significant that he hadn't once, since they'd met, remembered her name? She too, was expendable. As he swung up behind, she tried hard not to shake.

Who had he harmed, this man? What might he do to her!

Calm down, she urged herself. *Think, think.* He'd had plenty of chances to hurt her, if that had been his plan. Plucked her from a scene of danger and destruction, too. Saved her! Yes, remember that.

Had he, though? The man was an outlaw. Now that she thought about it, hadn't his appearance on the scene been a little too opportune?

'Not far now.' Behind her back, his deep drawl, probably due to some awful outlaw diet of hard liquor and fat black cigars. Fear squeezed her chest. Where was he taking her? For once, she couldn't speak.

Light was fading. It was that time between light and dark. Landscape drained of colour, outlines and distances blurred. Heading into strange and unmarked territory, in thickening dusk, Annie felt frozen with fear.

Her shaking hands, pale as ghosts, gripped the saddle and she tried to keep some sense of direction.

'Is this still Texas?' she said, over her shoulder.

'Sure is.'

'We're going towards Missouri, though. Aren't we?'

'Nope, New Mexico. We're headed west.'

'So ... is Missouri that way?'

'Oklahoma. Lucky you're not leading the way.'

She didn't say anything else, didn't dare. Her mind though, was whirling. If he wondered at her sudden silence, McCall made no comment.

Eventually though, exhausted by her thoughts and desperate to make sense of them, she spoke up again when he brought the horse to a halt, at the top of a ridge. 'You buy and sell horses, then?' Her voice wobbled.

'Yep.'

And steal? Slaughter? She felt sick. 'Where do they come from?'

The answer came readily enough. 'Here and there. We round them up wild, saddle-break and sell 'em. I've a mind to do something else, though.'

'Oh?'

'Cattle have been running wild since the war, un-branded, unclaimed. I'm aiming to start a herd. The North is crying out for beef.'

'Where ... will you do that?'

'There's a canyon, not far from here. Well-watered, good pasture. I've staked a claim.'

How did he do that, she wondered. How could someone so wicked, sound so reasonable? Was he trying to wash the blood from his hands? 'Do you have a family?' she asked, affecting nonchalance.

'No.'

'A wife?'

Behind her back, the slightest pause. 'I live single. You?'

'I beg your pardon?'

'Do you,' he said, 'have a husband?'

'No. No, I do not.'

'What were you thinking of then, running round Texas unescorted?'

Now, there was a question. 'My aunt,' Annie murmured. 'My aunt wanted to make the journey.'

'What about your folks?'

'My mother died when I was born. My father left soon afterwards. He came to this country, as it happens, to America.'

'He left you behind?'

'With my aunt,' she said, quickly. 'I had every advantage. My father was just overtaken by grief.' As well as being thoroughly feckless and irresponsible, of course, according to her relatives.

'It happens. Guess that hurt too, though, leaving you.'

'I don't think so.' Her voice was flat. 'He didn't write, ever. People said he was afraid I'd remind him of my mother. He couldn't have borne that, they said.'

'And are you? Like your mother?'

'Not at all. She was beautiful, apparently. Gay, charming. I'm more like my father's family, I think. The hair and - '

What had got into her? Confiding! In an outlaw!

Wheeling the horse round, he kicked them off to full gallop again.

Silence brought back anxiety. How could he converse so naturally? Was this the poise of a patient killer?

'So, what do you do all day?' he asked, unexpectedly, the next time they slowed to a lope. 'Back home. In England.'

'*Do*? Err ... I play the piano-forte and paint. Sew, write letters, organise the household. That sort of thing.'

A pause. 'That's it?'

'Well ... ' Annie hesitated. What did he mean, that's it?

'Women out west bake and sew. Till the soil, tend animals, raise kids. Work long and hard as their men. Most end up looking hard and used as a plough-handle mind, but they sure don't have time for tinkling on the piano-forte. So hard to keep one in good tune, doncha know.'

All fear forgotten, Annie was tempted to aim a sharp backwards kick at his shin.

'Are you suggesting,' she said, 'that I lead an idle life? You know nothing about me. Once, I very nearly joined Miss Nightingale in the Crimea!'

'What stopped you?'

'My aunt. She said I was too young.'

'Do you always do as your aunt says? Sounds kind of lily-livered.'

'You don't know my aunt,' Annie muttered. Nor, she prayed, ever would he. She serviced the needs of her family, that's what she should have said, that was what she did all day. More standing than a servant, less than a favoured pet.

Somewhere between a doormat and a dogsbody.

'Women in our family don't work, Mr McCall.' She felt driven to point that out, outlaw or no outlaw. 'They marry. Anything else is considered unseemly.'

'You accept that?'

'I have no choice.'

'There's always a choice.'

'No,' Annie insisted, irritably, 'there isn't. Not in England, anyway. Single women have no freedom to choose. Our standing in society depends wholly on some man. Surely it's the same anywhere.'

'Most women here seem to think pretty much for themselves.'

Oh well, they would, wouldn't they. And this man was undoubtedly a world authority on what most women did.

Retreating into silence, she suspected that she was being measured. Measured and found wanting. A spoiled English spinster, that was what he thought of her. Pampered, protected, retiring at the merest hint of a headache.

He didn't like Englishwomen, did he? He'd made that clear. She didn't know why, and didn't care, either.

Every so often, he reined the horse in and sat still in the saddle, just listening.

'I guess you single ladies just sit around sewing samplers,' he said, at one of these stops. 'Until a suitable beau happens along. That about it?'

Oh, how *dare* he! Mr Horse-Thief. Mr I Know Best. 'I visit the infirm,' Annie said, 'carry food to the sick and call on all my aunt's tenants.'

'Crumbs to the deserving poor? Guess they're missing you real bad.'

She gave up. Why try to justify herself? To this wastrel.

'Y'know, there's a shortage of women out here,' he

announced, airily.

'Strange,' Annie said, 'when they have such a wonderful life. Ploughing and reaping and sowing and everything. Such considerate, charming men, too. I'm amazed that women don't flock here in droves.'

'Just making the point, that you could get a husband here if you liked. Real easy.'

'Thank you,' Annie muttered, 'for the gracious suggestion.' She had a strong sense of him grinning behind her back.

'Just an idea. You can take it or leave it.'

'I'll probably leave it.' Hardly surprising this man had ended up in trouble. She'd almost been driven to violence herself. And if he thought her such a useless article, why didn't he just shoot her and get it over with?

They didn't speak again until the horse slowed to a trot, and McCall waved a hand at the scene ahead. A straggle of dilapidated buildings bordering a dusty main street. Red Rock.

Relief at arriving unharmed was tempered by sharp disappointment. Annie had expected more. 'It doesn't look much,' she spluttered, as yellow dust blew full in their faces.

Dirt, dust, squalor. Rough and tumble sort of town.

'Best keep that opinion to yourself. People here reckon it's a real up-and-coming place. No sheriff yet, but they're starting a school, building a church.'

Another blow to her hopes. She'd planned to fling herself at the nearest law person - sheriff, whatever - tell her tale and beg for assistance. Who would help her now?

Flicking the rein gently against his horse's mane, McCall steered them along the main street, stirring dust with each step. Staring at clapboard shanties, false store-fronts and creaking signs, Annie half-expected her aunt and cousin to come rushing out to greet her.

In fact, hardly anyone was around.

A few dogs, raw-boned and ragged, padded the empty street. A particularly mangy, three-legged one bared its teeth at them. All other life seemed confined to the saloons. There were at least three, full of smoke, raucous laughter, jangling pianos.

'Is this a friendly place?' she said, suspiciously.

'Oh yeah.' McCall nodded in the direction of one of the saloons. A woman lounged in the doorway, hennaed hair elaborately coiffed, throat and shoulders bare. As they passed by, she called out to him, boldly. 'Yeah, ree-al friendly.'

Shifting self-consciously, Annie fingered her own clothes. Shirt and pants were now stiff with dirt and she felt as if she'd been wearing them for ever.

He stopped the horse in front of a tired-looking hotel, two stories high and needing paint, between the Dry Goods Store and the Cattle Merchants Bank.

Annie was on the ground in a trice, avoiding his touch at all costs.

Instinct urged her to shrink away. Instead, she allowed herself to be led inside and waited meekly while he arranged two rooms.

The open door of one revealed an iron bed, clean sheets. Luxury after way-stations where you were lucky to find a thin curtain separating women from the men.

'Cattleman's hotel,' McCall said. 'Not fancy, but respectable.'

Annie avoided his eyes. What would he know of respectable?

'Take time to freshen up, then we'll eat. I'll ask around, try and get news of your relatives.'

'I don't want to eat,' she said, quickly. 'I'm not hungry.'

'Still feeling bad? Is it your arm or your guts?'

She shook her head, trying to think of something half-way plausible to say.

'Those clothes.' He sighed. 'Look, this isn't San Francisco, nowhere like. No-one gives a toot about style here. I could try and get you something else, if you'd like.'

'No!' Annie said. 'No, I am ... I'm tired, that's all, I need to sleep. I haven't slept well for days, you know, what with the shock and ... ' She thought of plans to get away. 'I'd rather not be disturbed.'

'I shan't disturb you,' he said, drily, 'but what about your aunt? Wouldn't you want any news tonight?'

Biting her lip, she reluctantly met his gaze. 'Of course. Yes. If you have news ... '

A long pause. Dark eyes considered her, carefully. 'Just a wild stab,' he said, 'but is something bothering you?'

A quick breath and Annie was tempted to challenge him there and then. But what would she say? (*'Well you see, Mr McCall, I've discovered that you're a murderer. A dirty thief! What have you to say about that then, eh, eh?'*)

'It's been tough.' He broke the silence. 'All in all, you've done pretty good.'

She couldn't help staring. 'For an Englishwoman?'

'For anyone. Anyone hurt and on their own. You looked so frail back there, thought you'd blow clean away. Get some rest.' His tone was unexpectedly gentle. 'Reckon you've earned it.'

Kindness? Annie blinked at his retreating back. Courtesy? Please, not now.

Heaven knows, it would be hard enough to run. This outlaw had delivered her safely, knew the way, knew where the Indians were. What did she know?

She would wait. Yes, that was what she would do. To see if he came back with news of her relatives. But why would he bother to keep up the charade? Did he think she'd be some sort of foil for him, was that his plan?

She paced the room, panic rising, until a vision in the mirror's speckled glass stopped her dead in her tracks. Dull hair straggled from beneath the battered hat, dirt-streaked face was pinched, eyes heavy. She looked as if she'd had a good rub down with dust every day.

Taking off her hat, she pushed the rat's tails back, then rammed it back on again. There was more at stake here than her scary appearance.

And then, she waited. Waited and waited.

Wide-brimmed hats passed below the window, boots clattered on boarded walkways. Men rode in, rode out along the rutted main street and voices rose, in easy laughter and conversation.

The flickering lamp cast a depressing glow. Perched on a hard chair next to the table, Annie flicked through an abandoned catalogue from Chicago. Better lives! The tattered pages promised. Brighter futures! Illustrations of ladies undergarments had been ripped out.

Another world. Not hers. She didn't know anyone here, not even anyone who knew anyone. In fact, no-one else had the faintest idea where she was. Ah yes, one person. A murderer.

McCall was back in less than an hour. It felt like days.

'Good news, I guess,' he told her. 'Your aunt and cousin were picked up by the Army. They're at Fort Mackenzie, south west of here.'

Clutching at a chair for support, Annie searched his face in the lamp's dim light. Was he lying? His expression was unreadable as ever. But oh, she wanted to believe him, she really did.

'Are they … all right?'

'Far as I know. If you're up to it, we can make an early start tomorrow.'

She nodded politely, averting her eyes.

Considering her thoughtfully, he reached for a stray strand of her hair and tucked it behind her ear. As the breath caught in her throat, his thumb lightly traced the curve of her cheek. 'Will they know you now, d'you reckon?' His mouth widened into a slow smile. 'Your relatives.'

Annie stood perfectly still, a pulse beating in her throat.

For pity's sake, she told herself, this person is dangerous. Lawless, out of control. He's already killed one man and might mean to kill more.

In spite of the evidence, she was still wracked by doubts. Could someone who looked this good, be so bad? No cloven hoofs, no horns, just dark hair flopping thickly over his face. Pushing it away now, he slanted his hat low over his eyes.

'You look like some sort of desperado,' she said, begging silently: *Deny it! Go on. Explain yourself, before it's too late.*

His eyes flicked over her. 'You don't look much like a Sunday school teacher, yourself.'

That was it, then. Nothing explained, nothing changed. Shutting the door on him, a thin, bare silence closed around her, and she found herself shaking.

McCall had gone.

She was utterly, entirely, on her own.

Chapter 9

'Let no lady traveller ever forget the vulnerability of the single woman alone on the road, or the limitations that her sex presents.'
– p.94

Annie had no idea what to do now, none. More than anything she wanted to cry, but fumbling for a handkerchief, finding she hadn't got one, made everything worse. She had nothing. No money, no means. Barely even a hairpin.

Come *on*, she scolded herself, pull yourself together. Crying's no good. Aunt Bea and Charlotte were safe. Well, McCall had said so, but he may have been lying. Oh, *stop* it, stop crying.

Fort Mackenzie? That name rang a bell, she'd seen it somewhere on a map. That was where she must go, then. Even if McCall were not telling the truth, there'd be soldiers there. Men to trust, men to advise her.

Waiting for his footsteps to fade, she stared around the room. The narrow bed, dresser and pitcher dissolved before her swimming eyes. It was no good. She couldn't do this, not on her own.

Look, common sense. Hadn't she always been sensible? *('You may be a plain piece of goods, Miss Annie, but your head's on the right way.')* In a crisis, she wasn't completely useless.

Before leaving home, hadn't she pulled two children from a frozen pond, pounding their backs to force out water, then half-carrying, half-dragging them back to the Hall?

Aunt Bea had been less than complimentary of course, about sodden silk, ruined petticoats and the inconvenience of half-drowned children of the lower orders cluttering up the kitchen.

But then, Aunt Bea would make a row out of anything to do with Annie. Everyone else had been sincere in their praise, hadn't they? Even the curate.

As Annie's thoughts touched on that particular young man - the cheery face above the dog-collar, the sticking-up hair, the gaiters - she felt a stab of regret. Having asked God for an angel, she'd truly believed He'd sent John Dickon.

Not that he'd ever confessed to fond feelings toward her, not in so many words. Oh, he admired her mind, and had confided his own hopes and aspirations, at length. And they'd walked together. Talked and read Greek together.

Surely, that counted for something. And if he hadn't stirred her blood, exactly - well, he was sensible and kind and *why* had he never spoken out?

So instead, Henry Hewell. The only man now, likely to offer for her. Clammy hands, an unpleasant disposition and tendency to gout.

And then this trip, and here she was, and what in the name of sense and sanity, was she doing here? Thousands of miles from home. On her own!

How could she ever have thought that she wanted a wild, free life? She was utterly unfit for it. The urge to cry welled up again and she clamped down on it.

Hoisting McCall's pants up to her armpits, she ran. Out of the room, down the stairs, into the street.

A short distance from the hotel, black stillness pressed in and she strained to see in the darkness. Where now, who to trust?

Behind her, shouts and raucous laughter from one of the saloons. Ahead, a heavy smell of straw and steaming horses led her to the livery stables.

McCall's horse, in a gloomy rear stall, pricked his ears and jerked his huge head at her. Could she just take him? She hesitated. Did she dare! The animal was still smoking and sweating, hardly fit for another ride. She needed a fresh mount.

'Looking for someone?' A voice made her whirl.

'Oh, I err ... pardon me, sir. I need a horse.' Adjusting her hat, Annie tried to roughen her voice.

'In the right place then, ain't you?'

'Thing is ... I have no money at present. Would you ... would you loan me an animal? Just until I – '

The man lifted his lamp. Squinty eyes peered down at her. He smelled of the barn and had a nosy small-town air. 'Do I know you, son?'

'No. I'm, um ... just passing through.'

'Not on one of my horses, you ain't. I don't give credit, not to strangers. Where ye headed anyways?'

'Fort Mackenzie.'

'Joining up, huh. War's over, boy. Get back to your maw and paw.' He shook the straw from his shoulders. 'You want to git there that bad, better walk.'

Annie barely heard. She was considering her next step. As horses moved restlessly against the stall boards, she said, 'Are there sign-posts to the Fort?'

'Folks knows where they's a-going. Don't need no sign to say where they's got.'

Ho, ho. She stepped back into the alleyway. A real wag. Pity she no longer had a sense of humour. It was somewhere back there beside the trail, along with everything else she'd once owned.

This end of the street was black as pitch, all respectable dwellings shuttered and sealed. A dog whined and scratched somewhere. The light breeze, too hot to cool the air, whipped up dust.

A shuffling in the shadows made Annie start. Horses hitched to a nearby brace-post were snorting and shifting, while two men lurched unsteadily round them. Peering into darkness, she saw a flash of brass-buttoned blue. Blue flannel? A uniform!

'Excuse me? Excuse me, gentlemen. If you wouldn't mind … '

Shuffling stopped. The street was eerily still again.

'E-excuse – '

'Yeah, yeah. Heard you the first damn time.' The scrape of a boot brought one man weaving into the open. Big-boned, forearms like hams. 'What the hell you want, boy?'

Struck by a fierce smell of whisky and his rude animal stare, Annie took a step back. Warning bells began to ring.

This person was drunk, his pock-marked face set in deep, mean lines. In uniform though, wasn't he? Soiled and slovenly, perhaps. But still, Army issue.

'Would you happen to know Fort Mackenzie?'

A humourless yap of laughter rose up from somewhere behind the horses.

'Maybe we do.' Fumbling in his pocket for a thin cigar, the man drew his tongue along the edge. 'And maybe we doan. What's it to you?'

'I err, may have a proposition for you.'

'Uh-huh. You got a name, too?'

'I … beg pardon, sir?'

'Name boy, your goddamned name.'

'It … um, Arnold. Arnold Haddon.'

'You're a mite puny for the Army, Arnold.' Heavy eyes flickered over her. 'What y'all want with us?'

'I need a guide. To the Fort.'

'Hear that, Rafe? Two-bit kid wants guiding to the Fort.' A high-pitched laugh was wheezily withdrawn. 'You're on your own there, kid. Button up them britches and git home to your mammy.'

'Please!' Annie said. 'I've no horse at the moment, but a relative at Fort Mackenzie would pay you well, once we arrived.'

The man scratched at his beard stubble. 'Lessee if I got this right. You ain't got no horse? And you ain't got no money, neither.'

'No. No, but you see, my *relative* ... '

'Relative, hunh? Some Yankee Captain or somethin'?'

'Erm ... ' Annie's trousers started to slip. As she tried to adjust them, the man stared. A match flared and he smoked for a minute in silence.

'Well now, Arnold.' Bloodshot eyes darted interestedly over her. 'Never let it be said that a Bailey wouldn't help a good ole feller out. Y'all wait there while I talk this over with ma brother.'

Touching a finger to his sweat-stained hat, he moved away with a whistle.

Feeling a pinch of unease, Annie wavered. Wasn't there a lesson here? Something to do with frying pans? Fires. Yes, yes, but what were her choices? Uniformed men, or the murderous McCall?

While she waited, a puppy wandered out from the stables, his gait as unsteady as the two drunks. Small spike of tail stuck hopefully up, eyes rolled, dark and trusting. He sniffed, then flopped sideways onto Annie's boot, preparing to scratch.

The man came back, his brother stumbling behind, and she saw a glimmer of something pass between them, something she didn't much like. When the heavy-set one lashed out with his boot - 'Git outta here, mutt,' - she yelped along with the puppy.

'You're a mite soft for the army, boy.' Sly smiles were slowly exchanged. 'Better toughen up.'

Dropping his cheroot stub in the dirt, the first man put a boot on it. 'Well now, Beau Bailey's the name, and this here's my brother Rafe. And if y'all wanting an escort, we'd be happy to oblige. Ain't that right, Rafe?'

Rafe didn't seem to hold much of an opinion. Shorter than his brother, he was stringier too, with darting eyes that reminded Annie of a rat. On that subject, wasn't there the faintest whiff of one here? 'What about the horse?'

'Don't fuss yourself. Cavalry allus has spare.'

'Cavalry?'

'We sho are.' Sucking stained teeth, the soldier spat downwind. 'Ain't we, Rafe?'

The mount they offered Annie was a brute, all rolling eyes, lunging head and yellow teeth. Apart from the leg at each corner, the head and the tail, it bore no resemblance to any animal she'd ever ridden before.

Stretching out a tentative hand, she jumped as it tossed its huge head at her, snorting and snickering. Pawing the ground, it fixed her with a malevolent eye.

'Hey! Don't spook him now, boy, if you aimin' to chew with a full set of teeth.'

Queasily, Annie moved back. Since her accident, she'd suffered a fierce fear of horses. A gentle, side-saddle canter on a quiet mare had been about all she could stand.

Clamped to McCall's chest had been a somewhat different experience, but she had no desire to dwell on that.

'Oh pish Annie,' Charlotte often snapped. 'Don't be so tiresome. Everyone rides. Even the most timid and pathetic of people.'

Maybe so. But as it had been Charlotte herself, bless her sweet heart, who'd deliberately placed the spiny burr that had caused the horse to rear and throw her off - Annie hadn't felt the need to pay much attention.

It was the worst thing anyone had ever done to her. She'd felt sick for weeks.

Now, sitting uncomfortably astride, waiting to start off, she grew more and more uneasy. Her injured arm had required her to be helped onto the horse. Had she imagined hands lingering?

And the uniform. Closer inspection revealed a rag-bag mix of blue and grey. What proper soldier would wear both?

Fool, Annie. Idiot! There was nothing about these men that she liked. McCall had been her first mistake, she couldn't afford another. Desperately, she tried to slither from the saddle.

'Easy. Easy now, kid! Whoa.' Grabbing her restless horse, Beau Bailey slipped the reins back over the brace-post. 'Kinda skittish, ain't you? Here.' He thrust a bottle under her nose. 'Take a tipple. To, uh ... let's see, now ... to army life.'

On firm ground again, Annie fought against her panic. 'I don't ... I'm not too well on whisky.'

'I don't give a hang what you're well on, Arnie.' He took a long, gulping swig. 'If I'm offering, boy – you're drinking.'

Screwing up her face, Annie sucked timidly at the bottle. A powerful raw smell met her nose, then fiery liquid caught her throat, rushing headlong into her empty stomach.

As she coughed and gasped, someone clapped her back. 'Thasser way, kid. Mite stronger'n sarsparilly, ain't it?'

Her eyes watered. The bottle passed round.

'To the South!'

'The railroad!'

Annie concentrated on swallowing as little as possible. Three quick gulps. A reeling head. Things sliding out of focus. 'Are we going to the Fort, now?'

'No all-fired hurry. Time enough to git your Yankee soldier suit and salute the damn flag. First off, we're doin' some hunting.' Shaping two fingers like a gun, Beau Bailey followed the path of a pretend target. 'Bang, bang. Y'all dead. Yip, buffalo hunting. For the railroad. We can use an extra gun.'

Annie's violent hiccup caused the horse to turn. Were these the Indian-haters McCall had mentioned? Men who slaughtered the herds? Rat-man was now checking an array of knives and rifles, and both men wore crossed gun-belts under their coats.

'Buffalo?' Her face was watchful.

'Yip. Kill 'em, skin 'em, sell the hides.'

'For ... the railroad?'

'In a manner of speaking. Meat rots, Injuns move off, track gits laid.'

Dear Lord, Annie thought, eyes darting round in panic. How do I get out of this?

No-one else was anywhere near. This end of the street, all dark and silent. The only sound a harrumphing and shuffling from the stables; the only light a cosy glow from the distant hotel.

Dizzy and off-balance, she stumbled. 'But, I'm expected. At Fort Mackenzie.'

Beau Bailey picked his teeth, idly. Rheumy eyes travelled over her. 'Your voice is kinda high for a boy, ain't it, Arnold? Hurry, hurry, hurry,' he mimicked, in whining falsetto. 'I'm hexpected. Hait Fort Mackenzie.'

Annie froze, and a hairy hand snaked out, snatching at her hat. Bone pins were sent flying, curls tumbled to her shoulders.

'Well lookee, lookee.' A long, low whistle, followed by a rebel howl. 'Told you Rafe, didn't I? Didn't ole Beau tell you? No boy has hips like that. Hellfire. We gonna have us some fun!'

'Hold on a minute, Beau. Railroad agent ain't gonna like this.'

'Railroad won't give a spit in hell, long as their track gits laid.' Stained fingers tweaked Annie's cheek. 'When you last see skin like thait, hunh? Like pastry.'

Too shocked to cry out, Annie inched slowly away. Whisky

may have dulled her senses, but she still recognised the idea forming behind those red-rimmed eyes.

If McCall was a pirate, these men were something else. Something she'd been shielded from her entire respectable life. Flotsam. A shiver ran through her.

'Purty little thing, ain't you? Y'all from hereabouts?'

'No. No, I'm ... I am English.'

'Yeah? Thought you was somethin'.'

Cautiously, she began placing one foot behind the other. 'Well, I ought to be going now. S-sorry to have wasted your time.' Desperately, she held onto a smile. 'So interesting hearing about the railroad and buffalo and skinning and everything. Good luck with – '

'Bad idea, Red.' Shaking his head, Beau Bailey gripped her arm. 'Little lady like you, out all alone? Temptation ain't it, in a land of men. Then there's our business plans, see. Wouldn't want folks hearing about them at no Yankee Fort an' getting the wrong idea.'

Tightening his grip, he jerked Annie to him, holding her with ease while she struggled. 'Whoo, brother!' A high-pitched cackle. 'We got us a real fire-cracker.'

Wedging her leg with one knee, he twisted her arm back - twisted and twisted, twisted hard.

'Please.' A shameful whimper of sound. 'You're hurting.'

'Stay still, then. Quit grisling. Be nice to ole Beau, or I'll – '

'Or ... you'll *what?*'

A new voice, slow and very sure of itself.

Beau Bailey's head snapped back. Annie's eyes flew open.

In the dusty street, everything seemed to be holding its breath.

Then, Beau swivelled round.

Chapter 10

'Personal experience leads me to advise that most perils can be avoided by the use of common sense.' – p.54

'Or ... you'll what?'

The challenge came again, and three pairs of eyes strained to make out the man, propped against the hitching-rail. Thumbs were hooked into pants, hat tilted loosely over his eyes. 'Want to play rough, Bailey? Pick someone your own size.'

'McCall!' The name was spat out, like a snake bite. 'Stick to hustling horses. This ain't nothing to do with you.'

McCall emerged from shadow, his feet planted wide. 'I'm kinda touchy about men handling women.'

'Handle plenty yourself, doncha?'

'Only when they want me to.'

'Well she don't mind, do you little lady?' Beau tossed greasy hair back. 'We was just having us some fun here. Ain't nothin' in the world wrong with that.'

Annie sensed McCall's stare. White-faced, she avoided his eyes.

'The lady doesn't seem to share your sense of humour,' he

said.

'Hell, y'all don't know a thing about it. She damn near begged us to bring her along, ain't that right, Rafe?'

'S'right, McCall. She came to us, we sho didn't go lookin' for her.'

'Well, you want to take her over, be my guest. Better treat her right, though, or the Army'll be sore. They're out looking for her now, all over.'

'We don't know nothing 'bout that.'

'You know now.'

Annie stood between them, consigned to the third person. Near to hysteria herself, she sensed that something more than mere words was affecting the Baileys. Something else. A reputation?

Rafe shuffled his feet. 'We ain't aiming to set up against you, McCall. We don't want no more trouble, swear-to-God.'

'Then don't start any. You smell too drunk to shoot straight. Get away from her.'

McCall's hand was on his gun-belt, Annie's eyes on stalks. As the grip on her loosened, relief washed her first, then confusion.

So, which foot was the boot now on? McCall had saved her. But, for what!

Just shoot me, she thought, heart limping in her chest. Get it over with now. Shoot me first.

'Oh, we're going. Best keep your big nose out of our business though, y'hear. Law's on your tail, McCall. And the Army. They gonna hang you out to dry.'

'Yeah? Army might be interested in the big bay, the black and the grey hitched up over there. I sold animals like that to the Fort awhile back.'

'That some kind of accusation? Ain't worth warm spit. You can't prove a thing.'

'Don't count on it. If ever a man had a buffalo by the tail, Bailey, you're it.'

'Well buffalo are disappearing fast, horseman.' Stumbling to his horse, Beau Bailey boosted himself up. 'Guess you ain't heard.'

Annie's eyes slid from one to the other. She was invisible now. A lone child in adult company. *Run! Go on! They won't notice, won't care.*

She didn't move. She wanted to, but for some reason her legs weren't responding to instruction.

Rafe stood his ground, plying a plug of tobacco between his teeth. 'Beau ain't all bad, McCall. He doan know how to act anymore, thass all. The war – '

'War's over. You don't like what he does, don't go along with it.'

'We lost everything. How's a man supposed to live? Tell me that.'

McCall shrugged. 'Still fit and healthy, aren't you? Carrying all your limbs. If you're willing to sweat, push a plough.'

'We want better'n that! We fought, McCall. Earned the right – '

'Rights aren't worth a lot here, Bailey. Not any more.'

'Know somethin'? You don't sound like a Texan no more, no white man, neither.'

'Shut up, Rafe.'

'Know how you sound? Like a dog-eating, flat-nosed – '

'Shut *up*!'

The Baileys rode off, hooves thudding away hard. A dog howled somewhere. Then, silence. Just warm wind soughing through from the south. In its path, frail buildings sighed and creaked.

Annie knew she had to say something soon. Yes, and any minute, she would. For now, she just rubbed her arm, summoning strength.

And McCall? His face, half-shadowed by the hat, told her nothing. Whatever he was thinking, he wasn't letting on.

What did he expect, she wondered. Whimpering gratitude,

a polite vote of thanks? How about screaming hysterics. Her mind went to wolves. Or was it bears? Animals with that same fixed sort of mask, so that you never knew what they were thinking.

She could almost smell the disapproval, though. His jaw was tight, shoulders set. A volcano about to erupt. Was he going to start spewing fire and smoke? Or just rear up and maul her?

Time passed, the world turned. The moon sailed out from behind a cloud, edging everything with silver.

Annie coughed and scuffed her feet.

'Well?' McCall broke the silence eventually, his voice a bored drawl. 'I don't want to blur your concentration or anything, but are you planning to tell me? Or shall I guess?'

She cleared her throat. It felt cracked and full of sand.

'In your own good time, of course. What? Didn't quite catch that.'

'How long were you there?' She eyed him, warily.

'Long enough. Trusted those mean-eyed drunks, did you? Over me?' Their eyes locked. 'We'd rubbed along well enough, hadn't we? I mean, you mistrusted me, I patronized you. What went wrong?'

Annie tried a smile. It wasn't returned. 'I saw the wanted poster. With you on it.'

'And that was it?' His sigh was reminiscent of a parent with a wilful child. 'You didn't ask, just high-tailed off?'

A minute shrug. She'd realised her mistake when he'd started lecturing the Baileys. Outlaws didn't have *principles*, did they? Ideals. Go on then, she thought, her stomach awash with whisky. Enjoy yourself.

'So, Miss English Prudence teams up with two roughnecks. Tell me, what did that prove?'

'I was desperate. They were in uniform.'

'A fool with one eye could see what they were.'

'I had to make a decision.' Squinting up at his face, she

looked for some sign of sympathy, or understanding.

'Yeah? You made a bad one. Did they hurt you?'

'Not really.' Not much. Just wrenched her arm almost off, that was all. Frightened her half to death. 'They ... who *are* they?'

'Jayhawkers. Ex-Army outlaws. Mighty mean, mighty drunk and paid to make trouble with the Comanche. That's how I ended up on a wanted poster.'

'I don't ... '

'I've crossed them, too many times. They want me out of the way. Them and the railroad. Nothing I can't sort. Takes time, that's all.'

'Why not tell an officer of the law, then?' Her voice was now almost a croak. She'd ground her teeth so hard that her jaw ached. 'A sheriff, or somebody?'

'There *is* no sheriff. Not for miles. Law and justice aren't always the same thing here, anyway.'

'The Army?'

'You don't want to hear about the Army.'

That's right, she didn't. What she wanted, though, was to be awkward. 'My ears are connected to my brain, Mr McCall. I can make up my own mind what I do and don't want to hear.'

'As you say.' His polite calm was far more threatening than anger. 'All right. The Army's been persuaded to make the plains safe for trains and profit-making.'

'Sounds reasonable enough.'

'When treaties are violated, buffalo wiped out?'

Ah, yes. *(Yawn)* McCall's Very Own History Of The West. Well, she'd asked for it.

'Tragic.' She shrugged. 'But isn't that progress?'

'Nothing can stop it, huh? Roll over and die, without a fight.'

His blood was up, for some reason. Well, sorry. She couldn't face another lecture. Her mouth felt like rat fur. She found herself wondering what it would take to get this over with. Grovelling?

'What about safe havens, then? Reservations and things?' She yawned again.

'Indians don't conform to lines on a map! They've been here thousands of years and never put up fences. It's whites who want to parcel it out.'

Annie's attention was caught, suddenly. 'What makes *you* so different, then? How you think. Doesn't it set you apart?'

'Lady, I was born apart.' Taking off his hat, McCall pushed black hair slowly back. 'Father was Irish, mother Sioux. That enough?' His lips tightened and he growled in the telling. Like a bear who'd been poked with a stick.

'You're Indian?'

'Part. Part Indian.'

Which part, wondered Annie, open-mouthed. 'But, you're so ... so ... '

'Civilised?' he suggested, bitterly.

No. She stared. That wasn't the word for him at all. Quite the opposite, in fact. But - an Indian? A wild ... red ... Indian? Of course. She could see it now. What he was. That mix of charm and menace. The dual loyalty, the sense of mission.

The underdog defending the downtrodden.

Goodness. If she got home in one piece, she could dine out on this for months. *('I travelled with an Indian, you know. No, no, it's perfectly true. A wild, red Indian. Part Sioux, I believe. The finest horsemen on the Plains. So thrilling.')*

She felt a flash of admiration. 'Well. That's wonderful, isn't it.'

'Who for?' he said, drily. 'You or me?'

'Aren't you proud of your heritage, Mr McCall?'

'I'm not apologising for it, if that's what you're getting at.'

'It's not a problem, though, is it? I mean – '

'Is it hell! It's been a problem since Columbus got here.'

Annie cleared her throat. 'Well, we have to think of the

present now, don't we? Not get stuck in the past.'

'Well pardon me, I stand corrected.' He shot her a slant-eyed look. 'Guess we're done talking. You'd better go.'

For a moment, she was shaken. He wasn't proposing to leave her there, was he? 'But, I need to go to the Fort.'

'Nice night for a ride. How will you get there?'

She stared. 'I was hoping you might take me.'

'I'm not a big believer in second chances.'

No, Annie thought, he wouldn't be. All right, humble pie, hair shirt. She would smear herself with ashes if it would help.

'Look,' she said, with as much dignity as she could muster. 'I'm really sorry to have put you to so much trouble. I've been naive. A perfect fool, in fact.'

'A fool with spunk. By the way, those pants are falling down.'

'Yes, I ... ' Red-faced, she hauled her trousers back up to her armpits. 'Sorry?'

'It took guts to go off like that. Didn't think you had it in you. Something else has come up, that's all. There's a game in the next town. Poker. You know it?'

'Cards!'

'Well, we throw in a few coins, just to make it interesting.'

'Oh, quite.' Annie paused. 'Well, I wouldn't want to come between you and anything *really* important. I can make my own way to the Fort. If you'd be kind enough to arrange the loan of a horse and point me in the right direction, I'll be off.'

'The hell you will! Ah yes.' His eyes rolled. 'I'd forgotten. You can look after yourself, can't you? A regular little pioneer. Listen, wandering off on your own is a real bad idea. Go anywhere here, you take precautions. Taking off without water is dumb, getting lost is a death sentence. Don't try it again.' Grasping her wrist, his eyes glittered. 'Promise?'

She drew back. Did he want her to cross her heart and spit

or something?

'Look,' he said. 'I found you. I don't want to be blamed for getting you lost again. I'm in enough trouble.'

'Well if *you* won't take me, how do you suggest I get there?'

'The Army. Those fifty-cent-a-day professionals can fetch you. We'll get a message through. Right,' he said, briskly. 'Let's close the book on it, shall we? I'll see you back to the hotel. If you're about ready.'

Annie's mouth and throat were paralysed, suddenly. Any minute now, she was going to crumple and cry and confirm all his rotten prejudices about her. 'This is goodbye, then?' she managed to croak.

'Afraid so,' he said, with heavy irony. 'But I'll always hold a special place for you in my heart.'

Back into view suddenly - ears up, tail down - tottered the puppy. Heading straight for them, he sniffed Annie's boots hopefully.

'Hello, pup.' Welcoming the distraction, she bent to scratch an ear, while he whimpered and rolled with joy. 'You're too young to be out on your own.'

'He's not the only one.' McCall's voice was desert dry.

A wave of exhaustion swept Annie. Hostility she could handle. But, condescension? 'I am twenty-seven.'

'You're kind of small for twenty-seven.'

'I was kind of small for seven and seventeen, too. What's that to do with anything?'

He grinned. She wished he wouldn't. It made her want to bolt for safety.

Straightening up, the blood roared in her ears and she swayed. The puppy whimpered against her legs, its coat rough and patchy. 'Who looks after it?'

'How should I know? On its own, I guess. A stray.'

Just like me, thought Annie, feeling increasingly frail.

McCall was muttering again, something about bad

company and not knowing any better. The blood thumped harder and faster and she stopped listening.

Of course, a proper gentleman wouldn't behave like this. McCall wasn't proper though, was he? He wasn't a gentleman, either. *Apparently,* he wasn't an outlaw. What he was ... what he ...

Her mind whirled, black sky began to spin and spin. She blacked out.

Chapter 11

'In uneducated, low-class company, the influence of a refined, self-respecting woman should never be underestimated. It is second only to the influence of religion in its benefits.' - p.80

What happened?

One minute, Annie's knees were buckling. The next, she was in strong arms, being carried into someone's parlour.

She remembered some things. Shouts, blurred faces. A buzz of voices.

'What's wrong with her? She's white as paper.'

'Shock. Fatigue. She'll be OK. Seems to swoon pretty often, though.'

What! Who said that! Why, she almost never -

'Is she sick? Loosen her stays.'

'She isn't wearing any.'

McCall. It must be. He had this unnerving habit of mentioning the unmentionable.

Annie struggled up. The room had emptied. So who was hitting her head with a hammer?

'Drink this.' McCall offered a glass. Something brown

swirled round inside it.

'No, no.' She started to shake. 'Water. Just water.'

'This is better.'

'What is it?'

'Trust me,' he said, drily.

Draining the glass, she coughed and spluttered. As its slow warmth spread, she hiccupped loudly. 'I beg your pardon!'

'Granted.' He refilled her glass. 'Here. Southern cure.'

'Am I drunk?' Her mind looked for excuses. (*'I couldn't help it, Aunt Bea. No, really! A most unfortunate set of circumstances. Quite beyond my control.'*) 'I've never been drunk.'

'Glad to hear it.' He gave her a measured look. 'You need to eat. Are you hungry?'

She shook her head. Not hungry, sick, sick. Three months on the rolling Atlantic, and she'd never felt as nauseous.

'You'll feel better if you eat. Food first,' he said, considering her carefully, 'then the doctor. I don't like the look of that arm.'

Shifting uncomfortably, Annie thought it probably wasn't all that he didn't like the look of. She felt like something abandoned by tinkers.

'There's a doctor here?' she said vaguely, examining scuffed and dust-splattered boots. Such a pity. They'd been custom-made. Black kid, high cut.

'Out front, in the saloon.'

Saloon! Her head jerked up. 'Is he sober?'

'About as much as you are.' McCall moved towards the door. 'Now, just stay put.'

Annie choked on the last of her drink. Strong liquor left an oily slick round the glass. She set it down with difficulty, missing the edge of the table several times, then stared around.

A room crammed with furniture, smelling of smoke and cheap scent. Plush chairs, a pair of maroon brocade ottomans, polished table. Damask drapes framing deep crimson blinds. So much red, so much *tassel!* Her head swam.

Sinking back into tongue-coloured cushions, she squinted at ornate wall-coverings. Portraits in dusty frames stared primly back. Blurred prairie scenes, a picture of a bull - huge horns, glittering eyes. It glared at her, belligerently. Colours and patterns ran giddily together. She felt sick.

Her hair, frizzing in wild puffs round her face, felt like dandelion fluff. She toyed with it nervously. Skin was dry and flaky, too and her teeth felt like flannel.

Well, she'd been warned. This was what happened if you failed to keep up the endless, boring maintenance of yourself, that was such a chore at home.

Skin stuff and hair stuff and unmentionable stuff. More and more stuff and who could be bothered in this heat?

Fat lot of good it did, anyway, battling with the forces of nature. Aunt Bea's voice seemed to echo in her ears. '*Quite, quite lovely, Charlotte. Annie – oh, dear!*'

Her head buzzed. She let it droop. A scuffling outside the door brought it sharply back up again.

'McCall?' Whispers and muffled giggles. 'Yoo-hoo, you in there?'

A soft knock, a flurry of petticoats and two heads poked round the door. Two girls with bright hair and hard, pretty faces. As they inched inside, curious eyes darted all round the room.

'Ooh, s'cuse us!' one said, adjusting her dipping neckline. 'We're waiting on a friend, a ... partic'lar friend.' She pouted and twirled her hair round her fingers. 'McCall? He was reckoned to be in here.'

McCall had friends? Annie struggled to focus. Until now, she'd seen little regard for anyone except his horse. Of course, these girls were prettier than his horse.

'Miss?'

Annie flapped a hand. For some reason, her tongue and lips wouldn't do what she wanted them to. 'Mishter McCall? He *was* here. Where is this ... eggsactly?'

'Here? This here's the Alhambra.' Beadily, the girls took in Annie's odd choice of clothes, her wild hair and exchanged glances.

'You, err ... travelling with him, lady?' One dug the other in the ribs. 'I'd nail his feet to the floor pretty damn quick, if I was you.'

More giggles. A flash of diamond tooth, rattle of cheap gewgaws, and they were gone. Well. Thank goodness. A suffocatingly heavy scent though, lingered a long while afterwards.

Annie took a breath. Ouch. This pain was getting worse. Her forehead felt as if it was about to split open. She thought of her aunt, (*'No-one knows how I suffer! I have headaches where I pray for death!'*) and vowed to show more sympathy, in future.

Supposing - imagination bolted off like a wayward horse - supposing she were to up and die here? Any minute now, considering how she was feeling. Who would worry?

No-one had ever cared for her, had they? Father, aunts. All her life, she'd been a burden to someone or other. Best thing now - a tear trembled in one eye - a swift and sudden demise. Easier all round.

Relatives would be free of a burden. (*'God's good grace, Eugenie. I mean to say - that unsightly limp! A merciful release.'*)

McCall could claim he had done his best: (*'Not a thing more I could do, ma'am*) - as he bore simple souvenirs to Aunt Bea. Her silver locket? A strand of hair, some tattered shreds of underwear. (*'She just faded away before my eyes, real sudden-like.'*)

No mourning cards for her, oh no. No fans of black silk, no horses with plumes. The family would close over her passing, like water over a pebble. Smoothly, without a ripple.

A few maudlin moments and Annie had herself dead, buried and disposed of. Lost forever in some lonely resting place. Just bury me, on the lone prair-ee. Long grass over her grave, a distant foreign death.

She was fading, slipping away. She would never get out of here. She was drunk. *Drunk*!

Quietness settled, like a shroud. What time was it? And why was McCall taking so long? He'd been gone for ages. Perhaps he'd already had enough and skedaddled out of town.

Lamps flickered and somewhere, a clock struck. Annie tried to keep count of the chimes, but lost track. A door opened, letting through a gust of noise and raucous laughter, then closed again.

Silence.

She shook herself. McCall had told her to stay put. But, for how long? What if he *had* left already? A person could wither and die, just waiting.

Easing the door open a crack, she peered out. All clear and she made a dash for it, flinging herself at the rear door of the saloon, just managing not to fall flat on her face as it swung easily inwards.

It took a moment for her eyes to adjust to the dimness. A room full of men, a wild loud crowd. Under a sea of hats, some hunched over bottles at the bar. Others sprawled at tables, bent on serious card games.

Someone shouted out bets. 'Straight draw poker suit everybody? Threes, straights, flushes. No fancy hands.'

'Hey you! Put up or shut up, will ya.'

Annie's eyes darted round, her head reeling. Painted mirrors lined the walls, lascivious paintings. Naked ladies in serene poses. Who are *you?* The people in the pictures sneered. What are you doing here?

Perspiration formed above her lip. A hard, dry feeling in her throat.

'What's your poison, friend? Whisky, warm whisky?'

She jumped, shrinking against the wall. Any minute now, everyone would turn and stare at her.

'Whisky, yip. Whisky all round.'

Not a soul bothered, no-one did.

An ancient parlour piano jingle-jangled, voices laughed and jeered. And over it all, a floating fog of thick cigar smoke fairly choked the breath out of you.

And the girls! Gaudy and bright as painted birds, all spangles and frothy petticoats.

Annie stared round, with a sort of stunned curiosity. How *could* anyone have brought her here? Speaking of McCall, no sign of him anywhere, none.

Hard to be sure, because her eyes were all blurry, but she scanned the room several times before sliding slowly backwards, towards the door. *Get out. Now.*

Then, something happened. Something that stopped her in her tracks and reduced the volume of noise in the room to a cough.

The newcomer attracted no attention at first. Not until he sauntered to the bar, demanding a drink. Bold as brass, calm as you please.

An Indian - no doubt about that - braided hair to his shoulders, a bright tight bandana. Curiously though, he seemed to be wearing the blue flannel coat of a Cavalry soldier. 'Whisky?'

At his muttered request, there was stunned silence. Music ceased, the buzz of conversation died down and Annie saw the piano player sidle away.

'You smell somethin' in here, Abe?' The barman turned his back, moving glasses, wiping the back counter, rearranging the bar.

'Sure do. Something stinks real bad.'

'Whisky?'

'No whisky, no way.' Turning back, the barman's voice rose. 'Ain't you seen the sign? No horses, no dogs and no stinking savages, neither! Savvy?'

'Yellow-bellied vermin can't read, Deevy. These dogs drink where they can.'

What was happening? Annie had no idea. She was terrified though, when tempers flared and a full glass of whisky was flung into the Indian's face. 'Here. Now, git. Back to your peyote and mescale. No fire-water here.'

The man - his skin the colour of copper, eyes intelligent and cold – didn't move or speak. He simply stared ahead, stony-faced, while whisky dripped and the stain spread on his coat.

'You ever see a honest injun wearin' a Army jacket?'

'Ain't never seen a honest injun. Throw the dog-eater out!'

The barman, Deevy, wiped his hands back and forth on his apron and reached for something behind the bar. Something heavy and metal, glinting dully in the lamplight.

Go, Annie willed the Indian fiercely, *go, go.* In his place, she would have slunk out like a whipped dog. Holding her breath, she watched while the barman checked his gun, turning the cylinder slowly, *click … click-click.*

'Waitin' fer me to put a bullet in that red hide, huh? Hell, ah'll oblige, I got legal right to kill scum-sucking hostiles. Ain't that right, fellers?'

No reply. Bystanders were too busy jostling to get behind each other. Feeling sick, Annie edged towards the door.

'I got a better idea. Lessee him jump.' Another man emerged from dim, boozy darkness waving a gun. His face was red, huge belly quivered and several chins seemed to have a life of their own. Like a character from one of those dime novels, Annie thought. A cliché, a joke.

No-one laughed though, as two sharp retorts sent everyone scurrying for cover. Bullets ricocheted right and left, men dived under tables and glass shattered, hailing over everything. Someone squealed.

Annie froze. In her panic, she didn't know whether to run, hide or throw herself under a table. She felt too unsteady for any sudden moves. As the gunman moved back for better aim, she found herself trapped, a hypnotised rabbit, staring in horror at the back of his thick, red neck.

'Dance, ya piece of dung.' Bullets chipped the ground, *ping … ping-ping.* 'Or I'll blow both feet off.' Raising an arm, the man stumbled backwards over Annie.

She did her best to duck away, but a stream of raw expletives nailed her to the spot.

For a sickening second, she thought he was going to shoot her. As he took in who, or what she was though, his jaw dropped and hand fell slackly to his side.

Every eye in the room now turned their way, and the atmosphere slowly changed. Someone laughed, mirthlessly, 'Nice one, Morg. Hurr, hurr.'

That made Morg madder than ever. His beet-red face jutted aggressively and Annie was reminded of one of those massive bull buffalo. Pounds and pounds of snorting meat on the hoof. Shouldn't someone be leading him round on a string?

Bloodshot eyes took in her frizzed hair, baggy trousers, bruised eye and he lowered his head, like a bull about to charge. 'Outta ma way, you dumb squaw. Let me see to this redskin.'

Annie's muscles locked. She wasn't afraid of bulls, she'd been brought up with them. Nasty pampered brutes with nose rings and a tendency to violence - (*'Don't clank 'is chain, Miss Annie, 'e bain't like it.'*) - who could smell a heifer five miles away. 'He's not an animal,' she heard herself mutter.

'No better'n dogs.' The man spat a yellow stream of tobacco juice in the direction of the Indian. 'Dirty, wild dogs.'

Yanking up her britches, Annie jammed fists deep in the pockets to hide their shaking. 'I wouldn't treat a dog that way.' She swallowed convulsively, a frog gulping down a fly.

'Oh, you wouldn't, huh? Run your mouth kinda reckless, don't you missy?'

'Just … voicing an opinion.'

'Voyacing hain oh-peen-ion! Well, there ain't no call for no women's opinions here. Only two things a woman's fit fer out West, wife'in or whore'in.'

'You tell her, Morg.' A beery voice from the bar. 'Next thing, they'll be runnin' fer sheriff.'

A hoot of laughter and Annie caught the curled lip and scornful sneer of one of the girls who'd been looking for McCall. Flushed at their contempt, she pulled self-consciously at her collar.

People were stirring again, conversations starting up and Annie knew what to do, now. Duck her head, make herself scarce. It wasn't her trouble, after all. But there was something so feeble about just standing and watching while a man was spat on and booted out, like a dog to the kennel.

Unexpectedly, her gaze clashed with that of the Indian. His eyes held hers for a moment. Something remote glittered there, something disdainful. That look reminded Annie of McCall. Flustered, she turned away.

'Talk kinda fancy, don't ya?' Morg was still swaying in front of her. 'Got that school-marm way about ya. Well, you got a lot to learn, school-marm.'

'Dammit Morg, you gonna deal or just stand there looking ugly?'

'Y'all hold on a minute. She needs teachin' some manners.'

'Look girlie,' one of the card players advised, wearily, 'just git while you can. This is a serious game, know what I mean? Real high stakes and a pot building.'

Morg brought his red face close to Annie's. 'What stupid no-good bum brought you in here, anyways?'

'This stupid no-good bum, here. You got a problem with that, Morg?'

A heavy hand squeezed Annie's shoulder.

Whirling round, she ran straight into a cold, formidable stare. McCall, rolling his eyes to the roof in a pantomime of despair. 'This just isn't my day, is it?'

Chapter 12

'Although eccentricity and originality of character may be admired in an Englishman, few will allow the same departure from convention in an Englishwoman.' – p.82

Once more, the room was plunged into silence. Not a sound, no-one stirred. Just the clink of a glass being carefully put down, and one person's extremely nervous cough.

Uneasy glances were exchanged. 'She with you, McCall?'

'Yep.'

'Tarnation!' Annie distinctly heard the sound of shuffling feet. 'We didn't mean no disrespect. See, she talks like a lady. Sure don't look or act like one, though.'

'S'right McCall. We got mothers.'

'Did I say she was my mother?'

Oh, ha! Blotchy with agitation, Annie shook free of his restraining hand. 'Look,' she said, 'are you going to help me here?' Because if not, he could go and boil his head. Morg's too, while he was at it. 'Are you going to do something? Or just stand there and insult me?'

'Do? Do what? Sell tickets?'

'Protect that man, that Indian! If you'd seen!'

'Isn't she a peach?' McCall drawled, to no-one in particular. And to Annie: 'You sure like to stir things up, don't you.'

'What do you mean? He had a *gun!*'

'Everyone in town has a gun.'

'It was pointing at me!'

'Shush. Enough. You're done.'

'Well, thank you,' Annie muttered, losing her grip on her trousers. 'You've been a really great help.'

'You telling me what to do now? I don't believe this.'

'I'm entitled to an opinion.'

'Reckon you're a mite too fond of your own opinions. Here, Deevy.' McCall tossed a coin over the bar. 'Give the scout a drink, and let him go. Army's due here soon. They won't be too pleased, if you beat up on their best tracker.'

It seemed a life-time before the piano started up again. Cards were cut and dealt and most men turned their backs. Business as usual.

Feeling clammy and light-headed, Annie swayed. Milky spots swam in front of her eyes. As she offered up a silent prayer of thanks, McCall's voice came hard in her ear. 'Now is definitely not the time to swoon, you hear? Listen to me for a change.'

She looked round for the Indian. Gone. Melted softly and silently away.

'Do you have any idea how they treated that person?' Her voice rose. 'What they said?' Mutinous eyes blazed up into cold, blank ones.

'Some,' McCall said, evenly.

Annie had the grace to blush.

'Right now, though, I don't give a damn who did what to who and in what disgusting manner. Understand? Right now, all I – '

'Hey, hey - hey!'

If she hadn't been about to fall over, Annie would have

welcomed the interruption. As it was, she reeled round to stare at the girl swaying seductively towards them.

'Hey, McCall!' A husky voice floated through the smoke cloud. 'Where in the world you been hiding?'

Would any man hide from this woman? Almost as tall as McCall, she was very striking. Clouds of copper-coloured hair (was *this* his redhead, then?) drifted round a creamy complexion, bare shoulders emerged enticingly from off-the-shoulder satin.

'Where you been all this time, honey?' Throwing slender arms around McCall's neck, she rubbed his cheek and purred.

A long, low whistle of appreciation rippled along the bar. ('Whoo-hoo! Over here, over here, Stella!') Someone cat-called something shocking.

Ignoring them all, Stella locked arms lazily behind McCall's head and planted a long, hard kiss, full on his lips. His surprised lips, his appreciative lips? Who could say? Annie saw no sign of struggle or protest, heard no yelp of outrage, either. Just a squelch of kissing.

Not that she was watching, nothing so vulgar. Hotly embarrassed, she'd looked away long ago. Unfortunately, her scandalised gaze just happened to land on a painted scene of naked nymphs, cavorting.

Only one thing to do – just stand there, looking silly. Not that it mattered. No-one was taking any notice; she was no longer worthy of anyone's attention.

After an excruciatingly long interval, (was this *necessary*; it certainly wasn't decent) McCall disentangled himself. 'Hi there, would've done just fine, Stella.' He raked the hair back from his eyes.

'Well, *hi!*'

'And 'bye, I guess.' He reached for Annie.

'You just got here, darlin'!'

'Now, I'm just leaving.'

'Ooh.' Stella's tongue flicked over her full, pouting lips. 'Not yet. What's been keeping you, anyhoo?' Aggrieved eyes turned on Annie, drifting from mussed-up, matted hair to dusty boots. Her look said it all. Something the cat dragged in?

'She's from England,' McCall said.

'Yeah? How'd she get here? Walk?'

Annie knew that she'd never felt worse. Sick, unsavoury. Stupid, too – mustn't forget that – misguided, interfering. Anything else? No, that probably covered it. She kept wishing the floor would open and swallow her up.

McCall probably wished that, too. Gripping his charge's good arm, he pulled her through the door behind him, trailing disapproval like a bad child. A smattering of applause floated after them from the bar, along with a cloud of beery smoke.

'Ouch.' Annie hopped frantically to keep up. 'That hurts!'

'Good. I'd get a move on, if I were you.'

'What ... why?'

'Those pants'll be down round your ankles in a minute. Unless you're aiming to give another side-show.'

'Why are you so angry?'

'Hiya Yancey.' A curt nod to a passer-by, then to Annie, 'You haven't even seen my hackles rise yet. Didn't I say to stay put? Wouldn't listen, would you?'

'How long did you expect me to wait?' They were back in the parlour now. Nose-to-nose. Any minute, Annie thought, he would shake her until she rattled.

'After our short acquaintance, Miss Hayden, not long! Sure picked a fine time to play hero, didn't you? For the second time today. Next time you're in a jam, don't count on some poor sap risking his neck to haul you out.'

'Given time,' she said, stiffly, 'I could have sorted things out, by myself.'

'And exited stage left, without britches? Oh yeah, I really wish I'd let you try. It had nothing to do with you. Didn't know a thing about it, did you?'

'Not really, no.'

'Then why get into it? You have to stick your thumbs into every pie you see?' He had the irritated air of someone to whom a scruffy stray dog had attached itself.

Annie stared at the floor and considered saying sorry, but she wasn't - not for speaking out, anyway - and McCall probably knew that she wasn't.

All right. Since San Francisco, she'd lurched from one calamity to another, each of almost Biblical proportions. What next? Fire, plague, pestilence? Outbreak of boils?

Dragging her eyes away from the threadbare Turkey rug, she met his grim gaze. 'Err, there's ... um, face paint,' she said. 'On your ... '

He wiped his mouth roughly with the back of his hand. 'Should've left you to the buzzards.'

'Yes,' she said. 'Sorry. It won't happen again.'

'That's right! It damn well won't!' Frog-marching her to a chair, he slid a tray of food under her nose. 'Here ... eat!'

'I can't manage all that.'

'Try. For such a small fry, you seem to have a pretty big mouth.'

She flushed. 'Please don't shout.'

'Why not? It makes me feel better.'

She stared down at her plate, piled high with brown mush. 'Can I ask a question?'

His look said it all. It had better be good.

'That Indian. Wasn't he wearing an Army coat?'

'He's an Army scout. Eat up, don't let those flies settle.'

'But those men wouldn't let him drink in the bar.'

'They don't drink with dogs. Didn't you pick that up?'

She shook her head. 'I don't understand. Why let them humiliate him, why didn't you step in?'

'Because that's how it goes with Indians. That's the situation.'

'But you're half-Indian,' she wanted to say, 'you're the same kind.'

'It didn't cross your mind, that you were insulting him yourself? Defending him ... a woman?'

She shifted, uneasily. 'There you are, then. He needed your help, not mine.'

'You needed it more. And next time you see a man paw the ground like a steer, get the hell out. However strong your opinions. What were you thinking?'

'If a thing is unjust,' she said, loftily, 'people ought to speak out.'

'With odds of thirty to one?'

'That man was a bully.'

'Yeah. A six foot four, two hundred pound bully.'

'He should be hung from a meat hook. Anyway, I was taught to ... to stand up ... for what I believe.'

'Very noble. Someone should write a ballad about you. A word of advice. If you're going to shoot off your mouth, learn the customs of the place first. Start with the one where you see a fight brewing, you run like hell.'

'But – '

'Enough! Lady, you may be itching to start another speech, but I'm real tired.' His voice was flat, his eyes red-rimmed. 'Just eat, will you.'

'So, I should just mind my own business?'

'Unless you're asked for help, yes. And go easy on the English righteousness, if you don't mind. Gives me gut-ache.'

A flat silence. Annie swallowed, thickly. 'You don't much care for the English, do you, Mr McCall?'

'Not much, no. Now, you going to eat or just sit there and yatter?'

He looked as stonily inscrutable as some Sphinx or Aztec God. What would appease him now, Annie wondered? Human sacrifice? Soggy with sympathy for herself and her situation, she gave a faint, self-pitying cough.

'I wouldn't cry into that food either, if I were you. It's salty enough already. Here,' pointing to the supper tray, he gave her a level look. 'Stop feeling sorry for yourself and eat. It'll make you feel better.'

Oh, but she didn't want to feel better, things were too far gone for that. Wiping her eyes with the heel of her hand, she gave the meal a fierce prod with her fork. 'It still wasn't right. Treating another human being in that way.'

'You don't know what you're talking about.'

'I know what's right and what's wrong. It was like a bear-pit in there.'

'Then, why go in?'

'I was looking for you!'

He gave a heavy sigh. 'It wasn't the time or the place to challenge. You – '

'… don't know a thing about it,' she said.

He sent her a long blank stare. 'Will you eat? This is getting silly.'

'Just an Englishwomen passing through. What would I know – '

'Eat! Just eat! For *pity's* sake.'

Annie ate. Fortunately, the meat was so hard and so tough that it took all her attention.

'Doctor will be right along,' McCall said, when she'd almost finished. 'Better now?'

'Yes,' she mumbled, her mouth still full. 'Thank you.'

A lie, but there didn't seem much point going into it. Her jaw ached as she chewed and chewed on the last few pieces of meat.

'Is this buffalo?' Or old saddle blanket? It took a gallon of water to get rid of every mouthful.

'Beef, probably. Good old Texas steak. About the only thing left in the South, since the war.'

'Those men.' She pushed the plate away and tried to un-stick her teeth. 'The Baileys. They talked about the War. As if it wasn't over.'

'To them, it's not.' His fingers drummed the table. 'They may have lost the fight, but they're dammed if they've lost the argument.'

Another yawning silence.

As flies settled on Annie's abandoned plate, the food sank in her stomach like a stone. She felt sick and heady. Slumped in her seat, she glanced at McCall. Half-asleep himself, he looked dull-eyed with fatigue and irritation.

'Sorry,' she said, and this time, she meant it. 'I'm not sure what got into me.'

'About a quart and a half of whisky, I'd guess.' His voice was lifeless, his mouth a thin line.

Annie's heart sank. Security gone; everything she knew and trusted, gone. Nothing familiar or friendly left. No-one to lean on, except herself.

'Clarice says you're welcome to stay here, instead of at the hotel,' he said, with a mammoth yawn. 'If you like.'

'Clar-eece?'

'Owns the place.'

'Oh. Well, I'm not sure.' Her mouth a prim pucker, Annie caught his baleful stare.

'She's offering shelter.' His voice was dry. 'Not putting you on the payroll.'

'So, what sort of people stay here? You know, mostly.'

'Cowboys, gamblers, railroaders. Men who want a good time and women who'll give it to them. Keep your shirt on,' he said, slapping Annie's back as she choked on a gulp of water. 'OK, they don't sew for the Baptists, but you won't be on your own, that's what matters now. Trust me, there's worse places. Some sweep up the body parts at closing. Just be sure and lock your door, that's all.'

Tipping back his chair, he squinted at her. 'So, where do you reckon you'll go, after the Fort?'

Annie shrugged. What did he care? He was off to play

poker. 'My aunt wanted to travel to New York by way of Texas. She didn't say why.'

'Maybe now your aunt will see sense and arrange an escort.'

'Maybe.' But knowing her aunt, maybe not. She sat up, trying to look sensible. 'Anyway, isn't it sometimes safer to travel unarmed and unaccompanied? I've heard that waving weapons can stir up violence. Whereas kind words, a ... a friendly appeal can ... you know, appease people.'

He didn't comment, didn't need to. Was that the look he reserved for small children and halfwits?

'Take monkeys.' She ploughed on. 'Faced with aggression, they smooth things over with gestures and gentle touching.'

This fascinating observation was greeted with a wintry stare. 'Is that a joke?'

'No, a fact.'

'I take it there's a point to this then, looming somewhere on the horizon?'

'I'm just saying, that conciliation sometimes works.'

'I'll put that on your tombstone.' His face was a picture. 'Some may squat on their haunches here, but don't let that fool you. We're talking about men, not monkeys. Where'd you hear that, anyway?'

'I read it. In a book.'

'Yeah, well unfortunately, Miss Haddon, Comanche and dirty drunks don't read the same books. The only way to appease the likes of the Baileys, would be to beat them over the head with a copy. Haven't you just had first-hand experience of their gestures and gentle touching?'

'I'm just *saying* ... '

'You don't picnic with rattlesnakes. Tell me, how were you aiming to handle the Baileys, if no-one had happened along? Turn the other cheek!'

Annie studied his knowing expression. 'No,' she said. 'I would have wrestled them to the ground and strangled them with the string from my trousers.'

McCall's mouth twitched. 'In a caring, Christian sort of way, I guess.'

'Weapons make me nervous, that's all. Guns and ... '

'You'd be a helluva lot more nervous here without one.' He eyed her, narrowly. 'Real life doesn't come from books. Take my advice. Meet up with your relatives and go home. This isn't the time or the place for women to be wandering about, unaccompanied.'

The arrival of the doctor put paid to any further discussion. Just as well, thought Annie. Nothing cosy about McCall's company. Or his conversation.

Chapter 13

'It is a good rule to try and take care of minor injuries oneself - e.g. cuts and bruises – and only seek help from a local physician if absolutely necessary.' - p.66

Moose Monroe was introduced.

Moose? He didn't look like a doctor either, none that Annie had ever come across. Doctors were elderly and greying, weren't they? Pince-nez and an air of authority.

This one had stiff shirt buttoned to the neck, a long black coat and wild hair. More like a priest from some Gothic novel. Or a huge dishevelled bird.

She studied him from behind her glass of water. Too young, too unhealthily pale and thin. A distinct air of dissipation about him, too. There was something so unnerving about an unfit physician.

McCall seemed to agree. 'You look lousy, Moose.'

'Oh yeah, I've missed you, too.'

'A lick of string with a knot in the end. You eating regular?'

'Sure. Got me a liking for prairie chickens. Danged hard to

catch though, it's chasing 'em keeps me thin. Well now.' The doctor's dark eyes shifted to Annie, listening warily to their exchange. 'How's the injured party?'

'She's kinda fragile.'

'That right, ma'am?'

'No. I am ... much improved,' mumbled Annie. 'My head and ... much better.'

'English?' Raising an eyebrow, Doctor Monroe shot McCall a quizzical look. 'Well, well. You surely pick 'em, Colt.'

'I didn't *pick*. I fell over her on the trail.'

'First visit here then, ma'am? How're you finding it?'

Annie was tempted to tell him. Oh, an unbridled pleasure. The whole trip. Abandoned to wild strangers. Mr McCall doesn't like me, doesn't like anything I say or do.

'Wouldn't advise asking for an opinion on anything,' McCall said. 'She's plumb full of information.'

Not any more, thought Annie, feeling her personality dribble away. Aunt Bea was right. A brain was a heavy curse on a woman. *('You require accomplishment, Annie, not knowledge, if you are to grace an English home.')*

She caught a strong whiff of rubbing alcohol, liniment and liquor as the doctor leaned over her. Two buttons hung loose, cuffs were all frayed and a bottle clinked in his coat. His hands shook, too, as they explored her arm.

'What in the world happened to you, sugar?' His soft Southern drawl was slow and easy and rolled over Annie in a syrupy stream. Her eyes blurred. This was the most concern anyone had shown her in weeks.

She felt an overwhelming urge to bury her head in his chest, and howl. Wouldn't get her anywhere, of course, and McCall would hate it. Perhaps that was why the idea seemed so appealing.

'So.' Tut-tutting at her rough sling, the doctor gave a smooth wink. 'Who's been at this then, darlin'? Some old horse doctor?' Slitting her shirt from wrist to elbow, he gently eased it away from her shoulder.

Annie's face turned the colour of a freshly-boiled lobster. Oh, the shame and humiliation of revealing so much bare speckled skin. In grey and grubby camisole, too.

And McCall, just standing there, staring with such interest.

Aunt Bea would have had a seizure. Hadn't she stopped Annie from rinsing underwear at a way-station? For decency's sake. *'It may be seen,'* she'd declared, scandalised. *'By a man!'*

Not that McCall seemed concerned. 'Is it still in line?'

As he squinted over the doctor's shoulder, Annie's breathing became laboured, breasts rose and fell unevenly and she fixed her eyes to a spot on the wall.

'Pretty much. Bad bruising, though.' A sling was efficiently tied. 'Pass those scissors, Colt.'

'Will it knit straight?'

The doctor shrugged and wiped his palms on a cloth. 'Can't say for sure. May grow back a bit bowed.'

It's true, then, Annie thought. I'm turning into some sort of curio. Somewhere between the bearded woman and the wolf man. *'Ladeez and gemmum. Step inside. See the freak.'*

'No busting broncs for you then, ma'am. Just plenty of good victuals. You need some meat on those bones.'

'Good advice, Moose. Why not take it yourself. Takes more than liquor stew to keep going.'

'Hey, cut me some slack, Colt.' The doctor gathered up scraps of lint and liniment. 'I'm doing just fine.'

Annie closed eyes and ears to the to and fro of their voices. Giddy waves started to whirl. Squinting blearily, she heard, 'Time for a game, later?'

'Poker?' she asked, after Moose Monroe had bade her farewell.

'Chess.'

Drat the man. Why must he confuse her? Why couldn't he just conform to a type - rough and raw and rude - and be done with it.

Her shirt was in tatters - beg pardon, *his* shirt. As she tried to burrow into its folds, he went off and found some sort of mantle to drape round her shoulders. Red devorè velvet, lined with satin. Perfect for a night at the opera. Where in the world had he found that?

'Better?'

No. Half-naked in the company of strangers? Rigor mortis setting in?

'Why Moose?' Cool satin slithered over her skin and slipped off one shoulder. Stifling a yawn, she yanked it back. 'Why is he called – '

'Ever seen any?'

'Pictures. And a head I think, on someone's wall.' Huge horns, unforgiving glass eyes. Probably bad breath and a terrible temper, too.

'Moose's similarities start the other end.'

Annie stared, then flushed and examined her fingernails. *Checkmate.* 'Are all doctors here drunkards?'

'You've been reading too many yellow-back novels.'

'He drinks though, doesn't he. I could smell it on his breath.'

'Everyone here drinks. Except the Ladies Temperance League.'

'I don't. Not alcohol. Everyone knows … '

'Got through enough today, didn't you?'

' … that it weakens the constitution. That was medicinal! For temporary invigoration, after … '

'Same goes for Moose.'

' … a shock. But he's a doctor!'

'Did all right for you, didn't he?'

'I just … doesn't anyone ever comment on it? Surely it affects his faculties, or something?'

'He buried his wife and baby daughter last year. Cholera. Guess he wants his faculties to be affected. Wouldn't you? He'll come out of it, eventually.'

Shocked and sinking slowly back into the mantle, Annie caught a whiff of faded scent. Something familiar. Attar of roses? Nostalgia brought back tears to her eyes. How much longer must she put up with all this?

There was a brief, uneasy peace. Her eyelids drooped, stomach was fluttering and her arm hurt, a low dull ache. Her head? About to explode.

'Hey, Colt.' Another voice, light and musical. 'How's it going?'

Another woman. Annie passed a hand over her eyes. Soon, very soon now, she was going to slide under that table and disappear.

'Clarice,' McCall murmured. 'You up to this?'

No. Just ... bed. Lie down. Sleep. Maybe soon, die.

Still, a whisper of silk and sweet heady scent brought Clarice rustling into the room. Taking in cobalt-blue eyes and perfectly coiled silver-blonde hair, Annie blearily acknowledged that this wasn't McCall's redhead, either.

And where *did* these women find their clothes? Not in any frontier corner store, that was for sure. In comparison, Annie felt like that puppy, all scruffy matted hair and bad breath.

With an enormous effort, she met Clarice's polished cerise smile - the human equivalent to a pat on the head.

'Feeling stronger, honey?'

'Yes, better. Thank you.'

'Oh.' A wide-eyed stare. 'You're English. Well, Colt says you'll stay the night.'

Annie plastered on a smile. 'Ah. *Most* kind, but ... '

'She's a little finicky about her reputation,' McCall said.

'Suit yourself. I've a front room free and one of the girls could fill a bath. Looks like you need it. Fifteen minutes suit you?'

And that was that. Discussion over. Clarice had better fish to fry, apparently. Turning to McCall, her voice dropped at least an octave to become a breathy, dove-like coo.

'Stay a while yourself, Colt?' Hands and lashes fluttered, prettily. 'Reckon you need a little looking after, too.'

'Sorry sweetheart, have to see a man about a horse.'

Annie's ears pricked. Would that be a poker-playing horse, then?

'You'd have a better time with me, darlin', than with some old horse.'

Caught in this cross-fire of teasing glances and husky laughter, Annie started to feel quite sick. Was this McCall's effect on all women? Oh, bound to be. After all, he looked like some sort of Aztec God.

Right again, Aunt Bea! Good looks were such a snare. For herself, Annie decided, she preferred more refinement. An appreciation of culture, yes, and plain good manners. Why then, this pathetic urge to bleat, '*Me! Look at me! Listen to me!*'

More words, back and forth. Voices fell to a murmur. Annie's eyelids flickered and drooped. Door opened, closed. Clarice gone?

For a while then, they sat without speaking. Time ticked sonorously by.

Moths hurled themselves at lamps, casting flickering shadows into dusty corners and across the ceiling. Bursts of laughter struck their ears from outside.

When a bloated black thing scuttled across the floor, Annie was too tired to even jump. Everywhere you went here, she brooded bitterly, there was something deadly and dangerous waiting to leap out and get you.

Too tired to move or speak, she was quite sure that McCall wasn't going to bother himself with small talk. Why was he still here, then? It wasn't exactly comfortable anymore. Didn't he have a poker game to go to?

She studied her fingernails - bitten and black - and dredged her mind for something to say.

'What are your own plans then, Miss Haddon?'

Plans? She had no plans. Except to stop biting her nails. She was an English spinster. Hadn't she told him as much? 'I haven't any. Why do you smile? It's perfectly true.'

'All women,' he said, propping his feet on a chair and locking hands behind his head, 'make plans. It's in their nature.'

His knowing smile irritated Annie. Weary as she was, she felt inclined to be argumentative. 'Not unmarried English ones.'

'I don't believe that for a minute.'

'Oh, some women have choices. Pretty ones, with feminine wiles.'

She could hardly believe she was saying all this. Was it the whisky? She shifted under his scrutiny.

'I've never had those. Just a head full of irregular verbs and verse. I,' she said, solemnly, 'must wait to be chosen.'

'Tough.' His mouth twitched.

'Oh, it's not so bad being unmarried,' she said carelessly, half expecting to be struck down for such heresy. 'Once you get over the disgrace of it.'

Well? It was true, wasn't it? Hadn't she resigned herself to being an old maid? Accepted the shame of it, the lack of standing in society. Then Henry Chewton Hewell had come coiling down her apple tree.

Weeks ago, she'd decided to keep him in the very furthest corner of her mind. If she left him there, refusing to think or speak of him, he might just go away.

'I do not much ... like him,' she recalled telling her aunt, tentatively, back in England. Nor trusted an inch or respected either, but she hadn't risked mentioning that. This news had been received with her guardian's customary tolerance and understanding.

'Like?' Aunt Bea had thundered. 'What has *like* to do with it? I know a great many couples who heartily detest each other and still lead perfectly comfortable lives!'

The storm had raged for some time. Duty was a word often used to beat Annie into submission. Obligation, another. And of course, ingratitude. Such were the nature of her aunt's sermons.

'We will make no other match for you, you are twenty-seven years old. What is there to recommend you?'

'You prefer books to men, I guess.' McCall's voice cut into her thoughts.

Oh, unfair. Although on reflection, some dusty old tomes would have been preferable to the suitors her aunt had dredged up for her. Social climbers, cads and bores. Stiff as sticks, shy and silent, or old and doddery, their red-veined cheeks a testament to too much claret.

'I refuse to talk to that awful person a minute longer,' she'd once heard Charlotte mutter to her mother. 'Even if he is incredibly grand. He'd bore the bustle off Queen Victoria.'

A gentleman's dullness, she'd been reminded, severely, is often in direct proportion to his distinction. 'Is that so?' Charlotte had smiled, sweetly. 'In that case, he'll do for Annie.'

No, on the whole, she did not prefer books to men. How depressing though, to be dismissed as some dry old stick of a spinster. She would have given eye teeth to convince this man that she was out every night, supping champagne from a satin slipper.

'Well, like I said, you could get a husband here, if you change your mind,' he said, helpfully. 'There's a real brisk business in mail-order brides.'

Annie's cheeks tinged with red. This was how he saw her, then. A resigned, but hopeful old maid. Would he think differently if she broke furniture over his head?

'Marrying some whiskery old miner in the Klondike, is not something I'd want to consider,' she said, kicking moodily at the chair leg.

'It's a choice.'

'So is herding yaks in Patagonia, but I wouldn't do that, either.'

'Do they have yaks in Patagonia?'

'Yes,' snapped Annie. 'I - '

' - read it, in a book?'

His mouth curved complacently and she gave a drawn-out sigh. Where was this leading? He was reeling her in, like a fish on a line. It wasn't fair. The fight had long ago drained out of her.

'I'm not blind,' she blurted, gracelessly, 'or a fool. Whatever you may think. I know what I am.'

'Oh? And what's that?'

Plain, bookish, lame - but even she had too much pride to say it out loud. 'An unsupported female.' She met his gaze, squarely. 'With no useful connections. And ... a disability.'

'A ... what!'

'I hobble.'

'Hardly surprising with that chip on your shoulder. It's a wonder you can stand up straight. Stop beating up on yourself.'

No need, reflected Annie. There were plenty of others willing to do that for her. He wasn't making such a bad job of it himself.

He leaned forward. 'A word of advice, Miss Haddon.'

'No, thank you,' she said, quickly. 'I've had more than enough of that for one day.'

For some reason, he found that funny. Grinning appreciatively, he took her small, creased hand in his own. 'Truce, then?' he said, eyes crinkling.

Annie stared. He was only inches away, close enough to smell his skin and faint hints of leather, soap, outdoors. Unlike herself - she swallowed, thickly - he must have found time to take a bath.

'Stop selling yourself short,' he was saying. Or something like that. It was hard to concentrate. 'You've shown real spirit.'

She blinked. Should she be pinching herself, or something? Surely he saw her as a sort of privileged half-wit, with slop for brains. Why so nice, all of a sudden? *Don't be nice,* she thought. She couldn't deal with it. Being petted, then pushed aside, like a kitten.

'That was a fair thing you did in the bar,' he said. 'Speaking up for the Indian. It surprised me. Lately, it's taken a helluva lot to surprise me.' Absently, he started stroking the inside of her wrist, with his thumb.

She looked down at her hand, lying limply in his, like a half-dead herring.

Lamps flickered, flared and steadied themselves. She tried hard to do the same. 'You don't have a great deal of faith in people, do you Mr McCall?'

Dark eyes came within inches of her own, and she found herself bitterly regretting her boiled complexion and birds nest hair. If only she'd listened to her aunts and bothered with herself a bit more - creamed her skin, tamed her hair. Too late, too late!

'Colt,' he corrected, dropping her hand. 'It's a little late for philosophy.'

Was it over, then? Slowly, her stomach righted itself.

'How's your head, now?'

'A little improved.' It wasn't her head she was worried about.

'And your arm?'

It wasn't her arm, either. 'Yes. I ... think so.'

'Bed, then,' he said, standing up. As if he'd suddenly exhausted his supply of patience and good humour. Annie prayed that it wasn't because she smelled of boiled mutton. 'You need rest. I'll call one of the girls.'

'So ... tomorrow?' she ventured, casually.

'You go East, I go West.'

'Will we ... will I see you again?' *Hussy, Annie! Brazen,*

forward chit.

'Guess not.'

If only he'd had the grace to look a little less pleased about that, she might not have felt quite so shamed. As it was, he'd be glad to see the back of her. Off on his own, while she returned to the bosom of her family. Aunt Bea and Charlotte. Henry Chewton Hewell. Why did her spirits sink?

McCall was still staring down at her. 'Amazing hair,' he said, curling his fingers into the heavy knot at the nape of her neck and testing the weight. 'Never seen such a colour.'

'Except on your friend,' Annie pointed out, her skin prickling.

'Who? Oh yeah, my friend.' He turned and headed for the door, muttering something about seeing if her bed was ready.

Amazing? she repeated to herself, when he'd gone. This wild, scratchy bush? It was the sort of thing people said, of course, to particularly plain women. The sort of kind, pitiful thing. Such beautiful hair! Such fine eyes!

Clearly, McCall had a partiality for red hair. Who was she then, his red-head? Where was she now?

When he came back five minutes later, she was already asleep, her head sunk low on her chest.

Chapter 14

'When selecting lodgings, attention should be paid to certain particulars. The room must be clean and well-ventilated. To ensure safety and privacy, a trunk or heavy item of furniture should be placed against the door.' – p.71

It was not Annie's best night's sleep since San Francisco, nowhere near, in spite of the blessed comfort of sheets and a pillow. Sleeping in a tree would have been preferable to the row which rocked the saloon for the rest of the night.

First, she was woken by carousing under her window and giggling on the stairs. Then whoops and yells, and in unison the dogs began to howl. *'Stop thait unholy racket! Y'all setting off the dogs!'*

Later, with fingers already in her ears, a wild splatter of gunshot brought drunks reeling into the street.

'Hey, a dollar ah cain hit that sign. C'mon! Where's ya money!'

When things finally quietened down outside, loud snoring started up behind the thin partition walls and Annie felt a murderous urge to grab a gun herself and rampage through the sleeping drunks. *Blam, bam!* See how you like it!

Somewhere, a cock crowed.

Through a tangle of bedclothes, she squinted blearily at sun struggling round a red calico blind. Strange stuffy room, strange bed and a strange chemise, soft as silk on her skin.

Where was she? No idea. How had she ended up like this?

Ah, yes. A soft groan. That terrible taste in her mouth, the thudding at the back of her eyes. The room. Over the saloon. Somewhere in Texas.

A fly buzzed sleepily at the window. Wagons creaked by outside. What was the time!

When the door squeaked open, Annie snatched a sheet up to her chin, but it was baby blue eyes, not challenging brown ones, that peered back at her.

'Come in.' Relief followed a rush of nausea. 'I'm awake.'

A young girl inched into the room, fixing Annie with a sullen stare. Pale and scrawny, her loose hair was crimped and caught in ribbons.

Annie smiled, woozily. 'Good morning.'

'Howdy.' A cool nod. 'Clarice sent these.' Her arms were full of clothes.

'What happened to *my* things?' Why was it so hard to remember?

'McCall took back his britches.' The girl lifted the pitcher from the dresser. 'We threw the rest out. Ah'll fetch water. Y'all want something to eat?'

Annie stretched. 'Is anyone else up?'

'Just Clarice. Others'll lie low 'til noon. Bad heads.'

The girl left and Annie picked primly through the clothes. Soon, she would be back with her relatives, and frills and ostrich feathers would not impress Aunt Bea, whatever the circumstances.

But Clarice it seemed, had taste and tact as well as good looks. Well, as a close friend of McCall – Annie's lips pursed - she would have, wouldn't she? The pale green silk dress she'd provided, full-skirted over a fitted top, was respectable enough for any church picnic. Not a spangle in sight.

Underwear was a different matter. Gingerly, Annie inspected a selection of silks and satins in shades of oyster and pearl, all with delicate inserts of ribbon and lace.

Guiltily, she held soft straps to her skin. *('Quite right, Aunt Bea - so shocking, most improper - but well, modesty had to be served by something!')*

No bath last night and she tried to think why. Her hair was all knots, a wild mess down her back. Amazing hair? Ha!

Look, the sooner she got McCall and his unsettling penchant for redheads into proper perspective, the better. He'd held her hand, that was all, touched her hair. Nothing more. Given her history with men, or rather the lack of it, that should have been crystal clear.

The girl, Susan, returned with water.

'Has Mr McCall taken breakfast?' Annie asked, splashing her face.

'Guess so. He left at dawn.'

'Left?' Glancing up, Annie met her own reflection in the gimcrack mirror. Red-nosed, rumpled, a real beauty of a black eye. The Hag from Hell. But ... gone? Already! 'When will he be back?'

The girl shrugged. Dull eyes held a trace of scorn. 'What's to bring him back here in a hurry? There's rags over there miss, to dry yourself.'

'Will Mr McCall be coming back?' Annie asked Clarice, wondering how anyone who'd slept so little, could look so good. What was this woman's secret? How old was she, anyway? Lace, braid, bows. Her clothes were smart enough for any city out East.

'As I recall, he didn't say. Fresh coffee on the stove, Miss Haddon.'

It was possible of course, that Clarice hadn't taken part in any of last night's revelry. She could have been challenging McCall to an absorbing game of chess, instead.

Speaking of games. 'He's gone to play poker. Hasn't he?'

'Poker?'

'He said ... that was why he couldn't take me to Fort Mackenzie.'

'Well don't fret yourself, hon. Army'll be here soon. Seems they'd already set out to look for you when someone pointed them this way. Ain't that lucky? You may only need one night with us.'

'So ... the poker game?'

'Colt wouldn't ride off at dawn for any two-bit card game round here.'

'Ah.' Annie tried hard to control the dying fall in her voice. McCall had wanted rid of her then, he'd had enough. She'd guessed as much. Even so. 'I had no opportunity, you see, to ... to say goodbye. He left no message?'

She met Clarice's guileless blue gaze.

'Now darlin', don't go pinning your hopes on Colt. Chasing that man is like chasing the wind. Look, don't feel too bad. Lots of females moon and sigh over him. It's debilitating, but it ain't fatal.'

Annie flushed. Would Charlotte have been fobbed off like this?

No, she would have clung to McCall like a limpet. Chances are, he would have let her, too. But then, Charlotte knew how the world worked, and the minds of men. Had done, since she was fifteen and first tossed her curls and pulled in her waist.

Anything Annie knew had been gleaned from books. And that was precious little. Twenty-seven years old, and what did she have to show for it? Achievements, none. Prospects, nil.

'Hope the hootin' and hollerin' didn't keep you awake last night,' Clarice said. 'A gang of railroaders came in late.'

'Well ... thank you for putting me to bed, anyway. I must have been very tired. I don't remember a single – '

'Don't thank me, honey. Colt carried you up.'

Was it always so hot? This pink, peeling heat.

'Good morning.' Annie spoke to an old man in a rocking chair, under the awning of the saloon. 'Is it always this hot?'

'Howdy.' He chewed his pipe. 'Hotter.'

And dust. Dust, everywhere.

'Does it ever rain?'

'Once in a while.' He nodded vigorously, a few times. 'Yip. And when it does, it rains Biblical.'

She opened her mouth to ask more, but he'd already dismissed her, clamping teeth round his clay pipe and fixing watery eyes on the horizon.

Head down against the glare, Annie walked on.

She'd felt in need of air. A chance to clear her head and gather her wits - the few she had left, anyway.

As far as the saloon was concerned, she was clearly not a welcome guest. Hardly surprising, when she had no means of paying the bill. First sight of Annie last night and Clarice would have guessed as much.

'Close that door, honey,' her hostess had snapped, as Annie dithered on the threshold. 'You're letting in a heap of dust.'

Out here, the main street was already busy. Horses and wagons clogged the road, dogs darted hither and thither. Skeletons of half-constructed buildings stood on almost every corner, some already boasting swinging signs. It really was an up and coming town. Hadn't McCall said so?

McCall carried you up? That thought ricocheted round in Annie's head like a ball in a barrel, and kept her gnawing at the sore side of her thumbnail.

'Good morning,' she said, smiling and nodding at a few more folk.

As an unattached female, she was already attracting more than a few frank stares. No-one here to disapprove, though, was there? She could do whatever she liked.

'*Look, aunt! No hat! No gloves!*'

Her full skirt billowed out and she was glad to be wearing a dress again. Even here, in the middle of nowhere, fashion was clearly more than just calico and aprons.

Whatever McCall had said about silk and hoops being fancy dress - bonnets were definitely trimmed, skirts worn wide and waists nipped in.

So, were corsets worn? Trying to decide, she almost collided with someone heaving a sack from a store.

'I beg your pardon. Good morning.'

'Howdy, ma'am.'

Well, she guessed so. Surely Clarice's shape wasn't solely due to the gifts of nature? Against her, Annie felt about as alluring as an antimacassar.

Walking on, a hot dry wind pestered her skirts and whipped up the everlasting dust. Everywhere was parched and glaring, this hard, dry Texas landscape.

She felt a sudden longing for England. For soft rain, damp breezes, mist. It was the first time she'd felt any sense of exile. In spite of all that had happened.

The walkway ran out. Here and there attempts had been made to grow vegetables and even flowers. Dusty plants struggled valiantly through parched earth, behind proud picket fences.

Amazing, Annie thought, what could be done when love and attention was lavished on something. Or someone. Not that she'd had much experience of either. She wasn't bitter about that, though.

To rear a relative's child, as Aunt Bea had done, without gratitude or reward, was a thankless task. Annie had been reminded of that often enough. However hard she'd tried, she'd been the cuckoo in the nest, wrestling with dos and don'ts and constant disapproval.

'You're such a trial to me, Annie,' her aunt had once said.

'What am I going to do with you?'

'I could go away; I could ... I could ... work.'

'Don't be ridiculous, you're just a child.'

'I could go to my father.'

'I hardly think so! He fobbed you off on us in the first place. What would he want with you now? No.' A heavy sigh. 'This is my Christian duty. I must endure it.'

Anyway, she had survived, hadn't she? And tomorrow would see her back to that regime. Courtesy of the Cavalry.

In the heat of the afternoon, a Sunday stillness settled on Red Rock.

People lazed, mopping their brows. Windows were wide, blinds belled out in the breeze, then fell back, exhausted.

Well out of the way, at the back of the saloon, Annie sat on a cane chair in the shade. Waiting, waiting. Waiting for the Army.

'Clarice says, d'you want a drink.' A pink and perspiring Susan appeared with a tray. 'Cordial? Sarsaparilla?'

'No, thank you.'

'Suit yourself. Ain't you hot out here?'

Hot? Annie was broiled. Clothes clung to her skin, damp hair wilted round her ears. Better out, than in, though, she'd decided, with the rank odour of stale liquor. Plus, the faint but alarming possibility of being mistaken for one of Clarice's girls.

'Army'll be here soon.' Susan sighed, glummer than ever. 'Then we'll be chasing our tails.'

'Just a few men, surely. A trooper or two, as an escort?'

Susan wagged her head. 'Regiment, at least. Case of Indian attacks. Red Devils are riled up 'cos railroad's pressing in on their territory.'

'Mr McCall mentioned that,' murmured Annie. Well, not so much a mention, more a diatribe. Not that she hadn't been interested. Up to a point.

'McCall don't like the Army. Reckon he left early so's he wouldn't have to meet up with any of them Army officers.'

Undoing a discreet button or two, Annie fanned herself with an old almanac, the only thing she'd found to read here, apart from some awful yellow-back novels.

If Susan was right, didn't it make McCall's tale about the poker game a little more palatable?

Another girl sauntered out. Celie? Sara? Annie knew a few of them by sight, now - the tall, the short, the cigarillo-smokers. No-one bothered with introductions. Whatever-her-name flopped down, flapping skirts to set up a breeze.

'Weren't you with McCall last night?' The girl blew damp curls from her forehead. 'You look a sight better today, that's for sure. Whatever happened to you?'

'Phew!' she said, after Annie had told her. 'Lucky then, it was McCall that found you.'

Lucky?

'Oh, look.' Annie clicked her fingers, and at her voice, the puppy from the previous day perked up and waddled over, snapping at a fly on the way. He stopped short of them, with the wary look of an animal who'd been kicked once too often.

'Damn nuisance of a dog, town's full of 'em. Yeah. I mean, could've been any man-jack of them crazy cowboys. Injuns, even.'

Annie held out her hand and the puppy licked it gratefully. 'Poor thing.' Picking it up, she settled the soft bundle on her knees. It was too weak even to wriggle; she could count all its ribs.

'Do you need a drink,' she cooed, 'do you? Not that I'd cast Mr McCall as the steady, dependable type exactly.'

'Kinda ungrateful, aren't you?' said the girl. 'I'd count on him ahead of most men here. He was a hell-raiser once, I'll give you that. Always round trouble. Heartbreaker, too.

Course, that was before ... well, he's different now.'

Annie slid the puppy from knee to knee.

McCall had changed? All right. No point pretending. She was interested in the man. Purely as a specimen for study. Like a moth on a pin, or something. Natural curiosity. Nothing wrong with that. 'So, Sara ... '

'Sally. Sara's short, brunette.'

'So ... Mr McCall. He's changed?'

'No secret. Everyone knows. Since his wedding.'

Annie sat perfectly still. McCall hadn't had a wedding, had he? He'd told her ... what? Something about being single. *'I live single.'* That was what he'd said on the way to Red Rock, she would have sworn to it. Had he lied?

Not such an outrageous idea, of course, his being married. He must be thirty years old or so, with a past. There would have been women. From what she had seen and heard, lots of them. Why not a wife?

'Are you *sure?*' she asked. 'About his wedding. Mr McCall's ... '

'Sure, I'm sure.'

'So where is his wife, now?'

'Oh, he don't have one. Wedding was all set and plans made for bell-ing and fussing and all them things. Then McCall upped and left, night before. Must be three, no, two summers ago now.'

'He left his bride? At the altar!'

'McCall wouldn't do that. Rode out, night before.'

Annie rolled her eyes. She knew nothing about him of course, nothing that mattered, she saw that now. Intimidatingly handsome, yes. Short of fuse, certainly. And, he'd saved her endangered bacon.

But to abandon a bride, whatever the story! Heartless, simply heartless!

'Went crazy, as it happens. Turned moody as a rooster.'

'The lady?'

'Nah! McCall.'

'Was she local to the town, then? His bride-to-be.'

'Nope.' Sally stood up, shaking out her petticoats. 'She was English, like you.'

Putting the puppy carefully on the ground, Annie leaned over to scratch its ears. McCall had made a promise to an Englishwoman, and *left* her? Shamed and humiliated her. No wonder he was edgy about the English.

'Don't give that mutt anything, miss. Clarice'll be mad if he starts hanging round the back door. Best not mention what I said to anyone, neither. Not in McCall's hearing, anyway. He gets red raw real quick.'

Well yes, thought Annie. That would be guilt. *'Tell me, Mr McCall, how does a man sleep at night, knowing he's laid an innocent person open to scorn and derision? How can he live with himself?'*

Oh, she didn't want to think about it, anymore. About the man or his morals. It was too hot; she was too weak.

McCall carried you up? She didn't want to think about that, either.

He'd carried her upstairs. That much, she understood, although she'd almost eaten through her thumbnail now, with the tension. Who, though – and this was what was bringing her out in hives - who had undressed her?

Chapter 15

'*The sooner one falls into the ways of a country, the better. Try to blend in with the local population as much as possible.*' – *p.63*

'Well, well. Here they come.'

Horses hooves drummed up the dust and a well-drilled formation trotted into town, the front rider's ensign fluttering frantically in warm wind.

'Men in dirty shirt blue.'

'I beg ... sorry?' Annie said, keeping one eye on the line drawing near. The men looked exhausted, their uniforms grimy and dust-caked after long hard days in the saddle.

'Cavalry.'

After the order to halt, she watched as one soldier steered his horse towards the saloon. An officer, she assumed. Tall in the saddle, immaculately turned out, extremely polite.

'Ladies.' Tipping his hat, he spoke with a soft Scots burr. 'Captain Andrew Wallace. At yurr service. I understand ye have an Englishwoman here.'

'That's me.' Moving forward, Annie gave him a shy smile. 'I mean ... I am she, Captain. Miss Annie Haddon.'

The officer blinked, making Annie wonder about her aunt's

description of her. She could guess at the gist of it. (*'You'll know my niece Captain – small freckled person, hair the colour of carrots.'*)

Removing his hat, the man regarded her, gravely. 'Glad to know ye, Miss Haddon. I'm here tae escort ye to Forrrt Mackenzie.' He rolled his rs with relish.

'And my aunt and cousin, Captain? Are they well? I've been so worried about them.'

'Safe and well at the Forrt, ma'am. They seem to have suffered few ill effects.'

There was a slight edge to his voice that made Annie wince. Was Aunt Bea being difficult? Since leaving San Francisco, she'd made no secret of the fact that in her opinion, the West was a barren wilderness, its occupants ramshackle colonists.

'The West?' she'd scoffed on more than one occasion, and never sotto voce. 'That is not a place, it's merely a direction.'

Experience on the stagecoach would not have mellowed those feelings, either. Now, they would be set in stone.

'You'll stay awhile, Captain?' Clarice butted in, her mind on business. 'Let the men have a little fun?'

'Just overnight, ma'am. Must get back. Hostiles urr giving us trouble.'

'Trouble?'

'Nothing the Army cannae cope with,' the Captain said, smoothly. 'Deal with 'em firrrmly and the others'll come to heel. Och, but we dinnae want to worry Miss Haddon now, do we? Spoil her wee visit oot West.'

'Better make the most of this, then.' Clarice's shrewd eyes were on the line of uniformed men moving off toward the livery stables. 'You like parties, Miss Haddon?'

Annie never did decide what it was. Party, hoe-down, frolic? Saturday night social?

'What exactly do you call this?' she asked breathlessly, a

long while later.

'Well, it sure ain't no quilting bee,' her nearest neighbour replied, with a grin.

Whatever it's name, it took her by surprise. 'Party?' she'd repeated blankly, to Clarice.

'Yip.' The prospect of good business had made Clarice much more amenable towards her guest. 'Few flags on the walls, lay the dust with a sprinkle of water, we'll have a high time yet.'

And the guests?

'The Army, honey! Pockets jingling, eyes a-popping at the thought of anyone in a petticoat. Not many females at Army posts. Better polish up them dancing slippers.'

'Oh. I don't dance,' murmured Annie. 'What does everyone wear?'

'Calico's usual,' Clarice said, 'since the war. Won't do for me though, nor you neither, not tonight. We've the Army's morale to keep up.'

'I don't think – '

'No need to think honey, just wear something pretty.'

'I don't have anything.'

'Oh, but I do, I do.'

What Clarice had, was sapphire silk trimmed with ruffled ribbon. Skirts spread wide beneath a tiny top, neckline dipped fashionably low and a hundred tiny buttons cascaded down the back.

A dress that demanded to be noticed. It rustled enticingly as Annie walked, with a painted fan dangling at her wrist.

She squinted down at bare shoulders. 'Doesn't it need lace?'

Clarice was aghast. 'You a Methodist, or something? Hmm, feet are kinda small. Try those French kid slippers over there. They're tight on me, pinch when I dance.'

'But, I don't ... '

Frowning at Annie's complexion, she insisted on rouge. 'Ever try anything on those freckles? Oh, my Lord – they're everywhere! Powder your shoulders, honey, cover them up.'

And the hair, the *hair*. 'Pity sakes, it's explodin'!' Clarice pulled, yanked and eventually subdued it, fixing sleek ripples up with combs.

When Annie peered into the speckled mirror, wide eyes - one green, one bruised - stared back. A shimmer of silk over foaming petticoats, shining coils of hair. Kid gloves, oyster-coloured stockings.

Where was that mouse of an hour ago, all self-conscious shrugs and twitching whiskers?

It went without saying, that this was a far bolder look than Aunt Bea would ever allow. At that moment though, who cared? Who would tell? Captain Wallace? Somehow, Annie thought not.

'Cute,' Clarice said, her head on one side. 'Perfect for your colouring. And the skirt swirls out real wide, when you're dancing.'

Clarice herself, wore something startling and crimson with black lace and ribbon trimming. Hair piled precariously high, while her neckline plunged, and pale skin was enhanced by the glimmer of jet.

Annie stared, in admiration. In the midst of dust and dirt, this woman looked amazing. A mix of brittle sheen and glossy paint, together with that enviable independent air that she'd observed in some American women.

Clarice and McCall. What was she to him, then? Or he to her, for that matter? Friend, confidante or ... ? Somehow, she couldn't imagine McCall lecturing Clarice on the wearing of whalebone. But then, what did *she* know?

When one's own experience of flirtation has been limited to the flutter of a fan; when your aunt considers even a naked hand at the window of a carriage to be risqué, what can you be expected to make of situations such as this?

She was just too ... too English, Annie decided. Too dull and stodgy, too straight-laced. Compared to Clarice and Stella anyway, and all those other saloon girls. And McCall's redhead, too, most likely, and his English bride. Unless they were one and the same. Was that a possibility?

Stop it, stop there!

The saloon had been transformed. Flags on the walls, drapes covering lewd pictures, dust over the puddles of tobacco juice. A trio of perspiring fiddlers, elbows flying, wore grins from ear to ear, as toes tapped to accordion, banjo, jew's-harp.

The rest of the room was crowded with men and thick with smoke. As ever. Floor and walls though, weren't the only things spruced-up.

Annie noticed a great many stand-collar shirts, tight new boots and slicked-back hair. A strong scent of cologne and hair pomade, too.

Still, the entrance of Clarice and herself caused something of a stir. Saloon girls nudged each other, heads turned, and Annie sent up a private prayer that no-one would recognise her from the night before. Plenty did.

'Ain't that the little loud-mouth McCall brought in? Can you believe they rode together?'

'Last night, no ... but she's cleaned up pretty good, ain't she?'

Uniforms were everywhere, dark blue and dazzling. Polished boots, glittering sabres.

'That little red-head's new, ain't she?' Passing close to a cowboy and a sleekly chignoned saloon-girl, Annie caught this sour exchange.

'She ain't permanent.' It was Stella, the girl who'd half-eaten McCall. 'All gussied up now, but she was wild as a witch last night.'

Spectators clapped and stamped, as couples pranced energetically past. 'Coming through. Hoop-de-doo.'

A gallop, shuffle, a reel? Hard to tell. There was less concern with style and steps, and more with enjoyment, than Annie had ever seen before.

'Your feet won't touch the floor tonight, honey,' murmured Clarice.

'Look,' Annie said, feebly. 'I won't … I can't dance.'

'Are you crazy?'

'No. Really. I have a limp, you must have noticed. And a … weak arm, at the moment.'

'Two heads and a club foot wouldn't stop anyone tonight. Now I can understand a lady turning up her nose at rough old cowboys and red-necked rail-men, but honey, you can't disappoint the Cavalry!'

'I'm ungainly. I make partners look stupid.'

'Oh, I reckon *that* horse has already left the barn.' Clarice waved at two men galumphing past, one awkwardly clasping the other.

'The poor saps are desperate. Shortage of gals, and one has to play female. Half are drunk, others have two left feet. Don't take this wrong honey, but just who d'you think's the lame duck round here?'

'Do me the honour, ma'am?' A young trooper appeared in front of Annie, buttons gleaming, hair plastered down. He offered his arm.

'Dee-lighted.' Clarice pushed her forward.

For the next few hours, Annie didn't think about her disability again. Or about who she was, or what people might think. The only things on her mind were her partner's feet, the waltz, the polka or scottische.

Big-bodied men swept her around the floor in a ceaseless whirl, swinging, circling, changing partners, treating her like delicate china.

When had she last abandoned herself to music like this,

without feeling foolish or worrying about her partners dignity? She couldn't remember. A lifetime ago.

Captain Wallace finally broke the spell, guiding her to a quiet corner for refreshment. 'Yurr enjoying yourself,' he said, smiling.

'Yes. Oh yes, I am.'

'Nae suffering too much then, after yurr terrible ordeal?'

'Erm ... ' Annie peered over her fan. Sarcasm? Surely not. His smooth face seemed empty of censure. A handsome face too, in a well-groomed, military sort of way. Skin burned brown by the sun and not a single hair out of place.

As he strode off in search of refreshment, her eyes followed his tall figure.

Two ladies teetered across her line of vision. Collapsing into nearby chairs, they fanned themselves frantically with their hands. Annie was sure she'd seen them earlier that day, in drab calico and poke bonnets.

'Well,' one said, breathing hard, 'say this for Miss Clarice Adams. She gives a good party. Law and Order league won't like it, mind, not one bit.' A young man was waved away. 'Not now, son. Must catch my breath, else I'll expire!'

'Pity Cavalry didn't delay 'til next week,' the other remarked. 'I've two nieces coming in from Chicago.'

'For the air?' Wry nods and winks. 'For their constitution?'

'A husband a-piece, more like! Sister was fretting about Indians and I says to her, Martha, I says, you'd be better off worrying about rough old trail hands who haven't seen a woman for a month, than them red devils. Tsk. Would you look at that neckline! Barely decent.'

'Cavalry now, they're different. Least they've some notion of manners. What they here for, anyways?'

One nudged the other in Annie's direction and she looked quickly away.

A few whispered words were all she could catch. 'Stagecoach

hold-up ... whisper ... McCall.'

'Good thing my nieces aren't arrived, then. Letting that man near our gals, is like letting a fox in the chicken coop!'

'Fair's fair, Louisa. He's a changed man since that wedding.'

Annie never did find out what Louisa thought of that, because Captain Wallace was edging his way back through the crowd with cordial. Offering a glass to Annie - 'Careful now, that's a mite full' - he pulled his chair closer.

A pleasant man, she decided. Nice and polite, he even smelled fresh and clean. A welcome change, when most men here carried a strong whiff of horse and hard labour.

'Soo. Except for yurr arrrm, of course, and that eye - you have nae been too ... distressed?'

Annie sipped the syrupy liquid. 'I believe I was most fortunate, Captain. I had a lucky escape.'

'The stage-coach was attacked? Indians, of courrse.'

'Well – '

'And then ... ?'

'I'm not sure. I hit my head, you see and when I recovered, everyone had disappeared. Luckily, Mr McCall happened along and – '

'McCall?' Captain Wallace leaned forward. 'McCall ... did ye say?'

'Mr McCall, yes. He found me, brought me here. If it hadn't been for him, well ...'

'Colt ... McCall?'

Too late, Annie remembered McCall's opinion of the Army. The wanted poster! *Stupid.* She nodded, her lips dry.

'He's still here?' Andrew Wallace shot a suspicious look over her shoulder.

'No.' At least she could be truthful. 'He left before dawn. You know Mr McCall, then, Captain?'

'Not personally, noo. We've never met. I mind well who he is, though.'

A shadowy figure appeared behind the Captain's back, to prop up the wall. Someone tall and thin and dressed all in black. Annie's view was half-blocked. She couldn't see who it was.

'I have to tell ye, ma'am.' Captain Wallace frowned. 'That ye made a most unfortunate alliance. It's a miracle yurr here safe and sound. McCall is a horrrse-thief, among other things. When we find him, we'll string him up. Steady now, watch that glass!'

Annie's trembling fingers dabbed at the sticky stain, spreading like a bruise over her skirts. 'You're not ... ' Her voice came oddly out of her dry throat. 'You don't mean ... that you would hang him?'

Captain Wallace's eyes, two blue pin-points, bored into hers and he inclined his head slightly, in assent.

She stared, with a sick sort of feeling. 'Here and now, without trial? I mean, I am all for law and order, but isn't that uncivilised? Brutal?'

'We'll hang him right enough.' His voice came back, brisk and cool. 'The man stole horrses, shot someone, too.'

In her mind's eye, Annie saw McCall's gun. He'd said that he would use it, told her so himself. Who then, had he shot? Dear Heaven.

'It's what we do wi' wrong-doers and horse thieves oot here.' The cold voice cut through her thoughts. 'Our civil duty. Rustlers are just another forrm of vermin. Did he tell ye anything about himself? Aboot what he did?'

'He was ... rather vague, about his exact line of business.'

'Aye. Ah'll just bet he was.'

Annie tried to change the subject. Whatever McCall was supposed to have done, he deserved a fair trial. She owed him that much. 'Have you been long at the Fort, Captain?'

'Not long, ma'am, noo. Now aboot – '

'And your wife? She is with you?'

'I have nae wife. You ken, I really – '

'Do I detect a trace of accent? A Scots accent?'

Andrew Wallace waved the question aside, irritably. 'Chances are,' he said, 'that McCall himself had something tae do wi' yurr stagecoach hold-up.'

'Oh, really Captain, I hardly – '

'The man's thick wi' too many savages. No need tae worry yurr pretty head, though.' He showed a tight smile. 'Now yurr under our protection, he'll nae likely bother you again.'

Annie felt a dart of irritation. Every time this man opened his mouth, she liked him less. And she wanted to like him, she really did. He was one of her own sort, after all.

'Mr McCall doesn't bother me, Captain.' Not in any way that she wanted to discuss. 'I don't think I have anything to fear from the gentleman.'

Did she believe that? Captain Wallace clearly didn't. His smile vanished, eyes were polished as mirrors. 'Dinnae be under any illusions, ma'am. McCall is no gentleman and in no way tae be trusted. Ye probably ought to be told, he has Indian blood himself.' He paused, dramatically.

'His mother, yes. Is that relevant?'

'Ye know already? Well! You learned a powerful lot about him, Miss Haddon, in a short time. Ah'm surprised his savage side didnae show itself. His people are marauders, you know. Aye, barbarians. A breed apart.'

'Didn't the English once think the same about the Scots?' Annie was amazed at her own cheek. 'We built a wall, I believe. To keep you out.'

The shadowy figure behind Andrew Wallace moved away, clapping a hand over a laugh. Annie still wasn't sure who it was.

'Well, actually it was the Romans, wasn't it? They built it, but ... '

What, the Captain's suspicious look said, are you talking about now, woman?

'And surely the Scots have some sympathy with the Indians,

Captain. After the Highland Clearances? You know, being dispossessed and ... everything?'

He clasped two hands together, to stop himself, Annie suspected, from reaching over and giving her a slap.

'A savage is a savage is a savage,' he said, grimly. 'But och, let's no' waste time discussing the man now.' His smile was bright as the edge of an axe. 'He's a maverrrick.' He rolled his 'rs' with distaste. 'My superiors at the Fort will want to talk more to ye about him, of course. Later.'

A warning? Annie bit her lip.

It didn't worry her too much. By the time they reached the Fort, McCall would be well out of the Army's reach. Miles away. Miles and miles.

Of course, she would never, ever see him again. Goodbye then, McCall. And God Speed.

Chapter 16

'Ladies of strong constitution will always be better suited to expedition, and experience fewer bodily discomforts, than those of delicate and sedentary habits.' - p.62

Shouts, screams, oaths, a frightening exchange of blows. Another quiet night in Red Rock. How did ordinary law-abiding citizens manage to sleep, Annie wondered. After they'd put the cat out.

Luckily, she didn't feel tired. The dance had been too much fun.

Back in her room, one of the girls had helped undo the hundred or so tiny buttons on her dress and she'd slid gratefully out of it, still humming one of the catchiest reel tunes.

The air was stale and stuffy and she considered throwing open the window, but whatever was going on outside sounded too scary.

Sponging herself down with tepid water, she brushed her hair into sleek ripples. It hadn't yet gone back to its wild gypsy state and her face still glowed with colour.

After that, still wide awake, she was desperate for distraction. A book, any old book would suffice, but there were none, she was sure of that, having scoured the place thoroughly, several times.

The only reading matter she'd been able to find was the almanac, with its advertisements for *Ayer's Medicinal Sarsaparilla* and *Celebrated Stomach Bitters,* and a tattered two-year old copy of *Atlantic Monthly.*

She needed a proper read. Something to stop her mind wandering in the direction of the Cavalry, and McCall, and gibbets.

Her eyes drifted restlessly round the room, noticing for the first time, an uncommon number of insects. *Live* ones. Where had they all come from?

From a safe distance, she watched a huge black thing on the window ledge. It didn't move, just sat there, staring back.

Flies too, mosquitoes and other things – fat brown things, with wings. These weren't scuttling round the floor either, keeping a respectful distance; these were sauntering over the walls in leisurely fashion, flaunting themselves.

Sliding into bed, Annie pulled the sheet up to her chin and immediately started to itch. Fleas? What to do about that? (*'Pardon me Clarice, but there are bugs in my bed?'*) No, suffer and scratch at the little bloodsuckers in silence, that's what.

Cowboys - like the fleas - frolicked freely throughout the night. Saloon walls shook and Annie slept fitfully, dreaming of her father, Aunt Bea ... McCall.

She was in swirling mist, facing mortal danger. A thunder of hooves and a steaming black stallion struck to her side. Astride, a man, all in black. Friend or fiend? She couldn't see. The horse reared, the man lifted a hand. A gun!

She screamed and screamed and then ... woke, in a twist of bedclothes. Damp with sweat, sore-eyed. Conscious of the mildewed mattress and sore places where she'd scritched and scratched at bitten skin.

The sound of splintering wood and gunshots struck her sore ears. Something yowled in the darkness. A cat? She hoped it was a cat.

She felt like howling herself.

On waking, she felt better than she had any right to expect. And today - she told herself, brightly – soon, very soon now, she would be on her way to the Fort. First step, towards home and safety.

And Henry Hewell? The fact that she'd been reserved for him, almost branded with his name, like a beast? She wasn't going to think about that, not until she had to.

Clarice greeted her with another armful of silk - a soft shade of violet, this time - and Annie eyed the sweeping skirts.

'Oh, I couldn't. The green will do perfectly well.'

'Take them.' Dress and jacket were bundled into Annie's arms. 'I've a cupboard full. No-one here appreciates 'em, anyway.'

'I'll send money back. Soon as I reach the Fort.'

'No need. Colt's settled up. Yep. Left a heap of money for your keep. Reckon there's a hat to match that, someplace. Give me a minute and I'll find it.'

'You're very kind.'

Clarice met her gaze. 'Just forget anything you've heard about golden-hearted saloon gals, honey. This is for Colt.'

So, Annie wondered. What had happened to last night's smiley-smiley-let-me-do-your-hair-for-you manner? Where had *that* gone? And did people always do what McCall wanted?

'About Mr McCall,' she said, carefully. 'Someone here mentioned his wedding, and I was wondering – '

'Don't believe anything those gals tell you. They love to gossip and tattle.'

'It's not true, then?'

'Depends what you heard. There was a wedding planned and Colt rode out. As to the whys and wherefores – you better ask him.'

'I doubt I'll ever see him again.'

'Don't need to know then, do you?'

Not really, no. Except for her own curiosity, of course, and to try and make sense of the myth and gossip that hung, like a cloud, round his name. 'When I get to the Fort,' she said, 'they'll ask questions. I need to be sure … '

'About what? About Colt? Saved your neck, didn't he? What more do you want?' Clarice's tongue clicked. 'All of a sudden, because of tittle-tattle, you've decided he's some feckless, lying cowboy?'

Something like that. Or some wild Indian. 'If people here hate Indians so much, why do they accept McCall?'

'Respect. In the Rangers, he fought alongside and proved himself. No-one gives a hang about his kin. To everyone here, he's Texan.'

'But … to himself?'

'Lady, you don't know diddly-squat. You kill me, you English, you know that? Buttoned up tight, laced so stiff, that full-bloodied men turn into ramrods and icicles at the sight of you.'

Annie blinked. Hadn't the war with the English ended eighty years or so ago? And far be it for her to point it out, but surely it was an Englishwoman who'd been wronged here? The jilted bride?

She waited for the dust to settle. 'So … what happened to the lady? McCall's bride. What happened to her?'

'Married some Cavalry officer or other.'

'On the rebound?' Oh. That poor, broken-hearted girl.

'Something like it. Look, you want more information, ask someone else. I don't give nothin' out for free.'

Having brought water for washing, Susan came back with the matching hat and jacket for Annie's dress. This time, she was inclined to linger.

'Looking forward to seeing your kin?' she said, making the most of the opportunity to nose about in someone's boudoir. Not that there were any clues to Annie's character in here. Nothing belonged to her, not one single thing.

'Of course.' Annie's answer came a little too quickly.

'It ain't your Ma and Pa at Fort Mackenzie though, is it?'

'My aunt,' Annie said, tipping up her head and brushing her hair. 'And my cousin.' One, two, root to tip. Three, four. Brushed and buttoned up. Ready for Aunt Bea's inspection. Clean hair and fingernails.

'They must be wanting you back, real bad.'

Ah. They would want what was right, Annie thought. They wouldn't have enjoyed confessing that they'd lost her, somewhere between San Francisco and St. Louis. *('Rather remiss of Beatrice Haddon, wouldn't you say? Somewhat careless.')*

'Ain't that outfit a mite fancy for rough travelling?'

'I daresay britches would be better, but my aunt would have a fit if I turned up in those.'

'She don't still tell you what to wear, do she?' Susan looked askance. 'At your age? You git scolded for biting your nails, too?'

Tearing her hand from her mouth, Annie held up the jacket. A deeper shade of violet than the dress, it had a narrow bodice, pinched sleeves and looped and braided fastenings. A tipped hat, with a flounce of net, completed the ensemble.

Charming. A little large, rather a loose fit, but still … charming.

'What's he doing here!' Susan jumped, as the puppy nosed out from the silken fringes of the bedcover. 'Ow, stop yer sniffing! Ain't planning on taking him, are you, miss?'

'I was thinking about it. Who'll look after him, if I don't?'

'Don't look at me. I got enough trouble looking out for meself. I'll fix that hat for you, though. Else it'll take off in the first breeze.'

Amidst a flurry of goodbyes, ('Thank you again, Clarice. Bye, Susan, bye-bye girls') a man appeared at Annie's side. Doctor Monroe, tall and spindly as a plant on a window sill.

In the yellow morning light, he examined her arm and seemed satisfied.

Look, Annie was tempted to say, enough about me, what about you? Drink less, eat more. Fresh air, exercise and all those sorts of things. The sorts of things you doctors always recommend to the rest of us.

A warm wind swept across the street, whirling dust round their feet.

Moose Monroe frowned. 'Before Colt left,' he said, brushing hair out of his sad, dark eyes. 'He asked me to say ... '

'Yes?' Go on, yes?

'Adios.'

Oh.

'And ... take care.'

'Take care?' she repeated, eyes drawn to the hanging thread on his coat where a button was missing. That was all?

The doctor's gaze went from Annie to the men mounting up behind her back. 'Cavalry'll ask questions,' he said, raising his voice above the noise of steel and leather and dogs yapping round horses' legs. 'You could help him, if you'd take the time.'

'I won't lie, Dr Monroe.'

'Wasn't asking you to, ma'am, wouldn't do that. More'n one way to milk a bull-frog. See right now, odds are stacked against our man.' The breeze blew curls back across his face. 'Reckon things need evening up a little. Only fair, wouldn't you say? Army act like they're hunting a mad dog, don't they?'

Annie glanced at the waiting line of Cavalry, the men erect on their horses, caps pulled low to shade their eyes. 'He didn't do what they say he did, then?'

'Guess you've got your own opinion on that. Whose side are you on, missy? Maybe it's time you showed your own hand.'

Annie's cheeks grew hot and she fiddled with the fastenings on her jacket.

She didn't want to betray McCall, of course she didn't, but it had to be said, he was alarmingly unpredictable. She barely knew him. How could she say with certainty, what he had and hadn't done?

'Is that a cock ah hear crow?' the doctor said, after a significant pause. He didn't bother to disguise his contempt. 'What will it take to convince you, lady? Reckon you owe the man.'

The wind flapped at his long, black coat, whipping the hair back from his face. He looked like an Old Testament prophet, Annie thought, railing against the spineless, the feeble, the weak. In other words ... her.

'What do you want me to do?'

'He needs time.'

To do what? Run away? 'How much? How much time?'

'As much as we can give him. He's no scat rabbit.'

And that was her responsibility? All down to her? Shouldn't her sole concern now, be safe reunion with her nearest and dearest?

Behind her back, someone cleared their throat, impatiently. Nodding at the doctor, Annie turned to take the arm offered by Captain Wallace.

Now, one more tricky item to be negotiated. She drew attention timidly, to the puppy. Could she bring him along? He was very small, hardly ate a thing, and was sure to be no trouble.

The officer swallowed his irritation. They would be travelling fast and rough, he said. The journey would be dangerous. No room for excess baggage.

But the pup wouldn't survive on his own, he would only last a few more days!

Tough. Captain Wallace didn't waver. 'Nae room for

sentiment in the Army, ma'am.'

The wagon was the best place for her, he said, considering her arm and all. One of his men would ride with her. He waved at the light buckboard wagon. Did she have everything she might need? Was she quite ready to leave?

Recovering her spirits and straightening her hat, Annie smiled, fixedly. Everything was fine, just fine.

Chapter 17

'On rough expeditions, it may be wise to dispense with most of the usual feminine adornments.' – p.88

One loud 'Ho-o!'

A wave of the Captain's arm and the thin blue line snaked sedately out of Red Rock, setting up a plume of red dust that spiralled towards the horizon.

Farewell then, Red Rock. Annie clung to her seat. So long, saloon.

She felt as if she'd been away from civilisation for years. On some anthropological expedition, perhaps. Lost up the Limpopo, stranded in the Steppes. ('Yes, the natives were friendly. Rather wild though, and lacking in culture.')

Once outside the town, the horses were pushed into a lope and then a gallop. Under her parasol, swaying beside a fresh-faced young trooper, Annie felt perfectly calm and comfortable. At first.

While the men were soon sticky and distracted in their uniforms, she was borne along in some style. Like an English memsahib in an elephant's howdah. Not for long.

Soon they'd set up a blazing pace. As they lurched and

bounced over rough tracks, she was forced to cling on with her good hand and steady herself with her feet.

First, she gave up the parasol, then any semblance of comfort. Later, the remains of last night's supper were abandoned by the trail, as well.

'Sorry, ma'am.' Her young driver was apologetic. 'We're taking a short cut. It ain't likely to be easy going.'

'How long before we g-get there.' Annie's voice wobbled along with the wagon, her face now a sickly grey.

'Sundown.'

Hours away! A lifetime. She would die first, get sick ... swoon.

The sun shone mercilessly in their faces and her little hat afforded no protection at all. She was so that glad McCall wasn't there, to mock or wag a finger at the whalebone restricting her ribcage.

Travelling, she decided, holding on for dear life, wasn't all it was made out to be. She'd been sick on a ship, stunned on a stage-coach and now battered and bruised by this wagon. Would the railroad have been any better?

Apparently, the first time Indians saw a train, they thought it was a fire-breathing serpent that had swallowed the men in its belly. Probably just about as comfortable, too.

'Oops! Hold on there, ma'am. Steady.'

Why, wondered Annie, had it seemed so much smoother riding with McCall? Even on one horse, even crushed against him. *Forget that, just forget it!* Even if it was likely to be your one close encounter with a desirable man.

(*'You never married, did you, Aunt Annie. But, surely you had beaux?' 'Ah, well now, chicks, once in America'*)

Yes, once in America, she'd felt the touch of a handsome man's hand. One casual caress, and it had to last a lifetime. As for Henry Chewton Hewell - she could almost hear his high-pitched, whinnying laugh.

The sky widened to a huge blue bowl, so blue that Annie's

eyes ached.

On, on over the prairie. Miles and miles of shimmering landscape, flat and endless as the sea. So big, so vast. She felt smaller and more insignificant than ever, a mere speck in the wilderness.

While they rested, Captain Wallace wheeled his horse round and trotted back to see how she was faring. Although most solicitous - 'This must be tough on ye, Miss Haddon. Ah'm sorry' - he didn't linger. Keen eyes kept scanning the horizon, and he seemed taut and tense as a coiled spring.

Just as well, thought Annie, furtively peeping in amongst flour sacks and supplies in the back of the wagon. Almost too weak to move, the small spike of puppy tail managed one waggle. When he whined, she shushed him, sympathetically.

He was enjoying this journey about as much as she was.

Her new driver had the foot-shuffling sort of good manners. Offering a bandana, he suggested she pull it right up, to the bridge of her nose. 'May help a little, ma'am.'

In this heat? She would suffocate.

No, no. He was very patient. It would mask the dust.

'Into line. Ho-o!' And they were off again.

At length, they began to climb. The rugged track zigzagged steeply, narrowing to little more than a shelf. On one side, sheer walls of massive rock, on the other - nothing. A yawning void. Inches from their wheels.

Carefully negotiating the rocky ledge, the wagon sent small stones flying into the gorge. Down, down, a precipitous plunge into the chasm. Far away at the bottom, Annie could see a thin, silver thread, the lead loop of a river.

Itching to bite her nails, she fixed her eyes up instead, on tight wavy bands of ancient rock. Giant buttes loomed over them, hundreds of feet high. Birds of prey erupted from dark fissures into dazzling sky.

'Look there, ma'am. An eagle.'

Thank you, very interesting, but she wasn't going to look

up. She wasn't going to move or breathe either, she was going to sit perfectly still and indulge in a few moments silent prayer.

Newspaper headlines danced before her eyes. *CAVALRY REGIMENT IN CANYON TRAGEDY! ENGLISHWOMAN PLUNGES TO DOOM! SO NEAR AND YET SO FAR SAY RELATIVES!*

And didn't eagles eat anything that moved? Pythons, prairie dogs?

ENGLISHWOMAN SNATCHED BY EAGLE! CAVALRY LEFT CLUTCHING BOOTS! FLAPPED LIKE WASHING IN WIND SAY HELPLESS ONLOOKERS!

A few boulders crashed down, startling the horses. No sign of who or what had dislodged them. 'How does one deal,' Annie asked her young driver, nervously, 'with falling rocks?'

'You duck, ma'am.'

Then, onwards. Downwards. Another burst of wide empty country. On, on, on.

At the next waterhole, the trooper helped Annie down, flexing as she stretched her own legs.

'The horses look exhausted,' she said, stroking the sweating neck of the nearest trembling animal.

'Yip. About done in.' The young man offered a canteen, then took off his cap, wiping his wet forehead on his sleeve. 'Them and us both, I reckon. Don't drink too fast ma'am, you'll be sick.'

Flapping damp skirts to set up a breeze, Annie turned to face the patrol. Men had dismounted, but girths were not being loosened, nor bits removed to allow horses to graze.

'Aren't we going to rest?' she asked her driver, in dismay. 'Why such a hurry?'

The soldier hesitated. 'An alert at the Fort. Seems Indians have been putting on paint and making raids.'

'Why are they doing that?'

He shrugged, uneasily. 'They're real mean when they want to be, ma'am. And right now, they sure want to be.'

An alert, an Indian alert. Oh, for England, Annie thought, where a person could wander the countryside in perfect safety, without meeting anything worse than an inquisitive cow.

Approaching the water's edge, she knelt down to splash her face. The water was almost as hot as the air.

Captain Wallace came to join her. Was she comfortable, did she need anything?

As he took his leave with a formal, choppy bow, she stifled a sigh. What was it about the man, that made her want to slap his back and say something unforgivably coarse?

Back on the wagon, she stared at empty landscape. Wind rushed through the sea of grass, sweeping it up one side of a distant bluff, rolling it down the other. No clouds spoiled the glaring brilliance of the sky, not one.

A world away from what she was used to. Narrow lives, closed rooms. Never again, would she be allowed to be this independent.

'What is your name?' she asked her driver.

'John Byrne, ma'am.'

'How old are you, Mr Byrne?'

'Eighteen years, ma'am. Near enough.'

Eighteen! And perfectly free to choose his own way, to come and go as he pleased. Oh, to be young, and a man.

'How far now, to the Fort?' That whine in her voice. Because she was desperate to reach her relatives? Or not? She didn't know anymore.

John Byrne, Annie observed, peevishly, was no longer giving her his full attention. He'd stiffened and was squinting hard at the horizon.

She followed his gaze. No-one in sight, just great open empty land.

Wait. There was something. Something fast moving in a pall of dust. Keeping his eyes ahead, the soldier felt slowly for his rifle, cocking it carefully with his thumb.

'What are you doing?'

'Just getting ready.'

For what!

'Whatever comes, ma'am.'

What came was a lone rider, careering past the sea of blue flannel. Swerving across the lead horse, he pulled his own mount up sharply, in a cloud of dust. Annie's eyes followed his path, along with everyone else's.

The newcomer, tall in the saddle, feet floating free, leaned slightly forward as he rode. The slant of a broad-brimmed hat hid his face. Annie stared and her pulse began to quicken. She knew that rider.

Neither Captain Wallace nor the newcomer showed any sign of wanting to dismount. Their horses shifted restlessly throughout a shouted conversation, a tense and heated exchange, and Annie watched, as wild arms waved and fingers stabbed to make fierce points.

It was no good, she couldn't sit still. Ignoring John Byrne's, 'Stay put, ma'am, please!' - she scrambled from the wagon.

Drawing near to the two men, she heard McCall's bristly brown growl. 'I'm telling you, there were Indians round that herd thicker than flies.'

'Guid, guid. They'll be too busy with buffalo then, tae bother us.'

'That was then. Now's different. That herd's been slaughtered.'

'Soo? Comanche have got their meat.'

'Not Comanche!' McCall shouted, as if spitting glass. 'Flesh has been left to rot, hides stripped. It's white hide-hunters.'

'I think nort,' Captain Wallace countered, coldly. 'Hide hunters have been orrderred tae stay norrth of the Arkansas River.'

'Tell that to the Comanche!' McCall wore a look of blue thunder. 'Well, you can't carry on the way you're going, that's for sure. If you were to strike out north-east, you might just — '

'That's for me tae decide, Mister. Dinnae think you can play hero at the expense of ma command. Ah have responsibility here and ah say we go on. It's the shortest, safest route.'

'You want responsibility for facing a pack of Comanche all fired up and hell-bent on revenge? Do yourself a favour, lieutenant ... '

'Captain.'

'Whatever. Check a little higher up the line.'

'An' who would ye suggest I consult with, laddie?'

'Your scouts, someone with a clear head. The Almighty. *Anyone!*

Andrew Wallace began to look hot under his hat. Angry, but uneasy. He fingered his collar, uncomfortably. 'Ah've two of the finest Osage scoots. They've told me nothin' – '

'Where are they now?'

'Up ahead.'

'Then wait 'til they report back.' McCall's eyes blazed to the horizon and back. 'At least, do that. Hear what they say.'

'Noo,' Andrew Wallace bridled, doubtless aware that he was beginning to look stupid in front of his men. Bad for morale, as well as his reputation. 'We're going on and that's all I have tae say. Ah don't propose to debate ma duty with – '

'What about the woman?'

The what? Annie blinked, then stiffened. Oh, the woman ... that troublesome piece of baggage. Well, don't mind me!

'Miss Haddon has been entrusted to ma care, and – '

That's right, she thought, crossly. Hadn't McCall himself passed her over to the Army? *His* idea.

'You'd be happy to see her scalp hanging outside some Comanche lodge?'

'Damn you mister, ye've gone too farrr!'

Annie dug ragged nails into her palms. All of a sudden, she was aware that McCall's dark eyes had floated round to engage hers. No sign of doubt there, either, just cold hard certainty.

'Perhaps we should ask the lady.' He studied her, coolly.

'Reckon she can speak for herself.'

Annie stared, her mind blank. Ask her what?

'Miss Haddon,' barked the Captain, huffing in the heat. 'Ah was engaged to escort you tae Fort Mackenzie.' *Forrrt Mackenzie*. 'And if ah take on a job, ah must insist ah am allowed tae finish it.'

'Yeah. He's going to escort you right over that rise, into the arms of Little Dog.'

'Dammit man ... ' roared the officer.

'Little Dog?' echoed Annie, faintly. This was the trouble with McCall. He had the unnerving habit, of sounding as if he knew exactly what he was talking about.

'One of Lone Cloud's young bloods. They're all painted up over there, looking for trouble. Dog soldiers. Comanche elite.'

'You seem awfully sure who they are, scoot.' Captain Wallace was grim-faced. 'Care tae explain why?'

'No, and I'm not your damned scout.' McCall's eyes flashed and the two of them locked horns again.

Like rutting stags, Annie thought. Except, she was no delectable doe.

'Just who the hell are ye then, Mister?' Captain Wallace said, suspiciously.

'Erm, I met this ... gentleman back in Red Rock,' put in Annie, hurriedly. 'So, do you know a safe route then, Mr er ... Mason?'

McCall's eyebrow quirked.

'To the Fort?'

'There are no safe routes.'

What were they arguing about, then?

A second's strained silence. As wind whipped silvery ripples through the flattened grass, Annie's skirts billowed out, and she had a sudden vision of herself blowing up, up, into the air and out of sight.

Something of a relief in the circumstances.

Because events had taught her to trust McCall, with her life, if necessary. He'd shown himself to have an unerring instinct for making sense, whether you agreed with him or not.

But, she had no wish to offend this officer, either. Or put him on his guard. Surely he was only a cat's whisker away from finding out who McCall really was.

And if she went with McCall, what chance would *he* have to get away and prove himself? He'd be lumbered with her all over again. She couldn't bear the humiliation.

'Weren't you going to play poker?'

'I changed my mind.'

'Ah.' Another idle thought. What was it like to have men fighting over you? She'd often wondered. Was it thrilling?

If only McCall had seen her before she left Red Rock. For once, she'd looked reasonably presentable. Now, her hair had fluffed and her nose was burned and look, look … *concentrate.*

Decisions. Life and death.

'Erm, well look, I appreciate your concern, Mr er Mason, but as things stand, I think it might be better for me to stay …'

Trailing off, she caught the Captain's eye. He had the infuriating air of someone about to be proved right. Confused, she turned back to McCall, sitting tall in the saddle.

Frustration showed in every muscle, but he allowed her less than a second to change her mind, before touching a finger to his hat and wheeling his horse away.

'Come back,' she wanted to call after him. *'Wait! I'm doing this for your sake, you know. Let me explain.'*

Too late. Dust from his horse's hooves drifted away on the breeze and he was lost from sight.

'Sound a call, sergeant. And put some spit in it, this time. Left front. March. Ho-o.' With a complacent nod, Andrew Wallace drove them on, his expression tinged with triumph.

Noting sour faces all around, Annie sensed a degree of

muttering in the ranks. Many of the men, apparently, agreed with McCall.

Back on the slow rumbling wagon, she felt full of foreboding.

Desperate for distraction, she looked for wildflowers in the tall, dry grass. On this trip, she'd seen so many that she couldn't identify. Birds, too.

As they came closer to the ridge, there were few birds in the air. In fact, there was hardly a sound, beyond the rush of wind, the soft fall of hooves and the creak of leather.

Just an eerie sort of silence, almost a stillness ... as if everything was holding its breath.

They heard the cries first and the shouts.

A split second, and two riders thundered into sight. Osage scouts and hot on their heels - Heaven help them all - Comanche ponies pounding over the rise, the braves on their backs yelling and screaming.

Pony after pony after pony.

Rooted to the spot, Annie stared transfixed at flashes of colour, feathers, painted breasts. Dimly, she heard someone scream, 'Dismount! Skirmish Line!' and men dropped down to the right and the left of her, rifles at the ready.

At 'Aim!' she had already been bundled behind the wagon by John Byrne. By 'Fire!' she was crouching down next to him, ashen-faced.

The air was suddenly filled with frightening noise - wild whooping and yelling, violent volleys of shots. Horses whinnied and the smell of burned powder drifted over to them on the wind.

'Ma'am.' John Byrne was pulling urgently on her arm. 'They need me up front. Now just stay put, y'hear? Don't move an inch and you'll be fine. Here.' He pulled his pistol from its holster. 'Take this. Just in case.'

Then he was gone, ducking down towards the front line.

Weighing the matt-black metal in her hands, feeling its

smooth frame, Annie caught her breath. Noise seemed to recede. *'Just in case,'* he'd said. In case … what?

Did he think she would use it? Did he? Could he honestly imagine that she'd hold it to her eye and aim at a man's heart? Her own heart thumped against her ribs.

Perhaps he'd meant her to turn it on herself! White women did that, didn't they, rather than risk captivity by savages? *The White Woman's Greatest Fear,* McCall had contemptuously called it. A fear greater than malaria and the pox. Easy for him, of course - a man.

Peering over the rim of the wagon, she took in a scene straight out of books that she'd pored over, back in England. Safe and snug in the parlour, hadn't she thrilled at the sight of half-naked red men, being routed by courageous cavalry?

She stuck her head up a little further. Whatever was happening here, did not - dear Heaven - look anything like a rout.

Fumbling for the puppy, she scooped him up, tucking him well inside her jacket. Warm and soft, his heartbeats mingled faintly with her own.

'Head down!' someone screamed and she hastily ducked down, pressing into the rough protection of the wagon.

A disturbance behind her back made her turn, in slow and stupid surprise.

She saw the pony first, a brown and white pinto, war-shield on its flank, stumbling up the slope. Her mouth fell open, knuckles whitened on the gun, but she was far too scared to call out.

As her eyes took in the near-naked man on its back, muscles swelling his shoulders and chest, a cluster of feathers behind his head – she heard her own sharp intake of breath. He held a knife in his hand, and had a lance and bow rifle.

Dear Heaven, Annie breathed, almost fainting in terror. This Plains Warrior coming through the smoke, was coming for her, coming straight for her. Dear Lord in Heaven.

As he swung down, every instinct screamed *run, hide!* But, where? She was helpless. A rat in a trap.

Everything she'd ever read about Indians rushed through her mind then, anything she'd heard. Every myth, lie, legend. Every superstition and gory tale.

He was close enough to see the sheen of sweat and grease on his skin, his cruel scarred body, the curious hawk-like stare.

She heard the crack of rifles discharging somewhere, wild yelling. Did a second pass? A minute, an hour? *'OurFather … whichartinHeaven.'* The prayer came to her lips, along with a flicker of courage. If she was going to die, then she had nothing to lose. If she had nothing to lose …

Letting the gun slip through her fingers, she moved towards the Comanche.

In spite of the whooshing in her ears, the cold sweat, she held his puzzled gaze. *I can do this. Dear Lord, help me to do this.* It was possible, it must be, somehow - to reach out, break down barriers.

Holding out her hand, she tried to smile as proof of good intent, but couldn't quite manage it. *Don't hurt me, don't kill me!* Her lips were trembling too much.

The Comanche's painted mask showed no expression. No crack in the ferocious hauteur, no sign of any softening. And the strong, sour smell coming off him made sickness rise up in Annie's stomach.

Then, as her eyes, heart and mind fixed on this terrible source of danger, another one entirely, overtook her.

A fearsome drumming fell on her ears and a heavy-breathing brute force launched itself at her so suddenly, and violently, that the screams were smothered in her throat.

Seized by the scruff of the neck, she was thrown over the back of a bolting horse and held down hard, the very life breath squeezed out of her.

Face down and panting, paralysed with fear, she saw red earth veer dizzily up to meet her, through wildly thrashing hooves. Stones and dust flew in her face, as the horse was spurred violently forward, snaking and swerving through dry gulches and gullies, round trees and rough brush, and through streams.

All she heard was the thud, thud and pounding rhythm of harsh breath. A foul stench - fear? rank sweat? - and pain in her arm and ribs as she fought for breath herself. Thud, thud, thud.

Against her chest, the puppy writhed and squealed and her life flashed before her eyes. Times when she'd been slapped and scolded. The time she was dragged behind the horse. Thud, thud.

'Not my fault,' Charlotte had sulked, *'just a joke. You're an idiot on a horse. Who else would have fallen off?'*

This time, she was going to die, she knew it. This time, no escape. *Sorry,* a voice screamed in her head, *for being a stupid disappointment to my family, sorry for being stubborn and self-willed, sorry, sorry.*

Squeezing eyes tight over tears, she braced herself. For something, anything.

Whatever was to come.

Chapter 18

'I strongly urge travellers to ignore such wisdom as – natives never attack unless they are first themselves attacked. Dear reader – they do, and they will!' – p.140

A lifetime later.

Annie's eyes stayed shut as the horse came to a halt. Bunched fists felt the slime of sweat on its back, its ribs rapidly rising and falling.

Her eyes were still screwed tight as someone slid her to the ground.

Let it be swift, Lord, she prayed, as the hair was pushed away from her face. *Let the end come quickly.* Panic threatened to choke her.

A violent spell of retching and coughing cleared some of the dust from her lungs.

'You have a real bad habit, Miss Haddon,' a familiar voice said, close to her ear, 'of being in the wrong place at the wrong time.'

Red-rimmed eyes flew open and she made out a blurred shape.

'Better get over it,' McCall said, his dry drawl dragging her out of shock. 'It's just not dignified.'

His face came into focus then, streaked with sweat and dirt, and Annie heard the rattle of her own laboured breathing. She closed her eyes, sensed him move away, and felt tears on her cheeks.

Tentatively, she touched the perfectly still, puppy-shaped bulge in her jacket. Then McCall was back with a wet cloth to wipe her face and neck.

'I'm amazed you've managed to live so long. What are you? Some sort of magnet for trouble? Hey, take it easy, take it slow. Move each arm and leg before you sit up.'

He offered water and she tried to say something, but her tongue felt swollen, and she choked.

He slapped her back. 'Haven't learned a helluva lot, have you? What were you planning to do back there? Shake that Comanche's hand and invite him round for muffins and tea?'

Another wheezy bout of coughing. Her eyes streamed.

'Well, you're consistent, I'll say that for you. Look, try to take it in, once and for all. They don't look like us, they don't talk like us. They don't think like us, either. To sign Comanche, you wriggle your finger like a snake. Get it?'

'But *you* … you are they!'

'Ma was an Indian.' He pushed his hat back with two fingers. 'Doesn't mean I wear buffalo blood or can make it rain.'

Annie was starting to feel like a rat, pulled out of the pantry by its tail to be interrogated about its motives.

Why had she done what she did? She didn't know. Wouldn't make any difference to McCall, anyway. He'd already marked her down as an ignorant idiot.

'I'd heard,' she muttered, when she felt strong enough, 'that Indians are afraid of insanity.' Her throat felt like parchment, but his stunned expression gave her some satisfaction.

'All right.' His sigh was weightily patient. 'Help me out here.'

'I've read that if someone's behaviour is really bizarre, Indians will leave them alone.'

'And that was your plan?' His mouth twitched.

'You find it funny?'

'I find it nigh-on incomprehensible.' The grin widened to a smile. A moment later, he was helplessly slapping his sides.

Annie watched, stony-faced.

'So,' he said, wiping his eyes, 'you learned all that from a book?'

'I couldn't have used that gun.'

'A gun is a tool, no better or worse than an axe or shovel.'

'You're saying I should have shot him?'

'If it's kill or be killed. You're a damn long time dead.'

'Aren't you supposed to be blood brothers, or something?'

'I'm a Texan. Any Texan is fair game to a Comanche. They don't give a damn about my ancestors. Comanche and Sioux aren't exactly friendly, anyway.'

She flopped back, exhausted. All this hating and chasing and murdering.

'I can't bear it,' she said, tears pricking again. She just wanted to sob and sob. 'Those soldiers could all be killed!'

'Nah. Looked like some pretty hard-bitten men in that troop.'

'But what if they're overrun?' She swallowed, thickly. 'I've heard of terrible things done to white people. They can't all be untrue.'

'They're not.'

'You told me they were!'

'I said some were exaggerated, that's all.'

'Children nailed alive to trees, women violated and disembowelled? How could anyone do that?'

'You're looking to me to justify them?' His jaw set. 'Don't demonise what you don't understand.'

'I'm *trying* to understand.'

'White? English? Not a hope in hell.'

'Please don't keep telling me what I can and can't do! I'm not a child.'

McCall was silent. Then, 'Indians want to take the white man's power, his strength. Any clearer?'

As she studied his face, soft paws scrabbled at her jacket. An ear emerged.

'What in hell's name's that!'

Sighing, Annie scooped up the slippery, wriggling bundle. A warm, wet stream soaked the front of her dress. 'Little dog?' Her nervous laugh wasn't convincing. 'It seems all right. Amazing it's not hurt.'

'That fool of a Captain let you carry a dog?'

'Not exactly. He called it a mangy, flea-ridden mutt.'

'Dead right. You'll be crawling with fleas yourself now.'

Annie scratched her neck. 'It wouldn't have survived back in Red Rock.'

'I hate to tell you, lady, its chances aren't that high here, either.'

Breathing unevenly, she squinted around.

They were in a deep hollow, in flat treeless grassland and quite hidden. Yellow grass, choked by rock, flanked a thin twist of water. Beyond that, open flats spread out to dark, shadowy hills.

Apart from specks floating high in the sky, nothing moved. No blur of motion, puff of dust. No hint of the bloody rout taking place behind those hills, neither sight nor sound of it. Just sky and sky and sky.

The air was still and hot, the sun fierce - a glaring, pulsating ball.

When her arm went up to shield her eyes, she saw her torn sleeve, dirty hem and an indecent expanse of stained hose. Pulling awkwardly at her petticoats, she glanced at McCall.

Sprawled on one elbow, hat pushed back, he was unconcernedly chewing a blade of grass, while the puppy sniffed round him. Chewing! As if this was a Sunday picnic.

The only sign that he'd exerted himself, were two damp circles under his arms.

'I should thank you,' she said, although her voice was lukewarm, and her limbs still shaking. Drowning relief had left her weak as the puppy.

'No obligation,' he said. 'I can see you're pretty much overwhelmed with gratitude.'

She flushed. 'Do you believe in Providence, Mr McCall?'

'Nope.'

'Angels then, guardian angels?'

'Whoa! Whatever you're thinking, leave me out of it! I'd just bet you do, though, huh? Well, he'd better hurry up and show himself then, we need all the help we can get.'

'It's not all wings and flaming swords,' Annie murmured. 'Angels are messengers, divine messengers.'

'And what message might you be expecting now?'

'That the Lord sent you to help me?'

'Try again. By the way, there's no Santa Claus, either.'

'Why come back, then?' she said. 'The Army said they were going to hang you, when they caught you.'

'Did they now. Unfortunately for them, I'm not of a hanging disposition.'

A heavy silence.

'I can't help thinking,' Annie's voice shook. 'If you *hadn't* turned back … '

'Oh, I reckon young Lochinvar would've come to your aid, eventually. The good Captain, whatever his name is. Pretty smart, isn't he? First tailored uniform I've seen in years.'

Bug-eyed, Annie stared at this new manifestation. The cowboy poet?

'I read books too,' he said sardonically, seeing her expression.

'Poetry books?'

'Occasionally. Most of us stopped wearing woad here some time ago, in case you hadn't noticed.'

'Sorry, I – '

'At Mission School, I was taught by an Englishwoman. She had this idea that a daily dose of British poets and Shakespeare was the best way to civilise little hell-raisers like me.'

Did it work? Annie wondered. Did she need to ask? 'Interesting idea,' she mumbled.

'Sure was. Along with treating me like a stray dog, not letting me speak my mother's language and daily beatings. Why the look? I was a wild child.' His voice held the faintest trace of bitterness. 'Real wild.'

'A *Christian* Mission school?'

'Oh yeah. Dead set on saving me from the ways of my mother's people. Shaved my head, beat manners and the Bible into me. Set me on the road to salvation. *Hal-le-lu-jah!*' He let the words hang. 'I grew up real quick, when I managed to stop puking.'

'I daresay they meant well.'

'Meant to wipe out all rotten traces of Indian, that's what they meant.'

She opened her mouth to say something else, but he cut her off with that look. The one that said: *Private. Keep Out. This Means You.* 'Better get going,' he said.

For some irrational reason, Annie had thought he was on the point of confiding in her. About the Army. His abandoned bride? Having escaped extreme danger, wasn't it just the sort of time when emotions were stirred up, and confessions came easily?

Not as far as McCall was concerned.

She thought, he lives like this, it doesn't bother him. If he had a nerve in his body, she'd seen no sign of it, so far. 'Aren't we safe here, then?'

'Only as long as the Army's keeping Little Dog busy. Comanche don't hang around. They go for surprise attack, sudden withdrawal.'

'That young trooper was only eighteen.' She came close to

tears, again. 'His name was John Byrne, he – '

'He'll be fine. That's what those blue-boys live for, isn't it? To whoop and holler and charge.'

She took a breath. 'You don't have much time for the Army, do you Mr McCall?'

'Colt,' he said, wearily.' C-o-l-t. Haven't we been through enough to do away with the Miss and the Mister? Oh, don't bust a gusset. It was only a suggestion.'

Annie's face grew hot again. She supposed she could get used to it. Against every rule of polite society, of course, and all her aunt's dire warnings.

'Annie.' The name jerked out from half-closed lips.

There. The sky hadn't fallen in, had it? Generations of dead ancestors weren't turning in their graves. Annie - her father's choice, after his red-headed mother.

Thoughts veered to Henry Chewton Hewell, someone she wouldn't dream of calling anything other than *Mister* Hewell, ever. Could you marry a person and never use their Christian name? Could you be close, share secrets, a bed? However hard she tried, she couldn't imagine herself as that man's wife.

McCall – err, Colt - nodding in grave acknowledgement, brought her back to the present with a bump. The corners of his mouth curled up, his impassive face was transformed.

It left her giddy, a little breathless.

His charm, when he chose to use it, was quite dazzling. He was utterly unpredictable, of course. The next minute, he might well bite your head off.

'You were saying,' she said, hurriedly, 'about the Army?'

'Was I?'

'You said you have no respect – '

'As I recall,' he said. 'You said that, not me.'

'You have had trouble, though?'

'Now and then. Haven't you? Look.' His tone was long-suffering. 'Those Union heroes who fought to free slaves are now fighting to put down Indians. Make any sense to you?'

'Anyway, you were extremely rude to Captain Wallace. You didn't expect him to just go where you pointed, did you?'

He shrugged. 'The man's a fool.'

'I can get no pleasure,' Annie said, 'from knowing those men are still back there, fighting for their lives!'

'You think that I do? That sort of skirmish won't even test their mettle. I'd wager every one of those good ole fighting men gets back to the Fort, covered in glory for killing a few Comanche.' He paused. 'They've lost you along the way, of course. That might take the edge off the Captain's swagger.'

'Do you *enjoy* intimidating people, Mr Mc ... Colt?'

'Do people find me intimidating?'

'You don't see much good in anyone, do you?'

He gave her a flinty look. 'Guess you've found a whole heap of people to trust here, huh?'

'The difference is, I *want* to trust people. You I believe, don't.'

'Is that so?'

'Why,' she snapped, 'do you always answer one question with another?'

'Do I do that?'

'Can't you ever find anything kind to say about anyone, anything nice?'

'Cute hat,' he said. It was still hanging on desperately, by one stout pin, to her hair. 'But useless. Better find something else. You about ready to move?'

No. She wiped split lips with the back of her hand. The idea filled her with dread. Gritting teeth, going on. Coping with McCall. The possibility of sudden, mindless violence.

'Two choices,' he said,' is what we have. Bad or worse. We can circle back towards the buffalo, head north-east across the river. Or try and rejoin the Cavalry. We know which way they're headed. With luck, the fighting'll be over and they'll offer us protection.' He watched her, closely.

'What's wrong with the first idea?'

'Sight and stench of hundreds of dead buffalo would gag a buzzard. And on one horse, we'll be real easy for Comanche to track.'

'They won't know which hoof-prints are ours, surely'

'Everyone has their own way of moving around.' He pointed at the ground. 'See, our prints show I weigh about 180 pounds and you put down one foot heavier than the other.'

They knew she was lame? She suppressed a shudder. 'Perhaps they won't bother with us now.'

'Anything's possible. Knowing the Comanche, it's not exactly likely.'

Dark pictures came into Annie's head. A band of Comanche rising up out of the long grass. Yowling, yelling, overwhelming them. Even so. She met his eyes. 'I don't think we should rejoin the Cavalry.'

'It may be safer.'

'Not for you, surely. But … thank you for asking.'

She caught a glimmer of something in his expression.

'OK. We need to travel light and fast. Make a run for it and hope we get lucky.' He looked meaningfully at the puppy.

'Don't ask me to leave him! I can't just abandon him here.'

'People risk death every day out here. Why waste sick sentimentality on an animal?'

'He's all alone,' she murmured. 'No-one cares. I thought Indians respected the rights of animals. Don't you believe everything has a spirit or something?'

His look was scornful. 'Guess that was in your book, huh. What's it called? *The Englishwoman's Guide to Savages?*'

Near enough. She reddened. 'Its author is highly-respected. World famous. An anthropologist. As a matter of fact, the entire text is considered – '

'Horse-piss.' He pulled his hat firmly down over his eyes.

Chapter 19

'A light veil of voile or cotton will protect the face and neck from dust, insects and sunburn.' – p.32

They rode as they had before - Annie at the front of the saddle, because of her arm - and McCall close up behind. Very close. He had to be. Sorry, but she couldn't get used to calling him Colt.

It was too friendly, too familiar, too … something else.

The puppy, too weak to wriggle, curled into the sling that McCall had rigged round Annie's waist. It was heavy and uncomfortable. Her bruises throbbed, sore places chafed.

She didn't complain though, she had more pressing concerns.

More and more aware of McCall's nearness, every nerve-end was on edge. She couldn't do anything about it either, except pray it didn't show. Every turn in the trail could hide danger, she knew that now, too.

So, why wasn't she more afraid? She puzzled about that. McCall certainly played a part. She trusted him now, to know what he was doing and where they were going.

Their lode star, their sheet anchor.

It was more than that, though. Having expected by now, to be back with her aunt, she'd suddenly been granted more freedom. It wouldn't last. It might explode in her face at any minute. But for now, it was exhilarating.

They'd been riding for about an hour when they saw the cloud of buzzards. Birds hung in the air like a mass of black flies - rising, mewling, falling over the slaughtered buffalo herd - and McCall swore under his breath.

Drawing near to the butchered mess, they came to a silent halt. Hundreds of carcasses, stripped of their hides, had been left for sun, ants and flies to do their worst.

The smell of blood had ripened in the broiling heat, and as McCall had predicted, the stench made Annie sick to the pit of her stomach.

As they skirted the bloody red mounds, with screeching birds quarrelling noisily over rotting flesh, she heaved and clapped a hand over her mouth. 'How could anyone do that?'

McCall gave an empty-eyed shrug and spurred the horse on towards the horizon. 'Violent ends are common here as in the Bible. For men and animals.'

'Those awful birds ... '

'They seek out the dead, the dying. It's what they do.'

Annie cradled the puppy closer.

It was another hour before they got to the river, and in that time, they barely spoke.

As far as the eye could see, the water was deep and wide and copper-coloured. Slow moving currents washed lazily over boulders, twisted round rocks, and the sound of rippling water filled the air.

Picking his way carefully along the water's edge, McCall's eyes were everywhere. Both banks appeared silent and deserted.

Annie watched a bird soar, swoop and plunge into bronze spray.

Until that moment, getting wet and risking death by drowning hadn't occurred to her. She'd imagined herself tripping daintily over stones, or being borne regally aloft by McCall as he waded waist-deep through the water.

Not a vision he shared, apparently.

'You can swim,' he said, sliding to the ground. A statement of fact, not a question. As if everyone could, everyone worthwhile.

Well no, she couldn't, as it happened. Water was yet another item on the long list of things she was afraid of. Something to do with her leg? She started to explain, but one look at his face and all excuses tailed away.

She knew what he was thinking. Foolish useless female – can't look after herself, can't even swim. Not like those ploughing, hoeing women of the West he'd gone on about. They probably swam rivers with their boots on and did the laundry at the same time.

Staring at the water, she shivered. Charlotte was right. A timid useless article, that's what she was, a pathetic ... *oh, dear Heaven!* McCall was loosening his belt, unbuttoning his shirt!

When he peeled off his pants to reveal long, tight-fitting combinations, she looked away. 'What about the puppy?' *And decency? What about that? Decorum?*

'What about it? Take off your dress.'

'I don't like deep water.'

'I don't like lots of things. We have to cross, can't stay here. See those wheel ruts? Wagons have forded here, it's quite safe. Now wrap your clothes round your neck. Stay on the horse's back and hold hard to his neck. I'll swim alongside. If you slip, hang on to me.'

'You might not catch me!'

'I've lightning reflexes. C'mon, time's short, make it snappy.'

Everything in Annie recoiled against it. She couldn't budge.

'Did I tell you about the snakes? When river's high like this, big old black snakes slither up trees, then drop down on your shoulders as you pass by.'

She looked wildly from the man to the water. 'Are you making that up?'

'Which'll get you in the water quicker, yes or no? Look, you'll be on my horse, you won't go full under.' Cursing, he dumped the dog on the ground.

'Here, give me your hand,' he said, and when she hesitated, 'suit yourself, I'm going over. Give my regards to the Comanche.'

As soon as her feet touched the ground, he was unhooking her dress, forcing it apart. When she tried to take over, he snapped, 'With one hand? We'll be here all day.'

Conscious of her heightened colour and unsteady breathing, Annie sensed he was perfectly at ease doing this. Something he was used to? Undressing women?

The dark silk of her dress fell away, leaving throat and freckled shoulders bare.

'Damned stays,' he muttered. 'Turn round.'

Unlacing her, he wrenched off her corset and flung it into thick brush. A billowing mass of lace and linen petticoat followed. Everything off, and she was down to camisole, lace pantalets, silk hose.

Her face scalded. Not that her saw her as a woman, he'd made that perfectly plain. She was a nuisance, that was all, a responsibility. Like a small child or wounded animal.

His eyes moved restlessly along the opposite bank. Weighing his gun flat in one hand, he seemed to be measuring the distance across the water.

Was he going to throw it? To keep that thing dry, Annie supposed. He was hesitating. It was some distance.

'Let me,' she offered, without thinking. 'I'll do it, if you like.'

'I don't.' He shot a sour look at her strapped arm. 'This is no time for jokes.'

'No, I'm left-handed, you see. And … you know cricket? Well, I've an excellent aim.'

'Good for you. If we were playing cricket, I'd be happy to applaud. As it is - '

Annie wasn't sure what devil drove her then, what she wanted to prove or why - but to McCall's startled grunt, she snatched the gun and hurled it in the direction of the opposite bank.

It was possibly the moment in her life when she came closest to strangulation. Certainly the sort of thing that caused apoplexy in her aunt. (*'Disobedience! Self-will! Thinking you know better!'*)

Luckily though, the gun's landing was marked by reassuring thud rather than a heart-sinking plop, and both she and McCall issued a collective sigh of relief.

'Pretty slick,' he said, showing remarkable restraint. 'Very entertaining.'

Annie was sure that given half a chance, he would have shaken her, like a rat.

'Any other skills you've a mind to demonstrate before we go on?'

Shrugging in weak apology, her eyes flicked up to meet his. He looked puzzled. As well he might. And still, he stared.

I must look odd, she thought. Boots, hat … underwear. Not her own substantial underwear, either. These flimsy things, transparent wisps on her skin, belonged to Clarice. In the heat of the moment, she'd forgotten that.

She was suddenly aware that gossamer-fine silk, cobwebby gauze and creamy lace didn't so much conceal a person's form, as display it. She'd never flaunted her figure, always considered herself too short and stumpy for that.

Even so, her colour rose.

Not see her as a woman? The expression on McCall's face said otherwise. Like a predator scenting prey, he caught on to her discomfort. And a chance to get his own back?

'No need to be shy.' Raking hair back, his gaze lingered on the soft swell of her bosom, rising and falling above a flounce of lace. 'It's not the first time I've seen you undressed.'

Annie sensed dangerous ground. Swamps, shifting sands. Questions started nagging, like toothache. When? Where!

Thank Heaven, she thought, adjusting a lace panel, that Aunt Bea was ... wherever she was. Somewhere else. Miles away. The Wrath Of One's Aunt Would Indeed Be Mighty.

Their heads came close as he tied her boots, draping them with her clothes round her neck. Annie was intensely aware of texture. The smooth sweep of blue-black hair, his pale gold skin and a small, vivid scar at the side of his mouth.

'How did you get the scar?'

'Bite.'

'A dog?' *Snake!*

'Woman.'

Gulp. 'So,' she spluttered. 'When did you ... you know.' The first thing to come into her head. Dolt!

His eyes flicked to her face, and she saw her own reflection swimming dizzily in dark, deeply amused depths. 'What?' he said, eyes narrowing in pretend ignorance.

'When you saw me ... '

'Undressed,' he finished, helpfully. 'Aah, is *that* it? Let's see now, let me think. Hey, your nose has gone all pink. Like a rabbit's.'

Annie made an odd sound, a sort of squawk. Like a cat with its tail caught in the barn door.

'Don't panic,' he muttered, heaving her unceremoniously onto the horse. 'I'd hate to offend any English sensibilities. That first night at the saloon? I carried you upstairs. One of the girls got you ready for bed.'

Relief shot through her.

'I just helped,' he said. 'Kept my eyes closed the whole time though, promise. Only peeked once. Maybe … twice.'

She was left staring helplessly at the back of his head, as he led the horse into the river. 'I'll say one thing. Clarice's underthingies are a hell of an improvement on those old lady ones we peeled off you.'

Chapter 20

'There is abundant evidence that many hundred Englishwomen, of independent means and without domestic ties, have travelled by themselves through foreign parts in perfect safety.' – p.14

The horse picked its way into the water, hooves plunging, head held high. Icy spray on Annie's skin, did nothing to stop her shaking.

Mid-river, with McCall alongside, the snorting animal stretched out its neck and kicked for the far bank, tail floating out, wild eyes everywhere.

There was a moment's panic when it shuddered, twisted, and Annie half-slid, half-fell into the foaming water. Flailing in confusion, she gulped, gasped, thrashed wildly about.

Swirling current sucked at her, greedily. Hands fluttered feebly, hair floated out.

Water filled her mouth, eyes, ears, and she surrendered to frighteningly fast undertow.

All sound ceased. Just a powerful watery world, and bubbles, bubbles. Sinking, sinking.

How McCall managed to grab both her and the dog, Annie would never know. Dragging them both to safety, he hauled them spitting and spluttering to the surface.

Spat out by the river, they scrambled up the opposite bank, water streaming from their shoulders, hair pasted to their heads and Annie retched there, painfully.

Minutes later, she was scrabbling in long grass for the gun.

When she couldn't stop shaking and shuddering, McCall said she should sit, calm down. Shock, he said, flicking wet hair out of his own face, like a dog. That's what this was. Breathe, he said. Deep breaths.

Breathe! She jerked away from his restraining hand. Sit about, in flimsy see-through underwear - breathing! With a near-naked, unpredictable man nearby?

Slippery slopes! She could almost hear her aunt's shriek. *Thin ends of wedges!*

Annie knew that she'd never been so vulnerable, so exposed and so utterly out of her depth. Any minute, she was going to laugh like a hyena, or sob hysterically, she wasn't sure which.

McCall spread his clothes out on bushes. Refusing to do the same, Annie struggled with her tangle of soaking dress. Still trembling, and a hiss away from hysterical, she fumbled with buttons.

'Quit fussing,' he said. 'Look, I know you're scared. That's OK, it's natural. No point trying to fly on one wing though, is there?'

Fear, Annie thought, was only part of it. This mix of shock, exhilaration and singing blood. She'd never known anything like it.

Nothing to do with McCall's well-displayed manhood, either. Well, not much, even though he was revealing bits of male anatomy she'd never heard of before, let alone had a close look at. Like someone sculpted by Bernini. *('Sorry, aunt. From now on, I'll keep my eyes averted, promise.')*

'Be sensible,' he said. 'Let me fasten you up, before my manly passions are inflamed.' The silk was creased and wet and took an age. 'You certainly managed to stirrr up the dourrr Scorts Captain.'

'I … beg pardon?'

'He was sweet on you, I could tell.'

'You only saw us together for five minutes!'

'Long enough to spot the lusty glint in his eye.'

Twisting her hair to wring out water, Annie flushed. 'He'd been on patrol for weeks.' A puddle formed at her feet. 'He wanted some feminine company, that's all, a little … civilised conversation.'

'I'll wager he was after more than that.' He watched her limp after the puppy. Step gimp, step sway. 'Does that leg ever ache?'

'Not any more. It's just unsightly.'

'Oh, I don't know. I kinda like imperfections in a woman.'

Well, how gracious of him. O Perfect and Able-Bodied One. What would he know about having a gimpy leg? This man who faced life with absolute assurance.

'For a whole year,' she said, coldly, 'I carried crutches. For one more, a stick. Dogs ran away from me, children called me names.'

'We all face those kinds of things. Part of growing up, I guess.'

'I was already grown up. Anyway, I can't imagine anyone calling *you* names in the school-yard. What would they dare call you!'

'Stinking savage, dirty redskin.' Eyes glittering, he held her gaze. 'Claimed it was the food we ate. Called me a dog and a dirty eater of dogs.'

Stricken silence.

'But, you're not – '

'What? Red-skinned or stinking?'

She shook her head. His skin showed little more than the healthy copper sheen of someone who lived mainly outdoors, that was all. If she hadn't known better, she wouldn't have thought anything of it.

'Other kids had skin white as bacon-rind. Mixed breeds were different. Different enough to get a good kicking.'

'You didn't kick back?'

'What do you think?'

Annie's eyes flicked over him. His bare, well-muscled torso reminded her of a prize fighter she'd once seen, outside a fairground booth. 'Clarice said, you'd earned respect.'

'Yeah, by swinging at everything in range. Took about twenty years to get rid of that hunted rat feeling.'

'It's made you tough, anyway,' she murmured. 'I wish I could claim the same.'

'Nothing wrong with vulnerability in a woman. Or being afraid, for that matter. For Pete's sake, sit down and stop footerin' around after that animal.'

Annie lowered herself onto a rock, conscious of a strong smell of river water and wet dog. As sand and grit dried on her skin, she stared back the way they had come.

It looked exactly the same. Empty, peaceful. Desert willow and tamarisk bordering the wide rush of water. Hills fluid and hazy in the distance. No sign of anyone else, no danger signals. Only the shadows had shifted.

'It's so wild here,' she said. 'And lonely. Almost Biblical.'

'Most white women have no taste for the wilderness. They see it as a threat.' His back towards her, he skimmed a stone across the glittering water.

A wide-open space was left for her to respond. The ignorant outsider.

She watched a bird rise in bright sky, heard its shrill call. Untameable. That was what she thought of the West. Much like McCall. And harsh and violent and tragic. All of those things. And yet …

How to describe her life until now? How she'd longed for space and adventure. How she'd waited and waited for it to begin.

'On the whole,' she said, 'I've enjoyed the freedom.'

He raised an eyebrow.

'At home, I'm rather ... hemmed in.' *Trapped, trapped.* 'It can be stifling.'

'Yeah, plenty of folks start out that way here. Bright-eyed and bushy-tailed about the wild free life. First black lonesome night, we have to wipe their noses, send them home.'

She chewed her nails. She'd led a pathetically sheltered life, she wouldn't argue with that. For instance, never before, had she been as aware of a man, as she was now. No man, for that matter, had ever made her as aware of herself.

Animal magnetism? It all seemed more complicated and nail-bitingly dangerous than that. She'd started to enjoy the deft fencing that passed for conversation between them. She was beginning - oh help - to admire his mind.

'You say you like it here?' he said, abruptly.

'I like feeling free. Until recently, I'd expected to spend the rest of my life as companion, to my aunt.'

'Worse ways to make a living, I guess. Nothing wrong with keeping a sweet old lady happy in her old age, bringing a little joy into her life.'

Annie almost choked. You'd be looking at Aunt Bea for some time before you thought of a sweet, fluffy old lady. The over-demanding voice, the constant nagging. In fact, if that dear old lady had been within earshot now, McCall would have been reeling from blows to the back of the head. Death by umbrella.

'Aunt Bea, is very regular in her habits,' she said. 'Our lives are conducted according to strict rules. Etiquette.'

'Yeah, I guess breeding's a terrible burden. Must wear a gal plumb out.'

Sometimes, she thought, I can hardly keep from screaming.

'All people have codes of manners. Men visiting a Sioux

tepee go in first and move to the right. Women go in, turn left. Men sit cross-legged, women don't.'

That shut her up.

Warm wind ruffled the halo of bright hair, drying to a frizz on her forehead. She felt like a damp and fluffy chick, tossed out of a nest and waiting, helpless, for someone to come and gobble her up.

'And, your cousin?'

Wonderful eyes, she mused, staring back at McCall. Smokey orbs in clear whites, smudged by thick, dark lashes. Seeing everything, missing nothing. What must it be like to look like that? To be envied and admired. Would a person ever get used to it?

Was he even aware of his own beauty? He seemed to carry it as carelessly as a beaten-up old saddle-bag, flung over one shoulder.

'Err, I beg pardon.' She flushed. 'My ... who?'

'There was a cousin travelling with you?'

Cousin? 'Oh, yes.' A cousin. 'Charlotte.'

'Is she wild for liberty, too?'

'No.' Annie shook her head. 'She fits in rather better than I do.'

'Strike out alone, then. If you're so against things as they are. Go, do whatever it is you want to do.'

'My relatives would fight me.'

'Fight 'em back. Don't let others make decisions for you. You're a grown woman, not a child. Or so you keep telling me.'

Annie looked at him, blankly. Fight? Overturn the rules? If only she could.

As it was, what choices did an unmarried woman have? Freedom came from being a man, or marrying one, neither of which appealed to her at the moment. Not that she hadn't had plenty of wild ideas from time to time.

She'd always been a dreamer.

Herself as heroine, screened by a sunbonnet, high on the seat of an ox-drawn wagon. Toiling over the Appalachians, facing adversity. *('An Englishwoman, you know. Such selfless courage!')*

As she day-dreamed, hot wind flattened the pale, bleached grass; sunlight danced on the water. Dragon-flies skimmed the river shallows and the puppy nosed after them.

Twisting away, McCall started to pull on his clothes.

Something nipped the soft skin between Annie's shoulder-blades. 'Something's crawling!' She flicked frantically with her hand.

Forcing the back of her dress apart, McCall prised a minute, wriggling creature out. 'A mystery how it got in, you're buttoned up so tight.'

As he touched her, she shivered - hating herself, but helpless. Now, fumbling for her falling neckline, she waited for him to move away.

He didn't move, he stayed where he was, stooping to blow the damp curls from her neck. When hands slid to her stiffly-held shoulders, exerting the lightest pressure, her nerve-endings burned.

An animal yelped somewhere, a bird clattered. She felt a flutter of anticipation.

'You're pretty stiff,' he said.

Oh, she was that all right. Was this the moment for a light-hearted laugh, an arch aside? No idea. No mother to guide her, no candid friend. Spit in his eye, box his ears?

Experience with Henry Hewell had left her wondering whether she was capable of responding to anyone. A queer, cold little fish, he'd called her, when she'd frozen in one of his furtive embraces, overcome by whisky fumes and the thick scent of pomade.

'No matter.' Wet lips had nipped her neck. 'I enjoy warmin' a woman up.' He'd seemed to think she should be grateful.

Was it her fault, she'd wondered? Was she too old, too cold, too desiccated for passion? An emotional cripple, as well as a physical one? She hadn't expected to find the answer here.

Here it was though, all the same. With McCall's hands in the bare nape of her neck, resistance was melting and a dangerous heat flooding through her.

'Better get going.' His voice husky, he slid the creased silk back up to her neck.

All over, and she was back on the horse, cradling the puppy. Imagination running wild and out of control.

Whoa. Annie felt the tell-tale flush lingering on her neck. *Keep your distance.*

Out of the question, at the moment. Damp clothes clung to every contour.

Back against McCall, she felt the heat coming off him. Enveloped by a smell of raw leather and warm skin, she started to shiver.

'OK?' He felt her jump.

She shifted as far forward as she could, without actually impaling herself on the saddle-horn. 'Not very comfortable.'

'Neither's my horse. Move back on the saddle.'

Tightening his arms, he drew her even closer, moulding himself round. His head above hers, long legs hard against her. 'Did you shake your boots back there? First rule of travelling.'

Boots, Annie thought, were the least of her worries. Sensitive to every part of him, conscious of each hard muscle, every movement, she could feel his heart beating evenly against her spine. Her dissolving spine.

'Somethin' bothering you, Annie?' His breath was warm on the back of her neck.

'Me?' Was that her voice, that high-pitched squeak? 'No. Nothing.'

He muttered something. It sounded like: 'Something's sure as hell starting to bother me,' - but Annie couldn't be sure, and had no desire to speculate, either. She wasn't going to risk another word.

Innocent maybe, but she could no longer ignore his hardness pressing against her, nor the sudden gathering heat between her own thighs.

This isn't love, ninny, she told herself. Nothing like. Love is … a meeting of minds, a mutual respect and regard, a growing understanding. She'd read enough books on the subject.

Real love, love of the soul, was the gift of God.

What was this, then? This strong, unhealthy interest in McCall. Carnal lust? Fleshly desire? No book had prepared her for the way her body was acknowledging this man.

She was not so much innocent, she decided, as ignorant. Not so much naive, as a fool. And McCall, Heaven help her, was sure to be an expert in every aspect of this.

Whatever it turned out to be.

Chapter 21

'It may be possible to travel at night. I recommend engaging a guide who can set a course, by observing the constellations and their shifting positions.' – p.147

The sun was setting in a crimson smear, when they finally made camp; the sky on the horizon blood red. Heat still hung heavy on the air.

'Cold camp,' McCall said. 'Better not risk a fire.'

'Why not?'

'I'd like to make it through the night, if at all possible.'

'You told me Comanche never attack at night!'

He shrugged. 'That's the trouble with Comanche. Damned unreliable. They're smarter than us and they don't fight fair. Like women, I guess.'

Annie let that pass. She'd had quite enough sparring for one day. 'We can't eat, then?'

'We could bite the bellies off a few ants. Joke,' he said, as her eyes stood on stalks. 'I've sourdough biscuits - may be a bit soggy - and jerky. That'll do fine.'

Jerky? That dried meat stuff, mixed with berries? Like chewing a stick. 'Give mine to the dog,' she murmured. 'I'm not very hungry.'

'Tender English stomach?'

No, nervous knots. To underline the point, a sudden rustling and scuffling in the bushes made her squeak in alarm. 'What's that!'

'Let's keep it down to a roar, shall we?' McCall placed a warning finger on her lips. 'Noise travels fast at night. Nothing to worry about. Something looking for a meal maybe, or a mate.'

Annie gulped. 'Something?'

Stiff and tense, she tried to ignore dark thoughts that kept creeping into her head. And that feeling again. Premonition? That someone, or something was close by.

McCall was now up and sorting out the horse. She wished she could help. Better than just sitting, imagining things. 'Anything I can do?'

'Try saying some prayers. Don't expect satisfactory results for me though, it's too late for that.'

She rolled her eyes. Why did everything he said, sound as if it should be carved in stone? She was about full to bursting with his folksy wisdom.

She wanted ordinary things again, everyday things. Clean hair and scented skin. Even that flea-ridden saloon had started to seem appealing.

Her hair had reverted to nature; complexion was all pink, and peeling. She now had flea-bites and nasty raw places where she'd scratched them. She must look like something that had crawled out from under a stone.

Not that McCall seemed to notice. He'd probably cast herself and the dog in the same unsavoury mould. Flailing yelping nuisances with frizzy coats.

Spreading out a blanket, next to his saddle, he indicated it was for her.

'What about you?'

'I'm used to sleeping rough. Here.' He held out his gun.

'Hold on to this and stay where you are for a few minutes. I'm going to take a look round.'

She dangled the gun, like a rat by its tail. 'What's it for?'

'If something moves, and doesn't call you by your first name, shoot it.'

Near-darkness swallowed him up. Then, nothing. No twigs snapping, feet padding, nothing. Just eerie silence and her own shallow breathing. And in the background, a million insects trilling.

Light failed and a huge moon came up, changing colour as it rose to full height. Hazy orange to yellow, then white. As a ghostly glaze settled on everything, Annie's eyes crawled over shadowy outlines. Trees, boulders, bushes.

Something hooted in the distance. Guttural grunts swelled into a howl. Wings unfolded, crashing through low branches. The business of the night was beginning.

The back of Annie's neck began to prickle and she cleared her throat, just to hear some small, human sound.

It didn't help.

No fire meant no warmth, and no security. She edged closer to the puppy, feeling its breath on her fingers. Then, tightening the blanket round, she scanned the sky. Huge haloes hung in the velvety canopy. Orion. The Great Bear. Cassiopeia.

What would she do, she wondered, if McCall never came back? Give up. Lie down. Die?

'You'll get dizzy staring at stars.' His low voice made her jump. 'Shhh! Name any of 'em?' He moved closer to catch her reply.

'A few.' She pulled the blanket up to her chin. 'My father was interested in astronomy, apparently. Perhaps I take after him. I can't be sure because he ... '

'Walked out?'

'When I was a baby, yes.'

A long silence gave her time to consider one thing that she could never admire in this man. He too, had 'walked out' on responsibility. How else could you explain his abandonment of a bride?

'I was a dreadful baby, they tell me. Did nothing but squall. Perhaps that had something to do with it.'

'Guess he was just trying to do the best thing,' McCall said, after a moment, 'leaving you with female relatives. What sort of life could he offer?'

'A better one than I had.' Annie's expression was set in stone.

He examined her face but made no comment.

She made a stab at politeness. 'Do you study the stars?'

'Enough to guide my way at night.' His eyes, faintly curious, were still on her.

'People here have a different education to ours, don't they? In Europe, we study literature and the Classics. You learn about the elements and how to survive. Natural wisdom.'

'You mean, we've got nature, you've got culture. The bone-headed meets the enlightened.'

'I didn't – '

'Amazing any of us got to be civilised, isn't it? A paltry few even manage to read music, hard to credit I grant you, and absorb other languages.'

She felt like a smirking child who'd been smacked. 'Do you ... speak other languages?' She should have learned by now. Never underestimate him.

'Spanish. Enough to get by. You?'

'French, and ... Latin and Greek.'

'They say Sitting Bull studies the tactics of Caesar,' he said. 'Maybe he knows Latin.'

'Oh, I wouldn't think so.'

'Why's that?'

'Well. It's hardly - '

'Yeah, right. Stop looking down your nose at people, you'll end up boss-eyed. Knowledge is power. You learn that real fast when you're fighting to survive.' Ignoring her sour look, he held out a biscuit. 'So. You still blame your Pa for leaving. Poor feller can't have been all bad, can he?'

'I don't know what he was. I just know that when I was small, I waited and waited for him to come back and get me. I thought he'd come, and everything would be perfect, and he'd understand me.' A small silence. 'He never even wrote.'

She brushed stray crumbs from her lips. Why she was telling him all this? She was bound to regret it later. These kinds of aching admissions were almost always a mistake.

'You're still angry with him?'

'I'm not anything with him, not anymore.'

'He came to America, is that what you said? You'd like to find him?'

For a split second, Annie was tempted to confess just how much. Yes, someone close of her own, immediate family. One problem. He'd never wanted her before. Why would he want her now? *'Hello there, Father. Remember me? Must be twenty-seven years and nine months ago now. I was in my crib. You were … running away, remember?'*

No. Bad stock. Feckless, her aunts said. Selfish, unreliable. She was better off without him. 'He's probably dead, by now.' She kept her voice carefully neutral.

He hesitated. 'Your father's name is Haddon?'

'No.' She shook her head. 'That's the family name, of my aunt. She changed mine early on. To avoid … what's that rustling!'

He listened, shrugged. 'You changed your name?'

'My aunt did it. To avoid any taint of scandal that might spoil my … any prospects.'

Aunt Bea needn't have bothered, of course. Dull looks and a limp saw off potential suitors more swiftly than any leper-bell. Except Henry Chewton Hewell, except him. But he had his own agenda. Whatever that was.

'Which part of the country did your father settle in, do you know?'

'I have an address, may be old one.'

'And, is that why your people made the trip here?'

'I've a vague suspicion it's to do with my father. No-one's said anything, but I daresay we're here because there's something to be gained by it.'

'Yeah, and let's take a wild guess, shall we? Money!' In response to her doubtful stare, he said, 'Trust me. No-one travels this far or takes these sorts of risks for anything else. You're here because a brood of relatives has their greedy beaks open.'

Annie chewed on a hangnail.

By now, the breeze had died down and all around was blue and silver and absolutely still. A few moths whirled over their heads, an occasional wild cry disturbed the silence.

In the hush, she found herself brooding. They could be the only two people on the planet. Survivors of some terrible catastrophe. Something awful, apocalyptic.

They were not the only two though, were they? Every sound, every scratch could be Comanche on the prowl. Was that the swish of moccasins now, on damp grass? The nicker of an Indian pony?

'Red hair runs in your family, then?'

Red hair, again. Was he obsessed with hair pigment? 'Just my father. Far as I know.'

'Father, huh.' He looked thoughtful. 'No-one else, no brothers, sisters? Well. Sure is an unusual shade. Very striking.'

He was staring so intently, that she was convinced he was going to say something important. He didn't. The silence just stretched on and on.

Night air was now a little cooler. Not to Annie's mind, that it offered much relief. The atmosphere between them was far too oppressive for that.

Another hysterically uncomfortable night together, then. Alone, un-chaperoned. If her aunt found out, *when* her aunt found out ...

She sat, hunched and miserable, words whining round her head like gnats. *Reputation, Virtue, Good Name.*

They sent shivers down her spine.

Chapter 22

'Ladies who take risks when travelling, must be prepared to face the consequences of their recklessness.' – p.198

'Cold?' McCall held his arm wide. 'Or just scared. Come over here.'

Annie wavered.

'C'mon, Annie. Don't get chilled.'

She thought, why worry? No-one need ever know. Anyway, McCall didn't see her as a woman. To him, she was just a pathetic scrap needing protection, like the puppy. Nothing else in his head.

She inched towards him, dragging her blanket. The staid and respectable English spinster.

A strong arm pulled her in, swathing them both in blanket. It was warm with the intoxicating scent of him, and straight away, set her emotions on edge. Aware of burning boats, she felt a sudden rush of blood to the head.

'Better?' His breath was warm against her cheek.

Worse. A brief nod was all she could manage; she didn't trust herself to speak. She felt jangled and nervy and incapable now, of moving away without fuss.

To stop herself shaking, she tried conjugating French verbs, in her head. Strong facts always worked. It was the concentration.

Not this time. *Stupid!* Reduced to this, by a man who could barely conjugate English verbs, let alone French ones. In desperation, she set her mind flipping through a list of English kings and queens.

Then his hand found her chin, forcing it gently upwards. As ebony eyes met hers, être, avoir and Edward the Confessor lost all their significance.

'Annie?' A silky sound from him, almost a sigh. Not the nasty snap-Annie-snap, that commonly came from the lips of her relatives. 'Try not to worry. It'll all work out.'

'I know.' She dragged her eyes away. 'I'm not worried.' Not much. Not about her physical well-being, anyway. It was her emotional state that was causing concern.

'This time tomorrow, you'll be back with your relatives. Nothing's going to happen to you. I won't let it.'

Too late. Something already had.

His eyes flicked over her, soaking up details she'd far rather he overlooked.

Blemishes, blots, freckles.

'If you can't trust me,' he murmured, 'better rely on that angel. Come to think of it, isn't he kinda overdue?'

They were quiet for a moment, breathing together. Then, 'You say you're smothered at home. Ever wonder if your father felt the same way? In a straight-jacket and desperate to be free.'

'He had responsibilities,' Annie said. 'Me, the estate. And he left my aunt remember, without a suitable male relative to conduct family affairs.'

'He'd just lost your mother. Maybe he couldn't face family affairs.'

'So, he upped and left? Even rats stay around long enough to lick their young.'

'Oh, face it, Annie. Whatever you've read, there are no snowy white heroes anymore. They've all been dirtied up. Guess he did what he figured was best.'

Oh, yes? And what made McCall such an expert? All this talk of her father was rubbing her raw. Old wounds were opening up and starting to hurt again.

'We've all,' he drawled, 'done things we're not exactly proud of.'

'We haven't all ruined other people's lives, in the process.'

'Hurting someone usually comes into it.'

What was he thinking about, then? Something he'd done himself? Something *bad*? 'And that's acceptable, is it, hurting innocent people?'

'Some things plain can't be helped. Most of us suffer one way or another.'

Curiosity, that ugly beast, reared its head, and she didn't stop to think before she spoke. 'Are you talking about your wedding?'

A significant silence. McCall's face closed, like a door.

Drat, Annie thought, as her words hung about shiftily, in the air.

'OK.' She heard his pent-up breath escape. 'Guess you've got something you want to say here. Put in your two cents worth.'

'People were talking,' she said, 'back in Red Rock, wondering – '

'Over-developed curiosity.'

'You don't care what they think?'

'I'm not responsible for what they think. It's a private matter.'

'Do men like you ever think they're responsible for anything?' she said, frustrated by his cold control. And once she'd started, she couldn't stop. Words raced out of her mouth, and kept on coming.

'So handsome, so sure of yourselves, you do just as you

please and never stay around long enough to face the consequences. Promises, wives, children – all shrugged off, like a …
like a … snake, with a skin. Someone else is left to mop up
the mess.'

She sputtered to a stop. *Snake?* This snake had saved her
life, hadn't he? Several times. Perhaps she'd been thinking of
her father. She rubbed her eyes. *Had* she been thinking of her
father?

Oh look, she was confused; McCall was too close.

In the deathly silence that followed, she had time to
appreciate her mistake. Not that it helped. When the
thunderbolt struck, it still took her by surprise.

'Want to get my back up?' McCall turned her roughly
round to face him. Hard, dark eyes blazed into hers. 'OK. It's
up. Men like me? What do you know about men like me?'

'Not a lot,' said Annie, miserably.

'Well let me lay it on the line for you. Maybe I'm not the
stay-around type. Maybe I'm not the reliable type, either. Just
maybe, I'm not the gentlemanly type. Get the picture?'

White-faced, she held her silence, feeling the anger coming
off him, and more. Hurts long endured. He seemed to be
fighting himself as much as her.

'You this personal with everyone you meet?'

Sorry. He hadn't been ready for marriage. Fair enough.
Didn't she feel much the same about Henry Hewell? She
gulped hard a few times, like a fish out of water. 'What I said
was … forgive me. Your affairs are no concern of mine.'

Prickly embarrassment followed humble apologies. 'I had
no right.' *Yes, sorry. Didn't mean to. Sorry.*

'Oh, stop grovelling!' His voice cut through her like a knife.
'Stop being so damned English.'

Annie's lips parted, but she had no chance to protest.
Resistance went unheeded as he slid a hand down her back,
pushed her hard to him and covered her open mouth with his
own.

As she panicked and struggled, he simply tightened his embrace. One hand slid into her hair to hold her head, the other arm clamped round her like iron.

Slowly, very slowly, her mind acknowledged something. Something missing. There was no passion in this kiss, no tenderness and no respect, either - just a strong desire to teach her a lesson. One that she would never forget. He was making absolutely sure of that.

Annie had been kissed before - oh yes, she had, once or twice - but never, ever like this. Nervous dry pecks from polite, well-bred partners, had required little or no response.

The demands McCall's lips were making on hers now, were savage. It was clear that he detested her. Hated the English, did he? So was this his way of getting back?

Willing herself to stay stiff and passive, she endured it. And as suddenly as it had started, it stopped.

As he drew back, McCall's ragged breathing almost matched her own. But, not quite.

'Is that the Indian way?' Annie's voice was barely audible, her body rigid. She didn't know which was upsetting her most. What he'd done, or her own reaction to it. 'Throw the woman to the ground and force yourself on her?'

The blood drained from his face, his mouth set hard.

'Next time you're this angry ... ' She wiped her mouth with the back of a trembling hand. 'Try a simple slap.'

'I don't hit women.'

'It might be better if you did.'

She saw him wince. Tense and quiet, he brushed her mouth gently with his thumb. 'Sorry if I was rough.' A muscle contracted in his jaw. 'Judge me on what I do though, Annie, not on what people say.'

'You hurt me!'

'I said I was sorry.' He gave her a dark fending-off sort of look. 'I meant it. That's an end to it.'

Confused and shaken, she stared at his face, trying to read

something in the half-shuttered eyes, controlled expression. Nothing. No wonder he was good at poker.

'Not going to talk feelings now, are you?' He sounded bored. 'Most women seem to want to, at a time like this.'

Annie opened her mouth. Nothing came out.

'Oh, come on.' He sighed. 'Spit it out. Tell me what code of etiquette I've offended here. See, we native boys are simple people.' When she didn't respond, he said, 'So, what's the English way? Should I shake hands now and beg your forgiveness, prithee?'

'We don't all stand round wearing wimples and speaking the language of Shakespeare,' Annie snapped. 'What's the American way? A hearty slap on the back and splinter of wood to chew on?'

A muscle flickered briefly in his face. He let a long silence pass, then said softly, 'We're on my territory now. Let's try my way, shall we?'

Angry and off-guard, she didn't see the danger until he'd closed the gap between them once more. Her focus blurred and for one agonising second, his mouth hesitated over her own.

Then as blood hurtled through her veins, he touched her eyes, brushed her neck, throat, face - and his mouth when it found hers, was warm and full and unbelievably sweet.

For a few seconds, she closed her eyes and leaned into him, abandoning herself to wild, unfamiliar feelings of delight. Then as his face, slightly rough, rubbed her own, she twisted away. 'What are you *doing*!'

'If you don't know, guess I'm doing it wrong.' Finding her hand, his fingers closed round it. 'It's more fun with two people, though. You want to join in?'

It's a game, Annie thought. With players nowhere near evenly matched. Men like McCall ate orphans for lunch.

What was *she* doing, that was more to the point. Drowning? Sinking fast. 'Mr McCall ... ' she said, stiff-backed as any dowager.

'Colt.' His mouth was back on her dusty neck. 'You make me sound like some bank teller.'

She pushed him away. 'I don't do this!'

'You don't kiss?'

'I don't kiss strangers. You do it all the time, I suppose.'

'I've done my fair share of tomcatting.' He couldn't resist a smug little smile.

Annie wanted to hit him.

'So, what sort of behaviour are you used to?' he said, feigning interest. 'Gestures and gentle touching? Or was that those monkeys?'

She examined her fingernails, black and bitten down to the quick.

'Oh, come on. I want to know how it works. What happens back home? In your English society. With men.'

Avoiding his eyes, she gave a shrug. 'We have to be introduced – '

'Can't hear, speak up.'

' ... introduced, then allowed to meet at certain functions. Private parties, card games.'

'Sounds a riot. Then what?'

'We meet in the company of friends, walk and talk together ... '

'When would – '

' ... get to know each other. I beg your pardon?'

'When would they get to kiss you?' His tone was mocking, faintly sardonic.

Annie felt spots of colour on her cheeks. 'My aunt,' she said, 'would ... '

'Try un-clenching your teeth.'

'My aunt would have to be sure of the gentleman's intentions.'

'All for a kiss? No wonder you're still single.'

She tried to think of a suitably crushing response. Nothing

ladylike came to mind. 'Plenty of women lead perfectly fulfilled lives, without a husband.'

'Yeah. Lonely, fulfilled lives.'

'They have friends and companions. Dogs.'

'None of those kiss you passionately on the lips at night. Unless it's a pretty strange set-up. So, you talk. Then talk some more. Then you get hitched?'

'More or less.' Even to her own ears, it sounded feeble. She shrugged. 'It's the way we do things.' *Oh yes, we English. We really know how to enjoy ourselves!*

'Well, I can see where I went wrong.' His laugh was low, and rather nasty. 'I'm no elegant, restrained English gentleman. My Sunday manners didn't fool you for a minute, did they?'

Annie's thoughts went to Henry Hewell - never elegant, rarely restrained and to her mind, no gentleman either, however you happened to slice him. Some of the things he'd suggested, hinted at, when they were alone together had made her shudder. In company of course, he was as circumspect and correct as any clergyman.

'That has nothing,' she said, wearily, 'to do with it.'

'Some of your best friends are natives, huh?'

'I believe all men are created equal, if that's what you're getting at.'

'Mighty big of you. I can hear you now - hey, you with the bone in your nose. Stop eating each other and come sit alongside me at the pianoforte.'

Shaken by his rough contempt, Annie stared. Which hobby horse was he riding out on now? 'I don't understand.'

'No, you wouldn't.' He sent her a brief, bitter-eyed stare. 'You are like you are. English?'

Annie stared back. 'Whoever this person was, this English person, and whatever they did to you - it wasn't me, was it?'

Disconcertingly silent, he neither shook his head nor murmured agreement, although something was surely called for. What in the world had happened then, to leave him hating an entire nation? 'What *was* it,' she said, 'that the English did to you?'

'I thought we'd agreed my affairs were no concern of yours.'

'Yes.' Annie nodded, several times. 'And I do understand how you feel. I have no right – '

'You have a right to stay out of my hair, that's what you have a right to.' He brushed something off his sleeve, probably wishing it was her. 'What was the other thing? Oh yeah. You don't know a damn thing about how I feel, either.'

'Tell me, then. It might help.'

'Hogwash! You want my opinion?'

Not particularly, thought Annie. His tone was hardly encouraging. She got it, anyway.

'Some questions are best left unasked. No point parading everyone's feelings in the open all the damn time, getting trapped in a web of talk.'

She didn't respond. Her heart had gone out of the argument, and she couldn't face getting drawn into another one.

A stony, wordless silence lasted for some time.

Then, 'Three people know what happened. That's plenty.'

The thin, yipping howl of a coyote echoed somewhere, and birds sounded a clucking alarm. Annie held her breath. 'Is one of them Clarice?'

'Clarice, yeah. We understand each other.'

'And we … don't?'

'Nope.' A sharp shake of the head indicated that as far as he was concerned, the subject was closed. 'We don't.'

It was true, of course. They didn't understand each other. Most times, they barely shared the same language.

So-and-so and blah-blah-blah - that was her - rattling on about everything. He rarely used joined up sentences. Different blood, different beliefs. Worlds apart. As strange to each other as a wild coyote and her aunt's pet Peke.

Another chill silence. You could almost feel the frost

forming.

A night-hawk flapped squawking from a nearby tree. The puppy's ears pricked. Straining to catch what was bothering him, Annie heard nothing. No sound, no wind. Nothing.

She stared out into the pool of darkness. What did it matter anymore, what did anything matter? They would die horribly here, be lost for ever, and who would worry? Not a soul, not for her anyway. Nothing left, except two piles of bleached bones. Three, counting the puppy.

Chapter 23

'Beware the lure of exotic life-styles. Freed from the scrutiny of society, the strictures of home and family obligations, some women succumb to this enchantment and cast aside all commonsense. These poor creatures then lay themselves bare – to danger, distress and disappointment.' – p.57

'I'm no good at this,' McCall said suddenly, his voice so low, that Annie had to strain to catch it.

'I ... beg pardon?'

'This open, sharing kind of stuff.' A minute passed. 'Look, a long time ago my life was real simple. Then an Englishwoman happened along. Name of Virginia.'

Annie sat absolutely still. *Now* they were coming to it. Virginia? Beautiful name. It suggested so much, didn't it? Charm. Quality. Nothing plain about that name, nothing dull.

'I was driving horses north. Got as far as ... '

'Did she have red hair?'

'What?'

'Virginia. Was she a redhead?'

He shook his head. 'Fair, she was fair-haired.'

'She was English though?' Her expression was rapt. 'Like me?'

'She was English, yeah. Not a bit like you. Virginia was kinda ... delicate.'

Never had Annie felt so squat and solid, so freckled. 'Was she ... she was visiting the West?'

No response. Two years on and still pining? Must be. So, what had gone wrong? Was he too wild for her, this Virginia? Had she tried to keep him on a leash?

'She was on a visit,' he said, eventually. 'Done the European Tour and wanting more excitement. Her friend's father was a colonel in the Cavalry and brought them West with his party. For a spot of sport and gentlemanly adventure.'

Sport, yes. Gentlemanly adventure? So why was McCall's mouth set in such a bitter line? 'Did she like the West?' she prompted. 'Virginia?'

'Liked the idea of it. Liked the idea of me, too. Wild cowboy with a bad name. And the hint of savage blood - well, that just thrilled her English soul to bits.'

Recalling her own reaction to the same discovery, Annie flushed. Sniffing her fingers, the puppy poked through them with his plush, velvet tongue. 'What happened?'

'She got scared, or wised-up. Maybe both. Me, I was blind to it. Her friends were real concerned for her welfare, though. Well, you know us wild half-breeds. Dangerous, the Colonel told her, unpredictable. Barely house-trained. Thought I might go native on them.'

Heavy eyelids drooped. His black hair looked almost blue in the moonlight. 'Anyway. She didn't take much convincing.'

'You didn't abandon her, then? That's what everyone says. It's what they all think.'

'It's what we agreed they should think. I rode out. She married a Cavalry officer four weeks later. The kind who encourages his men to take pot-shots at peaceful Indians. A year ago, he led a detachment into a village to shoot up old men, women and children. Got a medal for it too, that good old West Point boy.'

'I'm sorry,' she said. How lame. How she'd misjudged him. Sorry.

'About what, about butchered Indians? Most whites reckon it's the right thing to do. And Virginia,' he shrugged, studying the backs of his hands, 'was a long time ago. I was stupid. Lost my head, lost control. Won't happen again.'

Control? 'But, you loved her.'

'I didn't love her.' He cast the idea aside, impatiently. 'I didn't know her.'

'So … ?'

'No idea. A disease, I guess. Madness. Let myself get carried away. She built fantasies around me, how some females do. Then, when reality didn't measure up … '

'Is this why you dislike the English?'

'Partly. I'm only human.'

He was that all right. 'And, the other part?'

'In my blood, I guess. My Pa was starved out of Ireland by them. It's how he ended up here.' A pause. 'Better now? Now you've wheedled it all out of me? I told you, talk's best kept in the shallows. That way, it's easier to ignore.'

A brooding silence. The sort that follows thunderbolts or a fierce deluge of rain. This one didn't clear the air though, not that Annie noticed.

'Why aren't *you* paired up?' he said, suddenly. 'Never liked anyone enough, that it?'

She examined her hands. 'They didn't like me enough, in return. I don't suppose you'd know anything about that.'

'Lady, I know as much about hurt pride as anyone else.'

She stopped herself going off down that path again. 'Is today Sunday?'

'Feels like it. I'm being preached at.'

'I've missed church, then. I never miss, unless I'm ill.'

'Well, if we don't get lucky, you can apologise in person.

Now, how about we get some sleep?'

Attracted by the buzz of voices, the horse came closer, breathing damply between them. Putting up a hand, McCall caressed its velvety muzzle.

Lucky muzzle, thought Annie, before she could stop herself. Of course, he would never touch *her* again.

'Lie back, Annie. Rest your bones. I'll wake you at first light.'

The entire loose-limbed six-feet-something of him stretched out beside her on the ground. Annie stayed bolt upright, arms tight across her chest. 'I won't sleep.'

'Try. I'm not going to pounce, if that's what's worrying you. Look, let's not make too much of that, shall we. We were alone, in the middle of nowhere. It happens.'

He'd already shrugged it off.

Gingerly, she lay down. Their last night together, they'd been either side of a roaring fire. Now, there was barely a foot of ground between them. Of course, they were fully clothed. That must count for something. *('Of course, we were fully clothed, aunt.')*

'Can't we talk?' she said, desperately.

'About what?'

'Cows? The herd you want to start?'

A heavy sigh. 'Reckon there's about five million longhorns in Texas right now.' The hat over his face muffled his voice. 'Mavericks, mostly. Anyone who cares to, can round them up and brand 'em.'

'That's what you plan to do?'

'Yip. We'll drive 'em to the railroad. The North is real hungry for beef.'

'You're not against the railroad altogether, then?'

'I'm against the idea of Indians being swept aside, that's all. Sleepy now?'

'Tell me about the Sioux.'

The reply took so long, she had almost given up on an

answer. 'Why? So you can thrill your friends back home with tales of wild red men?'

Could he even begin to imagine her life at home? Dim rooms, dull conversations. Yawning silences. She'd met people here she'd never dreamed that she would meet, seen sights only seen in books.

She wanted to hold it all in her head. Each breathtaking view. Every conversation.

After all, these stirring times were just blank pages in her journal. It lay lost and abandoned, along with everything else, under the wreck of the stage-coach. Unless the Comanche had taken it. What would they have made of her entries?

FEBRUARY: 1867

Monday: *Rain. Stayed in, read book. (Fielding.)*

Tuesday: *Drizzle. Can't find Minnie, looked everywhere. Read, wrote letters.*

Wednesday: *Damp. Found Min, five kittens! Lost book. Started other.(Austen.)*

Question: Why does Henry Hewell eat here so often; why is he always seated next to me?

Thursday: *Hail. Lost kittens, found Taggart taking sack to river. Diverted him to barn. Aunt Bea FURIOUS.*

Friday: *Downpour. Losing mind! Furniture pressing in. Walked to town, got wet. Aunt Bea annoyed, Charlotte said I would catch chill and die, serve me right.*

Saturday: *Dinner, fish - twice this week. Henry Chewton Hewell, again! Do not like, ugh, yuk. Never smiles, merely smirks. Was he weaned on pickled onion?*

Sunday: *John Dickon admires my mind, said so twice. Wish he admired other bits. What else to admire though?*

And so and so on. Then Monday again and Tuesday after that and barely any difference between them. How thrillingly it could have been transformed.

AUGUST: 1867

Dear Diary ...

Sunday: *Hot, sultry. Slept with McCall, under the stars.*

Then, whenever life became too awful to endure, she could look back, and weep.

'Are you still awake?'

'I don't want to be.'

'Please. Tell me about the Sioux.'

He started, reluctantly at first, with tales that his mother and his mother's mother had told him. The power of stones and soil; man's kinship with nature and the earth, sun, moon and stars.

Annie listened spellbound.

'How can you choose,' she said, 'between the freedom of the Sioux and control of the whites.'

'Nothing free about the Sioux,' he said, drily, 'not anymore. I don't want to be parsed up and organised by whites, either. Lucky for me, there's no need to decide. I just need to make a living.'

'You're comfortable with that?'

'Pretty much. It's others that aren't.'

Rolling over, he propped himself up and pushed back his hat. 'Sure like to think things through, don't you?' He brought his eyes level with hers. 'Somehow I can't see you going back to your needlepoint and embroidery silks after this.'

No, Annie couldn't see it, either. French knots and feather stitch. Tedious conversations. 'I can't see you rocking on your front porch either, but I daresay you'll settle to it, eventually.'

'I'm settled,' he said, yawning, 'as I'm likely to get. What're you planning to do with that mutt, by the way?' He nodded at the pup, snoozing peaceably on its paws.

Annie had no idea. She hadn't thought as far as a name or a basket by the fire. 'Leave him at the Fort, I suppose.'

'Too many there already. All hair, teeth and yap.'

'Wouldn't you like a dog?'

He gave her an old-fashioned look, then stretched out again. 'No, I sure as hell wouldn't.'

'I don't think he'll need much grooming.'

'Well, isn't that a relief!' A beat. 'You aiming to talk yourself to death?'

'Have I done *anything* right since we met? In your opinion.'

'Wind's getting up,' he said, the hat back over his eyes.

'Because if there's one thing, I'd really like to hear it.'

He sighed. 'Do we have to do this? I'd rather pick fleas off your dog. What do you want me to say? Let's see, you teamed up with two outlaws, swallowed a quart and a half of whisky, started a bar-room brawl and tried to stare down a Comanche brave. That about covers it. But hey, don't feel too bad.' Another yawn. 'We all mess up from time to time.'

All around, the prairie lay blue and still and silent. The moon picked out planes of rocks and trees, and glinted coldly off the slant of the saddle. 'Why *do* you talk so much?' he said. 'As a matter of interest. Were you born that way?'

'No-one would want to just sit and look at me, would they? I learned that very early on. Conversation fills the gaps.'

She steeled herself for another wry comment, but none came.

'What do you think?' she said.

'About what?'

'About what I just said.'

'I wasn't listening to a lot of it.'

Sighing, Annie waited for the conversation to continue. It didn't. No more words, just the sound of McCall's slow, even breathing.

Some time later, she raised herself on one elbow. He was asleep. No doubt about that. Eyes were shut, his breathing selfishly regular.

She tried not to be alarmed by all the scufflings and rustlings. Rabbits, he'd said. Ground owls, coyote. But how could he be sure if he were snoring?

After a while, the night noises stopped worrying her. If *he* wasn't bothered, why should she be? Out of the question to sleep, though. Shifting restlessly on rough, uneven ground, she stared at stars, high above her head.

Recalling the names of a few reassured her. Perseus, Pegasus, Cygnus, Capella. Surrounding the high moon. There for a million years and there for a million years longer.

The air was hot, heavy with the scent of plants. The pulsing song of crickets, dreamily hypnotic. Why did she feel so restless, restless? A thin sheen of sweat on her skin, a shivering ache in her body.

Unfamiliar longings, vague desires. Feelings she recognised, but barely understood. Intimate relations? Ha. What did she know of those?

That sort of thing was never openly discussed. Not in her closed feminine society, anyway, and never within a million miles of her aunts. Bodily functions, intimate urges - even thinking about them seemed vaguely improper.

Not that any of her friends ever reached marriageable age without knowing what would be expected of them, on their wedding night. They weren't stupid; they'd read books, observed barnyard animals.

Disappointing though, when those same friends married and still failed to share any really meaningful insights into that state.

Take Meg Gilfoyle, Annie's best friend for years and years. Before marriage, she'd been happy enough to confide, hadn't she? Conversation had been frank and free, right up to the night before Meg's wedding.

They'd talked about everything. The dress - Brussels lace, with seeded pearls - hair ornaments, undergarments, flirting. Everything. Whispered too, about things they'd read or heard or vaguely suspected. Mouths opening into mouths, thrusting tongues. Swollen parts, immodest burnings.

Hadn't they giggled at Meg's mother's advice to keep furniture between oneself and one's husband, in the early days of marriage? She'd warned of strong excitements, violent emotions.

And afterwards? Had Annie's friend continued with her confidences? They'd spoken about furniture arrangements, mice and mutton, that was all. Nothing else from Meg, except a sly, half-shuttered secretiveness. With perhaps a trace, oh, just a hint of something unpleasant.

Had Meg been disappointed? Had the excitement of courtship settled too quickly into monotonous marriage? George Gilfoyle wasn't young, but then neither was Meg. Like Annie, she'd been the spinster of the family, past her prime and very much surplus to requirements.

Men, Annie sighed, were a mystery. Always were, always would be. Unless she allowed herself to be driven towards this ghastly union with Henry Hewell.

Otherwise, she'd stay an old maid, and end up all withered and frowsty. Shades of Miss Havisham. Or Miss Flite, with her parrots, from *Bleak House.* Spinsters who died waiting. One touch, one heavy breath, and she'd crumble and turn to dust.

('You never married did you, Aunt Annie? No grand passions then, no adventures?') ('Ah well, once my little chickadees, once in the American West ...')

Oh yes, once. A once-in-a-lifetime, never-to-be-repeated opportunity. And she'd pushed Colt McCall hard away. Why? *Why!* Good sense? Or gross stupidity?

Had Meg ever longed for George Gilfoyle to press himself against her, and part her lips with his own? Had she? Small stocky George, with his fussy ways, pasty complexion and sun glinting off his eye-glasses? You never could say for sure. And Meg was not about to tell.

Once, without warning, Henry Hewell had stuck his cold, flaccid tongue into Annie's mouth. She recalled it, vividly. A limp lump of wet flesh. She'd nearly gagged with shock.

A sense of the man now at her side, overwhelmed her. The set of him, the dusty scent, his raw strength. If he turned to her now, what would she do? If he put his arms around and pulled her close. Her body trembled. No-one need ever know.

Was she mad! She shifted restlessly, on the bone-hard ground. Was her brain starting to melt? Abandon herself to a man who would offer nothing. Not love, commitment or fidelity. Just the promise of emotional danger, and a reputation in ruins.

A hot night's sweat, that's all this was, a feverish aberration. Not, she had to admit, an altogether unfamiliar sensation lately. Sometimes, she worried about herself. Was it the humidity? Or just bad blood? If there'd been windows here, they would have been dripping with steam.

One thing she *had* learned from all this. It was blood in her veins, not water.

'Don't,' she confided to the dog, 'tell anyone about this. There'd be terrible trouble if anyone ever found out. You hear?'

The puppy didn't answer. He licked her ear happily.

She would never sleep, Annie thought. Not tonight.

Less than a mile away, beyond scattered boulders, tangled brush and trees, there was movement. No prints, no tell-tale signs, no noise. No warning at all of anyone coming.

Chapter 24

'In order to establish good relations with indigenous tribes and native peoples, it is often necessary to speak English, slowly and clearly.' – p.37

Waking in sudden panic, Annie found a hand - cold as ice - over her mouth, hot breath on her cheek. 'Hush up, Annie. Don't scream!'

McCall pressed in close, his whole body cocked alert. Not quite the scenario she'd been imagining.

Nothing else, no other sound. Just the silent shadow looming over them, blue-black and threatening. A lean, wolfish face. Oiled hair woven with feathers, falling to wide, bare shoulders.

Annie's mouth fell open.

'Don't scream!' McCall's voice was low, urgent. 'You hear me?'

She heard. Along with the roaring in her ears, the frantic thump-thump in her chest, the trembling limbs.

One easy movement and McCall was on his feet.

It was over then, all over. For him – a brutal and violent end. For herself, trouble just beginning.

Rolling onto her knees, she bowed her head, clasped her hands. Sharp stones pricked her flesh as she muttered, 'Dear Father, Merciful Lord ... '

'Shush, Annie! Get up.'

'The Lord,' she said, 'will deliver us.'

'The only place the Lord's going to deliver us is Fort Mackenzie, and he'll have a real hard time doing it if you stay down there on your knees.'

Annie looked up. Two pairs of eyes, dark and brilliant, stared back. As she got to her feet, she was shuffled to one side and the two men grasped each other, warmly.

'You *know* this man?' Wary eyes on the newcomer, she addressed McCall.

'Grey Eagle. You know him too. The saloon bar? Red Rock?'

He didn't look like the person from Red Rock. Red pigment stained his nose and cheeks and he wasn't wearing many clothes. 'You didn't *say* you knew him.'

'You didn't ask. Smile, Annie. Act friendly. And button those boots. You'll be riding hard in a few minutes.'

Her mind racing, she fumbled clumsily with boot fastenings. As McCall bent to help, she hissed, 'Why has he come?'

'To help us out of here. You'll take my horse. Don't worry. He's a real good ride, nothing spooks him.'

'What about you?'

'We have to split up, it's the only way. I'll go on foot.'

'What about me!'

'Grey Eagle'll see you safe. I'd trust him with my life. Often have.'

'You don't ... no, I can't ride.' She sounded desperate. 'Not on my own.'

That stopped him. Realisation quickly dawned that she wouldn't make jokes at a time like this. Both men stood over her. Brooding disbelief followed blank incomprehension.

McCall ran a hand through his hair. 'Man has two legs, he

can ride.'

'I can't.' She made a helpless gesture. 'Since my accident.'

'Why didn't you say before? He's a good animal, won't let you down.'

'He's huge. Frisky!'

'I'll give him a good talking to.' He eyed her narrowly. 'Ask him to spare your delicate nerves.' Loping to the horse, he slid an affectionate hand over its flank. 'Come over here and look him in the eye. Show him who's boss.'

Reluctantly, Annie approached the big, frothing horse. She looked him in the eye, saw his yellow teeth, flared nostrils. She smelled his rank breath. The horse blinked back.

They both knew, with absolute certainty, who was boss.

'I never used to be like this,' she said. 'Before. It's panic. I ... just can't.'

Grey Eagle cleared his throat and spat eloquently.

'You have to,' McCall said. 'You must.'

'Can't I ride with Grey Eagle?' Desperation drove her to say it. The last thing on God's earth that she wanted, was to ride pressed up against that Indian.

'Nope. It'd slow you down. Ride him or carry him. Up to you.' Sliding a firm arm round her waist, he heaved her up into the saddle. A violent jerk of its head and the horse skittered sideways. 'Easy, easy boy. I could tie you on if you like.'

Ah yes, the crowning touch, the final humiliation. Given the slightest encouragement, she would have burst into noisy tears and fallen off. Shaking her head, she drew an unsteady breath.

He shortened her stirrup-treads. 'Never figured you for a quitter.' His tone was the jolly, encouraging sort people adopt with nervous infants.

'Now, bunch the reins, hold them high. Move your hips with his. Your hips. You know where your hips are, don't you?'

Loose-legged on his own horse, Grey Eagle sat straight-backed and still as a statue, contempt oozing from every pore.

Annie stared down at McCall. This was goodbye, then. For good. Sensing his impatience to be away and put all this behind him, she held out her hand, felt his firm grip.

'I must thank you,' she said, concentrating really hard, as the horse jerked its head.

'No need. It's been … interesting.'

Purple plain stretched out all around, dark and vast as the sea. Passing ships, she thought, that's what we are. It wasn't McCall's fault that his passing had rocked her on her heels.

Was this how he'd remember her, then? A shivering, scruffy scarecrow on a horse? Stiff sprouts of orange hair, pale freckled face?

'Annie.' He hesitated. 'At the Fort, they'll ask questions. About me, about the stagecoach.'

'What should I say?'

'The truth … except for the medicine bundle. Remember? Someone left it there to stir up trouble. Don't tell them about that.'

She nodded, gravely.

'And Annie, what was your name?'

'My … what?'

'Family name,' he said, offhandedly. 'Before your aunt changed it. What was it?'

'Carlyle.' Was he writing his memoirs or something? 'Annie Carlyle. But the –'

'I or y?'

Did his expression change, when she answered? It may have done, she wasn't sure, the hat was too far down over his eyes.

The moment passed. Handing her the wriggling bundle of puppy, he merely touched a finger to the brim of his hat, and turned away.

Grey Eagle's huge horse reared. Low over its back, the Indian urged the animal on, and when Annie glanced back over her shoulder, McCall had already disappeared into the darkness.

'Will he be all right?' she cried out to Grey Eagle. 'Mr McCall, will he ... ?' Her words were lost, blown away on the wind.

It was the smell she would remember most. His smell, Grey Eagle's. Acrid and stinging, warm sour flesh.

They were side by side for a time and Annie's eyes, rounder by the minute, kept darting towards the Indian. She'd always considered herself enlightened, liberal with other races. Here was proof that she was nothing of the kind.

Smile at the man? Be friendly?

At the saloon, with him in buckskin breeches and a Cavalry jacket, it had been easy. He'd looked like any other soldier. Here, with paint and pigment across his cheeks and nose, and glistening arms all bare and brawny, he looked different. Cruel-bodied. Primitive.

A hint of something else too, something she'd seen in the eyes of that Comanche brave. Something unfamiliar, frightening.

ENGLISHWOMAN SLAUGHTERED BY SAVAGE! SAD LIFE BROUGHT TO CRUEL END SAY RELATIVES!

That wasn't how it would be. She knew how it would be, didn't she? How it always was, with captive white women. She'd read enough about it. Passed round among the braves and left broken, disfigured. Violated.

But McCall told her to trust Grey Eagle. He would have known that it wouldn't be easy.

And the horse? Even harder. Reluctant to pretend to be even remotely in charge, she let the animal have his head and just clung on grimly. In this way, she rode for miles in Grey Eagle's dust. Miles and miles.

Stars swarmed around them in the blackness. Ghostly

shadows reared up, then melted away into the night.

Dust made breathing difficult. Her nose stung, throat filled up and eyes were blinded. No way of knowing where they were going or where they'd been.

No fences marked their way, no creeks or trees. No fields. Just wind-scoured plains and ancient tribal grassland, rolling northwards.

Here and there, they splashed through stagnant water collected in old buffalo-wallows, scattering squawking birds from night cover as they passed. Mostly though, over it all, mysterious, breathless silence.

Just the relentless thud of their hooves, the crack of breaking brush, creak of leather and an occasional wild yowl of a coyote.

Two things kept Annie on that horse. Pride, and Colt McCall. Plus, the niggling suspicion that Grey Eagle wouldn't notice if she slipped to the ground, but simply leave her there, coughing and swaying in a cloud of dust.

Wouldn't notice, wouldn't care?

On high ground, as a line of light on the horizon heralded dawn, he called a halt. A burst of wide country unfurled below them in the mist.

The sun started to strengthen and grey landscape took on colour. Birds began shrill wake-up calls; insects started stirring.

'Is it far now?' Annie asked, faintly. Every muscle ached. She felt weak and sick. Twigs clung to her hair, sundry flying insects darted round her head.

No reply.

Motioning that she should dismount, Grey Eagle beckoned her on. He led the way, silently loping and she trudged behind, ducking when he ducked, obediently keeping pace.

'Shall we rest?' she puffed, a queasy feeling in her

stomach.

Nothing. He padded on, not the least bit out of breath, his sharp animal scent on the breeze. His broad back was unbowed, his expression impassive. Probably didn't give a fig if she lived or died.

As worn out and confused as Annie, the puppy whimpered reproachfully. Poor thing. Why should it have to suffer? How would it survive now, who would look after it? She was having enough trouble with herself.

Having hobbled both horses, the Indian offered water from a canteen, then lay prone on his belly, eyes level with the ridge.

Observing that stern, hawk-like profile, Annie kept her distance. Wind rippled through the long-stemmed grass, rustling in eerie silence. The horses grazed peacefully, flicking flies with their tails.

All she wanted now, was to stay here on the ground and close her eyes. Purgatory would be getting back on that horse. 'Will we be staying here long?' she said, palely.

Stolid silence. The glorious gift of conversation seemed to have passed Grey Eagle by. Perhaps these people communicated in a different way. Telepathy?

'Um ... you no speak English, Mr err, Grey Eagle?' she enunciated carefully, as if he were deaf, or dim-witted. *'For the benefit of natives, always speak English slowly and clearly.'*

Rolling his body slightly from its prone position, Grey Eagle fixed her with a dark stare. Stained skin, and cheek bones like daggers, made him look menacing and dangerous.

Annie quailed. 'Because, I'm afraid ... me no speak ... '

His expression grew even more disdainful. 'You are afraid?' The voice seemed to come from somewhere deep in his throat.

'No, I ... ' Drat. Near-perfect English. 'I mean to say, that you ... we ... have not spoken. I thought – '

'Sioux believe silence meaningful.' He regarded her,

narrowly. 'Thought before speech. No-one quick with question ... or ... pressed for answer.'

Ah. Annie coughed, uneasily.

Flicking stems of grass from her ear, her mind went to McCall. Was that why he was like he was? She never stopped talking; he rarely got started.

'You are Sioux, then? Like Mr McCall. I don't know a great deal about the Sioux. Except that you're very fine horsemen. Would that be ... ?'

'Many words,' he said sternly, cutting his hand sharply in front of his body, 'much noise. Too loud. Be still, listen.'

Yes, yes, sorry. 'I know,' she mumbled. 'Bad habit, sorry.' Nerves, she wanted to say, make me like this. Did he know nerves? She didn't think so. His expression resembled the rock face behind him.

'Can I just ... ' she began, tentatively.

He didn't speak, just held his head stiffly in her direction. Weak sun glanced off painted skin and oiled hair, heavy eyes rested on her. She swallowed, nervously.

'One thing?' she went on, taking off her hat to wave flies away. 'What happened at Red Rock? Why were you in that bar? Do you understand?'

The Sioux Indian's eyes were on her hair. She had a sudden picture of ginger scalps hanging off saddle blankets, and hurriedly pushed damp strands away.

His lip curled. 'I go ... meet McCall,' he said. 'At Red Rock. He not come.'

No, Annie thought. Probably because of her. He'd been off somewhere, saving her from something.

'So, you went to the saloon? But if he knew you, and you knew him ... why didn't he help?'

'Grey Eagle need no help.'

'No. Of course not. I didn't mean – '

'And red-hair ... '

'Me? You mean me?'

He muttered something in his own language. Then, haltingly, 'Red-hair ... make ... trouble.'

Annie sighed. Putting her hat back on, she fussed over the puppy and plucked at the harsh yellow grass. They sat in silence.

'Grey Eagle had vision,' he offered, suddenly.

Annie's jaw went slack. What was she supposed to say now? She tried looking sympathetic. Well, yes, happens to the best of us. This heat would make the Devil himself delirious.

'White-eyed woman with wagging tongue buzzed round McCall's head like insect.' He spat politely into the grass.

Annie frowned. Joke? So far, she hadn't seen much to suggest a sense of humour. What was she in his dream, then? Horsefly? Hornet!

He stared with interest at her flushed cheeks. 'White woman stupid,' he observed. 'Brave, but stupid. Come, we go on.'

He swept horse droppings into scrub brush to hide their trail, then led them off again, off in a mad trot. Sky above was hard blue, and already a promise of cruel heat in the air.

For a while, they were side by side.

'What about the Comanche?' she asked. 'Are they behind us?'

'They follow McCall.'

'But he has no horse! Who'll help him now?'

'He help himself. On foot, Indian tread lighter than fall of feather and leave no trace of passing.'

'He's not a proper Indian though, is he?' She raised her voice, as he went ahead. 'I said, he's not proper ... '

'He has the blood of his ancestors.' His words came threading back. 'Father of his grandmother was Holy man. The old ones run with McCall, always have. His visions strong.'

Old ones? Dead ones ... was that what he meant? Ghosts. Annie chewed her lip. Out here, she could no longer distinguish between superstition and reality. Boundaries were blurred.

Anything seemed possible.

Hours on, in the middle of the treeless plain, Fort Mackenzie shimmered into view. Hazy in the distance, high wooden palisades standing proud, flags fluttering in the wind.

Annie almost wept with relief.

Grey Eagle turned his enigmatic face towards her. 'Go. I watch.'

'You're not coming?' The croak came out of her hoarse throat. 'Wouldn't you like to rest? My relatives will want to thank you, and - '

'Sioux do not stay behind pointed sticks.'

Ah. No. Well, she hadn't been too sure about the other part, either. The relatives. How would Aunt Bea respond to a bare-chested native wearing feathers and streaked with paint? (*'Tea, Mr Grey Eagle? Jam tart?'*)

Not the woman who'd given the gardener at home a severe dressing down, for passing the terrace with rolled up sleeves and a button undone. It had been enough to give her conniptions. Put her right off her breakfast kipper, apparently.

How should you take leave of a Sioux brave, then? One who has more than likely saved your life. *Thank you so much? So nice to have met you?* Handshake, salute, small bow?

As she fidgeted, he extended his own hand, uncurling a fist to reveal something nestling in the palm. Something odd. She peered at it, dubiously. 'What ... ' It was hard to see, her eyes were so hot and dry.

'Eagle claw. You take. Strong medicine.'

'Most kind, but I really don't need ... ' Annie's limbs twitched. Burning hot, she was starting to feel unwell.

'At Fort, you need.' He nodded. 'Grey Eagle's visions also strong.'

She felt a quiver of unease. Myth, magic? Silly! Hadn't she sailed here from a place called the 19th Century? Witches charms were in fairy-tales.

'Eagle claw.' Grey Eagle pressed it firmly into her hand. 'You take.'

Not wanting to offend, Annie's fingers closed round it. Harmless gewgaw. Couldn't do her any injury, could it? Strangely enough, her hand began to tingle.

'Go.' He gestured, impatiently. 'Go now.'

She started down the slope, halting half-way to look back.

No hand lifted in salute, no nod or wave. His horse just wheeled sharply round, kicking up dust.

Struck by a sudden sense of loss, Annie trotted on towards the Fort.

Who at home, would ever believe it? *('A full-bloodied Sioux, you know. Several scalps on his saddle. More game pie, Vicar?')* No-one. Not in a million years. *('Have you heard Annie Haddon's tall tales? She's such a mouse, you may be sure she made them all up!')*

Nearing the Fort gates, in full glare of the sun, she felt more and more delirious. What was that chanting, those echoing voices? She glanced over her shoulder. A whirl of wind, that was all, wind whining.

No wonder she felt so peculiar. When had she last eaten? Slept? Bare legs. And no gloves. Lost her hat. Where had she lost that? McCall would be furious. No, he wouldn't. Wouldn't know, would he. Wouldn't give a fig anymore, if she were to fry.

Don't cry, she warned herself. Don't, don't. Not now.

Sliding from the horse, a wave of unsteadiness swept her. A drowning sensation. Then, legs buckled and she fainted right away.

Emerging from the wooden stockade, a fresh-faced and startled young trooper gathered Annie up. This crumpled bundle of odd clothes. Mangy scrap of a pup, too. Trotting nervously behind, out of kicking distance.

Chapter 25

'Portmanteaux may be used for the transport of personal effects. They should be strengthened with iron rims and must carry a strong lock and key.' – p.47

Mists eddied and swirled round her head. Strong arms bore her aloft. She heard voices. Soft murmurings. 'Alone? What's the story?'

'Beats me. Yip, out of the blue! Turned up at the gate with - hear this - some big, buck Indian on her heels. Cool as you please.'

'Not Comanche then, she'd never've broke loose.'

Mutter-mutter ... blah-blah. A shock to hear English words again.

Then, another voice. Sharp as a needle. Charlotte?

'The medicinal leech,' Annie mumbled, 'can live for twenty-seven years.'

'Oh, it's my cousin, all right. Head full of rubbish. Mercy, how brown she looks. How coarse!'

Struggling to speak, Annie's voice died away. Red mists burned behind her eyes, a prickly growth had taken hold in her throat. She was hot, hot. Hot as fire with fever.

'Burning up right enough ... face as red as her hair.'

'What's that in her hand? Some filthy Indian charm or somethin'. Land sakes! What kind of company she been keeping? The poor mite.'

People drifted in, out ... coming, going. Who? She didn't know. Voices rose and fell.

'Come to visit with your cousin, honey? That's nice.'

'I can't stay long. Not contagious, is she?'

Annie threshed and writhed on a narrow cot for days. Cool cloths were placed on her head, salt broth held to her lips. 'Try a little dear,' someone coaxed.

'No, no.' She couldn't eat, couldn't drink. She fell back, exhausted, helpless.

'Please. It may help.'

No! Swallowing hurt, really hurt. Go away. Too weak to be grateful, too sick.

The doctor came. Least, that's who they said it was. No Moose Monroe this time, all dark charm and curls. Older man, with veiny hands. Hairy ears and nostrils.

'Keep her comfortable.' A solemn voice. 'All we can do for her, now.'

Was her end nigh? *Ha*. No-one laughed, just scared faces. No-one answered, either. Wretched enough to die, that was for sure, wracked and wretched. Give in, she told herself, give it up. Surrender. What was the use?

Such dreams, she had too, so vivid and real. Indians hunting, ponies running, and strange birds - red-backed hawks - swooping and screaming over her head.

In the midst of one, and weakly trembling, she raised her head from the sweat-soaked pillow.

'Eagle claw?' Lips quivered and her breath made groaning noises.

'Lord bless her. That's what she's after, look. That bit of old bone and fur.'

'Strong ... medicine.' Annie's hand closed round and she gripped it tight.

'Yes, dear. If you say so.'

She slipped back into the dream.

Days later? Months, years? Forcing sore eyes open, she faced the thin morning light.

A miracle. No more sharp hot pokers piercing her brain. Her forehead felt cool, and limbs had stopped quivering. Joints - she tested them, cautiously - were aching and tender, but praise be, she was even hungry!

Sunlight filtered round the blind, filling the air with radiant dust. A still silhouette sat sewing at the foot of her bed.

'Aunt Bea?' Struggling up, Annie rubbed her eyes - her voice a crackle of leaves in her throat.

Someone else. Someone brown-haired and plump, who murmured kindly, 'Just lie back and rest, dear. You've been *very* sick.'

Annie had already flopped back. Her throat felt like parchment. How long had she been sleeping? 'How long ... ?' Her breath a painful gasp, she waved at the bed, and its blue quilted coverlet.

'Three weeks, near enough. Here, take a drink. Small sips now. Anything else? Could you manage a morsel of something, maybe?'

'Eggs?' Annie croaked.

'See what I can do.'

'Is my aunt here?'

'Not at the moment, dear, no. I believe she's in Missouri.'

'Don't know why she went.' Charlotte yawned. 'No idea. Why anyone would want to go anywhere here is beyond me.'

'When did she leave? I mean, does she even know that I

... '

'Hate this place, hate everything about it. The weather, the people. We *have* to leave, have to, as soon as Mama gets back.'

'I'm not sure Charlotte, I'm still so weak – '

'Oh, for pity's sake, how can you be, you've been in bed for weeks.'

'We rode so hard to get here, though, we had no – '

'*You* had a hard time, you! What about us? Stuck here, in this wilderness for more than a month! No theatres, parties, balls.'

'But – '

'No drives or daily post. No milk, no *vegetables* except for boring old potatoes!'

'I know, I know, but – '

'You *don't* know, you have no idea how awful it's been. No amusing conversation, nothing to do. No gossip, nothing interesting happens.'

'What *did* happen?' Annie said, suddenly. So far, no-one had bothered to tell her. 'At the stage-coach?'

'What? Lord, I don't remember. Something to do with the railroad. A gang of men with masks. They talked of shooting, burning, pinning the blame on savages. Mama spoke to them of course, she told them we were English.'

'That must have impressed them.'

'They were more interested in the man opposite, as it happens - you know, the one who drank whisky all day? Apparently, he'd been making maps for the railroad and for some reason, they daren't hurt him. So they herded us all onto horses instead, and took us away and then the Cavalry came, and that was that.'

'What about the driver?'

'Who? What about him?'

'Was he all right? Was he hurt in the wreck?'

'Hard to say, isn't it? Half of him appeared to be missing

before we started. Yes! Yes, he survived.'

'Did they catch the men?'

'How should I know? The officer who gave me a ride here - oh, he had the handsomest face, the most divine ... anyway, he told me not to worry my pretty head about it.' She let out a sigh. 'Pity he turned out to be married.'

'What about me?'

'What *about* you? Is this the time to point out that your hair's gone berserk and there's a peculiar splodge on your face?'

Annie gave Charlotte a look. 'You left me! Under the stagecoach.'

Charlotte met it, innocently. 'We thought you were dead. Oh, don't be silly, of *course* we were concerned, of course we were. But when soldiers went back to check, you'd gone.' Charlotte suppressed a smirk. 'We thought you'd been eaten by a wild animal.'

'I almost was.'

'What? Henry Hewell will be here soon, by the way. Oh, I can see you're just thrilled about that. And do something about that dog, it won't move from your door. I had to kick it really hard, before I could get in.'

'What did you say his name was?' Charlotte's head poked round the door to Annie's quarters, some time later. 'That man who found you at the stagecoach?'

Annie hadn't said. She'd been deliberately vague and tried not to mention his name to anyone, least of all Charlotte. The least said, the better.

'I ... ' Struggling to get into her dress, Annie's good arm waved awkwardly through the neck opening. The other one still hurt, if she twisted. No help was offered. None expected, for that matter.

She paused under folds of falling muslin. Until now,

Charlotte had shown little interest in anything that had happened to her cousin. *('The stagecoach hold-up ... yes, I was there, wasn't I! The thrilling rescue ... yawn, yawn ... pursuit by Indians ... zzzz.')*

Was this a trick question?

'Forgotten already?'

A wagon creaked by. Annie could hear the puppy fretting and whimpering the other side of the door.

'McCall,' she said, reluctantly.

She wriggled her shoulders, and twelve and a half yards of sprigged muslin slipped slowly into place. It smelled stale and unaired. Hadn't anyone bothered to open her trunk, since the Cavalry recovered it?

Perhaps they really *had* thought she was dead and had planned to bury her with belongings, like the Egyptians.

'Not ... Colt McCall? That's his name, you're quite sure?'

The puppy nosed a crack in the door and ducked round it. Dodging Charlotte's shoe, he skidded sideways and launched himself at Annie, in an ecstasy of panic.

'If you don't do something about that filthy animal, Mama will. So, how long were you in his company?'

'Who?'

'I'll slap you in a minute!'

Sighing, Annie told her.

'Three? Three days! How many nights?'

'Fasten me up, Charlotte?'

'But you've barely mentioned him!' Hooks and eyes were jerked violently together. 'Oh, what a nuisance. How long are you going to be this helpless? Go on then, tell me, tell me *everything*.' She rolled her eyes, dramatically.

'Nothing to tell.' Annie smoothed her dress. 'He just came along, that's all, escorted me here.'

'But what was he like, what did you talk about?'

'He didn't say much.' Annie felt a flush stain her cheeks.

Her cousin saw it. 'And that's why you called out his name?

When you were tossing in feverish torment, on your bed of pain? Not - Henry, Henry. Colt! Colt!'

Annie bent to fondle the puppy.

'Oh come on, Annie. You can tell me. Turned your head, didn't he? Go on, confess it. Rough, dark brooding man, a naïve, impressionable woman. No-one would *blame* you, you were bound to be girlishly besotted.'

Straightening to meet her cousin's inquisitive eye, Annie still said nothing.

Charlotte folded her arms. 'Oh, don't tell then, see if I care. Dumb faithfulness always was your strong suit. Like that stupid dog.' She aimed a kick at its head. 'That's how you'll end up, if you're not careful. Are you listening, Annie? The faithful companion. Fetching Mama's slippers, begging her to throw you a stick.'

Much more of this, Annie thought, and she'd certainly be sinking her teeth into somebody's ankle.

'Anyway, Ma won't rest until she gets the truth from you. Not if she hears about that man's reputation with women.'

'What reputation?'

'Now who wants to know! This place is rife with rumour. For your information, miss, I've met someone here who knows him, someone who nearly married him! A someone by the name of Virginia Rose Lee?'

Annie's jaw dropped.

'She's stylish,' Charlotte said, grudgingly, 'I'll allow that, for an *older* woman and reasonably charming. And *she* says this Colt McCall just has to walk into a room, for all the women to start up and try to catch his eye. What d'you say about that, then?'

'She's here?' Annie said, her mouth still agape. 'Now?'

'He gives a you a look, she says, and you start to twitch.'

Charlotte eyed Annie, consideringly. 'You know, you've had all the luck on this trip. Why couldn't he have found me, instead of you?' She yawned. 'I borrowed some of your underwear, by the way. Well, your trunk was just standing idle and Mama was concerned that men would be driven wild by the sight of something of mine fluttering in the breeze.'

'Is Virginia Lee here now, Charlotte? Is she with her - '

'Oh, I forgot. Colonel Ruane wants to see you. He's in charge here, the big white chief, in case you didn't know, so I'd hurry up if I were you.'

The Colonel's face held the coldness of pride and authority and Annie disliked him on sight. Introductions were polite enough. With two junior officers present, there were stiff bows, shy smiles, brisk nods all round.

Was she quite well now, they asked, drawing up a chair. Recovered from her terrible ordeal? Such a frightening experience and such debilitating fever, too.

Colonel Ruane's concern seemed genuine enough, his tone polite. Eyes though, were chips of flint. Sure enough, he swiftly turned to business.

'Is it true,' he asked, eyeing her keenly, 'that you came part way here with a man by the name of Colt McCall?'

'You know him, Colonel?'

'Mostly by reputation, ma'am. I know what he is. A man to avoid, at all costs.'

Annie kept her eyes steady.

'No sooner out of one scrape, than into another. Pays no respect to the law hereabouts, and is wanted by the Army right now, for selling us horses, then stealing 'em back. He shot a trooper, too.'

Annie's gaze began to falter. Could it be ... *might* that possibly be true? He'd been wild once, people said. How much of that wild boy remained? Certainty drained away and she stared at the wall beyond the Colonel's head.

The room was stuffy and airless. There wasn't much furniture. A large desk covered with piles of paper, a canvas basin. Dust floated in the air and something was buzzing between the shutters.

'I can only say ... ' she croaked, and then stopped. If she had any faith in McCall - and she did have, didn't she - then she owed him the strongest defence. It was the least she could do.

'He was my protector, that's all I can tell you, my good Samaritan?' She pressed a hand to her throat. 'Mr McCall could have passed by, Colonel, but he went out of his way to help me.'

Her side-ways glance took in sour expressions, set lips. Parables it seemed, carried little weight here.

'My dear Miss Haddon, you cannot compare McCall to anyone in the Good Book.' The Colonel's drawl was cold and condescending. 'Not on the side of right, anyway. He can't be trusted, ma'am, not at all.'

I trust him, Annie thought, I do.

'Oh, I'm well aware he's a ladies man. But that pretty face hides the fact he's a renegade and hustler. Now, I don't blame you for having your head turned, ma'am.' He shook his head, with a mix of amusement and sympathy. 'You're by no means the first. That man's left a trail of broken hearts plumb across the territory.'

He thinks I'm a fool. 'This is most confusing,' Annie said, sweetly. 'I experienced only kindliness and concern at Mr McCall's hands. At no time did he try to take advantage.'

'He's a half-breed ma'am. With half-breeds, you can never be sure where their loyalties lie. Times like these, that's dangerous, real dangerous. His father was Irish, his mother Sioux. Not a mix to gain respect round here. Sioux is a French word, y'know. Means cut-throat.'

'But, Mr McCall fought in the war.'

'For the South? They were whipped, ma'am. Forced to submit. Plenty here are still sore about that. We're not talking about someone who broke the Sabbath. Man's an outlaw, deserves to hang.'

Annie flinched, and the Colonel held her with a long look. 'Now, I need to find him.' He shuffled papers on his desk. 'Where exactly was he headed?'

'I've no idea, Colonel.'

Well? He could be here, there, anywhere, couldn't he? Injured. Dead, even.

Raised eyebrows showed exactly what the Colonel thought of her answer, but he was too much of a gentleman to challenge. The temperature in the room dropped several degrees though, and he started to get impatient.

More questions. What, in her opinion, had happened at the stagecoach? Any sign of Indians?

'Colonel, my cousin told me that white men wrecked the stagecoach, hoping to lay the blame on Indians.'

'Strange sport for a white man wouldn't you say, ma'am? What advantage would there be in that?'

'I'm not sure. The railroad? I've heard ... '

'Railroad's way north of here. No, red trash are responsible for ambushes hereabouts. They're after guns, trinkets. A threat to civilised values. What about the one who brought you here?'

'Erm, a friend of Mr McCall's, I believe. A scout.'

'Grey Eagle? Well, I'll be speaking to Grey Eagle! Just as soon as I catch up with him.'

Annie started to feel uncomfortable. Partly, in truth, because she hadn't worn a corset for days, and that morning, Charlotte had laced her up so tight, she could barely breathe.

'Well, if you'll excuse me Colonel,' she said, uneasily. 'I still get quite tired.'

'As you wish, Miss ... something scratching out there, Sergeant?'

'The lady's dog, sir.'

'Sorry,' murmured Annie. 'He's not trained yet, you see, and I – '

'It's a problem ladies face when travelling alone here, Miss Haddon.' The Colonel kept a straight face. 'They attract an uncommon number of pests. We've had a telegraph from Captain Wallace, by the way. His men have escorted your aunt to Sedalia and they're on their way back. Accompanied by your fiancé, I understand. My congratulations, Miss Haddon.'

Henry Chewton Hewell. Oh bull-feathers. How had he got here so quickly? Hadn't she suffered enough? And *Sedalia*? When Annie left the room, she was shaking.

Chapter 26

'Flowing trousers or 'bloomers' have been advocated by some as a sensible costume for lady travellers. I myself concede them to be useful under certain circumstances.' – p.52

Fort Mackenzie was a self-contained settlement, with one of just about everything - saloon, sutler's store, farrier. The temporary encampment started during a winter campaign had become a permanent outpost.

There were lots of men, of course, but apart from the usual complement of wives, daughters and visiting relatives, few women. So Annie's first sight of the person outside the Colonel's quarters the next day, stopped her in her tracks.

Girls as pretty as Charlotte, with their frills and flirting, were rare as hen's teeth in the middle of the plains. This though, was something else. No woman, Annie thought, had the right to look this good. Not here, in the wind and dust and heat. It wasn't fair.

Gawping at amazing gentian eyes and a china-doll complexion, Annie was certain this woman's skin would never tolerate a spot. Let alone a freckle.

'Miss Haddon?' Rose-petal lips parted prettily. 'Oh, I'm

Virginia Rose Lee, Miss Haddon and I've been longing to meet you.'

She had? Annie stared. No wonder McCall had been bowled over.

A heavily ringed hand was graciously extended. 'You see, I understand you were recently in the company of a *very* dear friend of mine. I haven't seen him for such a long time, and you know, lately, I've found myself wondering ... you *do* know who I'm speaking of, Miss Haddon?'

Oh, Annie knew all right. She was taken aback, that was all, by this unexpected womanly confiding. She wasn't sure what Mrs Lee was getting at, either.

A dainty silence grew.

'You see, I'd half-hoped Colt might just ... turn up here.' A light laugh. 'Eventually. After all, he has friends amongst the scouts. Am I misguided, Miss Haddon? Have you any encouragement for me? You saw him quite recently, I understand.'

Sun burned cruelly down and the wind sighed round them. Ribbons on Mrs Lee's bonnet fluttered prettily. Two dogs sprawled nearby, asleep and twitching and a wobbly-wheeled wagon creaked past.

Then, hot afternoon silence settled again.

The sky was brilliant blue. Against the violet of Mrs Lee's eyes though, even that colour seemed washed-out. How cool she looked, Annie thought, how fresh. Even in this heat, she wouldn't be so vulgar as to *perspire*.

So, why bother to seek the opinion of a person with perspiration on their forehead and hair fluffing out under their hat?

And what about the infamous Captain Lee? What did *he* think of his wife's concern for McCall? Where was he, for that matter? Out somewhere, taking pot-shots at peaceful Indians?

Arranging a smile, sympathetic and sisterly, Annie waved a

hand at far-off hills.

'I'm afraid that Mr McCall has left the territory,' she declared, in tones of ringing confidence. 'Gone away. Yes. On business, I believe. It really is most unlikely, that he will pass this - '

Behind her back, a sudden commotion. Orders shouted out, dogs yapping.

Fort gates creaked open, and a herd of horses - black, bay, skewbald, piebald, foals trotting along beside - streaked in, the ground shaking as they ran together.

Out of the corner of one eye, Annie saw three men following on. Two were motionless on their mounts, their clothes grimy and dust-caked. The third, all dark clothes and brown leather, drove the animals ahead of him, whooping and whistling and waving his hat.

He was tall in the saddle, this man. A particular way of riding, too. Loose and easy, feet floating free of the stirrups. The two women watched while he whirled a rope around his head, lassoing the lead stallion with seemingly effortless skill.

'How did he do that?' Annie murmured.

'It's all in the wrist apparently, a wristy flick, or so I've been told. Tell me, Miss Haddon.' Virginia Lee stared thoughtfully ahead. 'The man on the grey. I may be mistaken, but isn't that ... ?'

Annie froze. Never come back? Never say never, stupid. But why in Heaven's name would McCall risk coming here?

'Ladies.'

There was no mistaking that slow, dark drawl. Replacing his hat, he tipped the brim towards them. 'Taking care of yourself, Miss Haddon? Buttons buttoned, underwear all clean?'

Her face grew hot. How could he be so casual? As if he'd just dropped by to take tea with the Colonel's lady. Didn't he know they were all looking for him, wanting to hang him?

'Colt!' Mrs Lee showed no such constraint, she just glowed prettily. 'How wonderful! It really is you.'

'McCall!' Annie's own voice was low and urgent. His gaze though, had already passed her by, and come to rest on the perfect, upturned face of Virginia Lee.

'So, how *are* you, Colt?'

'Still kicking, Ginny.' The pet-name spoke volumes. As ever, though, his expression gave nothing away.

'You look tired,' Mrs Lee said, softly.

'Yeah? Well, it's kinda hard running a thirty-horse string.'

Could this be the reason he'd risk everything, Annie wondered. Had he known Mrs Lee was here? He was still hooked on the lady, and all she had to do was reel him in?

She felt a pang of the purest envy.

'Mr McCall,' she hissed, again. 'I must speak with you.'

'You are speaking to me, aren't you?'

'Not here,' she muttered, crossly. 'Alone!'

With easy grace, he slid from his horse, letting the reins trail loose over its glistening grey hide. Taking off his hat, he slicked his hair back.

'So.' Ignoring Annie, he fixed Virginia Lee with that straight unblinking stare. 'Guess your husband's got a commission here, huh?'

'You haven't heard?' A furled hand was pressed to her heart. 'Why, Colt. He passed on.'

'On? As in … passed in, through and out? Or … '

'Dead,' Mrs Lee whispered. 'Sadly.'

Another silence.

Counting the beats, Annie looked uneasily over her shoulder. All very well, but any minute now, McCall would find himself pinned to that wall with the point of a sabre. *Then,* he'd wish that he'd listened.

'An Indian skirmish. He was killed by Sioux.'

'Oh, sweet irony.' The words were so soft under McCall's breath, that only Annie heard. She sent him a shocked, disapproving stare. Didn't seem to bother him, one bit.

'How long?'

'Eight months.'

For a moment, Annie was distracted. No widow's weeds for Mrs. Lee, then. No dull taffeta draped to the ankles, no sad hat swathed in veiling. No funeral crepe.

'Listen.' She tried again, 'McCall. Oh, this is ridiculous!'

'What is?'

'You're in a lot of trouble, that's all. Colonel Ruane is looking for you, and when he finds you, he's going to hang you!'

'He isn't.'

'He is! He told me so, just a day ago.'

'Things have changed. Remember that pair of railroad clowns?' He nodded at the two men on horseback. 'The Baileys? They've been bad boys again. Comanche caught them skinning buffalo and set them to roast over a fire. Flames had just reached their butts when I hauled them out. They're kinda … grateful.'

Annie stared at the two men. 'They don't look grateful.'

'They're sitting on raw asses, that's why.'

'Why, Colt!' Virginia Lee giggled.

'I thought no-one ever got away from the Comanche,' Annie muttered. 'How did you manage that?'

'He's one of them, that's how,' one of the Baileys snarled, rousing himself. 'Murdering red scum are close kin. He knows their pet names, eats their stinking food.'

'Yeah.' McCall glanced over his shoulder. 'Real grateful. Now, they're going to tell the Colonel about all the bad things they've done. Stealing horses, and shooting people. Isn't that right, boys?'

'Buffalo.' He turned back to Annie. 'I came downwind of another herd. Comanche were happy to exchange two dumb, ugly brutes for a hundred or so others.'

'How is Grey Eagle?' Annie said.

'Taken with you, for some strange reason. Excuse me now, ladies.' Swinging back on his horse, he reined the grey's elegant head in a tight circle and trotted off.

Wild horses shied and reared all round them and Mrs Lee clutched Annie's arm.

'Do horses frighten you, too?' Annie said.

'Oh no. I'm extremely fond of nature myself. Just as long as it's tightly tethered.'

Annie half-expected McCall to seek her out.

He didn't. Probably left already. Why bother hanging around? Things to do, people to see. She longed to know if he'd made his peace with the Colonel, but was afraid to ask.

And what about Mrs Lee? In horse-flesh terms, Annie decided, Virginia Lee was a thoroughbred. Warranting special care and attention. She, on the other hand, was what? A sturdy Shetland pony? But rather less winsome. More of a donkey. Everyone's beast of burden.

Her life was narrowing down again, by the minute. Soon, she'd be back to the thrill of darning stockings and playing patience. Her sewing bag, her daily lists, her afternoon nap.

The night McCall had kissed her seemed a million years ago. A figment of her over-active imagination. Whoa, little horsey. *Don't think about it.*

'I can't *believe*,' Charlotte said, flopping down on the bed, a perfect vision in wild violet silk, 'that you didn't mention that man to anyone! *Why* didn't you?'

'I ... which man?'

'Mr Bun the baker. Who do you think, stupid? The cowboy hero. Three days alone together. Or was it four? You sly, sly thing!'

Annie eyed her cousin, thoughtfully. Was it imagination or had Charlotte taken extra pains with her appearance this morning? She seemed more animated than usual, and extremely pert and pretty.

Mating plumage? Something suspiciously like it.

In contrast, Annie looked a fright. She knew this because she'd stared into the mirror for a long time that morning, she wasn't sure why. Very depressing it had been, too, seeing huge dark circles under her eyes, a peeling nose and hair like knotted string.

'Everyone admires him,' Charlotte mused.

'Yes. Well, all females admire the biggest bull in the herd, that's long been observed.'

'What are you talking about now?'

'Females compete for the leader of the pack. It's what they do, they can't help themselves.'

'Sarcasm is *such* an unpleasant trait in a woman, don't you agree?'

'Not sarcasm,' Annie muttered. 'It's anthropology.'

'Jealousy, more like. Anyway, I don't care, I want to meet him. You *have* to introduce me.'

'I can't, he won't be here that long.'

'That's where you're wrong dolt, he's staying for the dance. Mrs Lee asked him. It's clear as day she's trying to get him back.'

'Dance?' *Get back!*

'It'll be awful, of course. I'm surprised they know how. Probably the Texas two-step, or something dreadful. What? Oh, stop muttering. Look, I have to be introduced today, because it's all being planned for tomorrow and Mrs Lee already has a running start on me.'

'Charlotte ... '

'Now don't start being stuffy, Annie. Mama will be back by then with Mr Hewell, so there's no need to worry about not dancing yourself, you'll have someone to sit and talk to, won't you?'

'Bliss. We can discuss his ague and gout.'

'Oh stop whining. It's not my fault you have to go through life dragging your leg behind you in that unsightly fashion. Well, I didn't mean it, for goodness sake, it was a joke. You can't still be bearing a grudge. Look, are you going to introduce me or not?'

'Stick to those young officers, Charlotte. They're all smitten with you anyway.'

'Pouf. Oh, they're fine enough in their uniforms, riding out with those pennants fluttering, but they're little more than boys and so ... so brash. I want to meet someone dashing before I leave here, someone *dangerous*!'

'I'd go and lie down if I were you, until the feeling passes. If your mother hears, she'll lock you up.'

'Well she won't hear, will she, and you'd better not tell her either, or I'll tell her a few things about you, Miss Prim! Some of the things you shouted out in fever made married women blush, I'll have you know. Soldier's wives! Don't ask. I wouldn't *dream* of repeating them out loud.'

'I don't believe you.'

'Colt McCall might though, mightn't he? If I told him. How you called out his name, how you begged him to – '

'You wouldn't!'

'Just watch me, dear thing.'

'Have you no scruples at all, Charlotte?'

'No, thank Heaven. You've quite enough for both of us. And a particularly nasty something on your neck, if you want to know. There, just there. Ugh. Can't you feel it?'

Annie tried to pretend that she didn't care, but in the end bitten nails betrayed her. Accepting defeat, she decided, was wiser. In the circumstances.

'Lord, what's this?' Screwing up her face, Charlotte snatched something from the small table that served as Annie's dresser, dangling the offending article between thumb and forefinger.

Annie's eagle claw.

'Don't touch that! Put it back this minute, it's mine!'

'All right, keep your wig on! I don't want the smelly thing, do I? Needs burning.'

An uncomfortable silence settled. It lasted for some time.

Then, 'When do you want to meet him?' Annie muttered.

Parading around, waiting to be noticed, wasn't something Annie was used to. She felt deeply uncomfortable.

'How long must we wander about,' she muttered, 'pretending to take the air?'

'Oh, stop fussing.' Charlotte adjusted her bonnet. 'Nothing else to do, is there? Lord, it's hot. This must be the vilest climate under heaven.'

'I'm getting quite used to heat and the flies.'

'Mmm, I can see that from your complexion. Now, sooner or later we're bound to stumble across him, and you can say that you wanted me to meet him and - '

'*I* wanted *you* to meet *him*?'

'Something like that, yes. Stop dragging your leg, you're bound to tread in something.'

'Then, what?'

'Oh, don't worry, I can manage him myself from then on.'

'Take a tip, Charlotte. No-one *manages* McCall.'

'For goodness sake, he's just a man, isn't he? A simple cowboy. Not the Great Panjandrum.'

'His people,' murmured Annie, 'eat snakes. Watch where you're stepping, Charlotte! Oh dear … too late.'

'Eergh.' Charlotte scraped her foot along the ground. 'If I didn't know better, I'd think you were trying to put me off, cousin mine! Why, I ask myself, why?'

'He's wild, that's all, he has a very bad name.'

'Cute, though.'

'*Cute!* Listen Charlotte, women are drawn to McCall, it's true. Swooningly drawn. He scares people, though. I've seen it, he's like a … '

'Wonderful. I'd rather have a rake than a milksop any old day.'

' … manacled tiger. A whole cage of tigers.'

'Ooh goody, I'm so tired of sissies. Anyway, he's bound to be trainable. All men are.'

'I'd wager this one isn't.'

Charlotte's lips pursed. 'Wouldn't have anything to do with wanting him for yourself, would it? Ha, thought so, you're jealous as a cat. Well, I don't care, I need an adventure. It's horrid here, I'm bored.'

'Read something then, occupy your mind.'

'Oh, that's just the sort of stuffy thing I'd expect from you. Makes any normal person want to give you a slap. Why don't you read *less,* occupy *your* mind with something else? Mr Hewell, for example. He's only asking for a little loyalty and devotion.'

'A cocker spaniel could give him that.'

'You really are a fool, aren't you Annie? Joking about finding a husband, at your age. Lucky for you that Mama takes it seriously. Look ... is that him? Quick, quickly. Over there?'

'Where?'

'There. Stop craning your neck, he'll see! Oh, no ... no, it isn't. Walk on.'

'Look. I didn't jump into this ... thing with Mr Hewell. I didn't fall, either. I was pushed.'

'Entirely for your own good.'

'I'm not convinced that he likes me anymore than I like him.' Annie's voice sharpened. 'Is money involved in this, Charlotte? Is it?'

'How should I know?' Charlotte's tone implied that she couldn't care less. 'Ma never tells me anything, you know that. Nothing important, anyway. You're far too suspicious of people Annie, too quick to smell a rat.'

'Speaking of smells.' She held a lace-edged handkerchief to her nose. 'Have you noticed the permanent whiff of ordure here? Horses, cows ... it's perfectly sickening. I can't decide which I hate most – horses or blue wool uniforms. Look there, Annie. Let's ask that soldier at the gate.'

They asked the soldier at the gate. Did he know of Mr McCall's whereabouts? He did. Mr McCall, they were reliably informed, was picnicking, with Mrs. Lee.

'Picnicking!' Charlotte was driven to stamp her foot. 'On their own? Really, they might have invited us; they know how little there is to do here.'

'I expect they wanted to be alone,' observed Annie, bleakly.

'Well! How utterly selfish of them.'

Chapter 27

'It has long been observed that an excess of mental excitement weakens the constitution, and reduces one's power to exercise caution and restraint.' – p.67

The dance was going to be wonderful.

Fort Mackenzie, bathed in moonlight and velvet shadow. Light, laughter, music wafting out on warm night air from the drill-hall. *Everyone* was looking forward to it.

Everyone, that is, except Annie.

Leaving their quarters, Charlotte linked arms - not out of any affection - but to make absolutely sure that Annie didn't turn tail and scuttle away.

'You're pig-selfish, you know that, Annie? Just because *you* can't dance, you don't want anyone else to enjoy themselves, either. It's not fair.'

Annie gritted her teeth. Was life ever fair?

Seeing rocks in their path, she couldn't help wondering what would happen if Charlotte didn't notice, and - whoops - tripped right over one of them. Nothing serious, of course. A bloody graze, torn hem. Just enough to send them scurrying back to their quarters.

'Always thinking of yourself.' Charlotte skirted the obstacles, daintily. 'What about me? If you don't come, I won't be able to make an impression on Mr McCall.'

'You don't need help for that, Charlotte. You look lovely.'

'Think so?' Preening, Charlotte adopted a half-pleasant manner. 'I couldn't decide between this and my rose organdie, but this colour does seem to make my eyes look, well ... wider.' She batted long lashes. 'Don't you agree?'

Wider yes, and the bluest of blues. While beneath round white shoulders, the creamiest, plumpest bosom peeped out from stiff net ruffles and a low-cut basque.

'I'm *such* a difficult fit at the moment, my waist's no more than seventeen inches! Everyone's remarked on it.' She twirled round, and yards and yards of baby-blue taffeta belled prettily out.

'I'm not worried about the Colonel's daughters, or any other women here, for that matter. Waists like sows most of them.' She patted the curls at the nape of her neck and looked so insufferably smug, that Annie wanted to jump up and down on her hem. 'It's Mrs Lee I'm bothered about.'

Ginny, McCall calls her, Annie might have said, but didn't. She was still having trouble dragging her feet.

Oh, her own dress suited her well enough – pale green silk trimmed with Chantilly lace - it wasn't that. Who'd be looking at her? Compared to Charlotte, she was about as exciting as a milky drink at bedtime.

'Such a pity you lack height, Annie,' Charlotte had remarked, as they left their quarters. 'Height is essential for a woman, don't you think? You're so small, and ... and spriggy. And your ankles. Well, they have grown rather thick and shapeless, haven't they?'

'Tell me, does Mr McCall like bold women?' Hearing hearty laughter ahead, her voice softened with excitement. 'You must have *some* idea. Should I flirt? Perhaps I'll simper.'

'No,' Annie said. 'I wouldn't, if I were you.'

'What, then? Quick! We're almost there.'

'Just be ... oh. Oh, my. Look what they've done!'

At the door of the drill-hall, even Annie's heart lifted. Walls were festooned with flags and bright bunting. Banks of greenery scented the air and candles glowed in every corner and on each flower-strewn table.

The room was already noisy and full to bursting. People had turned up from all over the territory. Cigar smoke mingled with feminine scents, as spruced-up cowboys and ranchers sauntered through the array of best silks and satins.

The Cavalry looked splendid. Buttons and boots gleamed, sabres shone and braided collars and cuffs glittered in the light from the candles.

Gaggles of girls stood around in billowing dresses - a sea of silk and tulle and organdie - and every woman in the room, knee deep in men.

For a few moments, the cousins took in the buzz of voices, hearty greetings, rising laughter. Then fiddles, banjo and harmonica started up, with a medley of knee-slapping, foot-tapping tunes.

'Oh, my.' Charlotte's voice rose above the din. 'This may just turn out to be fun.' She tossed her curls to make her earrings dance, and heads swivelled in their direction as she sashayed into the hall, wide skirts swinging.

Annie's eyes raked the room. No Aunt Bea, then, nor Mr Hewell. Yet.

'Your mother isn't here,' she said, to Charlotte.

'Neither's Colt McCall.' Charlotte's own eyes were everywhere. 'Nor Mrs. Lee. Lord. Do you suppose they'll come together? Colonel Ruane said Mama may be delayed. Something about those wretched savages being frisky.'

'Mr McCall has Indian blood,' Annie said, she wasn't sure why.

Charlotte snapped open her fan. 'That little green-eyed

snake isn't raising its ugly head again, is it? Take this in, cousin dear, once and for all. I don't care if he wears feathers and a loin-cloth. He's beautiful as a full-bloodied stallion, and I want to meet him. *Comprends tu?*'

'Miss Haddon?'

Both girls swivelled round. 'Why, Trooper Byrne! I'm so happy to see you! I was worried for your safety.'

'Same here, ma'am. Reckon we both had a lucky escape.' His words were directed at Annie, but eyes kept drifting towards Charlotte, who was already looking round in bored, impatient fashion. 'Won't you introduce me to your friend, ma'am?'

'I beg your pardon. This is my cousin, Charlotte.'

John Byrne swallowed heavily. 'Mighty pleased to meet you, ma'am.' Like all young men, he was utterly entranced and stared at Charlotte, longingly. 'May I ... may I have the pleasure of this dance?'

Charlotte bestowed her most dazzling smile. 'I *would* have been delighted, Trooper Byrne, but ... ' She turned to stare boldly at a group of officers nearby. 'Unfortunately, I'm already promised ... '

On cue, two officers approached, almost at a trot and Charlotte graciously took the arm of one.

'Ma'am?' The other bowed to Annie. 'Will you do me the honour?'

As Annie swept a low curtsey, Charlotte cut in. 'Oh, my cousin doesn't dance,' she said, smiling piteously. 'It's her leg, you know.'

Hotly embarrassed, the officer clicked his heels and backed away, while a sweetly-smiling Charlotte floated off with her partner.

Rooted to the spot, Annie's smile grew fixed. Being classed a 'poor thing' didn't get any easier, neither did public humiliation.

John Byrne had disappeared, and who could blame him

after being so rudely dismissed. Her own instinct was to crawl away and hide, because she'd long ago learned that the floor wasn't going to open and swallow her up, however much she wanted it.

She couldn't creep away either, not tonight, because Charlotte would object. Instead, she slunk round the dancers, like a wounded animal, seeking cover.

Cover, as usual, was provided by the Fort matrons - the older married, the elderly unmarried and the incapacitated - sedate in dark silks, cooing together and fanning themselves, like poultry on a perch.

It wasn't that Annie minded their company. She was almost one of them, after all. If only conversation wasn't so limited to babies and sickness and gossip. Cluck, cluck.

'So I asks her - straight out, you know - I says to her, Sybil, I says, how long did it take him ... to ... well, you know. You know what she said? You'll never guess. Not in a month of Sundays.'

Never guess, no. Cluck, cluck.

If only her foot didn't tap, Annie thought, if only she didn't know all the tunes. If only she could dance. Watching the whirling crowd, she saw Charlotte turn from one besotted partner to another in the reel. Between sets, soldiers squabbled for her hand and her attention.

Another nightmare scenario? This was just what had happened at Fort Reno. Jealous men, the worse for whisky, fighting over a flirtatious Charlotte. Herself ministering to bloody noses, Aunt Bea apoplectic.

Not again. She couldn't stand it.

As fiddlers struck up a waltz, Charlotte was seized by the biggest, boldest officer and whirled away. She laughed up at him, he smiled down at her. The tune was haunting, melancholy.

Dancers dipped, swayed. Annie swayed too, closing her eyes. When she opened them again, music had stopped.

Her gaze was drawn to a corner of the room, where girls were fluttering around one man, like moths to a flame. There was a crackle in the air, an outbreak of preening, pouting and eyelash fluttering. Annie even saw one girl employ a sharp elbow to get closer.

Oh, here was head lion, all right. The biggest bull in the herd, the kingpin. Chock full of cowboy-chic and Yankee-diddly-something. She craned her head for a better look.

'Mr Dixon's going for ... you know, cordial, dear. Would you like some?'

'Oh ... yes, please.'

Peering through the pall of smoke, Annie squinted at the newcomer's back. At least half a head taller than anyone else, he certainly dominated the room. Slicked-back hair still wet from washing, burnished skin against fine white shirt.

'No!' As he turned and Annie saw his profile, she was up and stumbling towards the door. 'No, thank you.'

'My dear, your fan! You've dropped your fan. Your purse is down here somewhere, too.'

Blow the fan, pouf to the purse, Annie's mind was on escape. Yah-boo to Charlotte, too *and* Colonel Ruane and his tobacco-chewing crew. And McCall, and all other perfect specimens of manhood.

They should be rounded up and driven off to some wild, uninhabited place, where they wouldn't wreak havoc amongst silly, impressionable women.

She closed the door on the noise and the music and skipping feet. On the everlasting smiling and nodding and pretending to enjoy herself. Her face ached with the effort of it.

It was cooler here. Quiet. A chance to lick her wounds.

Wandering through darkened rooms, she mumbled apologies to a trooper and his sweetheart, who she'd disturbed in a corner.

Muffled giggles followed her, until she ended up in the place where Sunday service was held. Chairs set in rows, a simple cross on the wall, piano in the corner.

Moonlight streamed through the window, glancing off the dusty cabinet and ivory keys. A rosewood stool was just low enough for Annie to prop her weak arm on the keyboard and pick out a few notes.

Tinny, out of tune, but never mind. She should have brought a candle. Stupid rushing out like that. *Stupid. Stupid.*

She sat and played in the dark, played for some time - *dolente, adagio* - oblivious to everything, ruffles and flounces billowing out around her.

Melancholy airs that took her back to England. To watery sun on Lebanese cedars and emerald lawns. To a time when she wasn't so mixed up and confused. When life was orderly. Dull, but orderly.

She was oblivious to doors quietly opening and closing, to distant bursts of noise as someone slipped through, to footsteps creaking on wooden floorboards.

The first she heard was the voice, *basso profundo*, then a slow hand-clap. 'Very pretty.'

No need to look round, she knew that dry drawl. The room suddenly seemed crowded. 'No it isn't, I don't practise enough. My fingering's weak.'

There was a pause, as he took in her stiff back and unsteady voice. 'Something wrong?'

'No.'

'You're not dancing?'

'I *don't* dance,' said Annie, bitterly. 'My leg, you know.'

'Didn't stop you in Red Rock.'

Stunned silence. 'Who told you?'

'Moose. Feet barely touched the floor all evening, he said.'

'I'm amazed he noticed. He doesn't like me.'

'He barely knows you. Why wouldn't he like you.'

'Anyway,' she said, quickly. 'No-one was watching me there. I can't skip step or anything, anymore. Once, I kept perfect time.'

'We're not talking gavottes here, are we? Everyone's just galumphing about out there, as far as I can see.'

'Sounds enchanting.'

'Oh, it can be, it can be. Come here and I'll show you.'

'Look,' she said, more and more on edge. 'Please don't linger on my account. I'm sure you can find more exciting ways to spend your evening.'

His stare didn't waver. Moonlight lit up the planes of his face, giving it a dark, saturnine air.

'At the dance,' she said, in case he hadn't grasped her meaning.

'What I had in mind requires a partner.'

'Dominoes?' she suggested, half-heartedly. 'What about Mrs Lee, then, where is she?'

'Dancing.'

'There you are, then. I'm sure she'd much rather dance with you. Go on, please. I'm all right on my own.'

'So you keep saying. Where are your relatives, as a matter of interest? Your aunt.'

Her relatives. Why did they have to hover over everything, like terrible wraiths?

'Aunt Bea went to Sedalia,' she said. Broomstick due to descend any minute. 'And my cousin ... ' she hesitated. 'What goes on in Sedalia?'

'Northern buyers meet southern cowboys. Herds get loaded on the railroad bound for St Louis. Good news then, I guess? She's tracked down your father?'

Annie shrugged. What could she say? No idea. Not the faintest.

'Have you sorted things out with Colonel Ruane?' she asked, to fill the lull until he went away.

'After a fashion. He's got his horses back, the Baileys are in the stockade. I'm free to go. He even came up with a proposition. Wants me to work with the Army, help subdue hostiles.'

'What did you say!'

'That he's got a tough job. That I'd think about it.'

She stared. 'But, you *won't*, will you?'

'Sure. I'll give it at least half-a-second's serious consideration. I want to stick around for a while.'

Of course, Annie thought. *Of course, you do.* For Mrs Lee. She cleared her throat. 'Well, I really think you should go back now.'

'C'mon, then. I'll escort you.'

She shook her head. 'I can't dance because I'm lopsided. And nothing's worse than just watching. Red Rock was different, I don't know why. It was … special.'

'I've been to dances in Red Rock,' McCall said, drily. 'They're not that special. Humour me, will you?'

Lifting her off the stool, he circled her waist and drew her close. Docile now as any rag doll, Annie couldn't deny a guilty pleasure at his touch.

'What happened to your hair?' He addressed the top of her head.

She coughed. 'Brushed. Washed?'

'I liked it wild. Reminds me of my friend.'

Ah yes, his friend. What a lot of friends he had, too. His red-headed friend, whoever she was, and Clarice and Stella, and Mrs Lee. Did he have to bring them all up now? Her eyes fixed blindly on his shirt.

His head bent over hers, his mouth next to her ear. 'One two three, step; one two three, turn. You try.'

'I can't.'

'Sure you can. Look at me, not your feet.'

A few times, they circled the piano and stool.

'That's not so bad, is it?'

'Who taught you?' she said.

'Same person who taught me to kiss.'

Annie hated that person. Hated Clarice, hated Virginia Lee.

There wasn't much space, they didn't need much. Holding her tighter, he pulled her even closer. Close enough to feel his rough cheek, smell his skin. Cute? she thought. Ha!

He didn't seem to be counting, anymore; he wasn't dancing, either. She wasn't breathing. Her face, buried in his fine white shirt, was flushed and pink; her body responding to his, in a manner that was positively indecent.

This must be improper. Illegal. Something. Permitting oneself to be pressed so hard and intimately against a man. 'Mr McCall ... '

'What happened to Colt?'

'My reputation ... '

'Oh, I think your reputation's already shot, don't you?' A short beat. 'You don't want to do this?'

'No.' *Liar, liar!*

'OK,' he said, loosening his hold and lightly tracing her spine with his thumb. 'Better find something we can both enjoy, then.'

'Look,' she said, breathing hard. 'Just because I'm naive and inexperienced, doesn't mean I'm easy game.' She forced herself to meet his blank, smoky stare. 'I was weak out there on the trail. You ... ' her tone was accusing, ' ... you took advantage.'

'I kissed you, that's all. Any warm-bloodied Texan male would've done the same. Don't say you didn't enjoy it.' An amused pause. 'Why are you blushing?'

'It just happened. You said that yourself. Didn't mean anything.' She heard herself swallow. 'I didn't kiss back.'

He stared. 'The hell you didn't!' Hands slid across her shoulders, bringing her back to him. Bending his head, he grazed her lips again and again, until her eyes fluttered shut and her hand curled tightly around his shirt, clutching him to her.

Sensing the change, his kiss became slower, harder and more demanding, until her body arched into his and her lips parted under his own. He tangled his hands in her hair, then lifted his head. 'Not kiss back, huh? Quit finger-wagging.'

She leaned weakly against him, her breathing shallow. 'Why waste your talents on me?' she said, in a muffled voice. 'Do you enjoy tormenting lame ducks?'

'I don't enjoy all this poor-little-me stuff, that's for sure. You'd do well to dump it. Never held much store by modesty myself, false or otherwise.'

'Look,' she said. 'I'm sorry I was foisted on you, back there at the stage. But I'm all right now. I ... absolve you. You're absolved.'

'From what!'

'Responsibility for me.'

'You're missing the point.'

'The point is, I'm easy to bully. Try picking your own scabs for a change. I daresay you can find a few.'

That spat of temper brought on another flash of razor-sharp grin. It didn't stop there, either. His mouth started to soften. 'Annie?' Pulling her gently back to him, he grazed the side of her cheek with his knuckles. 'Don't ever try to play poker.'

His palm cupped her cheek and she knew she ought to say something. *Stop!* Before he kissed her again, before this went too far. She closed her eyes.

Yes, yes. Any minute, she would.

Chapter 28

'Lack of opportunities for laundering and bathing can cause discomfort. If rainwater is unavailable for washing hair, well-water can be softened with borax.' – p.98

Annie didn't have to stop anything, slamming doors did that, and the sound of flat-heeled slippers skimming over wooden floors.

Then, the voice. 'Annie! Where are you hiding? Better show yourself, you hear? Mama's arrived. Answer me, dummy!'

'Who the deuce,' McCall said, lacing fingers with hers, 'is that?'

'I think ... someone who wants to meet you.'

He didn't say what he thought of that idea, just hissed sharply through his teeth.

As footsteps came closer, Annie tried to push him away. He wouldn't budge. It was like being tied to a railway track and hearing the whistle of an oncoming train.

The door was flung open.

'Annie!' Charlotte's voice could have shattered crystal. 'What in the world do you think you're doing? Didn't you hear? I've been looking everywhere. Who's that, who's there with you?'

As recognition dawned, her demeanour changed. Hawk to dove, in the blink of an eye. An attitude was struck. Right there, in the doorway.

'Well,' she fluttered breathlessly, taking careful stock of the limpid eyes and lean, muscular frame. 'This must be Mr McCall. I'm right, aren't I?'

McCall pushed back hair that had fallen on his forehead. 'You know me?' he said, with that lazy, liquid Southern drawl.

Seizing the opportunity, Annie slid out of reach.

'Well, I certainly feel as if I do, sir. You're quite a legend here.'

'Don't you have to be dead for that? Reckon you've been misled, ma'am.'

'Oh, no. Not in this case. I'm perfectly sure you're all the man they say you are.'

'Depends what they say, I guess.'

Depends, Annie thought, what Charlotte meant, too. She'd never seen her cousin look at anyone in quite that way before. Greedily. As if he were food.

With Charlotte's gaze safely elsewhere, she smoothed her hair, straightened her clothes.

'They say you rode into an Indian Village and brought out four white women and a boy held captive. That you returned them to safety, unaided. Isn't that so?'

Annie stared. McCall shook his head. 'It was three women. So, you are, Miss … ?'

'Charlotte Haddon, Mr McCall.' A gloved arm was graciously extended. 'Dear Annie's cousin. She must have mentioned me. Why, she's hardly stopped talking about you.'

As a dull flush spread over Annie's face, McCall's lips twitched. 'Your cousin's had a pretty rough time.'

'Yes, well, we've all faced dangers here. I've just adored it myself, this wild, untamed country. The adventure! So thrilling.'

'Pity Annie doesn't feel the same way.'

'Oh, Annie has always preferred dull old reading to any excitement, haven't you Annie? She detests the outdoors.' A knowing, kittenish smile. 'Friends say, I'm far too pretty for books.'

A moment was left for McCall to agree with her.

Someone really should be offering her cousin a saucer of milk, Annie thought. Somewhere to sharpen her claws. Anyone could see what she was up to, any old fool. Not McCall though, apparently. Too smitten, probably.

She fixed her eyes blindly on the wall, wishing she was somewhere else. Let these two flatter one another and flirt. She didn't have to watch, did she? She was as much a part of this conversation as that out-of-tune piano.

'My one regret,' Charlotte was saying, 'is that I haven't met any real Red Indians. Such a fascinating native people.'

'Oh, I daresay that could be arranged,' McCall said, smoothly. 'Leave your calling card with me. Like the smell of horse on a man, do you? Lice in his hair?'

Snapping back to attention, Annie shot him a swift, suspicious stare. He looked innocent enough, the very model of grave politeness.

'How old are you, princess?' he went on, pleasantly. 'See, you may be a bit long in the tooth for the Comanche. They mate their women real early.'

Annie drew a sharp breath. Charlotte just stared. 'What were you two doing out here in the dark, anyway?' she said, an uncertain edge to her voice. 'Not plink-plunking on the piano again, surely.'

'I was trying to persuade your cousin to dance with me. Isn't that right, Annie?' McCall exaggerated a wink.

Charlotte's brow furrowed, prettily. 'My cousin didn't tell? Oh, you goose, Annie! Why didn't you tell Mr McCall? Annie doesn't dance. Why, no.'

All warm-eyed sympathy now, she was practically crowing with satisfaction.

'Her crippled leg, you see. A tragic accident. Luckily long skirts hide the worst of the unsightly scars. It will keep swelling though, won't it Annie? Even regular poultices don't seem to help.'

Annie didn't respond. Let Charlotte sprinkle her poison pixie-dust, if it kept her happy. McCall didn't need reminding how pathetic and feeble she was, he knew already.

Even so, the sight of her cousin lifting skirts, to reveal as much as she dared of her own fine fetlocks, seemed bold, even for Charlotte.

Not that McCall seemed to mind. Dark eyes drifted appreciatively over trim ankles. 'A horse, wasn't it?'

'Oh dear.' Charlotte giggled and wagged a finger. 'Annie's been telling tales, again. A joke, a silly joke that went awry, Mr McCall. That's all it was. Pure accident.'

Her eyes slid to McCall, to gauge his reaction. 'Nobody blamed me, did they Annie? I'm a tease and everyone knows it, but I wouldn't harm a fly, let alone a hair of my dear cousin's head.'

'A joke?' McCall's eyes were still on her ankles.

'Prank, then?' Charlotte shrugged, tossing her hair. 'Silly fit of mischief? Call it what you will.'

'What does Annie call it?'

Oh, Annie didn't want to call it anything, thank you. It wasn't the time or place for extracting uncomfortable truths from people.

'Anyway Annie,' Charlotte said, perfectly poised again. 'Mama is most anxious to speak with you. Sorry dear, was that your shin? Don't let us keep you. Poor Mr McCall will have to find another partner.'

Her pretty face smiling up in sweet expectation, suggested that poor Mr McCall wouldn't need to look very far, either.

'You like to dance?' As she gazed up at him, moonlight

haloed her gleaming hair and traced the becoming curve of her smooth, white neck.

'Sure do,' McCall said, 'with the right partner.'

'Oh, so do I, so do I. I think I'd just die if I couldn't dance.' Charlotte's voice was now a purr of velvet. 'My dancing teacher says I have the perfect feet for it.' Arching an ankle prettily, she displayed one small, green slipper for him to admire.

They waited and waited then, but McCall didn't offer up another word, not one. No invitation, either. He just stood, sharpening up his own best choirboy smile, while a strained silence fell.

Smiles grew rigid. Eyes flickered and looked away. There was no mistaking the snub.

Deeply insulted, Charlotte made a sound, like a frog coughing in a bucket - her fingers twining round and round her tight curls.

Annie sighed. Charlotte was a spoiled madam, but would it have cost McCall so much to partner her? More times than she could count, Annie had been on the receiving end of a duty dance, herself. And very grateful for it, too.

'Well, it was interesting meeting you, Mr McCall, and I ... um, most interesting,' Charlotte blustered, with monumentally well-bred effort.

'Likewise, Miss Haddon.'

'We should go back, I think.' Her lower lip drooped, her expression grew sulky.

'Guess so.' He watched her wriggle, through heavy-lidded eyes.

'You'll accompany us then, sir?'

Oh dear. Charlotte was never one to leave a dead horse un-flogged. Not where a handsome man was concerned, anyway. She simply couldn't believe that she was being turned down.

'Reckon I'll sit this one out.'

'Oh, but hear? They're playing a waltz? You'd enjoy that, surely.'

'Wouldn't bet on it.'

The silence was only broken by Charlotte flouncing back to the hall.

In her wake, the door banged, walls shook, and Annie shuddered. 'You've upset her now.'

'I'm all misty-eyed,' McCall said, without a flicker of interest.

'Don't you care?'

'Oh yeah, I'm going to toss and turn on it all night. She's a bitch.'

'Please! You're speaking of my cousin!'

'She's still a bitch. What happened with your leg, what did she do? Guess you hate her, huh.'

'I can't afford to hate anyone. She's spoiled and high-spirited, that's all.'

'I'd spoil her, introduce her to one of those young bucks she's so eager to meet.'

Annie sighed. 'I'd better go after her.'

'What for? She give prizes for blind loyalty and devotion?' As she moved towards the door, he said, 'Not much good at loving or hating, are you Annie?'

The remark was tossed off casually, but it hurt, nevertheless. 'Lack of practice,' she managed to mutter. 'You appear to have mastered both beautifully.'

'Not really,' came back, roughly. 'Sometimes I find it hard to tell which is which.'

Annie didn't wait to hear more. She hadn't the heart for another emotional exchange. Lifting skirts, she trotted briskly after her cousin.

'That,' Charlotte snapped, in a fine old fit of the sulks, 'is no gentleman. What an ill-bred boor!'

'Now, Charlotte, he didn't mean anything - '

'Oh, shut up! Anyway, have you lost your mind? Alone

with him in the dark? It's lucky I found you, that's all I can say, before you made a complete and utter fool of yourself.'

Musicians were still fiddling up a storm and dancers spinning round - a swirling mass of rainbow colours, rustling silk, slippery satin. The atmosphere was hot and hectic; cigar smoke mingling with cologne and the scent of fresh bay.

'As if he'd look at you, anyway. Sad, freckled thing. Have you no pride?' Charlotte kept up the spiteful stream, as they edged round the crowded dance floor.

'There's Mama. Well, I wouldn't want to be in *your* shoes. She'll have the vapours. Trollop, she'll call you, fit for the gutter.'

'Now look,' started Annie. 'What – '

'Hold your tongue, miss, don't say another word. And Mr Hewell. What on earth will he think of you now?'

Henry Hewell? Annie squinted through the smoke.

Yes, there he was, under that portrait of President Johnson. Propped against the wall, upholstered in tweed and trussed up like a turkey.

A turkey about to roast, too. Perspiration gleamed on his upper lip, eye-glasses were all steamy. His suit, far too heavy for this climate, looked as if he'd slept in it.

He didn't seem in very good humour either, although his mouth twitched into a creepy sort of smile at the sight of Annie.

She felt herself go limp.

Beside him Aunt Bea, swathed in black with a cap of ostrich feathers, looking for all the world like a boiled beetle. Black fan flapped fiercely in a black-gloved hand.

Annie had forgotten how pinched and disapproving her expression could be. *Eye of newt, foot of toad.* 'Annie, here, here. Come here!'

Exhaustion swept her; all new-found sense of self seemed to drain away. She tried to compose herself. Fat chance, with her cousin's hand in the small of her back.

'Go on,' Charlotte snarled, giving Annie a really hard push. 'Get on with it. I can't wait to hear what Mama has to say about all this, just can't wait.'

Thankfully, Aunt Bea had other things on her mind. The stink and squalor of Sedalia, their nightmare journey from that awful place, the constant harrying and threatening by savages.

Well, no - she kissed the air adjacent to Annie's ear - she hadn't actually *seen* any of them with her own eyes, thank Heaven, but Captain Wallace warned that they were all around and on the rampage, too. Ranches razed to the ground, the very outskirts of towns threatened.

Annie leaned closer to catch her aunt's drone. Nothing was right with this country. It was going to hell in a hand-cart.

'Captain Wallace says … ' Lips pursed, eyes rolled. ' … Cavalry's bounden duty to rid the West … these wretches. He should know … inferior in moral and mental qualities … resisting the railroad inch by inch!'

The noise grew louder, crashing round her ears. Her aunt's lips were still moving, but Annie's own head was spinning. Somewhere, she lost the plot.

'Extermination's the only way … Captain Wallace says. Tribes-people … disgusting habits. Respectable white folk … live alongside? Pah!'

Captain Wallace, Captain Wallace. Annie wasn't surprised to learn that his views dovetailed nicely with those of her aunt. The oddest thing, was Aunt Bea's complete lack of interest in her own adventures.

As a rule, she could give the Spanish Inquisition a run for their money. Time to ask a few questions herself, then?

Why had she been abandoned at the wreck of the stagecoach? Under a heap of splintered wood and buckled iron. No-one had provided a satisfactory explanation, and surely, she had a right to know?

Abandoned! Her aunt's hands fluttered in horror. She had

not been abandoned! The stagecoach driver had insisted they leave her where she'd fallen. (Ha! Annie rapidly revised her good opinion of the driver.)

Hidden there, he'd said, her chances might well be better than their own. (Annie's opinion was grudgingly restored.) She opened her mouth then, to ask what her aunt and Mr Hewell had been doing in Sedalia, but thought better of it. The answer mattered too much.

And the music was too loud and people pressing too close, to afford any privacy. Their little group was already something of a side-show.

Tossing back another whisky, Henry Hewell caught Annie's eye. 'Don't hold with all this jingoistic New World rubbish,' he guffawed. 'Let's hear some good old English tunes!'

His beery voice could have carried to Cornwall, and wasn't winning him any friends. What was it about him, Annie wondered, that made her shudder?

Her eyes drifted across the room to the place where at that very moment, Colt McCall was inclining his dark head attentively, towards the fair Mrs Lee.

A wave of longing swept her. A dull ache started in the pit of her stomach, as she studied the two perfect profiles. McCall, darkly handsome. Virginia Lee, all scarlet silk and smooth alabaster skin.

She imagined intimate whisperings.

Mrs Lee opening her heart to McCall; he forgiving her. The two of them galloping off into the sunset, on one of those fine Appaloosa stallions he was so fond of. Happy Ever After. The End.

So why did she feel like kicking something? And why was Captain Wallace coming this way? He wasn't going to ask her to dance, was he! She couldn't bear it.

No, he was approaching Charlotte. Thank you, Captain. Yes. Dance attendance on my cousin, please. Pour some oil on those troubled waters.

Now. How soon could she reasonably leave this crowd and crawl back to her quarters?

Chapter 29

'Bonds I have formed with fellow travellers, have led to many happy excursions and some most fruitful friendships.' – p.136

Amazingly, the subject of Colt McCall didn't come up until the following morning. Perhaps Charlotte hadn't been such a tattle-tale, after all.

'His name, what was his name again?'

'Aunt?' Annie was all innocence.

'That tall, dark man. Your rescuer?'

'Oh, him. Oh. Mr ... McCall, Colt McCall.'

'*Colt!* Peculiar sort of nomenclature. Do we owe the gentleman?' Aunt Bea frowned. 'A vote of thanks? Anything.'

'Nothing!' Anger and hurt pride still clearly showed on Charlotte's face. 'We owe him nothing.'

Oh dear, thought Annie. Her cousin was still ruffled as a hen.

'He's no gentleman, Mama, he's quite unfit for polite society. Ask anyone.'

Her mother clucked. 'It's true that neither Colonel Ruane nor Captain Wallace speak well of him. What is it that he does, then? Precisely.'

'Erm ... '

'A scout of some sort?'

Horses, Annie muttered, something to do with horses. Cows.

'A cow-man? Well, most men here are crude and unruly. What more could we expect. I mean, who are their people?'

'Most arrived on the Mayflower,' muttered Annie, under her breath. She hadn't slept well. Eyes were all pink and puffy. 'And he's as honourable as they ever were.'

'What's that, Annie dear?' Charlotte hissed. 'Share your thoughts with us, do. Should I fetch his boots so we can lick them for you?'

'I only – '

'Half-savage, isn't he? Tell that to Ma! Hardly one of the Pilgrim fathers. Does he even know what knives and forks are for?'

'You see, there's no order.' Aunt Bea rambled on. 'No reasonable food and the climate is vile. Dust, heat, flies, we're on the very borders of civilisation here. As soon as our affairs are settled, we will leave.'

'Thank Heaven!' Charlotte rolled her eyes. 'Now, will you please, please consider the railroad, Mama? They do have trains going east, don't they? Why are your eyes all red, Annie? You look like a rabbit.'

Annie barely heard. 'Aunt Bea?' she said. 'Why *are* we in Texas?'

Her aunt coughed.

'Why did we come here?'

'I ... an appointment.' The unexpectedness of the question shook loose an answer, of sorts. 'Arranged long since. I missed the meeting, of course. Had to travel to Sedalia, instead.'

None the wiser, Annie frowned. No point pursuing the matter. Her aunt's expression hardly recommended it. Instead, a new name in the conversation.

'Now... you know my dear, *Mr Hewell* has been *so*

concerned for your safety. Beside himself, yes, on more than one occasion.'

Annie wasn't impressed.

'Soo concerned, soo distraught. I said to him, Mister *Hewell*, I said, take heart. Annie's a good strong gel. She may be small, but she's sturdy. Couldn't calm him, though. No. Try as I might, he was inconsolable, fearing you may have been harmed.'

Her voice droned on. 'You've realised by now, of course, that he's offered for you?'

Annie's attention, which had been wandering, was quickly caught. 'Offered?' She nearly dropped her book. 'Offered what?'

'I told you, Mama. Didn't I tell you? She's been like this since she got here. Deliberately awkward and difficult.'

'My advice would be to make haste and accept him. At your age, good offers don't come every day.'

'Who else would want her, for pity's sake? She can't still be hankering after that soppy curate. *Quel horreur*!'

'Why not allow those you trust to make the judgement for you, Annie. I only want what's best. Please don't squander my best efforts.' Aunt Bea rumbled on. Admirable man ... first-rate fellow ... so agreeable, so amusing.

Annie stirred, uneasily. Henry Hewell, her best effort? The last in a long line of misfits. What possible excuse could she dredge up for refusing him? Because this was what women did, wasn't it? Women like herself. Plain, impoverished ones. They settled. For what they could get.

After all, not so very long ago, unmarried women were often in danger of being burned as witches.

Racking her brains, she muttered, 'He has gout.'

'Good living! A recommendation, surely. How does that affect his eligibility?'

'It's sad. A sad, old person's affliction.'

'Nonsense! What do you know about it?'

'Noted by Hippocrates, named by de Vielehardouin in the thirteenth century.' She thought, he has a sad person's smell, too. An old person's smell. Not just here, with no soap and no servants. Always. Everywhere.

'Do you actually believe that reciting facts makes you interesting?' Charlotte snapped. 'Do you? Well, everyone hates you for it, you hear? You're plain and you're dull and you're stupid.'

'Charlotte! Enough.'

'Well! All this innocence and sweetness is so mawkish. Makes me sick, if you want to know. It's not fitting in a twenty-eight year old spinster.'

'Seven,' Annie said. 'Twenty-seven year old - '

'Oh who cares, numskull! It's too ridiculous.'

'*Enough!* And don't jerk your chin in that mulish way, Annie. What else could you wish for in a suitor?'

'Tomahawk?' spat Charlotte. 'Feathers? Tepee?'

Annie chewed on a nail. Common interests? By his own admission, Henry Hewell didn't read. Not a book, a journal, nor even a pamphlet.

'And that half-breed does, I suppose?' Charlotte hissed. 'Oh, I can see him now. Running a finger along the lines, his lips trying to shape the words.'

'Well, your own disposition has been ruined by books, miss. What use are books to a woman? About as much use as to a fish. A female brain is too weak for all those words. And what is twenty years of marriage? You'll adjust. Like the rest of us.'

Marriage, marriage. Annie closed her ears. The ultimate prize, almost a religion. Well, she'd rather not marry at all. She said as much too, impressed by her own daring.

Aunt Bea's expression, pinched and frost-bitten, soon put paid to that. 'In your present position, Annie,' she said, ignoring this imbecile talk, 'won't is not an option.'

'Why not hobble off and consider your choices then, Annie

dear,' Charlotte said, with a brilliant, hateful smile. 'If you think you've got any, that is. Discuss them with your ickle-wickle pet.'

'Pet, pet?'

'Didn't you know that she'd acquired an animal, Mama? La, Annie. So much to tell Mama! Bye-bye.'

Chapter 30

'Field glasses and telescopes can be most useful for observing the landscape.' – p.150

The next day began in a brilliant blaze, but soon slumped, into hot stupor. From mid-day, everyone languished indoors, dozing and drooping.

No escape anywhere from the brooding heat and their quarters were a gloomy furnace. Blinds fluttered in the window's hot draught, flies circled feebly. Round and round, zzzz … zzz.

Loosening her clothes, Annie tried to rest. She threw herself down on the bed, then got up again. Back in the chair – up, down, up again. It was no good, she couldn't settle.

The reason for all this restlessness? Henry Chewton Hewell. He'd been popping up like a bad fairy, all morning. Every time she looked round, he'd been there. Leering, no other word for it. As slimy and shifty as a snake-oil salesman.

And she'd tried to be polite, she really had. There was just something about the way he slithered so close, fawning over her, fiddling with his fleshy fingers.

So irritating to think that at home, Aunt Bea would have

been breathing, gimlet-eyed, down any suitor's neck. The only heavy breather here was Henry Hewell.

Why were his lips so wet, what did he want with her? Oh come on. She knew what he wanted, didn't she? She didn't want to think about it, that was all. Even back in England, he'd taken every opportunity to lunge at her.

As if given permission, as if he'd been promised something.

They couldn't have arranged all this behind her back, could they? Without her consent? Horse-trading, that's what it was.

No point fretting about it now. She had to get out.

In shade outside her door, Dog slumped in a dozy heap. Ears pricked as she came out and with a scrabble of paws, he lurched to his feet.

Her sweet little pup, she had to admit, was becoming a bit of a roughneck. Day by day, he looked more like a doormat. Perhaps that was why he'd been kicked so often.

Short bandy legs seemed better suited to a footstool, tail was frayed and there was a scar on his nose.

Annie scratched behind his ears. What to do with him, now? Aunt Bea wouldn't contemplate taking a scraggy thing of dubious parentage back to England - apart from herself, that is - and no-one else would have him.

Both unwanted, both oddities. Both should have been drowned at birth.

Their walk, beneath boiling blue sky, followed the path of the perimeter fence. Dry earth crunched underfoot. Shimmering noonday heat made everything hazy.

Dog lolloped ahead, tail up, tongue out. Annie pulled her hat down as far as it would go, but the hot breeze still caught her full in her face, stiffening her skin and drying eyes.

'Your complexion's gorn ruddy, Annie,' her aunt had remarked critically, that morning. 'Freckles all over.'

'She's never had a complexion to speak of.' That had been Charlotte.

How had *she* managed to stay so pale, then? By not venturing out at noon, stupid. In fact, by rarely venturing out.

'Hold, hold fast!'

What? Dog froze, sniffing the air and Annie's eyes screwed up against the glare.

Enter the villain. Again! Henry Hewell, trailing whiffs of sulphur. No escape either, nowhere to hide. And she couldn't run. Too hot.

As he panted up, all plump wobbling jowls and port-wine complexion, she felt some concern for his health. In spite of loud and bitter complaints about the food here, his weight and waistline seemed to be increasing by the minute.

He drank too much, of course, that was why the heat affected him so badly. But who wouldn't suffer in that thick suit, and high, tight collar?

Dog approached, ears flat, hackles up. He didn't like this person. The feeling, Annie observed, was entirely mutual.

'Like dogs?' Aiming a sly kick, Mr Hewell sidestepped smartly. 'I've dogs. Hounds, lurchers. Lap dogs? I'll get yew lap dogs. Something to fondle and pet, is that what you'd like, hmmm?'

'I like this one,' Annie said, quickening her pace.

'A stray. Can't trust 'em. Don't pet the mutt, he'll get attached. Hey, slow down! Ain't racin', are we? For someone gimpy, you move amazin' fast.'

A fat hand on her arm pushed her out of the sunlight, into the shade of the high wooden palisades.

'Now, Miss ... ahem ... your aunt's spoken to you, I trust?'

Finally. He was getting round to it. It was almost a relief. As his red face came close to hers, Annie's stomach knotted at the puff of whisky and stale cigars. 'She speaks to me every day, Mr ... '

'Vair good, vair good. Informed you of my offer then, yes? Always a great favourite with me, y'know.' He blinked behind his eye-glasses. 'Yes, for some time ... ahem, aware, I'm sure ...

of, well y'know ... my ardent attraction.'

Ardent *what*! Did he think her dim-witted? They'd barely exchanged two words until a month or so ago, and not many more since. Had they ever enjoyed a proper conversation? Shared a view, a joke?

Great favourite, my eye! This was close to comedy.

'I want a wife, Miss ... Haddon, *Annie* ... yers, that's right, and your aunt has led me to believe you'll look favourably on my offer.'

Oh, has she. 'What about the other one?' Annie muttered, trying to detach herself from his reptilian grip.

'Eh? I don't – '

'Other wife?' she said, playing for time.

'Dead. They didn't say? Died when she pupped.'

Poor wretched thing. 'You have a child?' Annie felt a smidgen of sympathy.

'Both dead. Said so, didn't I? When she pupped.'

'I am so sorry.'

'No need. Mistake to marry her. Always bloodless, always sickly. Money, of course. All gone. So, nothing to hinder us, eh?' He made a noise in his throat. 'Well done, yes, vair well done.'

He was the sort of man, Annie was beginning to suspect, who wouldn't shrink from jabbing a finger in your eye, if he felt it called for. The sort who considered women to be little more than large children, and treated them accordingly.

There'd been rumours at home, of course. Gossip. Something about servants and a taste for private violence. Brutality, *bestiality*. Both had been mentioned. Annie quailed. Help?

No-one around to, everyone else was inside, sensibly avoiding the heat. Just a whorl of tumbleweed blowing this way and that, and wide-winged birds wheeling lazily overhead.

What should one do then, on these occasions? Say? Should she be sensible of the honour or something? Even if it felt like a death threat?

'I'm … not sure that I – '

'Don't be coy! Modesty does you credit, but you're a fine healthy gel.' Another blast of sour breath. 'Good blood, y'know. Vigorous.'

Annie shrank back from those wet, rubbery lips. She didn't want them anywhere near her cheek. Or her hand, for that matter. The one he now raised to his mouth.

'Down. Down boy!' A furious blur of curly fur suddenly launched itself at her suitor, clamping its jaw round his ankle.

'Bit me! Damn dog bit me! I'll wring its neck, I'll shoot the – '

Annie's battered hero withdrew to a safe distance, growling through his whiskers.

With a supreme effort, Henry Hewell collected himself. 'Put a plan to your aunt today,' he went on, doggedly, 'and got her agreement, full agreement. Dotes on you, y'know. Why not bless the union here, was my suggestion. Without further ado.'

'I … pardon?'

'Tie the knot, wedded bliss. No objection to our union, so why wait, hmmm?' A thin smile appeared. The smile of the yellow-toothed snake. 'What say, um… missy? Eh?'

What say? Breakfast turned to bile in Annie's stomach. *Whoa, whoa stop.* That's what say. Not for the first time, she caught the rich whiff of ulterior motives. They clung to this man like camphor. If she could only work out what they were.

'Mr Hewell!'

'Henry.' Piggy eyes gleamed behind his eye-glasses. 'Know each other well enough, wouldn't you say? Or soon will, hey?'

'Mr *Hewell*! If I've given any encouragement, then I am sorry, truly sorry. But, I can *not* … ' Her voice faded.

'You're not refusin' me?' A mottled flush spread over his face. 'By what objection? What possible objection could you have!'

His resemblance to a toad struck Annie suddenly. Bulging eyes, a moon face and no neck. No frog prince hiding here, though. Not, to be absolutely fair, that she'd pass muster as a fairy princess, either. 'Well, er ... feelings ... feelings dictate - '

'Foolish humbug!' Throttled by his high collar, he began to wheeze. 'Don't try your wimmen's games on me! I insist you accept. Your bounden duty, understand?'

Annie felt a sense of foreboding. There was going to be trouble.

Lunging forward, he gripped her arms. 'Stop this silly blather and listen to me. Hmmm? Get ... away you ... stupid mutt.'

'Ouch ... you're hurting!'

'I want my answer.'

'You've had it, I've given it. Dog, come on!'

'Don't be perverse, missy!' Fat fingers dug into her arm and he shook her, roughly. 'My rightful answer!'

Annie squeaked and there was uproar. A fit of furious yelping, hackles and teeth, as a crazed, foam-flecked form flew at Henry Hewell.

'I'll kill the devil,' he swore violently, 'see if I don't! Swear-to-God.'

'Annoying someone else I see, Annie.'

The languid voice forced Henry Hewell to stop his windy threats and peer over the rim of his eye-glasses.

A man loped lazily towards them. As Dog gave him an enthusiastic greeting, Annie's bravado all but dribbled away.

'Well now, mister.' McCall's eyes moved over them. 'We've seen what you can do with a woman. How are you when they come a little bigger?'

'This is a private conversation.' Henry Hewell peered down his nose with practised British rudeness. 'Between meself and the lady. Nothing to concern anyone else.'

'It concerns me,' came back the slow drawl, 'if you're

shaking her and she's saying ouch.'

'Are you suggesting I'm not behavin' in a gentlemanly manner, sir? Eh, eh?'

'Not suggesting anything, bub, I'm saying it straight out.'

'My good feller, I am *English!*'

'Well, good for you.'

'He doesn't like the English,' said Annie, helpfully.

'How vair American of him! Well, see here fellow, I am Henry Chewton Hewell, and ... '

'Did someone sneeze?'

' ... I am affianced to this lady.'

'What's that, when it's at home?'

'Engaged, we are engaged! To be married, don't you know.'

After a brief, highly-charged pause, McCall turned to Annie. 'Any other secrets I'm likely to trip over?'

'It's not what it seems,' she said, dully.

'Go ahead. Surprise me.'

'He's not my fiancé, I have no fiancé.'

Henry Hewell held up a threatening finger. 'Why, you sly, deceitful little – '

'I wouldn't say any more.' McCall's voice was ominously calm. 'I really wouldn't. Be a pity to roll that fine suit in the dirt.'

'Oh stop it,' Annie said, before somebody punched somebody. 'There's no need for all this.'

'Quite so.' Henry Hewell fingered his collar, his forehead shiny with sweat. 'Let's not get heated. I doubt you'd hit a man wearing eye-glasses, Mr, er ... '

'McCall. Oh, only if it were absolutely necessary.'

'McCall! Aaah, I *see*. The half-breed fellow who brought Miss Haddon here, the native redskin?' He retreated behind prim parlour language. 'Well, err ... well. No need to concern yourself a moment longer, my good ... er, yes. She's in safe hands now.'

'That's a matter of opinion. Annie? You want to carry on with this conversation?'

'I can assure you, that she – '

'She's got a tongue, she can speak for herself. Annie?'

Ping pong, ping. Annie turned from one to the other.

'I ain't finished speaking!'

'Well she's sure done listening.'

'Oh, for goodness sake,' she said. 'Why do you have to be so ... '

'Me?!'

' ... belligerent!'

'Look fellow, I don't care for your manners. Noo! Your attitude to this lady is exceeding ... fresh and familiar.'

'A few nights alone together and you get kinda familiar. You want to teach me manners, mister? You'll sure learn more than you teach!'

They were nose-to-nose again. Or rather, Annie observed wearily, nose to snout. One - lean, dark and sardonic; the other, portly and perspiring. Impasse.

Henry Hewell started to splutter. Something about vulgar impertinence, and other gross slurs on Annie's character. He demanded, nay ordered, that she return to her quarters *immediately*, threatening dire and dreadful consequences if she didn't.

She didn't move, she couldn't be bothered. In full heat of the sun, it was hard to think. Overcome by drowsy numbness, she stayed where she was, chewing a knuckle.

'Well, let's see what your aunt has to say about this!'

Watching his portly figure mince away, Annie was aware of McCall's even breathing behind her back.

'Guess he's rich, huh?'

'I ... sorry?'

'Flabby, slippery, hypocritical. Looks like he swallowed a stick. Not exactly Prince Charming, is he?'

'He's not rich, just obsessed. Like a dog who's been promised a bone. Why me? I still don't understand it.'

McCall's eyes drifted over her, as if checking cattle at an auction. 'Many a man's ruined himself over red hair.'

Annie flushed. 'My aunt's set on it, too.'

'Money, then. Can't you sniff it? Never trust a man who's mean to your dog, by the way.'

'I haven't any money.'

'Well, you've sure as hell got something he wants. I take it you don't want to hitch up with him? No, guess you'd have to be pretty desperate. What *are* you aiming to do, then?'

Annie shrugged. Try to convince everyone that she could stay unmarried and still be a useful member of the household. She wouldn't eat much, honestly, wouldn't get in anyone's way.

'Kinda stifling, isn't it? Sewing handkerchiefs, writing letters. Not much to base a life on.'

'It's what unmarried Englishwomen do,' she said, wearily. 'It's how we behave.'

'So you keep saying. You'd be better off here, then.'

That took her by surprise.

As his words hung in the air, a question mark formed over her head. Was he *asking*? She felt a heart-skip of hope. It swiftly faded. Whatever he was suggesting, wasn't any sort of offer, was it?

'Give us time. To get to know each other.'

Pushing hair away from her eyes, Annie stared. He couldn't be serious. Look at her, now - half-broiled, red-faced, damp patches under her arms. A frizzy-haired cripple. While somewhere close by, lingered the cool, the fragrant, the ever-faithful Ginny Lee.

He was feeling sorry for her, that was all. Being kind.

Even so. 'What would I do here,' she said, cautiously. 'The only single women I've seen have been in saloons, or shacks on the edge of town.'

'Saloon or flophouse isn't the only choice. Teach school?

Enough being built. Plenty of opportunities here for an educated woman.'

'I don't think ... '

'Forget what you *think*, how do you feel? Here. In your gut. No point sitting round waiting for something to happen, your whole life. Go out and get what you want. No-one else'll do it for you, that's for sure.'

'You can't just come along and expect me to change my whole life, just like that.'

'Lady,' he countered, after a beat, '*you* came along. I live here, remember?'

And now, here they all were again. Trundling back, that grim little group. Henry Chewton Hewell, aunt and cousin, all heading their way, faces like thunder.

Storm warning!

'The Assyrian came down,' McCall observed, 'like a wolf on the fold. Byron,' he said, in response to Annie's blank stare. 'Looks like you're in for a hiding. Shall I stick around?'

'No.' It would be like poking a sore tooth. 'Please. Don't.'

Relatives loomed. Aunt Bea's voice held rising notes of outrage. 'I've had quite enough of this. Keep that animal back, keep him quiet, you hear! Annie, go to your quarters. Pride and obstinacy will be brought down. Do you understand me?'

Chapter 31

'When travel has been used as a means of escape from domestic entanglements, it may be wise to consider the method of one's return, as well as one's departure.' – p.212

'I will not marry Henry Hewell.'

Trapped in her quarters like a fly in a sticky web, Annie had been cajoled, brow-beaten, threatened. Relatives had closed ranks and were sticking together, like glue.

Ungrateful, Aunt Bea and Charlotte had chorused. Unladylike, unmarriageable.

And then, finally, 'All right, all *right*! We will wait. You don't have to marry him here.'

She was not, Annie vowed, when they'd left her alone, going to marry him anywhere. Why was everyone so set on it?

Henry Hewell wanted a bride, a respectable one. All right, she would do for that. *Cook and clean for you, sir? Keep house? Bear your children?*

He would carry on doing what he'd always done, of course. Gambling, philandering and drinking, not necessarily in that order. He probably assumed she would fit in with that, too.

She was such a mouse, after all.

'Well, you've done it now,' Charlotte said later, banging down a supper tray. 'You've blundered this time. We're leaving. First light, when the stagecoach comes through.' Stiff skirts swished wildly. 'Tell me, were you born stupid? If you hadn't been so stupid, we could have travelled by railroad. Mama won't hear of it now.'

Hot and fretful herself, Annie considered her cousin. Two spots of high colour on Charlotte's cheeks signalled very bad temper. Her usually perfectly-coiled chignon was mussed, blue eyes were chips of glass.

She looked ready to hit somebody.

Annie prepared to duck.

'Make the most of this slop and don't dare give any to that mutt, either! It's the best any of us will see in weeks.' She clicked her tongue, as Annie pushed the tray away. 'Mooning and dreaming over that roughneck, I suppose. Tell me, aren't you the *least* bit ashamed? Slavering over that ... that cow-person, that half-breed.'

Miss Pot, Annie mused bitterly, to Miss Kettle?

'Don't think I don't know what this is about, either.' Charlotte's eyes were blue slits. 'That creature made advances to you, didn't he? Did he kiss you? I can't believe it. A man like him, a man ... why on earth would he *want* to?' She rolled her eyes, genuinely perplexed.

'Perhaps I remind him of his mother.'

'And you *let* him? You actually let him. You're even more of a simpleton than I thought. Soiled goods now, Annie. You'll be turned out.'

'Oh, hardly ... '

'No man is content with kissing, dolt! Not one as rough and dangerous as McCall. Do you think I'm dumb? It leads on to things.'

'As a cough leads on to fever?'

'You dare to joke! What really happened? Tell me. You *have* to!'

Silence.

'Know what? You're as cold and closed-mouthed as that hateful specimen himself. Well, as long as you didn't show any signs of enjoying it, that's all I can say. Look at me, Annie, look me in the eye! You didn't give him the satisfaction of seeing how grateful you were, did you? Oh, you ... you cat's paw!'

A pulse started up in Annie's forehead. She hadn't any intention of letting Charlotte turn her memories into something shameful. They had to last a lifetime.

Having driven in the knife though, Charlotte gave it a couple more twists. 'I've heard about the men here, everyone has. Even ugly women bring out the beast in them. Tell me, in your wildest dreams, did you imagine it would end well? How did you see yourself? The plucky little one-legged wife behind your hero?'

'That's cheap, Charlotte.'

'La, Annie!' Blue eyes blazed. 'You dare criticize me?'

'It does you no credit, that's all and I'm sick of all this baiting. Unhook me?'

'Say you'll marry Henry Hewell, then, and put everything to rights. Oh, it's all shan't and won't with you, isn't it? All self. Well you *must,* can't you see, you simply *have* to.'

'Why does it matter so much?' Annie said, exhausted now. 'You've a queue of admirers yourself, you're bound to marry soon.'

'Don't you understand? If *you* don't marry, neither can I. You're ruining my chances!' Faced with a blank stare, Charlotte stamped a tightly-laced boot. 'Money. Money, money. We don't have any, in case you haven't noticed. If you marry Henry Hewell, he's promised to settle on me, too.'

Annie frowned. 'He has his own debts though, doesn't he? Whose money, Charlotte? What's it to do with me?'

'You're so clever, you work it out!'

'I've *tried*, I keep trying.'

Outside the open window, a steady shuffle of hooves as a routine patrol rode in. Staccato barks of command, the slither of men dismounting. A strong smell of horse wafted on in hot draughts of air.

Charlotte screwed up her nose. 'If you breathe one word to Mama, I'll kill you! Don't think I wouldn't, either.' She paused, her eyes meeting Annie's. 'It's to do with your father.'

Yes. Annie's pulse went wild. Lacing her hands, she braced herself. Still, the next words, spoken without a smidgen of sympathy, shook her to the core.

'He's dead.'

Annie's eyes closed, briefly. Outside, a bugle brayed.

'Mama had notice. Apparently your feckless father did something right for once and made money from the goldfields. A tidy sum we imagine, which comes to you when you marry.'

Dead! Annie's eyes blurred. All that waiting and hoping and now, he was gone. And she'd never known him, never even seen him. She'd half-expected it, though, hadn't she? So why was it so hard to take in?

'Dead, yes. Fathers die, mothers too, every day. And dratted puppy dogs.' Charlotte aimed a kick at Dog. 'If they're not careful. Why that stupid look, it's not as if he's ever meant anything to you, is it? You never knew him.'

Folding her arms, she stared irritably at Annie's white face.

'How did he die? How long ago?'

'Don't ask me.'

This was the trouble, Annie thought. She *didn't* ask, she just let them keep fobbing her off.

What had she really thought would happen here? That she would somehow bump into her father? At the railroad camp, or in Sedalia? What efforts had she made to find him? Always what if? Maybe? Perhaps?

'And, if I don't marry? What then?'

'Some trustee person doles the money out in dribs and drabs for the rest of your life. No earthly use to anyone.'

Money, Annie thought, always money. Money pledged, money due, money owed. Money held back. Now, she could see what should have been blindingly obvious from the beginning.

It was why they were here. And the reason, the only reason for Henry Hewell's dogged pursuit of her. McCall had been right, all along.

'Mama was due to meet your trustee, whoever he is, in Texas. They missed each other because of the stagecoach crash.'

'Where is the money now then, who has it?'

'The Sedalia bank. If you'd done as we'd asked and married Mr Hewell, claim could have been laid to it weeks ago. Your pig-headedness has delayed it for months.'

'And how long have you known all of this?' Annie tried to keep her voice steady.

'Oh, I don't remember. Since the stagecoach? I kept asking why we'd come to this God-forsaken place and in the end, Mama had to tell me.'

No-one had thought to tell *her* though, had they? Annie's throat was dry. They'd guessed she would be difficult.

Tears pricked her eyes - half regret, half rage - and that terrible churning started, the one she always felt when she thought about her father.

First, he'd abandoned her. Now, he was going to ruin her. Of course, he wouldn't have known how few suitors she would have, or how pitifully uninspiring they would turn out to be.

He'd have imagined her like her mother. Beautiful, charming. The pick of the bunch.

'So,' she said. 'Your mother and Mr Hewell went to Sedalia to lay claim to my inheritance? Is that right? *My* money. I can't *believe* they'd do that. Without a word to me.'

'Oh, for goodness sake! It's not as if we were depriving you of anything, is it? You'd benefit, too, you'd be married. Not stuck on the shelf with your fusty old books. Face it, no-one else will want you, not with your disfigurement.'

'Marry Henry Hewell,' Annie said, 'so that he can waste my money, as well as his own? Oh, beg pardon - support his estates.'

'You're not going to help me, then? After *all* we've done for you, all that depends on it? Just for once, can't you show some gratitude?'

'I *have* been grateful, all my life. And I'm tired of it, the awful burden of it.'

Charlotte paled. 'You! You're tired of it? Mercy, what about us? For years, we've suffered your odd little ways, your ... social gaffes.'

'Now that I have money, I could marry someone else.'

'Annie, you're boring. No-one likes you, no-one who matters anyway. And don't think a nobody like you is going spoil the prospects for somebody like me, you hear. You've *got* to marry him! Mama says.'

With monumental effort, she composed herself. 'Anyway, think of it. A place of your own, the importance of being a wife. Wouldn't that be better than staying at home with Ma? An old maid, pitied and derided?'

There was some logic to that, Annie acknowledged, wearily. And Charlotte certainly needed the confines of marriage, she was far too spoiled for anything else.

'Say yes, Annie. Please, please! I could never be content without a husband, I'd go mad. Look at me, it would be a sin, wouldn't it? Annie, I *beg* of you. This is so unfair!'

Annie didn't say yes and she didn't say no, but Charlotte clearly sensed her cousin was weakening.

'If you'd only agree,' was her parting shot, 'things would be so much easier. We could call in at Sedalia, you could marry there and we could collect the money. See? All settled, all done.'

What could be simpler?

Alone again, Annie wrapped her arms tightly around herself and watched a fly circle the congealing contents of her supper tray. Wasn't it sometimes better to stop fighting? To just hold up your hands, and give in?

In gloomy silence, she felt herself sinking. First, second, third time.

She was lost. The sacrificial lamb.

Running, she was running fast, in the middle of muscular Indian ponies. Legs tightened to a vertical leap and she was up, out of the rush and astride a pony. In moon shadow. Rhythmically rising, falling, floating towards the horizon. *Hey-a-hey-hey.* There was chanting. She wasn't afraid. She was meant to be here.

Chapter 32

'In bygone days, the rule that no lady should travel without a gentleman by her side, was doubtless a wise one. Opinions are divided on the subject, but some now believe the quality of travel experience to have been immeasurably improved, by the abandonment of that restriction.' – p.151

They were up before dawn, before the birds. Bathed in cold, blue light, their little group huddled together in the middle of the deserted parade-ground, surrounded by bags and baggage.

Colonel Ruane was there, Captain Wallace, too. Considerate of them, Annie thought, to get up at dawn just to bid a polite goodbye. Of course, good riddance may have been more in their line of thinking. That wouldn't have surprised her, either.

Two young officers that Charlotte had charmed to distraction, loitered palely, too. Poor deluded souls. No-one else was around.

Was it silly to hope that somebody … anybody … would be? Wasn't too late, of course. A person might still wander by to … wave them off?

Captain Wallace greeted Annie with a formal bow. 'Ah'm sorry to lose yurr company, Miss Haddon. On the other hand, I widdna wish your safety t'be compromised.' He paused, 'In any way.'

Annie blinked, warily.

'I'm tockin' about the savage unrest, of courrse,' he said, sharp eyes glinting. 'But dinnae fret. Indians have no future here. They'll soon go the way of the buffalo.' He drew a finger across his throat.

That he was describing McCall's fate and McCall's throat was obvious to Annie. She was torn between dislike and distress.

'Anyhoo,' he added, slyly. 'I understand yurr to be married.' His arrogant gaze flicked over Henry Hewell. 'May I wish you everry happiness.'

Every happiness, yes. From somewhere, Annie produced a watery smile. Her face though, was sheet-white. Struggling against a feeling of helplessness, she turned her attention to the Colonel.

Stagecoach lines had been unreliable lately, he warned, since fresh trouble with the Comanche. Routes of travel, times of arrival and departure - all likely to vary. Day to day, hour to hour. Discretion of the driver.

'Are you telling me,' Aunt Bea said, her fingers drumming on a portmanteau, 'that we're required to just stand here, in the vague hope that a stagecoach may sometime arrive?'

''Fraid so.'

'Preposterous!'

'A sight preferable, if I may say so ma'am, to the prospect of being taken captive by Comanche.'

That shut her up. Not Charlotte, though. 'Annie may be inclined to disagree,' she pointed out, silkily.

And Annie might, Annie thought, in her present mood, send her catty cousin to the Devil. She'd had some thin times in her life - oh, yes. Never though, had she felt so cast down, so alone.

Had she even one good friend in all the world?

Speaking of whining and one good friend - here he was now, at her heels. Dog, her faithful companion. What hope for his survival now?

Dawn was only a thin white line in the eastern sky when the Overland stage rumbled in, creaking and grinding to a stop. Two men stumbled out to stretch their legs while dusty mail sacks were thrown down, bags and portmanteau tied on top.

With teams of fresh horses buckled in the traces, farewells were exchanged, hands politely shaken. An officer clasped Charlotte fiercely to his bosom.

'Charlotte!' shrieked her mother. 'Unhand that young man, at once!'

Annie took a long, last look round. Everything was quiet. It was too early yet for morning work call and no smoke drifted up from any of the chimneys.

'Lost something?' Charlotte slithered close enough to say. 'Someone? Oh, stop looking so tragic. No-one's going to come now, are they? Accept it.'

Around the stagecoach, a sudden bustle of activity, calling and shouting, as they prepared to set off. 'Git ready fer a hot one,' their driver chimed, to groans all round. 'Hundred eight, hundred ten.'

'Dammit, I do hate to sweat in a new hat.'

'Well hey-ho bud, ain't you the dandy!'

Henry Hewell insisted on helping Annie up, his hands sliding all over her waist, the cad, while Dog whined and jumped at her heels.

Her throat constricted, the beginnings of tears pricked her eyes. 'Get down, boy. I can't take you.' She'd known this would happen, known it would be awful.

Then, an ear-piercing yelp and the sound of freshly-kicked

puppy, as Henry Hewell lashed out with his huge, shiny boot, the cad. Flattening shredded ears, Dog fell back, whimpering pathetically.

What manner of man actually was this, Annie wondered. Cruel unfeeling brute, that's what. Petty vengeful monster.

And he dared to plump down beside her then, as if nothing had happened, his fat thigh pressed hard against hers, in proprietary fashion. Nothing she could do about it either, except stare fixedly ahead, a sick feeling in her stomach.

Minutes ticked by, they sat and sat. The first light of dawn crept into the stagecoach. People shifted and grew restless. 'What in tarnation we waiting fer, now? The rainy season?'

'You up there, driver!' Aunt Bea's shrill voice rose above the rest. 'What's holding us up, pray?'

They soon found out.

A flutter of silk and some cooing apologies brought another traveller hurrying across the parade ground.

The cracked varnished door swung wide and to Annie's astonishment, Mrs Lee stood there, in a swirl of silk and claret-coloured velvet. A waterfall of lace at her throat, wheaten hair coiled up under a sprout of feathers and twist of net.

She was dressed for something. But was it travelling? Her entire outfit, the full fig, would have been more at home in the watering holes of London, Paris, New York.

Not that anyone cared. Covert glances of admiration quickly turned to slack-jawed stares and drooling. Not just the men, either. Even Charlotte's mouth fell open, as Colonel Ruane helped Mrs Lee inside.

Clouds of heady scent wafted in with her. Syringa, crushed lilies? Dazed from lack of sleep, Annie's lungs clogged and she started to feel dizzy.

She wasn't sure how she felt about Mrs Lee, either. Jealous? Oh, why try to hide it? Shameless, panting, jealousy, that's what this was. Didn't matter anymore though, did it? She suddenly felt old. Old beyond her years.

Then another late arrival, a lean young man with straight-brimmed hat and saddle over his shoulder. Swinging the saddle up top, he boosted himself inside, to loud complaints, as everyone had to squash up and dove-tail their knees.

Annie wondered how long she could bear this. Crushed hard against Henry Hewell for hours and hours. Through her misery, she heard Mrs Lee's gracious goodbyes. 'So kind, John. Goodbye, Andrew. Thank you for looking after me. Bye now. Bye.'

'So sorry to have delayed you.' Her sweet, easy voice beguiled the rest of them. 'A late decision. You-all know how it is.'

Does McCall? Annie couldn't help thinking. Know how it is? Why had he let her go, then? She hadn't left him again, had she? Was the woman deranged?

Another delay? Scuffling outside and muffled roars from the driver as he cracked his whip. 'Git that damn animal away from my wheels!'

Readjusting her dropped jaw, Charlotte smiled malevolently at her cousin.

A plague of boils on Charlotte. Annie was in no mood to be forbearing. *Let her hair fall out, let her develop mange.*

As the Fort faded to a dark smudge in the misty distance, she fingered the cloth round the eagle claw in her pocket, and shut her ears to Dog's heart-rending howls.

Dust started drifting in through the windows. Prairie undulated by outside. The driver threw pebbles at his lead horses, and with a rattling jingling clamour, the team pulled faster and faster.

Jolting and jarring gave way to bumping and swaying, and soon they were hurtling along at a reckless and dangerous speed. As if the Furies were after them. Peering out of the window into pearly mist and half-light, Annie saw no sign of anything in pursuit though, thank Heaven. Yet.

So, here they all were again, corseted, gloved, bowed.

Laces laced to straining, buttons buttoned tight. Almost a dozen billowing layers apiece, and barely an inch of skin left uncovered.

And England only a hop, skip and jump away. Before they knew it, they'd be back to porringers of broth and good red flannel. Annie's head itched. Had creatures already taken up residence? She rummaged under her hat.

'Annie! Where are my salts?'

'Here, Aunt.'

'My fan?'

'I have that, too.'

'And water? Colonel Ruane said that the flask must be kept full at all times.'

From beneath lowered lashes, Annie studied the other passengers. The only amusement on offer, unless you counted swatting flies.

Of the three men not with their party, the leathery one with the lazy eye was already sweating profusely.

Another, older and fatter, fugged the carriage with thick cigar smoke. His broadcloth suit was creased and he held a bulging bag on his knees.

Not the outdoors type, complexion was too pale. Banker? He kept checking his timepiece, checking, checking. Was that bag full of money?

The third and newest arrival looked to be much younger. Hard to be sure, because he seemed to be sleeping, his hat pulled down over his eyes. A person couldn't help noticing though, if they'd a mind to, that his skin was clear and bronzed and he had a good firm mouth.

Was anyone else engaged in the same game? Annie slid her eyes sideways to the delicate, heart-shaped face of Mrs Lee, and then wished she hadn't, when Mrs Lee caught her curious stare and smiled back.

'Miss Haddon.' She leaned forward. 'I had no idea you were leaving so soon.'

'What!' Aunt Bea raised her head, like a horse peering over a hedge. 'What say?'

Mrs Lee, to her credit, was not put off. 'You knew that Colt was planning to meet prospective buyers for his horses today?'

A small pause, as she fingered the flounce of lace at her throat. 'He's sure to make a good price, he's an excellent judge of horse-flesh.'

'Pity he's not so shrewd with women,' Charlotte muttered, under her breath.

Aunt Bea just sniffed. 'I can think of nothing more vulgar, than hearing how a person makes their money.' Then loudly, to Annie: 'Sit up straight, Annie!'

On, on, on then, through the early morning's thin haze. The world rushed by, the landscape a blur.

Wreathed in clouds of smoke, the cigar-smoker regaled them with long-winded accounts of his adventures across the frozen wastes. Canada, Alaska, the Yukon. His gold tooth flashed, his mouth jaw-jawed. He didn't falter. Except for checking his timepiece and coughing, appallingly.

Only Annie bothered to listen. Everyone else looked bored. Charlotte yawned most rudely and Mrs Lee stared out of the window. Mr Hewell - head thrown back, haunches splayed - slept soundly. His mouth was wide, his snoring loud and rhythmical.

Prairie passed. And more prairie.

Travelling at speed, they covered vast distances. Oceans of pale bleached grass all around. Immense blue sky arching over and above.

Before long, the sun was up and threatening to burn. As the curtain of heat inside the coach got thicker and heavier, its occupants grew crabbier.

Charlotte snapped first. No longer cool and collected, now damp and cranky. And bored, profoundly bored. A deadly combination.

Annie was the easiest target. 'What's that book? What are you reading?'

'About Piranesi.'

'Mountains! Bor-ing. It's so thick. Mama, she's weighing us down with books. Didn't Colonel Ruane say to leave anything we couldn't eat or wear?'

Then, 'They'll probably eat your wretched dog, you know. They eat anything here that moves.'

And, 'A grooming tip, Annie? Consider a wig. Your hair's a fright, even under that hat.'

Nice. Gnawing her nails, Annie told herself that her cousin couldn't help this. Not really. As a scorpion needed to sting, Charlotte was driven to torment. It was her nature, it was what she did.

So, later. 'Not still pining for that half-breed, are you? I've heard they pickle Indian heads in alcohol back East. For freak shows.' And, 'Oh stop breathing and fidgeting! Lord, it's like Elizabeth Barrett Browning, with palsy.'

At some point, when Annie was slowly coming round to the idea of strangulation, the young man opposite pushed back his hat. 'Lady?' he said to Charlotte, opening one bleary eye, like a tortoise. The eye was blue and very cold.

Charlotte brightened immediately, giving him the benefit of one of her own baby-blue, doll-like stares. Lashes fluttered coyly; it was clear what she was thinking. Why, here was the most attractive man, since, oh ... since Colt McCall, and she was trying so very hard to forget about him.

'You've got a tongue,' the young man muttered, 'like a boning knife. Go find the carcass of a dead animal somewheres 'n rip into that.'

Annie didn't look at her cousin, didn't dare. She heard a strangulated sort of sound come from Charlotte's direction, though. Like a sick pigeon.

No-one else uttered a word. Charlotte sat back, stiff and haughty, and Annie fixed her eyes on the middle distance.

How long had they been travelling? One hour, a day, a year? The sun was now high, the atmosphere, too. Soon, surely soon, they would have to make a stop.

'A month, at least a month before we take a decent meal.' Mr Hewell twitched awake, his taut skin spotted with high colour. 'By my reckoning.'

What?

'I've a fancy for a well-hung bird. Ripe pheasant. Or pork, yes. Side of bacon. Fat pork, with crackling.'

Pig, brooded Annie, picturing bacon fat dribbling down his chin. She'd done her best to ignore his slumbering form at her side, heaving and snorting like a walrus. Avoided all eye contact too, with Charlotte, Mrs Lee and the young man. And the fat cigar smoker.

Sorry, but she'd had enough of his travels in Alaska. His cigars were too large, his tales too long - like some endless, Icelandic saga. *Gather round brothers and sisters, throw another log on the fire.*

'If ever you meet a grizzly,' he'd said, nodding sagely, 'don't run.'

Don't? What, then?

'Climb a tree. Or play dead.'

Annie had started to say that she hadn't noticed many bears in the English shires, but someone else had snapped, 'Mister? Will ya keep that damn cee-gar outta my face!' - and polite conversation had all but petered out. For which, she'd been very grateful.

Rattling wheels set up a grating rhythm. Her eyes were dry and hot and she felt the beginnings of another bad headache. Really bad. Blinding.

Then, something started happening, something *bad.*

Her eyes jerked open. Gunfire? Staccato shots blasted out over the clamour of the stage and Annie flinched with each one.

Horses shied wildly. The driver pulled hard and high on

the reins. Stamping on the brake lever, he brought the stage to a shuddering, grinding halt and clouds of dust billowed up all around them.

Stricken silence settled, along with the dust. No sound. Just an air of sullen expectation inside the carriage, and faint smell of cordite on the wind. The smell of danger.

It couldn't be happening all over again, could it? Another attack, another ugly wreck? Ashen-faced, Annie's hand closed round her talisman, the eagle claw in her pocket. It just couldn't.

Chapter 33

'On encountering native peoples, offer cordial address, whilst expressing by one's tone and manner, one's own superiority.' - p.35

Hooves thudded up. Someone shouted outside.

Heads turned, uncertainly. 'What the hell we carrying?'

'Mail, only mail! I'd swear to it.'

'Indians, then. Surer'n hell.'

Eyes widened in shock, and they stared at each other.

Then, the lazy-eyed man swore, sweatily. 'Whip those nags on, dammit! What in blazes we waiting for? A pow-wow?'

'Can't afford no delay.' The fat cigar smoker squinted smoke out of his eyes. 'Told the driver, when I settled ma fare. Got real urgent business in St Louis.'

'This here's Comanche business, feller - taking the tops off our heads. Comanche haircut. Chew on that.'

'I don't hear no-one yowling for our hair,' the young man said. 'And Comanche don't use Winchesters.'

'No? Who's this then mister, you know so damn much? Buffalo Bill?'

All eyes went to the window, straining against the glare. Someone whistled, a long, low note; someone else blasphemed. Oh-oh! Danger! Danger!

'Oh-my-God – '

The towering figure outside had a hard, cruel body and wolfish face. Cheeks smeared with pigment, oiled hair falling to wide shoulders. A cluster of feathers at the back of his head was caught by an eagle claw.

A perfect match, for the one Annie now held tightly in her hand.

'Shoot it!' Charlotte squealed. 'Quick, quick, kill it someone!'

'Surprise, surprise. She's a screamer.'

'Do something! Make it go away!'

'What do they want?' Henry Hewell's voice was hoarse with panic. 'God in Heaven! Don't let them hurt us!'

Aunt Bea was praying, too. Or having a seizure. It was hard to tell which.

'Hush up!' the young man said. 'I'm tellin' you this is no Indian attack. That Injun ain't dressed for war.'

'It's Grey Eagle.'

'What! What say, missy?'

'Grey Eagle,' Annie said, her heart thump-thumping. 'A Sioux. He's ... friendly.'

Why here, she was wondering, why now?

'Don't look none too friendly, not from where I'm sitting.'

The door swung wide. Grey Eagle's huge bulk - buckskin leggings, bare scarred arms and chest - filled the frame and Aunt Bea and Charlotte shrank back, as if faced with leprosy.

'Sure he's tame, little lady? Cain't figure it.'

Grey Eagle wasn't going out of his way to reassure anyone, either. Slitted eyes swept the carriage, lingering longest on the women. The air filled with a hot animal scent and Charlotte began to whimper.

Minutes passed, long, silent minutes and Annie's mind

raced, as they sat in fearful silence. Suddenly, the Sioux scout backed away and disappeared.

No-one gave a fig about the whys and wherefores. There was a general shudder, as a horse was ridden away hard. Breathing gradually became more regular, but no-one dared move or speak.

A scrape of a boot brought their driver's grizzled face to the door. 'Y'all right in there, folks?' He rubbed his chin. 'Feller didn't scare yuh, did he?'

'We're paying you,' Aunt Bea's voice was high and trembling, 'to take us to Sedalia. Not stop and pass the time of day with every curious savage.'

'Beg pardon, ma'am, but you ain't paying me - stagecoach company is - and if a Army scout waves a Winchester, reckon I oughta hear what he has to say.'

'Scout! Scout, you say? What did he want?'

'Didn't say.' Swinging back up to his seat, the driver set them moving again.

Another anxious silence. It lasted for some time. The only sounds, the grinding rhythm of wheels, the creak of leather and someone's still-heavy breathing.

'Of course that native weren't dangerous.' Henry Hewell removed his eye-glasses. A slick of sweat greased his forehead. 'Anyone could see. The feathers on his head were half-chewed. Cavalry'll subdue those savages no time, no time at all.'

'Don't know diddly about redskins, do you mister? Want to hear what that means? Do yuh? Huh, huh? Them half-feathers mean he's cut the throats of his enemies.'

Silenced, Henry Hewell dabbed the side of his mouth.

A moment later, he turned to Aunt Bea. 'How many days must we suffer in Sedalia, hmm? When is the circuit judge due in?'

For her wedding? Annie didn't protest. A wedding in Sedalia, the next way-station or Waxahachie, what was the difference?

Never in her worst nightmares though, had she imagined anything like this. No hallowed church, no blossomy bouquet, no foaming veil. Just a hastily-arranged ceremony in some God-forsaken spot, in front of strangers.

To a man she barely knew.

The stage was soon swinging in a wide arc towards the next way-station. Around the rough hillside, through billowing dust. Ahead, squat buildings shimmered in the heat.

As they ground to a halt, there was a banging on the wooden roof.

'Thirty minutes, folks. Jest time fer a drink and stretch them legs.'

Ducking out into a brutal wall of heat, everyone brushed themselves off. In relieved silence, the men shook stiffness from their legs, the women smoothed their hair.

Annie was creased as a duster, her hair a disaster. She knew she looked a fright. Charlotte was fetchingly crumpled. And Mrs Lee? Still luminous, still lovely. Was she set in aspic?

Following each other inside, their eyes slowly adjusted to the way-station's dim interior. Bare white-washed walls, sour smells of liquor and smoke heavy on the air. Coffee bubbled on a old black stove, and bottles of pale liquid and tumblers stood waiting on a mahogany bar.

Pop-eyed and puffy, Henry Hewell gulped down two tumblers and poured himself a third. The coffee smelled good, but Annie could find no taste for it.

Listlessly, she drifted to the window. Flat land dotted with dust-covered mesquite stretched away in the heat haze. The rough slope of hillside disappeared in dusty, distant glare.

You couldn't just pass through this landscape, could you? It reached out and drew you in. Wide-open spaces, petrified rock and painted sky had somehow seeped in, under her skin. In spite of all that had happened.

But now, Sedalia beckoned. Life as Mrs Henry Chewton Hewell. No point feeling sorry for herself though, was there?

Brooding. She'd agreed to this marriage and that was that.

But when her intended's slurred, high-pitched voice reached her from the other side of the room, she couldn't help a cold knot of apprehension.

'Miss Haddon?' Mrs Lee drifted over to join her. 'Is your pretty cousin really going to marry that man? They don't seem suited.'

'Not my cousin, no.' Annie's voice was flat. 'Me. I am marrying him.' She nodded in the direction of her aunt. 'They may ask you to be a witness. We'll need two at least, won't we? I believe that's customary. Three?'

Close now, to losing fragile self-control and saying something stupid, she turned back to the window.

Her eyes glazed. Staring sightless at the view, she suddenly saw movement, the faintest blur on the hillside. Small specks, dots zigzagging down the slope, with a dust tail billowing behind them.

'Riders,' she said, and everyone turned to stare.

Chapter 34

'It is my experience that travel can give a woman time to reflect on the world around her.' – p.197

The two riders reined in their horses.

Mrs Lee recognised them first. 'That scout again,' she said, shielding her eyes. 'Grey Eagle? And ... why, looks like Colt!'

'What now?' Onlookers edged away from the windows. 'What they want?'

'Danged if I know,' the stagecoach driver said.

'Know about Indians, doncha?'

'Yip.'

'So? What they want?'

'Dunno.'

'Aw, shut up.'

Annie knew. Of course she did. McCall had come for his love, after all. How swooningly romantic, how sublime. Her knees went weak with envy. He must have ridden like the wind to catch up with them, too. 'Mrs Lee,' she said.

Charlotte stared. 'Are you telling me?' Words dripped from her lips like blood. 'That all this is for the benefit of

Miss Fancy-Pants over there? All that shooting and scaring us senseless. How *dare* they!'

Mrs Lee wasn't listening, she'd already disappeared. Annie watched through the open swinging door, as she picked her way round rock and brush and ankle-turning earth.

Towards McCall. Towards joyful reunion? Towards his hard embrace.

How *could* she have been so stupid? McCall had kissed her, she had kissed him back. She had confided ... oh, help ... she had clung to that man.

Well, hopefully, he'd ride away now and take Mrs Lee with him. No need to see either of them ever again. Until then, she didn't have to watch, did she?

Turning away, her eyes drifted blankly back to the dim room. Seeing, unseeing.

Western men, well-used to sitting things out, were hunkered over drinks, or in conversation with the station agent. They were in no hurry.

Aunt Bea, a little apart and now recovered from her fright, seemed unperturbed by this latest interruption. In fact, she looked pleased as a cat.

And why not? Things were going well. Her unmarriageable niece almost married! A satisfactory match, too. Mrs Henry Chewton Hewell. Who would have thought it?

And the bridegroom? Slumped at the bar, purple-faced and glassy-eyed, his waistcoat straining over his ample stomach. He'd already polished off one bottle of something, and was half-way through another.

Annie felt the life-blood drain out of her. What would they do, if she ran outside screaming? Drag her back? Chain her to the table leg?

The screen door banged. A huge silhouette loomed.

Not even a chair scraped the floor as Grey Eagle's eyes raked the room. When they came to rest on Annie, he beckoned sharply.

'Your party now, I reckon missy.' Blowing smoke unconcernedly into the air, the stagecoach driver nodded, sagely. 'Best get out there afore he gits edgy. Ornery critters, them Sioux.'

'Stop her, Mama! Before she makes fools of us again. You, go away. Shoo, shoo!'

'Ain't wise to wave threats at injuns, lady.'

Annie took no notice of any of them, she barely heard. She was far too busy wondering what on earth McCall and Mrs Lee wanted with her. A witness for their own wedding? Well, serve her right.

Fly too close to the sun, missy - you get burned.

At the door, she hesitated. The raw strength of Grey Eagle, the foreignness of his feathers and paint, unsettled her still.

'Come.' The big scout gestured, impatiently.

Straight-backed and erect, he walked steadily in front. Close behind, dust puffing from every step, Annie stumbled through the stunted brush.

The sight of Mrs Lee picking a careful way back, skirts held high to avoid the dust, stopped her dead. She saw no sign of triumph in Virginia Lee's face, just a sort of trapped, defeated expression.

Their meeting was brief. One minute at most.

'Take a tip,' Virginia Lee murmured, with that wide-eyed, gentian gaze. 'If you want him, you'll have to tell him. Sweet nothings and kissy-kissy just aren't his style. Lord knows why I'm telling you this, but ... don't do what I did.'

Turning daintily on her heel, she walked away. 'Better heed me, Miss Haddon,' she threw back, the wind tugging wisps of veiling over her face. 'Or live to regret it. Oh, yes.'

Annie stared after her. Then, turning back, she shielded her eyes.

Harsh sun dazzled, it was blisteringly hot. The horizon blurred in a haze.

Some distance away, a solitary figure watched and waited,

shimmering in and out of focus on waves of heat. High on a horse, he held the reins of Grey Eagle's grazing pony, while the animal's tail flicked lazily at flies. The rider's legs were long and loose, his back straight.

Annie would have known him anywhere.

Swinging down, McCall sauntered to meet her - his hat well down, thumbs hooked into his belt. He didn't look too pleased. He didn't seem in any hurry, either. Why then, the brouhaha? The chase, the gunfire.

A frown tightened his forehead. 'You didn't *say* you were leaving.'

Ouch, thought Annie. His voice was icy as Alaska, sharp as splintered glass.

'You want to go?'

'I have to.'

'Do you *want* to, is what I'm asking.' He sounded vexed.

She searched his face. As ever, no clue and no encouragement, either. Just narrowed eyes and that blank, unreadable expression.

She shrugged. 'What I want doesn't matter anymore.'

'Matters to me.' His gaze was steady. 'Ginny says you're going to marry that knucklehead. What the hell for? No backbone, no guts - you don't even like him.'

The roughness in his voice disconcerted her. 'It's best,' she said. 'My relatives - '

'Still letting them push you around? You're a grown woman, stand up for yourself.'

Annie shuffled her feet, like a pigeon. Well, she'd tried, hadn't she? A fat lot of good it had done her, too. 'Look, you don't – '

'Oh, I understand. Better than you think. That fool's on the hustle, sniffing round for your money.'

He knew about her money? How? How did he know? She said, 'It will benefit us. My entire family.'

'To hell with your family! They're selling you off and you're letting them do it. I ought to wish you luck. You'll sure need it.'

'It's *my* life.' That was what she kept telling herself, anyway.

'Yeah, and you're making a mess of it. I look at him, I see your future. And I tell you Annie, it won't be pretty. Turkeys don't come any plumper.' He paused. 'You think he's all you're worth? Don't look at me like that, say something.'

'What? That I'm the runt of the litter, the one that's been marked down? I have a duty. To – '

'You just don't get it, do you? Not one of 'em gives a damn for you, anyway.'

'If you don't mind.' Annie felt the colour rise in her face. 'I'd like to leave here with a little self-respect. Anyway … it's too late. I've made my choice.'

'Make another.'

He came closer. She wished that he wouldn't, it made it hard to think sensibly, anymore. Communing with a wild thing would be easier. A bear? Don't run. Climb a tree. Easy.

Loosening his hat, he gave her another hard stare. 'Look,' he said, 'it's tough on a woman here, I know that. Yeah. The life, the … ' His voice faded; he let the words drift.

A long silence then, a private, churning one. Hot wind whipped up the dust. A huge beetle ran out of a crack in the ground, and disappeared.

'This kinda thing hardly ever works out,' he went on, at last. As if the words were being dragged out of him. 'Too much against it.' Another pause. 'Swore blind I'd never get this way again. Anytime I felt myself getting caught up, I'd cut loose.'

He sighed and his voice shifted, from gruffness to hoarseness. 'I'm there though, aren't I, and I'm doing it. I'm asking.'

Asking? Annie's mind went round and round. Still no clue

in his expression, no sign of any barriers coming down. Just that closed, private look, as enigmatic as the landscape behind him.

Chapter 35

'It has been said that women have no taste for the wilderness and adventure. However, to travel abroad for curiosity's sake, to see nature in it's grandest forms, can stir such a sense of discovery that one's inner, as well as one's outer landscape is irreversibly changed.'
– p.204

A sudden displacement of air yanked Annie back to her senses.

Gritty reality arrived, with a swoosh of silk and a terrifying screech. 'Back! Get back inside, Annie. This instant!'

'Aunt, this is – '

'Silence!' Aunt Bea's watery fish-eyes gave McCall a thorough going-over. 'I am well aware who it is. You know what they say of you, young man?'

'Nope.'

'That you're a public menace. According to Colonel Ruane, men stand away from you, women's reputations are ruined by you!'

'Never believe anything a Westerner tells you, ma'am. Damn liars every one.'

'Well hear me now, hear this.' Well-bred nostrils began to quiver. '*Our* name, our family name has given rise to esteem and deference in England, since Henry the Eighth's time.'

'And very well-deserved, I'm sure,' McCall said, drily. 'Is there some point to this?'

'Clearly not to anyone here! Deplorable antecedents, lack of education. What do you people know about breeding?'

'We tend to be pretty good at it.'

'Wipe that smirk from your face!' Aunt Bea's jaw had the snap of an alligator. 'Don't dare be coarse and vulgar in my company! Have you no respect for your betters?'

'Respect has to be earned here, ma'am, not passed on by some monarch. And I am coarse. Isn't that what you're saying? Rough and rude and deep-down dirty?'

Annie winced. To anyone's eyes, he'd look formidable. In need of a shave, with that scar showing at the side of his mouth, and dark eyes glistening against Aunt Bea's starched respectability.

'What in the world recommends my niece to a libertine like you, then? Hmm?' Aunt Bea shook, as if confronted by cloven hooves and a sulphurous stench. 'A decent, refined, *Christian* woman.'

'A mystery.' Charlotte came close enough to coo, with bird-of-prey malice. 'Can't be her looks or her shrivelled limb. Must be her mind. Yes, yes, that's it. He aims to improve his mind. How sweet.'

'Her money, dammit,' Henry Hewell chipped in. 'What else? Who in their right mind would choose a cripple, eh? Exceedin' plain one, at that.'

'Shut your mouth or you'll find my fist in it.'

'Hear that! What'd I tell you? Fellow's an animal, he's … vile!'

'I'm warning you.' Aunt Bea clutched her throat. 'My nerves are very close to the surface. I'll not have a public brawl!'

McCall turned to Annie. 'Well? I've asked you to stay.'

'Don't be insulting, feller! You've gorn too far. Damned outrage, if you ask me.'

'I didn't. Annie? Something's going on between you and me. Been going on since we met. Will you give it a chance?'

'Young man, enough! Stop this nonsense. My niece is to be *married,* d'you hear? To one of her own kind.'

The wind died down, leaving an intense heat-vibrant silence. An other-worldly stillness.

Catching Henry Hewell's eye, Annie could see only cold, unblinking dislike behind his eye-glasses. No gratitude, no warmth. A glimpse into her future that made her blood run cold.

McCall was right. It would be cruel and achingly lonely. Prison, with no time off for good behaviour. Could she stand it?

A rough ball of woolly fur suddenly launched itself at her legs, yelping and demanding attention. 'Dog? You've got *Dog!*'

McCall swung her round to face him. 'P'raps I'm not doing this right. Annie? You want me down on my knees?'

She stared. 'I'm not sure what you mean. Are you ...?'

'Reckon so.'

'We *are* talking about ... ?'

'I sure hope so.'

He narrowed the space between them. 'Will you stay?'

Annie looked into his eyes and found herself somewhere else. Another place. Somewhere she'd been looking for, all her life.

She started to smile and before she knew what was happening, he'd pulled her to him, cupped her face in his hands and was kissing her mouth.

Her arms drooped in surprise, then laced round his neck. Pulling tighter, his hands curled round handfuls of her travelling jacket and held her so tight she could barely draw breath.

He rested his forehead on hers for a moment.

Then, as Annie waited for the world to stop spinning, and tried to wipe the stupid expression from her face, he drew slowly away and straightened her hat.

'Wanton, shameless immodesty! How *dare* you behave in so brazen a fashion! Have you no regard for the state of my health?'

A person had to admire the power of her aunt's lungs, Annie thought, as her own mouth burned, and blood rushed in her ears. Shameless? Oh, yes.

'Wretched ingrate!' Henry Hewell rattled, harshly. 'For some reckless, foolish infatuation, you'd defy God ... defy society! Defy ... defy your own, deah family!'

Yes, thought Annie.

'No,' said McCall.

'Who, pray,' Mr Hewell said, his indrawn breath whistling through his pinched nose, 'do you consider family, then? The family of man? Some damnable tribal brotherhood?'

Silence. Hot breeze shivered through the grass and Annie had that feeling again. The one that had been clinging to her since she got here; the one that wouldn't be shaken off.

Someone, something was watching. Waiting. *Ghosts, ghosts.*

'Annie.' McCall's voice came from a far-off place, and he took her hand. 'I have to tell you something. About my friend, my red-haired friend. Remember?'

She bit her lip. Not now, with tensions so high and words whirling round in her head and confusing her. Too many people here, were already grinding too many axes.

A growing sense of unease was made worse when she glanced up and encountered his very odd expression. An air of what? Anticipation?

'Annie, that friend. It was your father. I knew him well.'

Around Annie, everything grew still. She heard a cry of shocked surprise from someone, possibly her aunt.

Then silence. Just the murmur of the prairie, the rustle of dry, pale grass and those words left hanging on hot, dusty wind.

She cleared her throat. '*My* father?' Her voice was barely audible. 'Are you sure?' Her head turned, a fraction of an inch and she looked round, in bewildered appeal. For confirmation, reassurance? Someone?

A blur of faces, white as goose-feathers, stared back.

'Carlyle is common, I think ... a common enough name.'

'Thomas James Carlyle? Born 1812. Six-three, red hair, green eyes?'

'Why on earth didn't you say something before?'

'Your name was different. That put me off for a while. I needed to be very, very sure. And *my* friend had tried to keep in touch with his daughter. He wrote, sent money. Begged and begged for her to come out here. That didn't fit with what you'd told me.'

Whoa! Whoa, there! 'He *wrote*?' Annie had a strong sense of her aunt and Henry Hewell coiling up, like snakes in the grass. 'He sent *money*?'

'Yep. Regular as clockwork.'

'Didn't he wonder why I never wrote back?'

'He thought you didn't want to know him.'

'I can't bear that he thought that.' The blood drained from Annie's face. 'Now he's dead and I can never tell him how much I wanted to meet him.'

The silence grew strained. No-one moved an inch.

High, white sun beat mercilessly down on their little tableau, out of glaring afternoon sky. A lone buzzard flapped languidly over their heads and hung there, wide wings outstretched, on warm draughts of air.

Annie pictured its cold black eye. What did it see? The fallen, the weak? Well, she was both and everyone was watching her now, waiting for her to say something.

What! What did they expect? *Hypocrites!*

Her eyes went back to the bird. It circled round, then drifted off, effortlessly.

She was pale as a ghost. Something started to swell in her throat. She felt herself shaking and knew with absolute certainty that she was going to cry.

'Now, Annie ... ' Recovering herself, Aunt Bea bustled up. 'Look here, dearest girl ... now ... now, listen to me.'

McCall turned on her, sharply. 'I need to talk to your niece alone, ma'am. Guess you owe us that much, huh?'

Aunt Bea's eyes came together in a squint. Huge bosoms heaved, but she slithered into red-faced silence.

'Here.' McCall offered his neckerchief and waited while Annie dutifully blew her nose. 'Listen Annie, your father came out from England, mad with grief after your mother died. You were ... what? Four, five months old? Right away, he regretted leaving you behind. Hear that?' He examined her face. 'When he passed away, he was still raw.'

'They wouldn't tell me a thing about him.' All those years, all that wasted time! And had she complained? No. She'd just let them fob her off.

'They thought him an idle-good-for-nothing, from an idle-good-for-nothing family, that's why. That's how he explained it to me. Not good enough for your mother, for you, or the rest of them, either.'

'So they lied about his letters?' Annie's voice shook. All that strutting about on the moral high ground. And Aunt Bea had lied. Eugenie lied! Again and again.

'Ten years I knew him, Annie. He was a good man, a *good* man. Only thing left was to leave you his money. A helluva lot of it. He made me his trustee. That's why I had to be sure about you, d'you see? I was on my way to meet your aunt in Amarillo when the stage was held up.' He shrugged. 'You know the rest.'

'Tell me everything.' She was still struggling to make sense of it. 'What was he *like*?'

'First things first. How many of those bags on top of the stage are yours?'

Annie squinted up into the sun's glare. 'I'm not sure that I'm ready.'

'I'll help you get ready. Look, we've barely hit our stride. We need time together, time to get to know each other.'

'What if you change your mind?' She felt herself redden.

'Me? Nah.' Lifting her hand to his mouth, he kissed it. 'I never start anything I don't intend to finish. You were meant to be here.'

Yes, yes. She'd felt it, hadn't she? Something in the air, something other worldly. The strangest pull.

She turned to her relatives. No longer talking, they appeared as shocked and confused as she was herself.

Catching her glance, Aunt Bea bore down on them, lips quivering, red blotches staining her face. 'Whatever I did,' she said, trumpeting into her handkerchief. 'I did for the sake of your poor dear sainted mother. I hope you believe that.'

A throbbing pause.

'You can't stay here, Annie, it's no fit place.' Her voice dropped. 'This man, this McCall. He's handsome, I'll allow that, but ... foreign dear, *foreign.* Dissolute!'

'It's what I want, Aunt Bea. I believe my father would have wanted it, too'

'But Mr Hewell could offer so much more! He'd forgive you, I'm sure. In time. When he's not so upset. Let me reason with him.'

Annie looked round for the grieving bridegroom. He didn't look too tormented. He already seemed to have given her up and had retreated to the hot box of the stagecoach.

Lose one fiancée, Annie thought, get another. Prettier, possibly. Richer. She no longer counted.

Virginia Lee was in there, too, at the far side, by the window - her pale pretty face turned away, her back rigid.

Annie felt a stab of sympathy. She knew that feeling.

Hiding the hurt, pretending you didn't care.

'I'm meant to be here, aunt.' A new world. Freedom. 'I can be happy.'

'What in the world is that to do with anything?' her aunt flared. 'We're not put on this earth to enjoy ourselves. Well, you are of age, I can't prevent this. But you'll live to regret it, Annie. You know *nothing* of these people. How they live.'

Annie felt a brief stab of panic. It only lasted until McCall came back with her bags. 'Better come say goodbye,' he said.

She walked to the stage, Dog circling her heels.

Charlotte was buttoning her jacket and barely looked up. 'I still can't believe it,' she muttered, in less-than-flattering fashion. 'Why on earth would he want you? The cowboy hero. I'll never understand it.'

Annie assumed a saintly expression. 'God moves in mysterious ways, Charlotte.'

'Not as long as I live. It's not your face or your figure. Can't be. Your mind? What on *earth* have you two got in common? Ask him how he'll deal with that awful limp, ask him that.'

'Perhaps he likes to suffer.'

'Well it won't last. He'll leave you, just wait and see. I mean, look at him. Look! And look at you. You're such an embarrassment.'

Snapping out a smile, Annie waved cheerfully. 'Goodbye! Bye, Charlotte.'

'Will I see them again?' she asked McCall, as the driver climbed to his seat on top of the stage. She couldn't quite believe what was happening.

The coach creaked in readiness, its harnesses jingling.

'Do you want to?'

'I think so. They brought me up, they did what they thought was best.'

'Then it'll happen.'

'I hate goodbyes.'

'Me, too. Hellos are much better. Annie?' He watched her

face. 'You're sure about this, about me? So much has happened, so fast'

Something snatched at Annie's senses, then. Some fleeting presence, a passing brightness, without form. She blinked and it was there again, a mere flicker of movement.

Something or someone in the corner of her conscious mind, in broad hat and coat, with the collar turned up. Someone watching. Her father?

Catching her breath, she nodded. She'd come home.

The stagecoach started rumbling out. They watched it weave away, bumping and swaying in a billowing dust cloud, then gathering speed, the rattling clamour fainter and fainter until it disappeared from sight.

There was a moment somewhere between the end of the ceremony and the point where Colt scooped her up, carried her up to their hotel room and kicked the door behind him - when Annie thought, this is sublime. Perfectly heavenly, in fact.

It wasn't just the fun and the flowers and the sawing fiddles, although the wedding breakfast had been wonderful. Clarice had done them proud.

Nor even Colt holding her so close in their first dance that she was afraid they would offend public decency, then kissing her so hard that she wasn't able to breathe.

It was ... everything. Where she was, who she was with.

Comments as they left the saloon.

'Who just got hitched?'

'Colt McCall.'

'Dang me! Never thought I'd see the day. Someone local?'

'Sure is. Tom Carlyle's daughter.

It was belonging.

June Kearns second novel, *A Twenties Girl's Guide to Making a Match* will be available in 2013.

A Wet English Winter. A Hot Texan Summer.
An irresistible mix of style and fashion, land, love and cattle barons.
After the Great War

If you enjoyed this book, you might like other novels by the **New Romantics 4** – all available as e-books and paperbacks.

Tall, Dark and Kilted, by Lizzie Lamb
A Hollow Heart, by Adrienne Vaughan
Last Bite of the Cherry, by Mags Cullingford

3616585R00187

Printed in Great Britain
by Amazon.co.uk, Ltd.,
Marston Gate.